# ROMERICA

## ROMAN ARTIFACTS IN AMERICA

DAVID S. BRODY

Eyes That See Publishing

**Romerica**

**Roman Artifacts in America**



Eyes That See Publishing

Newburyport, Massachusetts

ISBN 978-0-9907413-7-4



Cover by Kimberly Scott and Renee Brody

Printed in USA

## Praise for Books in this Series

"Brody does a terrific job of wrapping his research in a fast-paced thrill ride."

—PUBLISHERS WEEKLY

"Rich in scope and vividly engrossing."

—MIDWEST BOOK REVIEW

"A comparison to *The Da Vinci Code* and *National Treasure* is inevitable....The story rips the reader into a fast-paced adventure."

—FRESH FICTION

"A treat to read....If you are a fan of Templar history you will find this book very pleasing."

—KNIGHT TEMPLAR MAGAZINE

"An excellent historical conspiracy thriller. It builds on its most famous predecessor, *The Da Vinci Code*, and takes it one step farther—and across the Atlantic."

—MYSTERY BOOK NEWS

"A rousing adventure. Highly recommended to all Dan Brown and Michael Crichton fans."

—READERS' FAVORITE BOOK REVIEW

"The year is early, but this book will be hard to beat; it's already on my 'Best of' list."

—BARYON REVIEW

## *Dedication*

*To Jeanne De Filippo Scott,*
*the best mother-in-law a guy could hope for.*

*And to think we used to laugh at you*
*when you bragged about Roman exploits.*

## About the Author

David S. Brody is a 6-time Amazon #1 Bestselling fiction writer named Boston's Best Local Author by the *Boston Phoenix* newspaper. His children call him a "rock nerd" because of the time he spends studying ancient stone structures which he believes evidence exploration of America prior to Columbus. He serves as a Director of NEARA (New England Antiquities Research Association) and has appeared as a guest expert on documentaries airing on History Channel, Travel Channel, PBS and Discovery Channel. A graduate of Tufts University and Georgetown Law School, he resides in Newburyport, MA with his wife, sculptor Kimberly Scott.

*Romerica* is his 14th novel.

**For more information, please visit DavidBrodyBooks.com**

Also by the Author

**The "Templars in America" Series**

*Cabal of the Westford Knight: Templars at the Newport Tower (Book 1)*

*Thief on the Cross: Templar Secrets in America (Book 2)*

*Powdered Gold: Templars and the American Ark of the Covenant (Book 3)*

*The Oath of Nimrod: Giants, MK-Ultra and the Smithsonian Cover-up (Book 4)*

*The Isaac Question: Templars and the Secret of the Old Testament (Book 5)*

*Echoes of Atlantis: Crones, Templars and the Lost Continent (Book 6)*

*The Cult of Venus: Templars and the Ancient Goddess (Book 7)*

*The Swagger Sword: Templars, Columbus and the Vatican Cover-up (Book 8)*

*Treasure Templari: Templars, Nazis and the Holy Grail (Book 9)*

*Watchtower of Turtle Island: Templars and the Antichrist (Book 10)*

**The "Boston Law" Series**

*Unlawful Deeds*

*Blood of the Tribe*

*The Wrong Abraham*

## Note to Readers

1. **Though this story is fiction, the artifacts, sites and works of art pictured are real. See Author's Note at end of book for more detailed information.**
2. **This is a stand-alone story. Readers who have not read the first ten books in the series should feel free to jump right in. The summary below provides some basic background for new readers:**

Cameron Thorne, age 46, is an attorney/historian whose passion is researching sites and artifacts which indicate the presence in America of European explorers prior to Columbus. His wife, Amanda Spencer-Gunn, recently died; she had moved to the U.S. from England and was an expert on the medieval Knights Templar. Cam and Amanda adopted Astarte, who is of Native American descent, when she was a young girl. Astarte is now seventeen and attending college in Montana. Cam resides in Westford, Massachusetts, a suburb north-west of Boston. This story is set in a post-COVID world, where the virus has been mostly brought under control.

## Map of Sites in Book

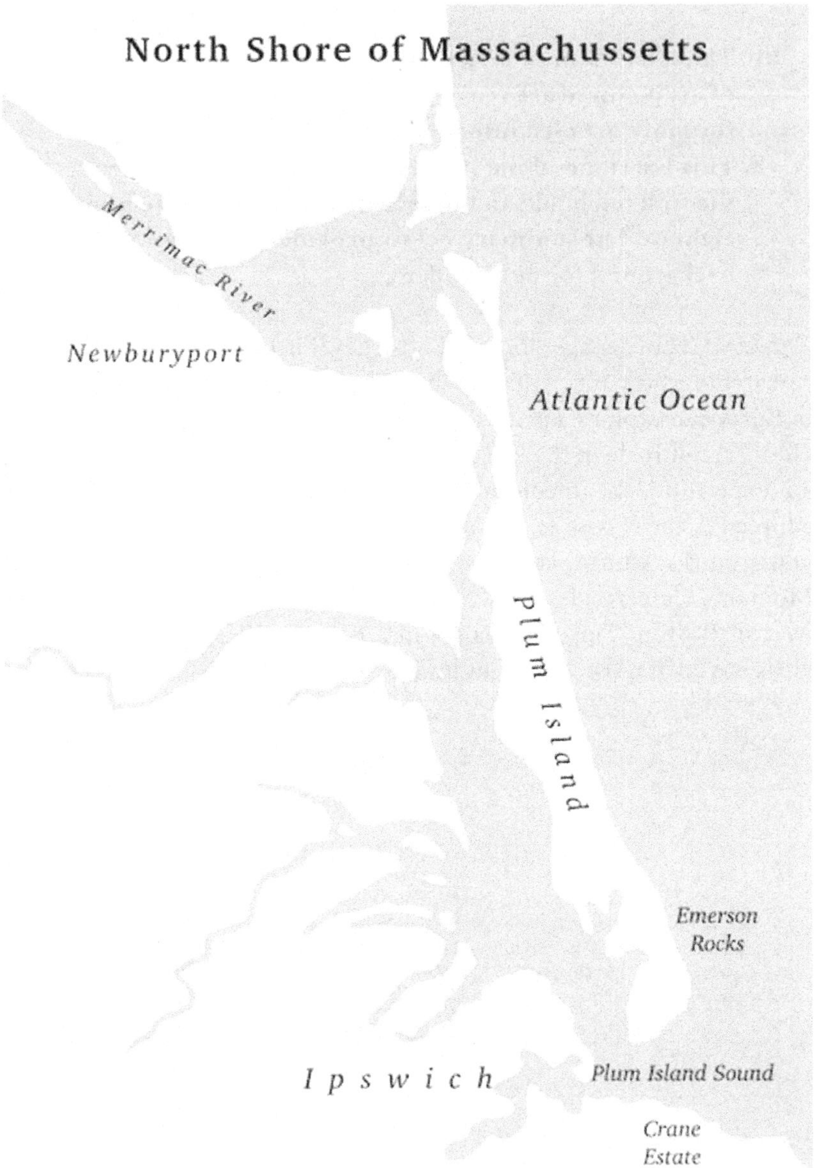

North Shore of Massachussetts

Merrimac River

Newburyport

Atlantic Ocean

Plum Island

Emerson Rocks

Ipswich

Plum Island Sound

Crane Estate

## Chapter 1

***Massachusetts***
***August, Present Day***

Cameron Thorne wound his way east, toward the coast, tidal flats of the Atlantic Ocean intermittently visible out the window of his SUV. He breathed in the cool, briny air, a welcome relief from the heavy August heat inland. He had not wanted to take this meeting. But it was never a bad thing to be near the ocean.

A bluff rose in front of him. He snaked his way up a winding drive, the final turn revealing a sprawling English manor-style mansion atop the crest. Cam tapped his brakes to admire the massive structure. Crane Castle, part of the Crane Estate. A fortune made from Americans needing to flush their toilets. Cam had toured most of the mansions of Newport, Rhode Island, but this dwarfed even those.

He continued his climb, half-expecting to spot hounds pursuing a fox in the woods flanking the drive. As Cam understood it, the 59-room mansion had been rescued from insolvency by the man he was meeting today, Mario Marconi. Marconi had stepped up to lease the property for the cool sum of one million dollars, essentially replacing the castle's yearly gross booking income, most of which had been lost to the COVID-19 pandemic. It had been a big story—many brides-to-be were distraught at losing their chosen venue, but Marconi's upfront payment had been the only way to keep the property afloat financially.

Marconi could afford it, and then some. The grandson of Guglielmo Marconi, the inventor of radio communication, he had taken his inheritance and parlayed it into a fortune by selling cars in the suburbs around Boston. Cam had heard Marconi's voice many times on the airwaves: *My grandfather gave you the radio; I give you the car to listen to it in.* It wasn't the catchiest of slogans, but the opulent mansion was evidence that it was effective. Cam parked.

The car dealer had contacted Cam about conducting historical research on ancient Roman artifacts. Ancient Rome was not Cam's area of expertise, and Cam had learned over the years that people wealthy enough to splurge on castles tended to treat everyone in their orbit as vassals. But Cam hadn't worked much over the past four months, focusing on recovering emotionally from the death of his wife Amanda and physically from the injuries suffered in the car accident which killed her. With his daughter Astarte heading off to college and his medical bills mounting, Cam had little choice but to accept Marconi's offer, especially when he offered to triple Cam's normal hourly rate. Which, Cam understood, merely made him a well-paid vassal. He just hoped the castle didn't have a dungeon.

A tall, elderly, grey-haired man in an Italian-cut beige suit and maroon tie pushed through the front door and strode down a set of stone stairs to greet him. Cam had half-expected a butler—odd how a man who would bother to lease a castle would choose not to stand on pretense. Marconi moved gracefully, his posture erect, his face familiar from his television commercials. He reminded Cam of the old *Fantasy Island* television show, with Ricardo Montalban as the urbane star. Of course, Cam realized, Montalban also played the arch-villain Khan in the *Star Trek* series.

"Welcome," his host said, offering a half-bow. Cam lowered his head in response. It would take him a while to get accustomed not to shaking hands, but he understood the new reality of life in the shadow of a pandemic. "Thank you for coming," Marconi said graciously. "Normally, I would have met you at my office. But I wanted you to see the site of the shipwreck. A Roman shipwreck, based on what I have learned. I will, of course, pay you for your travel time."

*Shipwreck?* Cam stopped. He had assumed the man had some Roman coins or perhaps a bust he wanted examined. "There's a shipwreck?" he blurted.

Marconi smiled and gestured for Cam to follow. "Come. I will show you. Then we will have lunch."

A lawyer by training, Cam had spent the better part of two decades wearing a suit to work and had reached the point where he let his work, not his clothes, speak on his behalf. But the elegance of his host, combined with the opulence of the mansion, contrasted sharply with Cam's khakis and blue golf shirt. He was glad he had at least tucked in the shirt.

Following a path, they circled the mansion, passing over manicured lawns and through well-tended gardens. Cam moved gingerly, using a walking stick. It wasn't like running free in the park like a kid, but it sure was nice to be out of his wheelchair.

A thumb of land north of Boston called Cape Ann jutted into the

Atlantic; Crane Castle, in the town of Ipswich, sat at the bend where the inner part of the thumb met the palm. Marconi gestured with his chin as they passed through a line of shrubbery, the Atlantic opening in front of them. "We're facing northeast right now. But if you sail due east, there is nothing between here and Europe beside open ocean."

Cam had done a little research on his host. "Speaking of crossing the ocean, it was your grandfather's company that transmitted the first transatlantic radio communication, right? From Cape Cod to England."

Marconi stopped, turned and smiled. "I am fortunate to descend from such a great man. There is a beach on Cape Cod named after him to commemorate that event. Marconi Beach. He would have been amazed at today's advances in wireless technology." Marconi stood on the slope below Cam, but his height allowed him to hold Cam's eyes. Cam smelled his earthy, sandalwood cologne. "I believe I have discovered something that will be almost as important as my grandfather's work."

Cam pursed his lips and nodded. A Roman shipwreck off the coast of Massachusetts would, as Marconi suggested, be a remarkable find.

"Please understand, Mr. Thorne. I am an American. I love this country. But I am also an Italian. It pains me to see how my people are depicted in this country. Americans think we Italians are all in the Mafia or are like those hideous *Jersey Shore* girls on television. And now even Christopher Columbus has been taken from us, his statues being taken down all across the country." He sighed. "We are a rich and proud culture. Rome was the greatest empire in the history of the world, and we are still world leaders in fashion, the arts, medicine, wine, automobiles. I want the world to think of these things when they hear the word, *Italian*." He sniffed. "Not Tony Soprano."

Now behind the mansion, they climbed half a flight of stone stairs to a terrace spanning the main floor of the castle. A lush, rolling green lawn, lined with evergreens, unfolded from behind the mansion like a carpet, descending almost all the way to the ocean in the distance.

"The lawn is called the Grand Allée. It runs for almost a third of a mile. I'll give you a few seconds to appreciate the view." He handed Cam a photograph. "And here is an aerial view of the property, taken by my drone." He smiled. "I believe in the movie business they call this an *establishing shot*."

Crane Castle, Ipswich, Massachusetts

And what a shot it was. This, Cam knew, was the panorama which attracted so many wedding couples.

Marconi led him to a waiting golf cart and sped down the Grand Allée toward the water. They dipped down a slope and then back up the other side. "From that bluff ahead we will be able to see a spit of land. That is Sandy Point, at the tip of Plum Island."

Stopping on the bluff, Marconi handed Cam a pair of binoculars. "If you look carefully, you can see rocks jutting out from the point, called Emerson Rocks. Some of the old-timers call it Ipswich Bar. Waves are breaking over them." Cam snapped a picture with his phone.

Emerson Rocks, Plum Island, Massachusetts

Marconi continued. "They are the only rocks along this coastline, and they are perfectly positioned to catch unwary sailors seeking safety in the bay. The currents moving south along Plum Island from the Merrimack River meet the tidal flow coming out of this inlet, called Plum Island Sound. Plus you have the pounding surf. This three-way convergence, coupled with the hidden rocks, has claimed scores of ships over the years." He paused respectfully. "Norman's Woe Rock, in Gloucester, is the most famous shipwreck site on the North Shore. But this is the more deadly."

"Wait," Cam said. "Norman's Woe. I've heard of that." He searched his memory, back to his undergraduate days at Boston College. "An old poem, Longfellow maybe?"

Marconi's eyes twinkled. "Correct. I admire an educated man. Longfellow's 'The Wreck of the Hesperus' tells the tale of a tragic shipwreck on those rocks." Marconi cleared his throat and recited the poem's final stanza:

*Such was the wreck of the Hesperus,*
*In the midnight and the snow!*
*Christ save us all from a death like this,*
*On the reef of Norman's Woe!*

"But," Marconi continued, "Longfellow just as easily could have been writing about Emerson Rocks." Cam eyed the reef through the binoculars a second time, its sharp rocks rising like fangs a couple of hundred yards off the point. As Marconi said, it could easily gash unsuspecting mariners. "And you think there's a Roman shipwreck out there?"

"I don't think it." Marconi tapped his chest. "I know it, here in my heart." He lowered his voice. "It is why I leased this castle. To keep an eye on things. To make sure others don't steal my find." He paused, staring at the reef. "In fact, I often wonder if the original owner of this castle, Crane, suspected something important was buried out there—there have been rumors circulating for centuries. He did not have the benefit of drones or other high-tech monitoring devices. But the alignment down the Grand Allée, from the widow's walk on the roof of the castle, is perfectly aligned to the wreck, like looking down a rifle sight."

Cam swallowed. There was a term for people who knew things in their heart—*wishful thinkers*. But sometimes wishes actually came true. And who was he to be skeptical of unlikely historical finds? He had spent the past decade making the case for remnants of the outlawed Knights Templar exploring America a century before Columbus.

"How do you know the wreck is Roman?"

"I dived the site myself." He smiled. "It was not an easy thing for a man of my age. Based on the design, I am certain the ship is a Roman trireme. The experts I have shown the photos to agree."

Cam knew the ship was so-named because it featured three ('tri') rows of oars. "Wasn't a trireme an oar-powered vessel?"

Marconi seemed pleased that Cam knew his ships. "Yes. But also with two sails. It was primarily a warship."

"Wouldn't an ocean crossing have been difficult?"

"It is true that Triremes were not designed for the open seas. But Julius Caesar sailed them to Britain, proving they were sturdy enough for the Atlantic." He gestured. "And, difficult or not, the proof is right out there buried off of Emerson Rocks. The ship is a trireme. Obviously it wasn't built by the Colonists."

Nodding, Cam stared out. If the ship indeed was a trireme, it would be tough to explain away. Triremes were not in use after the fall of the Roman Empire in the sixth century.

Marconi restarted the golf cart and spun back toward the castle. "We must proceed cautiously," he said. "If word gets out, others will try to poach my find. That is why I have not done more dives. I can't be certain people won't talk, won't gossip. The one dive we conducted, when I confirmed the ship was a trireme, I brought a dive team over from Italy. As I said, this is a delicate operation."

"If you want to salvage the wreck, you're going to need a permit from the state. I'm not sure I'm your guy for that."

"No." He waved the comment away. "That is not why I retained you."

"Why then?"

"I'm not a fool. I understand how this works. Even though I believe there is a Roman ship out there, I need evidence if I hope to attract a top maritime archeologist and dive team. Nobody wants to be associated with a fool's errand, no matter how much I might offer to pay them. As I said, I first need evidence to prove my case. That will be your job. You have made the case—convincingly, I might add—for the Knights Templar and other explorers coming here before Columbus. I need you to make a similar case for the Romans. To start with, I have heard rumors of Roman coins being found on Plum Island after storms. If so, that could be important evidence to prove our case."

Coincidentally, a friend of a friend had recently found Roman coins on a beach south of Boston and sent them to Cam for him to analyze. And Cam knew of other mysterious Roman-related artifacts scattered around New England. Maybe there really was a story to be told here of ancient Romans along the Atlantic coast.

"Okay, then," Cam said as Marconi stopped the golf cart at the castle's rear terrace. "I'd like to help. My only issue is that I am still recovering from my accident, plus I have some law cases I need to deal with, so I can't give this my full attention. But I'd be happy to put in, say, fifteen hours per week."

Marconi blinked. "I see." He stared out at the ocean for a few seconds before standing. "Please follow me."

From the terrace Marconi led Cam to a portico offering the same stunning views. A round table with a white tablecloth sat in the center of the space, two chairs facing each other on either side.

Marconi cleared his throat. A single object rested on the table, a copper box about the size of an ice bucket. Marconi motioned to it. "Please open it."

Leaning in, Cam lifted the hinged lid. He immediately recoiled. *What the?* A human skull sat inside. He dropped the lid, swallowed, and eyed his host. He tried to gather himself. "What is it?"

"It is a skull, obviously. You are a historian, so I thought you would appreciate it. It is the head of one of Columbus's crewmen. I purchased it many years ago while traveling in the Caribbean."

Cam stepped closer. "Are you certain?"

"As certain as one can be about these things. I had a fragment carbon-dated, and the time frame was correct. DNA testing shows the man was of Spanish origin."

The car dealer motioned for Cam to sit. "You are of course wondering why I showed this skull to you. Legend has it that the crewman disobeyed Columbus, and Columbus ordered him beheaded." He paused, letting his words sink in. "The head was displayed on deck as a message to the rest of the crew. Columbus demanded full obedience, full commitment." He leaned forward, his eyes darkening. "As do I." He paused. "As it turns out, the one luxury I do not have is time. I had hoped you would commit to this project fully. Instead, you offer me fifteen hours per week." He motioned the offer away with a flick of his hand. "That is, simply, unacceptable. I am no longer making a request, Mr. Thorne."

Cam's jaw clenched. The attack leading to Amanda's death was still both an open wound and a fresh memory. Who was this guy, threatening him with an old skull, demanding blind obedience?

Seething, Cam counted to three, waiting for his rage to subside. But he knew it wouldn't. Since Amanda's death, his fury seemed always to be looming, just beneath the surface, ready to erupt. He had learned to live with the monster inside him, even if he couldn't always tame it.

The monster surfaced. "I see," Cam said, standing. Slowly he pulled back his arm, and, eyes on Marconi, swept the container and skull off the table. They crashed and skidded across the stone floor, the jaw bone bouncing away from the head. A thick man dressed in black pants and a white shirt stepped from the shadows, waiting for orders. Cam held his host's eyes. "My apologies to your guest," Cam said, nodding toward the skull. "But everyone knew Columbus was a tyrant. Perhaps your man here should have been smart enough to sign on to a different ship."

Marconi lowered his voice. "Sometimes the tyrant is the only game in town, Mr. Thorne."

Marconi made a quick slashing motion with his hand and, before Cam could react, the henchman had closed on him. The cold edge of a sharp knife pressed against Cam's Adam's apple. He froze, suddenly all too aware that his head—like Columbus' crewman—might soon become separated from its body. "If you kill me," he said through clenched teeth, "I'm of no use to you."

"You're of very little use to me now, as things stand. Choose your next words very carefully, Mr. Thorne."

Cam knew he should back down, say what was necessary to remove the blade from his jugular. Astarte needed him. And, as much as Amanda's death had sucked the joy of life from him, he suddenly realized how much he yearned to live. Which meant acquiescing, submitting...

The knife edge turned another fraction of an inch, his hot skin no match for its cold edge. A rivulet of blood ran between his collarbones, pooling at his chest. It didn't help that his heart was pounding.

His brain screamed at him to surrender. Only a fool would make a stand when outnumbered and unarmed. Yet something in his gut, fueled by the monster, resisted. Marconi made his fortune closing deals, driving the best bargain he could while not letting the mark get away. Cam was the mark today. Marconi needed him. Brashly, Cam spat out the words. "If I agree to drop everything else, to put my life on hold, it will be because you convinced me it was a worthy project. Not with threats, but with words."

The two men—host and guest—held each other's eyes, the space charged with tension, the only noise the sound of the henchman's rapid breathing. Finally, Marconi exhaled. He leaned back and folded his hands together in front of his chest as if praying. "Very well. Please sit, Mr. Thorne," he said softly. "We will try this your way. You will hear my words. But you would also be wise to remember my threats."

Cam sensed disappointment in the knife holder, who roughly shoved Cam into his chair and stepped aside. Cam exhaled, the monster receding, leaving Cam alone in his trembling body.

"My son, my only child, died in Afghanistan two years ago. He was a fighter pilot. A few months later, my wife, her heart broken, committed suicide." Marconi spoke matter-of-factly, as if ordering his lunch. Cam listened, his fingers applying pressure to the knife cut. "Four months ago, I was diagnosed with pancreatic cancer. Incurable. I have, at most, a few months." He held Cam's eyes. "They say a man is nothing without his health. And also that love is the most valuable thing in life. By both these measures, I am bankrupt. Empty. But this emptiness is also empowering. I am not constrained by the things that constrain most men. I am free to spend my considerable wealth on the few things in life I still care about. And I am free to pursue these interests with all my zeal." He shrugged. "In short, I have nothing to lose. I can break laws, waste my fortune, make enemies, ignore social niceties."

Cam voiced the obvious retort. "Apparently so."

Marconi ignored the jab. "I am telling you this because I want there to be no misunderstanding between us. I will pay you well for your time—more, I am guessing, than you normally earn in a year. But, as I said, I require full loyalty and commitment." He leaned forward. "I lost my child and then my spouse. You recently lost your spouse but still have your child. Trust me, you do not want to follow in my footsteps."

Another threat. Leaning forward, Cam hissed, "Touch her, and I'll kill you."

Marconi shrugged and smiled sadly. "I'm close to death, anyway." He pointed his chin at the henchman. "And I am well-guarded, in any event. Trust me, Mr. Thorne, the wiser course is to simply accept my generous terms. Work for me. Make history. Keep your daughter safe." He sat back. "In a matter of months I'll be dead, and you can spit on my grave."

Marconi made a subtle gesture, and the thug circled again behind Cam's chair, blade flickering in the sunlight. Cam weighed his options and came to the immediate conclusion that he didn't have any. Above all else, he would not, *could* not, do anything that put Astarte in danger. Marconi had nothing to lose and the resources to carry out his threats. Unclenching his fists, Cam nodded. "Okay. I accept. But you do realize that you're behaving just like the Italian mob boss stereotype that you claim to hate, right?"

"I do. And I am past caring."

The car dealer resumed the conversation as if no threats had been made, as if no knives had been pressed to necks. He handed Cam his handkerchief, a host graciously offering succor to a guest who had scratched himself strolling in the garden. "This castle is actually the second one. The original was built in the Italian Renaissance style." He smiled sadly. "I have seen pictures. It was sublime."

Cam barely heard the words, instead focusing on controlling his anger. And getting his heart to stop racing.

Marconi continued. "But Crane's wife didn't like it. Too Italian, apparently, for a blue blood. She preferred the English style. So, after ten years, Crane tore it down and built this monstrosity in its place. Apparently, he was a bit of an eccentric."

"Maybe there's something in the water here."

Marconi allowed a tight smile to form. "Careful, Mr. Thorne. Your insults mean nothing to me. But I trust they do not presage any disobedience."

Cam merely stared back.

Marconi resumed. "Crane was a collector. He filled the castle with his pieces, many of them Italian. In fact, if you look above you along this terrace, there are a dozen Roman busts set into alcoves. I like to think of them as my countrymen watching over my work, guiding me. Perhaps, on another visit, I could show you the pieces inside the castle as well."

Cam forced himself to refocus. He had a job to do, and the faster he did it, the faster he could get Marconi out of his life. He took a deep breath and gestured toward Plum Island. "Is it possible Crane pulled some of the artifacts from the wreck site?"

Marconi pursed his lips. "Intriguing suggestion. It is certainly possible. If there was one Roman shipwreck in this area, it stands to reason that there may have been more. And they all would have had artifacts of some kind on board."

"Well, we're going to need to build a case with evidence, not speculation and supposition." Cam pushed back his chair and stood. "Which means, I'd better get to work."

Marconi cocked his head. "You'll not stay for lunch?"

"I'll not. I've lost my appetite and, like you, no longer see the need to observe the social niceties."

Astarte sat on the back deck of her Westford home with a book, a light breeze off the lake doing its best to cool her as the sun burned through the August haze. She had applied sunscreen before coming outside. Funny, when her mom was alive, Astarte—naturally almond-skinned—fought her on the need for it. Now she wore it religiously, as if her mother was watching from above and Astarte didn't want to cause her any aggravation. She sighed, tears brimming in her eyes.

Mum would always be with her. But it sure would be nice to have her here in person.

Astarte was not alone in that desire. Two nights ago she had awoken to use the bathroom. Through a partially open door she saw her dad sitting at his bedroom window, a photo of Amanda in his hands, tears running down his cheeks as he stared at the moon. He didn't sob or wail or moan. He just sat silently, tears flowing, lost in his grief. She had thought about going to him, but at an instinctive level she understood that the part of his heart which had broken was a part a daughter could not reach.

Venus, their yellow Lab, sat at Astarte's feet, a pair of sad brown eyes staring up at her. "Are you gloomy also?" Astarte said. "We can't *all* be mopey. You need to be the one to cheer us up." Venus had watched her spend a couple of hours packing this morning and was smart enough to know that the big green rectangular thing on wheels usually meant someone was going away. In Astarte's case, in three days—to start college in Montana. Astarte rubbed the dog behind her ear. "I'm going to miss you. But you need to take care of Dad."

She returned to her book, an account by a lawyer-turned-painter named George Catlin of the months he spent living with the Mandan Indian tribe along the Montana-North Dakota border in the 1830s. The Mandan were Astarte's people, almost all of them wiped out by a smallpox outbreak a few years after Catlin's visit. According to legend, the Mandan descended from a group of European explorers who came to America centuries before Columbus. As a young girl, before Cam and Amanda adopted her, Astarte had been taught that those legends were true. One of the reasons she was going to Montana was to immerse herself in the homeland of her people. And to determine, finally, if the legends were based in reality.

One thing she did know as fact was that the Mandan had not always lived along the Montana-North Dakota border. They had migrated north from the Ohio River Valley. She was going to Montana to reconnect with her past. But she had a feeling that answers to many of her questions would be found in the ancient Mandan lands, east of where the Ohio River met the Mississippi. If the Mandan truly did have European roots, it was there—in southern Indiana and Illinois—where the story likely began.

Rumors had long circulated among frontiersmen in the late 1700s of a group of European-like Indians who spoke a language similar to

Welsh. In 1804, President Jefferson, himself Welsh, sent Meriwether Lewis and William Clark to investigate. On their return trip to Washington, DC, they brought the Mandan chief—whom they dubbed 'Big White' because of his pale complexion—so that Jefferson could view the chief's European appearance with his own eyes.

Catlin, the chronicler of Native American life, felt strongly that the Mandan boasted a unique history, different from the many other Native American tribes he had lived among and studied. He was particularly influenced by the Mandan being the only tribe who used stretched animal skins to build their canoes, a design mirroring boats of the British Isles. More fundamentally, he noted that the Mandan differed in culture, religion, language and (most dramatically) appearance from the neighboring tribes:

> *I am fully convinced that they have sprung from some other origin than that of the other Native American tribes.... A stranger in the Mandan village is first struck with the different shades of complexion and various colors of hair which he sees in a crowd about him and is at once almost disposed to exclaim, "These are not Indians."*
>
> *There are a great many of these people whose complexion appear as light as half breeds; among the women particularly, there are many whose skins are almost white, with hazel, with gray and with blue eyes.*

Catlin also debunked the possibility that the tribe's appearance could have resulted from interbreeding with European frontiersmen:

> *Why this diversity of complexion I cannot tell.... Their traditions afford us no information of their having had any knowledge of white men before the visit of Lewis and Clark, made to their village thirty-three years ago. Since that time there have been but very few visits from white men to the place, and surely not enough to change the complexion and customs of a nation.*

Catlin's paintings backed up his conclusions. His portrait of a Mandan girl with Mediterranean features left little doubt in Astarte's mind of the tribe's transatlantic origins.

Mandan Girl Portrait, George Catlin (1832)

Astarte smiled as she studied the portrait. Only a few weeks before dying, Amanda had commented that the Mandan girl resembled Astarte, except that Astarte had wavier hair and blue eyes. And, her mother had joked, Astarte always seemed to be smiling. Astarte did the math in her head: It was possible that the girl in the portrait was her great-great-great-great-grandmother.

If so, that would have made the Mandan girl the 34th princess. As a young child, Astarte had been told that she was the 40th princess, destined to bring about some kind of spiritual awakening which would unite first the Native Americans and eventually all Americans. As the story had been told to Astarte, in the late 1100s a group of Knights Templar had crossed the Atlantic to the Catskill Mountains of New York and then traveled inland to the Mandan homeland. One of the knights, himself descended from the union of Jesus and Mary Magdalene on one side and Cleopatra and Marc Antony on the other, had broken his vows of celibacy and taken the daughter of a powerful Mandan chief as his bride. Their daughter, uniting the dynastic lines of Jesus and Cleopatra with Mandan royalty, had been the first princess in Astarte's line.

It was a fairy-tale story, one often repeated to Astarte by her birth mother when Astarte was a toddler. But how much of it was true? Fairy tales were often just that, stories made up to entertain children.

But Astarte also knew that even the most outrageous fables contained germs of truth. And in this fable, she herself happened to be the princess.

His body trembling in anger, Cam dropped into the driver's seat of his SUV. He cranked the air-conditioning, hoping the cold air would cool his rage. Part of his fury, of course, was directed at Marconi. But part of it was directed at himself. How had he put himself in danger again? And Astarte as well. As a single parent, he needed to be extra cautious.

His reflection stared back at himself in the rearview mirror. *What was I supposed to do? The guy seemed reputable. He wanted to hire me to do some historical research. How was I supposed to know he was a sociopath?* The answer was simple, he knew. Stick to practicing law. Stay away from unconventional historical research, which seemed to attract all sorts of fringe personalities. Well, it was too late now.

Angling the mirror, he pulled away the handkerchief and examined the knife cut. It had begun to clot, which was all he cared about for now. Exhaling, he shifted the car into drive and raced away, finding the highway on-ramp. As he drove, his rage lowered from a boil to a simmer. But simmer was as low as it would go. He was stuck. He couldn't call the police. Other than a flesh wound to his neck, Cam had no evidence. Plus, Marconi was a pillar of the community who surely had a team of high-priced attorneys on retainer. And Cam dared not call the man's bluff and refuse to work for him—what if Marconi responded by targeting Astarte?

Forty-five minutes later, he pulled into the driveway of their lakefront home. The lake, like the ocean, calmed him. He took a deep breath and rechecked his wound. A soupy scab, mostly closed. He tossed the handkerchief into a trash barrel. He would not bring Marconi's negative energy into his home.

Astarte greeted him from the kitchen table, half a turkey sandwich on the plate in front of her. "Hey, how was your meeting?"

He turned so she could not see his neck. "Interesting. I met the guy whose grandfather invented the radio. He was surprisingly poor at communication." It felt good to insult Marconi, even though he of course could not hear it.

"I had to stop packing. Venus was whining."

"I need to use the bathroom, be right back."

After taping a bandage to his wound, he dumped his briefcase in his study, grabbed the Roman coins from his desk, and returned to the kitchen.

"What happened to your neck?"

"Venus scratched me overnight by mistake. I think she was having a nightmare. I didn't want it to get infected." Moving closer, he dropped a ruby-red felt bag on the kitchen table next to the turkey sandwich. It jingled as it landed.

"You giving me a treasure to take to college?"

"Look inside," he said, before retrieving a can of seltzer water from the fridge.

Pushing her plate away, she loosened the gold drawstring and emptied the contents onto the table. A handful of coins clattered. She examined their odd shape and coloring. "How old are these?"

He eased himself into a chair to give his legs a rest. "They date back to the second and third centuries. Roman."

Fingering the rough edges, she studied them for a few seconds. Some had faded and tarnished, but most still featured discernible images. She looked up. "Shouldn't they be in a museum or something?"

"They're actually not as valuable as you'd think. That's why they're just in that bag. You can find them all over Europe."

She picked up a browned coin and held it to the light, examining both sides—the head of a Roman emperor on the front or obverse, an eagle on the reverse.

Roman Coin, Marshfield, MA

"I think that one's Emperor Aurelian, minted around 275 AD," Cam said.

She lowered the coin and spoke. "Let me guess. You're going to tell me these were not found in Europe." She turned to him. "Another mystery?"

"Right. They were found on a beach south of Boston."

"And you have them, because?"

He shrugged. "Because the guy who found them has been getting the runaround. You know the story. He spoke to someone at the state archeologist's office and she told him some collector probably lost them."

Astarte grinned, amusement brightening her expressive cobalt-colored eyes. "At the beach? Who brings their coin collection to the beach?" She shook her head. "Dad," she said in a theatrical voice, "you grab the cooler and sunscreen. I'll get the towels, umbrella and coin collection."

He chuckled. Seemingly overnight, his little girl had grown into a self-assured young lady. "Exactly."

"So are you thinking Romans were here?"

"That's what my meeting was about, a possible Roman shipwreck. There are literally dozens of Roman coin finds along the Atlantic coast and Ohio River Valley."

"And they're all supposed to be coin collectors who just lost them?"

"Actually, I've heard some other ... creative ... explanations also. One historian said sea gulls brought the coins across from Europe in their beaks. Another guy said Colonial-era ships might have used Roman coins as ballast. One archeologist said a bunch of coins were probably buried at the beach by someone so his grandkids could find them."

"Sea gulls? Ballast?" Astarte shook her head. "This is where Mum would have said the experts were bloody crazy."

"Yup." He took Astarte's hand and swallowed. "That's your job now."

She held his eyes. "I'm happy to do it, Dad. But you don't need me to tell you when people are full of shit."

"No, but it's nice when you agree with me."

"Seriously, go with your gut. You're usually right about this stuff. And who's to say some Roman ship didn't get blown off course and end up wrecking here?"

Cam scooped the coins back into the bag and stood. "You just want me to have something to keep myself busy when you go off to college."

"Damn straight. How can I enjoy myself knowing you'll be moping around here with nothing to do?"

That she could joke about him moping spoke volumes about how much his mood had improved over the past month. Getting back on his feet had helped, and the cliché about time helping to heal wounds had proven true. But he knew he still had a long way to go.

He squeezed Astarte's shoulder. "I'm going to miss you, honey."

She looked up, spoke in a low voice. "I don't have to go, Dad. I could stay local. Plenty of colleges in Boston."

This was not the first time this summer they had discussed this. "You chose Montana State because that's the best place for you. No reason to change your mind now. A psych professor told me once that decisions made from grief are rarely good ones. Seems like good advice."

Nodding, she replied, "Okay."

"Besides. If you stayed home because I was moping, Mum's ghost would probably kill me in my sleep."

She grinned and spoke in a British accent, as Amanda would have. "Bloody right she would."

## Chapter 2

Cam pressed the clutch tentatively, grinding the gears of Amanda's Subaru sport sedan as he veered onto the highway on-ramp on a hazy Saturday morning. His brain commanded his foot to depress the clutch, but his weakened leg muscles responded sluggishly. Amanda's voice came to him:

*It's bad enough that you Yanks drive on the wrong side of the road. But how hard is it to master a standard transmission?*

He smiled. He often spoke to her. Or with her. He patted the steering wheel affectionately. "Sorry about that."

The reality was that he needed to get used to driving the Subaru. He and Astarte would be leaving for Montana in a few days, driving his SUV packed with her belongings. Then he would fly back, leaving the SUV with her for her four years of college.

He drove east, back toward the Massachusetts coast, repeating yesterday's journey. Because of the trip to Montana, he needed to get started on Marconi's research right away. Plus, the city of Newburyport had great lobster rolls. It would be fun to surprise Astarte with her favorite meal for dinner.

He downshifted and merged into traffic, gears screeching. Amanda, mercifully, did not. He had thought about trading the car for something more practical. But he could occasionally catch a faint whiff of Amanda's perfume wafting through the vehicle, and that was easily worth whatever a new clutch might end up costing him.

Forty minutes later, he exited the highway near Newburyport. If the medieval Templars had come to New England, as he and Amanda believed, this old seafaring port, where the Merrimack River met the Atlantic Ocean, was likely their landing spot. It stood to reason that the Romans might have found their way here as well.

Cam cruised into the historic brick downtown area—Newburyport had been one of the few cities in America to resist urban renewal in the 1960s, and it boasted a picturesque business district to show for it. On the eastern side of the city, where the river began to widen to meet the ocean, he picked up the Plum Island Turnpike, a two-lane stretch running east across a mile of tidal flats and salt marshes to the

Atlantic. A few houses on stilts dotted the landscape, rising from the salt marshes, including a shabby pink Colonial sitting alone in the bog like some kind of forgotten dessert oasis. Cam shook his head—that house probably had a story.

The salt marshes gave way to Plum Island, a narrow barrier island protecting Newburyport from the angry Atlantic. Essentially a giant sandbar, the island spanned the gap between the Merrimack River to the north and the Ipswich River—and Emerson Rocks—to the south. Most of its southern portion had been set aside as a federal wildlife preserve popular with birdwatchers, but the northern two miles, split between Newburyport and the town of Newbury, was as densely populated as the salt marshes had been barren. Cam sighed. Amanda had loved it here, especially the secluded beach at the island's southern tip. "It hasn't changed in thousands of years," she used to say. "And yet it looks different every time we come because of the violence of the Atlantic."

As Marconi had explained, it was that violence which made the island a favorite for metal detecting. At a stop sign, Cam glanced at a map he had copied, showing more than seventy shipwrecks along the island's ocean-facing coast. Every new storm seemed to churn up the seabed, freeing its treasures.

It was one of those storms, in the late summer of 2016, which had resulted in Cam traveling to Plum Island today. He checked his watch. Just before eleven, a few minutes early. The turnpike had given way to a commercial strip consisting of restaurants, tightly-packed cottages, and a couple of parking lots. He paid to park, removed his shoes, rolled up his khakis, and wandered along the beach, stopping to allow the surf to wash over his feet.

A few clusters of beachgoers dotted the sand, but the tide was low and the beach long. Seagulls cawed while a toddler, his bathing trunks slipping down around his thighs, shrieked as he raced the waves to shore. The scene reminded Cam of a famous Warren Buffet saying: *At low tide, we learn who has been swimming naked.* Cam took it to mean that, eventually, the truth would reveal itself. Amanda had argued that it meant that some people just liked to swim in the buff.

He breathed in the ocean, dug his toes into the wet sand, and stared east. Would the truth reveal itself? Sociopath or not, Marconi was asking a reasonable question: Had ancient mariners—the Romans or others—made the Atlantic crossing? Historians accepted that Polynesians, using only canoes, navigated the Pacific Ocean hundreds of years before Columbus. Yet these same historians refused to entertain the possibility that ancient seafaring peoples such as the Phoenicians may have crossed the Atlantic. This despite that the Atlantic was only half as wide as the Pacific and that the Phoenicians possessed ships three times as large as what Columbus sailed.

A voice interrupted his thoughts. "You must be Cameron."

He turned to see a tanned woman with blond, dreadlocked hair wearing a yellow t-shirt and tight shorts. He immediately thought of the movie *10*, with Bo Derek; her poster had been the first non-sports figure to adorn teenage Cam's bedroom wall. He straightened himself and smiled. "How'd you know?"

Her hard blue eyes held his, and she spoke with a Boston accent. "Only someone coming to the beach for a meeting would wear khakis." Late thirties, he guessed, maybe a decade younger than him. Not as fine-featured as Bo Derek, her face harder and more angular. But still attractive.

"Fair point," he replied. He had wanted to appear professional, non-threatening. He gestured with his chin toward the satchel slung over one shoulder. "But I could say the same thing about your leather bag."

Sunglasses perched on her head, she sized him up, polite enough not to ask about the bandage on his neck. He knew he had a face which most people trusted, sort of the boy-next-door look. After a few seconds, she spoke. "Yeah, well, I like leather. I'm Denise, in case you hadn't figured it out."

She led him up the beach to a picnic table next to an ice cream stand and slid the satchel onto the table between them. "These are the coins." She removed a cardboard book from the bag and opened it; it was one of those coin-collecting kits Cam remembered from his childhood, with round holes cut into the cardboard where coins could be set. "I didn't know where else to put them." She laid a gray piece of construction paper on the table and one-by-one, with long, delicate fingers, began to set out the coins. "I had a coin collector look at them. They're Roman-era, though some are from Greece and other places around the Mediterranean." Cam snapped a quick picture as she laid the last one down.

Plum Island Coin Find, September, 2016

When she finished, she looked up. "So there they are. My ex got the Harley. I got these stupid coins and the TV. Not much to show for nine years of marriage." She sighed and looked out at the ocean. "But better than the pink house lady, I guess."

"Wait, you mean the pink house out on the turnpike?"

"You don't know the story?"

"No."

She smiled. "During an ugly divorce, the wife insisted on an identical house as the one they lived in. But she didn't specify a location.

So the husband built it out in the middle of the swamp, with saltwater plumbing. They call it the Spite House."

"Ouch."

She let out a long breath. "Life sucks sometimes."

Cam didn't know what to say. But he recognized the pain in her eyes. "I'm sorry."

She shrugged. "You married?"

"Widowed." He had never really used that word to describe himself before. It made him feel, well, old. And, of course, sad. "Just four months ago."

Neither seemed to want to continue this conversation, so Cam leaned in and focused on the coins. "Can you tell me again where you found them?" Cam had tracked Denise down after doing an internet search and reading about her find in the Newburyport newspaper. He didn't think this was a hoax, but he also couldn't rule out the possibility. Occasionally, people—sometimes mainstream historians—attempted to embarrass researchers who believed in pre-Columbus exploration of America by planting fake artifacts. A group of archeology students, hoping to score a 'gotcha' on supporters of the Kensington Rune Stone in Minnesota, carved a fake rune stone in 1985 near the original find and waited for it to be discovered; fortunately, their subterfuge was uncovered.

She gestured with her chin. "See that rock jetty going out into the water?"

Cam nodded. He knew the technical term for it was a 'groin' and that it was used to prevent beach erosion.

Denise continued. "My ex—his name is Pete—and I used to come out here after storms with our metal detectors. There was this one big storm that came up from the south. We started at the jetty and just walked down the beach, to the right. We got a bunch of hits right away. Then we came around to the other side and got a few more. The coins were close to the surface, like they had just been washed in." She angled her head. "We were thinking they were in some wrecked ship out there and got shaken loose by the storm. Maybe some sea captain's coin collection or something."

"Could be," Cam replied. But, if so, there were a lot of unlucky sea captains who lost their coin collections along this stretch of coastline over the centuries. He was inclined to suspect there was another explanation. "Did you ever find stuff like this before?"

"No. A wedding ring, once. We asked around and found out it was some woman who threw it off her balcony when she learned her husband was cheating on her." She shrugged and smiled sadly. "We melted it down, got $120 for it. Paid for a nice dinner."

It had been a long time since Cam had been single, but he noticed Denise kept turning the conversation toward marriage and weddings. Was she flirting with him? Cam was miles away from being able to consider being with another woman. Before Amanda died, he would sometimes look at other women and find them attractive, like a fine piece of art. But since her death, nothing.

"Anyway," she continued, "you're welcome to borrow them. They're not worth all that much, maybe a few bucks each. You can return them whenever."

"Thanks." He was still no closer to getting a sense of whether this find could be some kind of hoax. Not that he could see any reason for it. "Any chance you're a history buff?"

"No. My dad is, loves to watch History Channel. I'm more of a sci-fi girl. You see the new *Star Wars* movie yet?"

Cam smiled. It hadn't been *that* long since he'd flirted. "I did, in fact. With my daughter. She likes that stuff also." He moved to safer ground. "Just one more question, if you don't mind." He wanted to test her. "The newspaper article I read said something about an expert telling you he thought, based on the level of corrosion, that the coins had been in the water for a long time." Which would, of course, preclude a modern-day hoax.

She furrowed her brow. "I don't remember anything like that. Maybe that came from my ex."

He nodded. Good, she passed the test. It would have been easy for her to verify the corrosion story—which Cam had fabricated—if she had wanted him to swallow the bait.

He helped her put the coins back in the cardboard book, then stood and thanked her. "I'll get these back to you. I promise."

She held his eyes. "No rush. I hear they're already working on the next *Star Wars* movie. Maybe by then you'll be ready."

He smiled and nodded. There was no need to ask, *ready for what?*

Cam grabbed lobster rolls at the Bob Lobster seafood shack as he left Plum Island, then wound his way to Route 495 for the forty-minute drive back to Westford. The cardboard Roman coin book sat on the passenger seat next to him, taunting him. Had an ancient Roman ship really gone down off the coast of Newburyport?

He turned off the radio, sensing that Amanda had something to say. Cam's doctor said it was perfectly normal, part of his healing process. Cam wasn't so sure. It seemed so *real*, like she was in the car with him, British accent and all. And the frequency of their conversations had not decreased over the months.

*I agree, Cameron, she's telling the truth. That doesn't prove there really is a Roman shipwreck out there, but at least this is not some hoax.*

He replied aloud. "I have a couple of other people to talk to. Lots of Roman coins, it turns out."

*Lots of clumsy collectors, you mean. Seems like every collector on the eastern seaboard is dropping their coins at the beach. Who knew the Romans greased their bloody coins?*

"What did you think of Marconi?"

*I can see why he was so successful selling cars. He's very smooth. And he seems to be telling the truth.*

"You mean when he said he'd put my head in a box if I was disloyal?"

*Yes. And also when he said he had nothing to lose. Be careful with him, obviously.*

"He's totally obsessed. He leased the castle just to be near the shipwreck. Who throws around a million bucks like that?"

*The Italian heritage thing is important to him. Very. I think part of the reason that he tries to be so urbane is to distance himself from the wise-guy types.*

"He can try all he wants, but it's not working. Urbane people don't put a knife to their guests' throats."

*Well, it was sterling silver.*

"Very funny." He touched the wound on his neck and swallowed. "I'll be careful. I know Astarte needs me."

*Not to change subjects, but aren't you going to ask what I think about Denise?*

He felt himself blush. "Um, no."

*Sorry, you're going to hear it, anyway. One of the few advantages of being dead is I always get the last word.*

"I'm not ready to start dating, if that's what you mean."

*Why not? You know that I wouldn't mind, right? Especially once Astarte leaves for school, you're going to get lonely. And she was definitely interested.*

"Like I said, I'm not ready. It's only been four months." He lowered his voice. "I'm not sure there's room in my heart for someone else."

*I don't think that's how it works, Cameron. Did you love me any less when Astarte entered our lives? No. Your heart expanded to include both of us. Our capacity to love is limitless. It's like a candle—the flame isn't diminished when it lights another wick.*

He was always amazed when Amanda made an insight which had never occurred to him before. If her voice was just his subconscious speaking, as his psychiatrist said, how could Amanda possess original thoughts or insights? He replied, "That may be. But I'm still not ready. I'm supposed to go on a date and still have conversations with you in my head?"

*Fair point. My wit would overshadow hers, no doubt. She might feel like a dullard.*

"No doubt. By the way, do you agree with my Bo Derek comparison?"

*Of course. Nobody knows more about perfect women than you, Cameron.*

Grinning, Cam let his mind drift back to the Roman artifacts. Proving there was a Roman shipwreck on the New England coast would be an uphill battle. The mainstream academic types would fight the possibility at every turn. The effort would take perseverance and, most of all, money. Cam didn't like Marconi. But he had to admit the man had plenty of both.

Cam eased the Subaru into the driveway and exhaled, flexing his leg. The last ten miles on the highway had featured stop-and-go traffic, requiring a half-hour of constant exertion from his left leg. Just what he needed before his physical therapy appointment.

He shuffled into the house and found a note from Astarte. *Went to the beach with Venus. Home in time for dinner.*

After sticking the lobster rolls in the fridge and grabbing a granola bar, Cam changed into shorts and a t-shirt just in time to answer the doorbell. A tall, thirty-ish woman with dark hair pulled into a ponytail smiled at him from his front step. Something about the way she stood made Cam think military.

"I'm Rebecca." Cam stood five feet nine inches tall, and she was every bit of that, in sneakers. She wasn't pretty in the classical sense, but the overall effect was pleasing, in the same way many people found Megan Markle attractive. "Janice is sick today, so I'll be handling your therapy." She held up a laminated ID. "Sorry I'm a bit early."

"Oh. Okay." He didn't love Janice—she was a bit of a hard-ass. And the dark-featured Rebecca seemed pleasant enough. "Come on in."

He led her to a first-floor room on the side of the house which had been the dining room before Cam converted it into a home gym. Rebecca peered out the window. "Nice view." He noticed what he thought was a Middle-Eastern accent. Perhaps Israeli. "Pretty lake."

"When I was in the wheelchair, I couldn't see the water over the shrubbery. It was a big day when I graduated to a walker."

She glanced down at a clipboard she had unpacked, then eyed the universal weight apparatus. "Janice says we should do strength work, then range of motion exercises." Her eyes wandered to the corner. "And you have free weights also, I see."

"Even with my therapy, I want to keep my upper body strong also." He shrugged. "I like free weights better than the universal."

She nodded. "Me too. How much do you press?"

He smiled. "I read once that to be in good shape a guy should be able to bench press eight reps of his body weight. I weigh 175. So that's what I do. After the accident, I dropped to 130, but I've built it back up."

"That's what I press, 130."

Cam didn't doubt it; her shoulders were broad and her biceps pushed at the sleeves of her orange golf shirt. "That's a lot for a woman, right?"

"They used to tell us bench-pressing made our breasts smaller." She shrugged. "Whatever."

Cam couldn't help but check her out. 'They,' apparently, were wrong.

She looked around. "Who spots you?"

"Sometimes my daughter. But if she's not around, I can't really push myself."

"You want to do a set now? I can spot you."

"Sure. Great, thanks."

He sipped some water and placed his phone on the floor before stretching out on the bench. Breathing through his mouth, he lifted the bar off the rack and lowered it slowly to his chest before hoisting it back up again. Rebecca stood behind him, her hands under the bar, ready to grab it if he were to weaken. On the eighth rep, he lowered the bar and exhaled, marshalling his strength for the final push.

"Cameron," Rebecca said, leaning closer, surprising him, the curve of her breast only inches from his face. He could smell her perfume, floral and sweet. "I need you to listen carefully to what I'm about to say." Suddenly, she shifted and pressed down on the bar with both hands, pinning the weight to his chest.

*What the—?*

He squirmed, trying to wriggle out from under the crushing mass, the monster raging within him. But his muscles were shot, and she had both leverage and gravity on her side. The metal bar pressed down on him, bowing around his chest, threatening to collapse his ribs.

"What ... do ... you ... want?" he gasped. The Marconi attack had at least made sense. But what was going on here?

She eased off a bit on her pressure, just enough to allow him to suck in a breath of air.

"As I said, I need you to listen." She pressed down again. Surprisingly, he saw no anger or animosity in her eyes. If anything, he saw concern.

"O-kay."

"Good. I work for the Mossad. And my name is Rivka, not Rebecca."

He nodded for her to continue. He wouldn't have guessed it, but neither did it shock him. His research, centering on the Templars, often touched on issues dealing with both Judeo-Christian history and Israel. In fact, the Mossad had enlisted Amanda's and his help a couple of years ago in Belgium when they had been researching the Ghent Altarpiece painting which, they had concluded, was a secret map leading to the lost Templar treasure. *Enlisted* was actually the wrong word. *Strong-armed* was more like it.

"I'm going to ask once, nicely. Hopefully, I will not need to ask a second time." She spoke matter-of-factly, as if explaining something simple to a child. He squirmed, but it was like having a truck sitting on his chest. In response, she pushed down again. "Understand?"

Fighting against the pain, he nodded again.

"We need you to keep us apprised of your work with the Italian, Marconi. We need to know what he finds."

Cam didn't have a choice. His lungs could barely expand to get air, and his arm muscles were beginning to spasm, able to offer only minimal resistance against the weight. During the Salem witch trials, an accused had been executed by piling weight on his chest. Cam had no interest in sharing his fate. Even the monster seemed to acquiesce.

"Okay," he gasped.

Nodding, Rivka eased pressure on the bar. "I'm glad you agreed so quickly." She leaned closer, her face near his. "I don't enjoy this part of the job. Not one bit."

She seemed to be waiting for a response, so he nodded.

She continued. "To be clear, we don't take kindly to people going back on their words. Truly, I hope it doesn't come to that." He believed her. "But we will do what is necessary." He believed that as well.

With a final nod, she hoisted the bar off his chest and set it in the rack. He gasped, filling his lungs, his chest throbbing in pain.

Rivka wiped her hands on a towel and picked up her clipboard. "Okay. I'm glad that's out of the way." She lifted his phone from the floor and entered her number into it. "Are you ready now to do your leg exercises?"

"What?" *Was she serious?* "Please leave."

She looked at him quizzically. "It was nothing personal. And now that we are in agreement, why not get your therapy done?"

He sat up. "Are you even a therapist?"

"No. But how hard could it be? You can show me."

He shook his head. "Like I said, you should leave."

"Oh. Okay. I do hope you believe me that it was nothing personal." Turning, she began to walk away before stopping and smiling. "Nice job on the presses, by the way. I'd be happy to spot you again sometime."

Cam and Astarte sat on the deck overlooking the lake, dining on lobster rolls, potato chips and cucumber slices. The cloying heat of the August day had begun to fade as the sun dropped and a breeze stirred the water. He did not tell Astarte about the visit from the Mossad, but he could barely move his torso due to what he guessed were bruised ribs—hopefully they weren't cracked or broken.

Venus sat at his feet, hoping for another chunk of lobster to tumble from his bun as he struggled even to feed himself.

"You okay?" Astarte asked.

"Just sore from lifting weights. I overdid it and strained an oblique muscle." He smiled. "You're going to need to scoop the ice cream for desert."

"Okay. Then I need to do some more packing."

He told her about the Roman coins he examined today. "And, like I told you, the guy I met with yesterday is convinced there were Roman ships here. A lot of these coins were found along the Ohio River. I thought we could make a couple of stops at museums to look at some on our trip."

"Fine with me. I wouldn't mind taking a couple of detours to some of the old Mandan villages along the Ohio River also."

"Great. We have four days. Plenty of time for stops."

She leaned forward, as if something just clicked in her head. "You know, it makes sense that there are artifacts along the Ohio. That's part of the Mandan legends. I'm not sure if the explorers came up the Mississippi or down the Ohio from Pittsburgh." She shrugged. "Either way. I've been reading George Catlin. He makes a pretty compelling case that the Mandan have a different origin than the other tribes. Probably European or Mediterranean."

Cam nodded. "I'm beginning to think Roman is a possibility." He, too, had read Catlin and found his arguments persuasive. As to the question of how the explorers arrived in the Ohio River Valley, Cam was unsure. Crossing the Allegheny Mountain range to get to Pittsburgh would have been a challenge—the only access across the harsh terrain was via a single Native American trail. It was one thing to navigate inland along waterways, but an eighty-mile trek across a rugged mountain range in hostile territory would have been a daunting task. Except, that is, for a battle-hardened Roman battalion. Hell, Hannibal led his army—complete with elephants—across the Alps to attack Rome in the Second Punic War; surely the Romans, stinging from that defeat, would not have been deterred by the lesser Allegheny range. The more Cam thought about it, the more he favored an approach from the east rather than from the Mississippi.

But what would the Romans have been doing here? Until today's visit from the Mossad, he had assumed they had come for the same reason as other explorers—perhaps to colonize, but more likely looking to trade or fish or harvest timber or extract minerals. Yet why would the Mossad care about ancient banalities like trading and mining?

One possibility could be Israel's desire to find the legendary land of Ophir. According to the Bible, King Solomon received valuable shipments of gold, silver, pearls and other riches from Ophir every three years, accounting for Israel's vast wealth. Yet Ophir's location has remained a mystery. Historians have suggested the Philippines, India and America as possible locations. Was the Mossad hoping to prove the truth of the Ophir stories, thereby validating the accuracy and authenticity of the Old Testament? The stories in the Bible—and, by extension, Israel's claims to the Holy Land—had in recent years increasingly been called into question. Locating Ophir, perhaps through an ancient shipwreck, would be a coup for the Israelis. It may be that the Israelis believed that Marconi's wrecked ship was Phoenician rather than Roman, thereby potentially tying it to the reign of Solomon, who was known to trade with the Phoenicians.

Cam shrugged away his musings, the motion causing him to wince in pain.

"Wow, Dad, you look pretty miserable." Astarte stood and cleared their plates. "Can I get you some Advil?"

"Thanks, yes." He took a deep breath. He had been dreading Astarte leaving for Montana. Now, with the Mossad slinking around, it might be the safest place for her. He called through the sliding glass door to the kitchen. "Honey, I need to talk to you about something."

She returned with a pair of pills and a couple of bowls of ice cream. Mint chip, Amanda's favorite. It was one of the small gestures Cam and Astarte had adopted to keep Amanda in their lives. Astarte looked him in the eye and smiled. "I'll deal with it, Dad. Honest."

"Deal with what?"

"You starting to date. Don't get me wrong; I'm not thrilled. And I will not be happy if I come home for Thanksgiving and you're in a relationship." She shrugged. "But dinner and a movie, why not?"

"Astarte, where is this coming from?" Had Amanda told her? Was it possible that Astarte, like Cam, was conversing with the deceased?

She sucked on her spoon. "I just figured that's what you were going to ask. I'm going away, so you'll be alone. And why else would you be lifting all those weights?" She grinned. "Can't be out there in the singles world with a dad bod."

He shook his head. "That's not at all what I want to talk to you about." He sighed. "I'm not ready to date. Honest."

She shrugged again. "Okay, whatever." She took another bite. "So what *did* you want to talk about?"

"I told you about this Roman stuff. But what I didn't tell you was that it might be dangerous. The Mossad has taken an interest."

"Your research is always dangerous. I get that. But we can't stop just because people are afraid of the truth. At least, I can't." Her prophecy—that she was destined to bring about a widespread spiritual awakening—would surely inflame passions. She smiled at him. "You told me once when I was a little girl that it wouldn't be called courage if you only did things that didn't scare you."

Cam studied his daughter, turning away before she could see the tears pooling in his eyes. If nothing else, Amanda had left quite a legacy in the way she had raised Astarte. He reached out and squeezed her hand. "Thanks, honey." His chest tightened and a throbbing ache spread outward from his heart. But it had nothing to do with his bruised ribs.

## Chapter 3

Cam watched as Astarte buried her head in Venus' neck, kissed the dog on her nose, and trudged back to the SUV in the muggy morning air.

He smiled at her as she put on her seatbelt. "Venus will be fine. She loves staying with Brandon."

"But I'm not going to see her until Thanksgiving."

"I can only hope you miss me half as much."

"We can Skype, at least." She tried to rally. "And I think after four days in the car together, you and I will be pretty sick of each other for a while."

He put the vehicle into drive, his ribs still sore, and waved goodbye to his cousin, Brandon. "Off we go. Thirteen minutes after six. Montana or bust."

Actually, their plan today was to get as far as Louisville, Kentucky. It was ambitious, almost 1,000 miles. Google Maps estimated a fourteen-hour drive. But they had packed food and, by staying north of New York City, should avoid most traffic.

The Mossad agent wasn't riding in the back seat, but that didn't mean she wasn't coming along for the trip. Cam had brought the SUV in for service yesterday, handed the mechanic an extra hundred-dollar-bill, and asked him to check the vehicle thoroughly for any tracking device. Nothing. But who knew what other tricks they might have? Cam just hoped the Mossad didn't order him to do one thing and Marconi another.

"You going to let me drive?" she asked.

"Of course." Though inexperienced, Astarte was a careful driver. Cam had always believed that good baserunners also made good drivers—the decision-making was the same, weighing time and distance and speed. The only difference, which he made sure Astarte understood, was that it was acceptable sometimes for baserunners to take risks. "We'll switch after a few hours."

Cam handed her a book he had wedged in the gap next to his seat, the rest of the vehicle stuffed with Astarte's clothes and belongings. "Take a look at this."

She read the title. "*The Graves of the Golden Bear*. What's it about?"

"The author, a guy named Rick Osmon, lives out in Indiana. Long story short, he has documented a line of pre-Colonial forts running east-west across the Ohio River Valley. Basically, the forts go hilltop to hilltop. He found about 45 of them. The Smithsonian documented a bunch of them back in the 1840s." He handed her his phone. "I saved a picture of one of them."

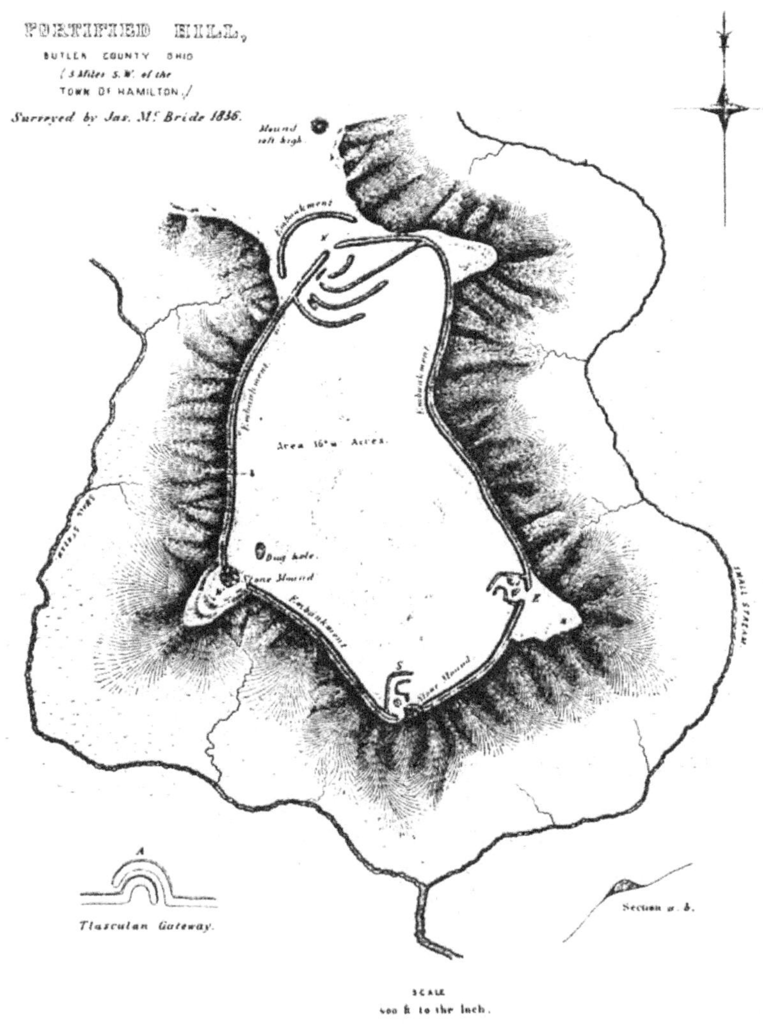


Ancient Fortification, Hamilton, Ohio

Cam continued. "He thinks the forts were meant to control navigation or levy tolls. He compares the whole thing to Hadrian's Wall."

"That's in England, right?"

Cam merged onto the interstate and set his cruise control to seventy. "Yes. The wall was the northern border of the Roman Empire. It's near today's border separating England and Scotland. Every few miles, there'd be a fortress, like this author found along the Ohio River."

She thumbed through the book. "I'm not getting the connection between Hadrian's Wall and the Ohio forts."

"Mostly it's the construction style and techniques. The forts look Roman. But here's the key point: The author thinks the same Roman legion that built Hadrian's Wall also built these forts. The legion disappeared from history in the second century. The author thinks they came here."

"Okay. But, why?"

"That's what we need to try to figure out."

"How does an entire Roman legion disappear?"

"Good question. Including camp followers, you're talking maybe ten thousand people. It's pretty hard to make that many people just disappear without a trace."

She lifted the book. "We've got forts. And a bunch of coins and other artifacts. And what Catlin said about the Mandan. Seems like, if you're willing to open your eyes, there are lots of traces."

Astarte took over driving after they stopped for gas late morning in Scranton, Pennsylvania, four-and-a-half hours into the trip. "Take a nap, Dad. I'm fine. I have Google Maps. Basically, I just drive west on Route 80." She smiled. "If you sleep too long, we'll end up in San Francisco."

"Okay," he said, reclining his chair. "Wake me when we hit the Golden Gate Bridge."

She settled into the middle lane and queued up her Spotify playlist. Within minutes, her dad began to snore lightly. Good. He needed rest. His body was still healing. Not to mention his soul.

Unlike most kids, Astarte often thought about her parents' marriage. She had never known her real dad, and after her birth mom died, she was raised by her Uncle Jefferson, who lived with his sister. So until she moved in with Cam and Amanda as an eight-year-old, she had never really been around people in love. It had all seemed so much like a fairy-tale to her, especially because she had always thought Amanda resembled one of those fair-skinned, bright-eyed princesses. They were so cute together, holding hands and finishing each other's sentences and drinking wine from the same glass. But now, with Amanda gone, her dad seemed, well, incomplete. And not just because he had temporarily lost the use of his legs. He seemed droopy and wan, like a flower in need of water.

Which was why she was glad they had decided to drive to Montana rather than fly. Just getting away from home seemed to help. And having a new adventure, a new mystery, had invigorated him.

A text flashed on her phone. Matthias. He of the chin dimple and deep brown eyes and tender kisses. She made sure she had good separation from other cars and quickly glanced down. A heart emoji, followed by, *See you in 81 hours!* Had Matthias, too, felt incomplete during her absence? Truly, she hoped not. They hadn't been together long enough—a total of five days over two weekends—for him to droop without her. She found herself smiling, singing along to the music. Maybe someday she and Matthias would have what her parents had. Or maybe, like most college romances, theirs would fade away. Whatever the case, she intended to enjoy the ride. That was one thing her mother had taught her—*savor the journey.*

Cam woke to the sound of raindrops pelting the windshield. He sat up. "You doing okay?"

She nodded. "Fine. We've been climbing. I think we just crossed the Allegheny range."

Cam rubbed his face. "Just like the Romans almost two thousand years ago." Smiling, he asked, "Did you see any forts?"

"Sorry. Eyes on the road, just like you taught me." She shifted in her seat. "I was wondering something. This guy, Marconi. You said he wants to glorify Italian culture. Do people really still think that way?"

"Surprisingly, they do. Remember when all those Confederate statues were being taken down during the Black Lives Matter demonstrations? Governor Cuomo, a liberal Democrat, refused to take down

Columbus statues in New York, even though Columbus was a racist who enslaved Native Americans. Cuomo wanted to keep them up as a symbol of Italian pride."

"So it's okay to be a racist, as long as you're Italian."

"Apparently, in Cuomo's mind."

"And that's where Marconi is coming from."

"Same kind of ethnic pride."

The rain continued. Cam checked his watch. Just after noon. "Why don't I eat my sandwich, then we can switch."

"Okay."

As he ate, Cam checked the map on his phone. "We still have a long way to go before Louisville. We're supposed to see that Roman coin tonight. The guy's meeting us at our hotel at eight. It'll be tight."

"Is that the Bar Kokhba coin?"

"Right. So I guess it would be more accurate to call it an Israeli coin from the Roman era." Cam explained that, after the Romans put down a Jewish rebellion in 70 AD, the Jews rebelled again—led by Simon bar Kokhba—in 132 AD. That uprising, too, was put down, but not before the rebels minted their own coins featuring the Temple of Solomon on one side and Bar Kokhba's name on the other. "So it makes sense that the Romans would have had these Israeli coins. After they put down the rebellion, they looted the city."

"Wow," Astarte said. "If that coin could talk."

"Right." He took another bite. "In some ways, it can. It tells us that the Romans didn't come over until after 132 AD."

She nodded. "And it might tell us who they were and why they came. There must be a list of which legions fought in Israel during the rebellion, right?"

Cam nodded. "But it's also possible some soldier brought it to, say, Spain and then somebody having nothing to do with Israel brought it across." He weighed the possibilities. "But you said something that I had been wondering about myself, about why they may have come. When the Romans put down the two rebellions, they brought a lot of the Temple treasures back to Rome. But a lot of other stuff was never found and seems to be lost to history." The Templars, in fact, excavated under the Temple in the early 1100s, hoping to find the lost or hidden Temple treasures and artifacts. "One of the Dead Sea Scrolls, called the Copper Scroll of Qumran, lists a bunch of treasures hidden during the Bar Kokhba uprising.

Like I said, they've never been found." He held out his phone. "Here's a picture of the scroll."

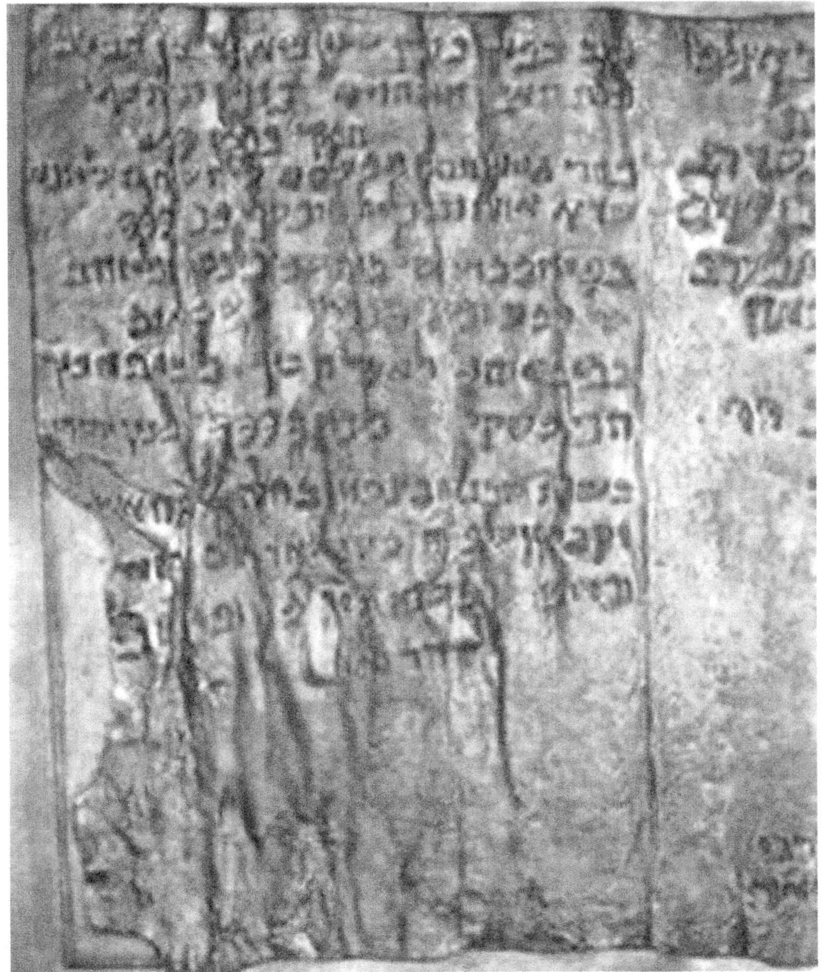

Copper Scroll of Qumran, Listing Temple Treasures

"Give me a second," Cam continued. He had never really gone down this rabbit hole before, but it now seemed important. "This is from Wikipedia, discussing the scroll." He read aloud:

> *The text is an inventory of 64 locations; 63 of which are treasures of gold and silver, which have been estimated in the tons. Although the scroll was made of*

*alloyed copper in order to last, the locations are written as if the reader would have an intimate knowledge of obscure references. For example, "In the salt pit that is under the steps: forty-one talents of silver. In the cave of the old washer's chamber, on the third terrace: sixty-five ingots of gold." There are those who understand the text to be enumerating the vast treasure that was 'stashed' where the Romans could not find it. Others suggest that the listed treasure is that which Bar Kokhba hid during the revolt. The Romans might easily have acquired some or all of the treasure listed in the Copper Scroll by interrogating and torturing captives, which was normal practice."*

"Wow," Astarte replied. How much are we talking about?" She smiled and fluffed her hair, as if posing on a Hollywood runway. "I know *talent* when I see it. But I don't know how much gold that is."

Chuckling, Cam punched at his phone. Amanda would have been quick to note that it was *his* fault Astarte made silly pun jokes.

"Here it is," he said. "A guy wrote a book in 1999. He placed the value of the copper scroll treasure at $1.5 billion in today's dollars." He stared out the window, through the raindrops. "If, say, a Roman battalion stumbled upon the Temple treasure, one possibility is that they would have high-tailed it out of there and gone someplace to hide their loot. Otherwise they'd just have to turn it over to the emperor."

"Someplace really far away, you mean? Maybe across an ocean?"

Cam nodded twice. "Wait for a few years for the dust to settle. Then come back to some fishing village or remote outpost where nobody knows you and live like a king for the rest of your life."

Astarte glanced sideways. "And I think you've just explained why they didn't sweat it much if they happened to drop a few coins along the way."

They had switched drivers just as the rain stopped. Cam cracked the windows as he sped southwest through Ohio, straight into the late afternoon sun.

Astarte had spent the last hour reading up on the Bar Kokhba uprising. Amanda had been an excellent researcher, but Cam had to admit that Astarte was almost her equal. She had the ability to go deep down rabbit holes but not get lost there, always able to return to the thread of her original query. In other words, she didn't get distracted by trivialities or minutia.

"Okay," she said, setting down her phone. "I think I have something." She smiled. "You're going to like this."

"Shoot."

"In that book you showed me this morning, the author said he thought the forts along the Ohio River were built by a lost Roman legion, right?"

"Yes. The one that built Hadrian's Wall."

"That would be the Roman Ninth Legion. In Latin, the 'Legio IX Hispana.' They were called Hispana because the legion was raised in and around Spain. Turns out that one of the legions sent to Israel to put down the uprising was the Ninth—"

Cam interrupted. "Wait, really? The same legion?"

"Yup."

"What are the odds on that?"

"There were, like, fifty legions at that time, and the Romans sent ten legions to Israel." She smiled. "So, by my calculations, the odds were around five-to-one."

"I can see why you aced AP Math."

"Five-to-one is not such a big coincidence. But, still. Anyway, like your book said, before going to Israel, the Ninth Legion was stationed in northern England, along Hadrian's Wall. After Israel," she shrugged, "gone from history. Some people think the entire legion was wiped out during the Jewish revolt. But there's no record of that, and one would think the loss of 10,000 Roman soldiers would be a pretty big deal."

Cam felt that familiar tingling in his arms and legs, his body signaling to him that they were on the verge of an important discovery. It was all still conjecture, but the pieces were starting to fit together in a way which defied probability. "That's a lot of coincidences so far." He counted them off on his fingers. "The author, Osmon, thinks the legion that build Hadrian's Wall also built the Ohio River forts. Then we find out that legion was in Israel during the Bar Kokhba uprising. Then the legion disappeared from history. And so does the Temple treasure. But one of the Bar Kokhba coins somehow shows up thousands of miles from Israel, near the Ohio forts."

"One more thing," she said. "From what I read, the Romans weren't great seafarers. They preferred to fight on land. But after they won the Punic Wars, they captured all the Carthaginian land and ships and, well, people. And the Carthaginians—the Phoenicians—were expert boat-builders and navigators. Eventually they became the Roman navy."

Cam nodded. "And Spain was part of the old Carthaginian empire. So the soldiers from the Ninth Legion would have been exposed to a sea-faring culture. Excellent point."

"They easily could have crossed the Atlantic. They were technically part of the Roman Empire, but many of them were ethnically and culturally descendants of the sea-faring Phoenicians. They navigated the oceans using the stars."

*The Phoenicians.*

Cam squeezed the steering wheel. Now things were coming together. He didn't need to run through the evidence with Astarte; she had heard about it enough over the past decade. But he made the case in his head, as if presenting it to a jury.

He had long believed that ancient Phoenicians—known in the Bible as Canaanites—explored America during the Bronze Age, around the year 1000 BC. Both artifacts and astronomical alignments indicated that the Phoenicians built the America's Stonehenge site in New Hampshire. An inscribed tablet reading, 'To Baal of the Canaanites,' dedicated the site to the Phoenician sun god, Baal.

Baal Stone, America's Stonehenge

Astronomical alignments further tied the site to the worship of Baal and the sun. On the summer solstice (the longest and therefore most important day of the year for a sun-worshiping culture), the sunrise aligned to both Stonehenge in England and also to Israeli Stonehenge, a circle of ceremonial standing stones in the Golan Heights region of Israel, home of the ancient Phoenicians. It appeared that the New Hampshire site had been 'reverse-engineered' to tie into these ancient megalithic sites as a way to mark the importance of the summer solstice sunrise.

Gilgal Rephaim, Israeli Stonehenge, Northern Israel

Furthermore, a stone platform at the America's Stonehenge site known as the Sacrificial Stone indicated that the site may have been used to make sacrifices to Baal—these sacrifices would have been animal and perhaps human, the ancient Canaanites/Phoenicians being specifically named in the Bible as sacrificing the children of their enemies to their gods. Grooves carved around the rock slab's perimeter would have served to collect the blood and divert it away.

Sacrificial Stone, America's Stonehenge

The America's Stonehenge site, Cam and Amanda had concluded, probably had been built as both a ceremonial center and a base of operations from which to mine and trade for copper in New England and the Great Lakes region, copper being needed to supply the voracious demand in Europe and the Mediterranean to make bronze (a mixture of 90% copper and 10% tin). A petroglyph of a Phoenician-style ship carved on a rock in the aptly-named Copper Harbor, part of Michigan's Keweenaw Peninsula jutting into Lake Superior, confirmed this theory.

Phoenician-Style Ship Petroglyph, Lake Superior

In addition to the petroglyph, copper ingots found in a Phoenician shipwreck off the coast of Turkey, dating back to 1300 BC, were of a purity found only in copper originating in the Great Lakes region.

Cam thought about Marconi's shipwreck. As Astarte pointed out, the Romans were not experienced seafarers. Eventually, they built a navy by capturing Carthaginian/Phoenician ships and copying their design. If Phoenician ships had crossed the Atlantic 3,000 years ago, Roman ships could surely have done the same a millennium later…

Astarte interrupted his musings. "Earth to Dad. You there? You want to get on Route 71 South up here. Don't go into Columbus."

"Sorry. Got it." He switched lanes and stretched his neck "I was just thinking about the Phoenicians. If they were here, and I think they were, no reason the Romans couldn't have come also." He shifted in his seat. "Sorry to sound like a lawyer, but the Romans had motive, means, opportunity and ability. Not to mention all the evidence we've found." He glanced across at her. "It's not an ironclad case. But it's getting pretty darn close."

Astarte had taken over the driving, Cam directing her to their hotel across the Ohio River from Louisville in Clarksville, Indiana. The river divided Kentucky and Indiana, and the museum they planned to visit in the morning was actually on the Indiana side.

"But we can't leave Louisville without visiting the Louisville Slugger factory," Cam said. "They have one of Babe Ruth's bats and it's almost as big as a tree trunk." He smiled. "I don't care if you have to miss your first day of classes."

"You do realize that I've never so much as touched a wooden bat?" She had played softball since moving in with Cam and Amanda in the third grade, but never baseball.

He angled his head. "I guess that's true." He shook his head. "There's something about the sound of wood hitting a ball."

She smiled. "How would you know? From what Uncle Brandon says, you usually swung and missed."

Chuckling, he pointed. "Up there. On the right."

She glanced at the clock. 7:44. "Sixteen minutes to spare."

"Just enough time to check in. We can grab a bite while we meet with the guy. You okay with ordering a pizza?"

"When am I ever not?"

Fifteen minutes later they greeted a middle-aged man with thinning dark hair and a white beard at the hotel front desk. As they sat on either side of a coffee table in the lobby, he pulled a small plastic bag from the breast pocket of his shirt. "Here she is," he said proudly, unsealing the bag and handing a silver coin to Cam. "My grandfather found this back in 1952 while swimming." The man smiled. "He saw something flash, reached down, and pulled it out. It's from Israel."

"You said swimming. Was he in the Ohio River?" Cam asked.

The man nodded. "Not far from here, in fact."

Cam examined the coin, then handed it to Astarte. She asked the man, "May I take a picture of it?"

"Of course."

She laid the coin on a white piece of paper she had requested from the front desk and photographed both sides.

Bar Kokhba Coin, Ohio River

The man continued. "That's the Temple of Solomon on the front with the name 'Simon' in Hebrew letters around it, for Simon bar Kokhba. On the back is something called a 'lulav,' a branch of the date tree. Around the lulav, it says, 'Year 2 of the freedom of Israel.' That would be the year 133 AD."

"Wow," Cam said, holding the coin to the light. "That's really cool."

The man grinned. "Isn't it?" He shifted. "I wish I had a nickel for every time I heard my gramps ask, 'How in the world did that coin get here?'"

"How indeed?" Cam replied, handing the coin back. "Do you know anything else about it?"

"Just that there have been other coins from that era found in the area. One of them is a match to this, I heard, but I've never seen it. And there are Indian legends about an ancient fort along the river in these parts."

"Really?" Astarte said. "Do you know anything about it?"

"Sorry. That's all I know."

"We're going to see some Roman coins tomorrow at the Museum of the Falls," Cam said.

The man nodded. "They've got some good ones there." He leaned forward, holding Cam's eyes. "You've driven a long way just to see these coins. And you seem like an educated fellow. Do you really think there were ancient people here on the Ohio River?"

Cam answered as honestly as he could. "If you had asked me a month ago, I would have said, well, maybe." He took a deep breath. "But these coins have a story to tell. And it might be a story the world has never heard before."

## Chapter 4

Brushing the sweat from his brow, Cam slid his keycard into their hotel room door. He had awoken at five and spent an hour in the gym lifting weights. As his drill sergeant of a physical therapist had said, "Only two people can control how much and how quickly you heal: you and God. And I think God has a few other things on his plate now." Cam was beginning to rethink his ambivalence toward her. The therapy was working. And, of course, she hadn't tried to crush his chest.

He gently shook Astarte, sleeping on the pull-out sofa in the living room of their suite. "Wake up, honey. It's almost seven."

He used the bathroom and put on a fresh t-shirt to go with his shorts and sneakers. He wasn't healthy enough to jog yet, but he had built up to a daily 3-mile walk in addition to the weight training. And today they had an important destination.

After a quick breakfast in the lobby, they strolled south, toward the river, the morning already hot and sticky. The interpretive center where the coins were displayed didn't open until nine. But the outdoor park opened earlier. The plan was to visit the park and center, return to the hotel for a shower, and be on the road by 10:30.

"I stayed up last night to do some reading about this area," he said. They had come to Louisville to see the coins, but the man they met last night had piqued Cam's interest with his comment about an ancient fort. Cam explained that the Falls of the Ohio got its name because the river dropped twenty-four feet over a two-mile stretch. It became a natural stopping point for travelers who needed to hire local guides to navigate the series of rapids. Before that, Native American tribes frequented the area, fishing and using the shallows below the rapids as a crossing point; the shallows also attracted bison, which made the area a fertile hunting ground. "Which," Cam concluded, "brings us to the interesting part."

"I'll be the judge of that," she said with a smile.

"No, I'm pretty sure I'm right about this one." He took a deep breath. "According to Shawnee legend, the Falls of the Ohio was the site of the massacre of the so-called 'White Indians.' They had a fort here, on high ground on this side of the river, with stone walls and five watchtowers. About ten acres in size. At some point, the Shawnee and other tribes banded together and attacked them. Most of the tribe was slaughtered. The survivors fled west, where they resettled along the Missouri River."

She stopped, turned to him and swallowed. "That's the story of my people."

"Yup. Sure is." He shrugged. "I don't imagine there was a *second* tribe of White Indians on the Ohio River."

She pointed at the river ahead. "So this is it. My people's ancient homeland. What are the odds we just ended up here?"

"Honestly, it's probably not a coincidence. We're here because of the coins. And the coins are here probably because the European explorers who became the Mandan tribe settled here and brought the coins with them."

Astarte picked up the pace, and they walked in silence for a few seconds. "This is crazy."

He struggled to keep up. "If you stop for a second, I'll give you more details about the fort. They call it the Devil's Backbone fort." He pulled out his phone. "This is from an Associated Press article from 1989." He read aloud:

> *Upstream from Louisville, Kentucky, the craggy hill rises abruptly from the Indiana bank. Fourteen Mile Creek runs behind the hill, carving out a narrow strip of land between the creek and the river. The peninsula is less than 20 feet wide at the top and falls off abruptly on either side to the Ohio River and the creek. The resulting pear-shaped bluff has a flat top five to seven acres across and is almost inaccessible.*
>
> *The earliest survey of the area, done in 1873 by state geologist E. T. Cox, found a prehistoric fortification on the hilltop. A manmade limestone wall, 150 feet long and 7.5 feet high in some places, stood along the front and one side of the hill where the cliffs could be scaled, Cox said in his report. The wall no longer exists, the area's early settlers having taken the huge, unmortared stones to build foundations, bridges and fences that can still be seen throughout the rolling countryside.*

*Excavations conducted by the anthropology department at the University of Tennessee concluded that one of the structures, known as Old Stone Fort, was built in the third century.*

"*Third century*," Astarte repeated. "A manmade wall over seven feet high. That must be the fort the guy was talking about last night."

"Right. And probably part of the line of forts in that book we looked at this morning. The dates line up perfectly."

She let out a long breath. "I don't even know the name of this town. I mean, I know across the river is Louisville. But you said the fort was on this side."

"This is Clarksville, Indiana. Ring any bells?"

"No." She paused. "Wait. As in, Lewis and Clark?"

He nodded. "William Clark. He lived here. The town was named after his family. In fact, the Lewis and Clark expedition originated here in 1803."

"Another coincidence which is probably not a coincidence at all. If Clark lived here, he must have known about the Mandan and the fort."

"Which explains why he spent so much time at the Mandan village in North Dakota. He wanted to see if the legends were true. Here's more from that Associated Press article."

*George Rogers Clark, the founder of Clarksville, Ind., first heard the story from Tobacco, a chief of the Piankeshaw. Some of Clark County's earliest settlers reportedly found ancient coins and European armor. Clark found some armor-clad skeletons that he thought were ancient Welshmen and jotted down his findings in his personal memoirs. A copy of this book, in Clark's own hand, was stolen years ago from the Jeffersonville public library.*

"Let me guess," Astarte said, "George Rogers Clark is related to William Clark."

"His older brother."

"Like I said, then. Clark must have known about the Mandan."

They reached a bluff overlooking the river. Astarte's eyes scanned the area, probably trying to imagine how it would have looked almost two thousand years ago. "Is this the bluff? Is this where the fort was?"

"I don't think so. The article said the location was upstream from here. But this whole area is beautiful." He pointed at the park. "From what I read, this is a popular spot to observe wildlife. And when the water is low, you can see fossils in the limestone dating back over 300 million years."

She took it all in. "300 million, huh? Makes a Roman fort from 2,000 years ago seem like no big deal."

He put his arm around her shoulder. "Actually, no it doesn't. It's the story of your people. It's a *really* big deal." He smiled. "And if it's true, it's an amazing story."

Astarte waited while her dad bought admission tickets to the Falls of the Ohio Interpretive Center. She was only vaguely aware of the center's striking architecture—stone and glass and the convergence of soft curves and sharp edges. She had hoped to catch a whiff of her tribe's history somewhere along their drive. Instead, on their first stop, they had struck gold.

Or, in the case of the coins they were going to see, 1,800-year-old bronze.

The coins were displayed side-by-side beneath Plexiglas in a corner of the museum. Both displayed the bust of a Roman emperor and both dated back to the third century. She snapped a picture of them.

Falls of the Ohio Roman Coins

Cam read from the information panel. "They were found in 1963 during a construction project in the next town over, along the river. Originally there were more, but the guy who found them gave some away."

"Hmm. That's a funny date," Astarte said. "If the Romans came over after the Bar Kokhba revolt, how would they have coins minted a hundred years later?" The revolt ended around 136 AD.

"Those coins I showed you at breakfast last week are also third century. I suppose one explanation is that a bunch of them came over after the revolt and some of them stayed. Maybe every few years a ship came back to bring supplies and trade, probably via the Mississippi."

She nodded. It made sense. "If they had as much gold as the Copper Scroll says they had, I could see why trade ships would come back to supply them. And," she added, "the third century date matches the date the archeologists give for the stone fort."

They both stared at the coins for a few seconds. Cam said, "The story is probably more disjointed than we think. Some of the Romans stayed, some went back. Some settled along the coast, others moved inland. Some brought wives from Europe, others married Native American women."

Astarte focused on a second information panel. "This one talks about how Clark—the older brother of the Clark from Lewis and Clark—found six skeletons clad in armor not far from the fort in the 1790s. Just like it said in that Associated Press article." She read aloud from a letter a historian wrote in 1824 discussing the find:

> *In 1799, six soldiers' skeletons were dug up. Each skeleton had a breastplate of bronze, cast with the Welsh coat of arms and a Latin inscription.*

She continued reading from the panel. "And then, in 1895, someone found more armor and a shield here in Louisville. The Smithsonian verified it as Persian."

Cam nodded. "Welsh and Persian. Makes sense. The Ninth Legion was in Britain, so some of the soldiers would have been Welsh. And the Latin inscription fits. Then the Ninth was transferred to Israel, where it wouldn't have been hard to acquire Persian armor."

"You know, Dad, this is pretty compelling. I mean, it's one thing to explain away some coins. But how do you explain the armor? The

Indians didn't work with metal. Either Clark was just making stuff up, or it's real."

"I doubt he was making it up. And what about the Smithsonian? They were making it up also?" He shook his head. "I agree with you. The armor is pretty compelling."

She sighed. "Too bad it's been lost."

Cam's phone dinged, indicating a text. He grinned. "Excellent. I have a Facebook friend who knows a guy who found a bunch of Roman coins along the river near here back in 2009. The guy died. But his niece has the coins and can meet us this morning."

"Even if it puts us behind schedule, it's worth it."

"And check this out. My friend sent me this map. He's been tracking these Roman coins for years. Every star on the map indicates a different Roman-era coin find. There's more than thirty of them. And it only lists one in Massachusetts—I know of at least five."

Map of Roman Coins Found in U.S.

Astarte studied it. "You know what's interesting? There's nothing west of Texas. If these coins were all 'lost' by collectors like the experts say, wouldn't they be equally dispersed across the country?"

"Good point." Cam smiled as they began to make their way to the museum exit. "The collectors in the western half of the country must have stickier fingers."

Twenty minutes later, sweaty from their walk in the heat, they were back in their hotel lobby, drinking bottled water and sitting around the same coffee table as the night before when they viewed the Bar Kokhba coin.

Cam smiled at Astarte. "You want to go shower and I'll handle this myself?"

"Not a chance. If I smell bad, deal with it," she said.

A woman with a hawk-like face in a dark business suit strolled into the lobby and marched over. About Cam's age, she carried a briefcase and fixed them with hard eyes. Astarte felt underdressed in her shorts and t-shirt.

The woman skipped the pleasantries. "Just so you know, the only reason I'm here is because your friend was always kind to my uncle. I only have fifteen minutes."

Sitting, she opened her briefcase and removed an oak storage box about the size of a college textbook. She unhinged the clasp, opened the box, tossed a couple of pairs of white gloves onto the table, and leaned back. "Have at it. There are nineteen altogether. My uncle found eight coins on one trip, then eleven a few months later. This would have been back in 2009."

Astarte put on the gloves and removed one of the copper-colored coins from its felt nest in the storage box. The lower portion of the coin had been broken off or worn away. She could see a man's profile; on his head, he wore a spiked crown.

Roman Coin with Solar Crown, Found in Indiana

"Almost all of them have those crowns," the woman said. "They're called solar crowns, or radiants. Part of sun worship. They identify the coins as third century."

"So all these coins are third century?" Cam asked. He, too, was examining a coin.

"Give or take a few decades, yes."

"Where did your uncle find these?"

"About fifteen miles east of here, most on the Indiana side of the river. With a metal detector."

Cam glanced at Astarte. "That's near where the fort was," he said.

Astarte wasn't surprised. "Can I lay them all out and take a picture?" she asked.

The woman exhaled. "I'm sorry, no. It seems like everyone profits from these coins in some way except us. Books, documentaries, magazine articles. My uncle was ridiculed in his last years, accused of perpetuating some kind of hoax. And that was when he wasn't being laughed at for believing the Romans were here."

Cam leaned forward. "I understand. I've seen it happen before. And we appreciate you going out of your way to let us see these. The truth is, I'm planning to write a book about these Roman coins." This 'truth' was news to Astarte, but she knew enough not to interrupt. Dad was adept at reading people and pushing the right buttons. "And my publisher gave me a budget for research. Would, say, two hundred dollars be a fair price for you to allow us to take some pictures?"

The woman's eyes narrowed. "Make it five hundred and you have a deal."

"Okay. Let me go to our room and get my checkbook."

She replied before he stood. "Sorry. Cash only."

While Cam went back to their room to get the money, Astarte laid the coins out and snapped a bunch of pictures, including one of the entire collection.

Roman Coin Collection, Found in Indiana & Kentucky

Cam returned and handed the woman a wad of cash. “Thanks. We appreciate it.”

The woman allowed herself a small smile as she counted it quickly and tucked the money into a pocket in her briefcase.

“Last night,” he said, “we saw an Israeli coin from 133 AD, from the Bar Kokhba uprising. “You probably know a lot about these Roman-era coins. You ever see any like it?”

She shook her head. “No, but I can ask around.” She stood to leave. “Everyone around here ties these coins to the legend of Prince Madoc coming over here from Wales. Some people say twelfth century, some say sixth century.” Astarte knew the legend—Welsh explorers crossing the Atlantic and finding their way inland from the Gulf of Mexico. In fact, many people, including President Jefferson, thought Madoc and his group might be the ancestors of the Mandan tribe, the genesis of the so-called White Indians. Astarte’s ancestors.

The woman continued. “But it seems to me that these coins are too old for Madoc. Why would the Madoc group leave behind nineteen coins that are many centuries old and nothing more modern? And why no coins from the British Isles?”

Cam nodded. "I agree. Madoc may have been here. But I'm guessing these coins tell a different, older story."

Less than an hour after Cam handed over the $500, he and Astarte were back in his SUV heading west. Cam had, begrudgingly, decided to skip the Louisville Slugger factory. They just didn't have time. "I really had my heart set on seeing those bats today," he lamented. "Oh, well."

Instead of getting back on the interstate, he turned onto Route 111, an Indiana two-lane highway which tracked the Ohio River. "There were also more coins we could see," he said as they put Louisville in the rearview mirror, "but I think we've got the picture."

"I agree."

"And we've got a couple other stops to make along the river here."

An hour later, they recrossed the waterway and stopped in Brandenburg, Kentucky, at the county historical society. There, they examined the Brandenburg Stone, a beige limestone slab about the size of microwave oven with a mysterious script carved across its face.

Brandenburg Stone, Kentucky

"It's an ancient Welsh script," Cam explained. He had researched the stone before the trip. "And it's highly weathered, so it's not modern."

"More Welsh," she said. "Just like the armor."

"We're back to the Ninth Legion. Many of the soldiers would have spoken Welsh."

"What's it say?"

"It talks about dividing the land among offspring."

"So a kind of boundary marker?" Astarte asked.

"Yes. And dividing land is definitely something ancient Europeans would have done. Especially if they planned on staying for a while."

From Brandenberg, they continued southwest along the river to a farm in the town of Derby, Indiana, where a retired, white-bearded professor from a local college society showed them a wedge-shaped stone anchor with a hole near the top. Cam was surprised at its size, almost as large as an outdoor trash can you'd see in the park.

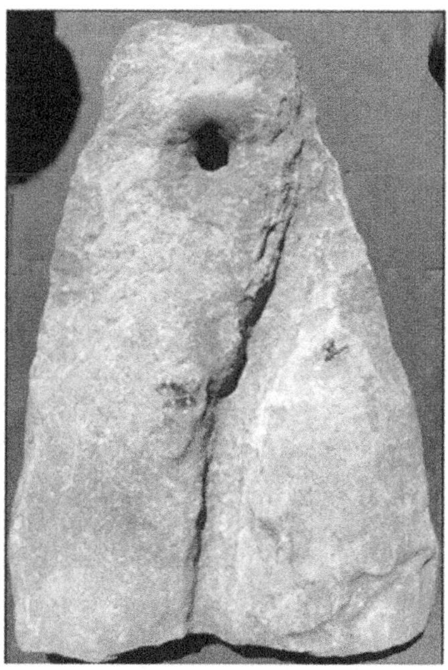

Stone Anchor, Derby, Kentucky

The professor pointed out that this type of stone wedge anchor was common in the Mediterranean during the Roman era. "The hole was not machine-drilled," he explained, indicating it was not modern. "The Native Americans, obviously, didn't need anchors for their canoes, especially one this large. And the Colonists would have used iron anchors." He shrugged. "It's a real mystery how it got here."

Cam looked around. "And we're not even on the river."

The professor smiled. "The river's about a quarter mile west of here. In the 1830s, a dam was built that changed the river's path. This would have been the old riverbank. That tells me the anchor must date back to before 1830."

"You said it's not Native American and not Colonial. So what could it be?" Astarte asked, playing devil's advocate.

The professor smiled again and stroked his beard. "You've asked the million-dollar question, young lady. Somebody used it. And it weighs four hundred pounds, so it must have belonged to a pretty big ship."

Back in the car, Cam drove north to pick up the interstate and continue their trip west.

He turned. "So, do you feel like all this gives you more insight into the Mandan past?"

"In some ways, yes. For the legends to be true, for us to be the so-called 'White Indians,' there had to be white people here. These coins and the fort and the armor and the anchor and the Brandenberg Stone all seem to confirm that." She chewed her lip, a habit she picked up from Amanda. "But there are still so many questions. Our legends don't say anything about Romans."

Cam replied, "I think you need to be careful about labels. To the Native Americans, a Roman was probably no different than a Scotsman or a Viking or a Phoenician. And, don't forget, the Ninth Legion wasn't from Rome. Sure, some of the senior officers were Roman. But the other guys were recruited from the local populations of the areas they conquered. Especially as time passed, the local people would have felt like they were part of the Roman Empire even if they weren't ethnically Roman. A lot of them became legal citizens of Rome. Marconi is not going to like this, but if we're right and it was the Ninth Legion who came over, they were mostly from Spain and Portugal and the old Phoenician sea-trading ports, plus all the guys they recruited while up in Britain. Not many true Italians."

She smiled. "So you're saying the Mandan are mongrels."

"Pretty much. The original Mandan were probably a mix from all across Europe. Not just Welsh or Roman or Iberian." He shifted in his seat. "Which brings us to our next destination. Burrows Cave."

She nodded. "Good. Our legends say the cave is important. And you know that my Uncle Jefferson agreed."

"In fact, that's how I first met him. You were only eight at the time." Hard to believe almost a decade had passed. "He wanted me to continue his research."

"Did you?"

"A bit. But Burrows never told anyone where the cave was." Russell Burrows, an Indiana prison guard and truck driver, claimed to have stumbled into the cave, filled with thousands of stone artifacts, in 1982.

Many of the artifacts were inscribed with ancient Mediterranean scripts and/or depicted a wide variety of ancient Mediterranean cultures, seemingly dating to the centuries just before or after Christ. Most experts believed Burrows somehow fabricated the pieces. "Without the actual cave," Cam said, "it's impossible to prove the artifacts are authentic."

"So how can we have a 'destination' of Burrows Cave if nobody knows where it is?"

Cam smiled. "Because I have a lead. I got an email from a woman in Illinois who read my book." *Across the Pond,* six years old now, summarized Cam's research concluding that waves of explorers, many with ties to the Knights Templar, came to America before Columbus. "She said everyone's been looking in the wrong place. Said her family owns a farm and they keep discovering stones with strange writing. I think this is where Burrows may have found his artifacts. I did some research and tracked down a magazine article from the 1920s talking about strange stones in the area around the farm."

"Well, if they were found back in the 1920s, Burrows couldn't have faked them. He wasn't even born yet."

"Exactly. I'm thinking the real cave is at this farm. Burrows told everyone the cave was in the town of Olney, which is fifty miles away. He was probably just trying to throw people off the scent."

Cam had never agreed with the so-called experts who dismissed the find as a hoax. He explained to Astarte that the historical sophistication of the pieces—often demonstrating knowledge of obscure and subtle points of antiquity—far exceeded the knowledge of the high-school-educated Burrows. And art experts who had looked at the artifacts concluded that the artistic quality of the carvings, along with the ability to work in various media, also surpassed Burrows' rudimentary woodworking skills.

Astarte shifted in her seat. "It's been years since I thought about Burrows Cave. Is the art really advanced?"

"Some of it. Search for 'African head' and 'Burrows Cave.' There's a cool marble head carving."

She did so. "Got it." She showed him. "You're right, that's well done. It looks African. And the decorations on his forehead look Egyptian or maybe Greek."

Marble Head, Burrows Cave

"Try another search with 'sandstone head,'" he said.

A few seconds passed. "Wow, that one is really impressive. The lines are beautiful; it could be in a museum. It looks maybe Sudanese."

Sandstone Head, Burrows Cave

"Try one more," Cam said. "Look for a Roman head. There are two, actually. One is on a black stone, the other on marble."

She turned the phone. "These ones?"

Roman Soldier Profiles, Burrows Cave

He nodded.

"I agree, those are Roman soldiers," she said. "But, unlike the other two, the artwork isn't that impressive."

"That's the point. Some are simple, some are advanced. But they don't look like they were all done by the same guy in his basement. And look at that marble piece. See how it looks like the stone was partially submerged in water, which washed away much of the detail —and dirt—below the soldier's neck? Erosion like this takes decades, maybe longer. Probably during periodic storms when the cave flooded. It would be nearly impossible for someone to fabricate weathering and erosion like this."

Astarte handed his phone back. "So, you think Burrows found these on some farm?"

"Yeah. Maybe he was trespassing at night or something. The reason he could never bring anyone to the site was because he didn't have permission to be there, much less take artifacts away. He couldn't very well show up with a team of archeologists and expect not to get questioned. Or arrested."

They drove in silence for a few minutes.

"You know," Astarte said, "Uncle Jefferson had these artifacts all over the house. He had hundreds of them. And he used to say to me, 'Astarte, the stones tell a story. We just need to learn how to listen to them.'"

"What story did they tell?" Cam replied. He had a theory about the Burrows Cave artifacts, but he wanted to see if Astarte would get there on her own—he knew that Jefferson had spent a lot of time teaching her about his collection.

"He said that each stone was a clue. Some of them had Hebrew writing, some Phoenician, some had hieroglyphs, some had Latin, some had Greek. Same thing with the images—some of the carvings were Egyptian, some Roman, some Jewish, some African, some Christian. And they all dated to around the first century. So he figured the people who carved them must have come from all over the Mediterranean and lived around the first century." She took a breath. "That's why the King Juba II theory became popular."

Cam was familiar with the theory. Juba II was the king of the African nation of Mauritania in the first century. He also happened to be the grandson of Cleopatra and Mark Antony. After Juba II died, his son Ptolemy of Mauritania succeeded him. Ptolemy was assassinated by Roman emperor Caligula in 40 AD, likely because Caligula wanted to get his hands on the Mauritanian wealth. The supposition was that the ruling class of Mauritania—consisting of seafaring cultures from around the Mediterranean—fled in ships with the Mauritanian treasure before Caligula's forces could arrive. They eventually made their way to America, the theory went, which accounted for the Mediterranean-themed carvings dating to the first century found in Burrows Cave.

"But what if," Astarte continued, "the Juba story is wrong. The artifacts wouldn't look much different if they were second century instead of first."

Cam nodded and smiled. "Keep going with that thought."

"It could just as easily have been the Ninth Legion." Her voice rose in excitement. "Like you said, the legion would have had soldiers from all around the Mediterranean—Roman, African, Greek, Iberian, whatever. They could have carved the artifacts just as easily as the Mauritanians."

Cam had never totally bought the Juba explanation. But the Ninth Legion timeline made sense. Put down the uprising in Jerusalem in 133 AD. Grab the Bar Kokhba treasure. Sail west to America. Make their way inland along the Ohio River. Create a museum-like collection of artifacts as a way to remember their rich and varied Mediterranean cultures. Bury artifacts to protect them from enemies. Cam smiled. Perhaps bury the Bar Kokhba treasure as well?

He spoke. "You said something that made me think. If some of the artifacts were Christian in theme, they couldn't be from around 40 AD. Christianity hadn't really gotten going yet. Jesus didn't die until around 33 AD. No way could it have spread all the way to Mauritania that quickly."

She leaned forward. "Another argument pointing to the Ninth Legion."

"Hey, try something for me, just for giggles. Do a search for 'Roman ship' and 'Burrows Cave.'"

He waited while she tapped at her phone. With a grin, she angled it to show him the search results. "Bingo," she said. "One Roman-era ship, just like you ordered."

Roman-Era Ship, Burrows Cave

He nodded. The carving didn't prove anything conclusively. But if they were correct that Burrows Cave evidenced a second-century Roman visitation, well, that's the type of ship they should see depicted on the cave carvings. Not, say, a twelfth-century Dutch cog or ninth century Viking longship. It was a subtle, but compelling, point.

They continued west along Route 64, the land flat and sparse with only an occasional wooded area breaking up the plots of farmland. Just over three hours after leaving Louisville, but only two hours on the clock due to crossing time zones, Cam exited. "We're about 100 miles east of St. Louis."

"Are we near where the Ohio River meets the Mississippi?"

"That's south of here. If we had followed the river, we could have gone to a place called Cave-in-Rock. It's a massive cave on the banks of the river. Look it up."

She found an image on her phone.

Cave-in-Rock on Ohio River, Illinois

"It says here that it used to be used by bandits who robbed people on their way down the river," Astarte remarked.

"In the 1830s, a doctor wrote a book and said the cave was filled with ancient carvings of animals and people. The people, he said, were dressed in Roman clothing. Unfortunately, the carvings are gone now, covered by graffiti. Otherwise, it would have been worth another detour."

He headed south toward the town of Makanda. "But there is something south of here I want to look at. We're a bit tight on time, but I think it's worth it."

Just over an hour later they parked in front of the Giant City Visitor Center, a rustic stone and dark-wood structure that reminded Cam of a Vermont ski lodge.

"This place is famous for its giant sandstone walls, which is where it gets its name. They're natural. But there are also some manmade stone walls in the woods that are a mystery."

They got out of the vehicle. "You're thinking Roman."

He nodded. "Not just me. The first settlers in this area were convinced the walls were built by some ancient culture."

They hiked up a steep incline to find a wide, six-foot high stone wall snaking its way along the apex of the ridge for the length of a football field. At its base, the wall averaged five feet in width.

Old Stone Fort, Giant City, Makanda, Illinois

"The thing about it is that the wall serves no obvious agricultural purpose," Cam said. "There's more than forty thousand stones, all of them apparently carried up a two-hundred-foot hill from the streambed below. It had to be for defensive purposes, here on the high ground."

"Could it be Native American?"

"Possibly. But the local tribes lay no claim to it, and there's really no other example of this kind of rampart work among the tribes. Remember, the tribes in this area were migratory. They didn't defend a particular territory."

"Except the Mandan. We settled in one place, like Europeans."

"Right."

"What's the age?"

"They did carbon-dating. Would you believe me if I said between first and fifth century?"

She smiled. "Of course I would. Otherwise you wouldn't have dragged me up this hill."

Cam and Astarte left the Giant City park and headed back north, toward what he hoped would be the Burrows Cave site.

"Tell me again why you think this farm is the spot?"

He handed her his phone. "Here's the email I got from the woman whose family owns the farm?"

Astarte read it aloud:

*Our farm is known as the Lowery Farm, in Romine Township. There's a large rock bluff running in a north-south direction on the farm alongside the Skillet Fork River. In around 1925, our ancestor, Orville Lowery, found a hole carved into the wall of a cliff face. A rock plug cut exactly to fit the hole blocked it. He removed the plug, crawled through and found a cave with numerous carvings which he thought were Indian—mostly black stones with strange writing and the faces of men wearing unfamiliar headgear. Some marble pieces as well. He also believed the cave had been filled with gold objects because he found gold dust on the walls. Over the years, we've found other cavities and small caves with the same kind of carved stones.*

Astarte looked at him. "Black stones with strange writing and men wearing headgear. My uncle had, like, fifty of those. And some marble pieces also."

"The Roman soldier carving you found online is one of them. You're right, there are hundreds."

"What about the gold?" she asked.

"I don't know. Burrows, from day one, claimed he found gold statues and sarcophagi hidden in the cave. But he also said he left most of it in there because the pieces were too big and heavy to carry out."

"So why did this woman contact you? I mean, why not call the authorities?"

"She heard me on a radio show, then bought my book. She says she went to the local college and they looked at her like she was a kook. I told her we were driving out this way. She agreed to show us the cave as long as we kept it's location a secret."

Astarte chewed her lip and stared out the window for a few seconds. "Okay, let's say this cave is some kind of repository for artifacts related to the Mandan. Maybe they fled west after being attacked at that fort in Louisville, or north from that Giant City fort, and they needed someplace to hide their treasures."

"Right. And the Skillet Fork River, the one running through Lowery Farm, flows into the Ohio via the Wabash River. So the site was accessible."

They picked at trail mix in the car, not wanting to waste time with a lunch stop. An hour later, following his GPS, Cam turned down a long, straight gravel drive leading through cornfields to a modest red-sided ranch house. The home sat atop an island of grass amidst the cornfields. "Number 4017," Cam said, "this is it." The mid-afternoon sun beat down on a white pickup truck in the driveway as a light breeze did little to cool the August heat.

A tall blond woman in blue jeans and a denim shirt waved from the porch. Cam and Astarte, knowing they were going to be exploring a cave, had dressed in jeans as well.

"Dad," Astarte said, "please tell me you're not going to wear the fanny pack."

He grinned, filling the pack quickly with granola bars, hand sanitizer, and the Roman coins he had shown to Astarte at breakfast a few days earlier in Westford. He wanted to show the coins to the owners of the farm. "In fact, I am. Never can be too careful. And it's a fashion statement."

She rolled her eyes. "I really miss Mum."

Chuckling, they exited the SUV. "I'm Fern," the woman said, walking toward them. She looked to be about forty. "You must be Cameron."

"And this is my daughter, Astarte. Thanks for meeting with us."

As she wiped her hands on a rag, Cam notice that they appeared smooth and blemish-free, not what he'd expect from a farmer.

"I was just doing some cleaning. We start harvesting in a couple of weeks. Once that starts, no time for anything but."

"If you want to just point us in the right direction, we can go look at the cave ourselves."

"No, now's a good time." She gestured toward the pickup. "Hop in. I'll drive. Too hot to be hiking around out here." She pointed toward a forested area rising to meet the horizon beyond the sea of corn. "It's back there, in those woods."

They bounced along a rutted track for about half a mile. "Like I said in my email, my great-grandaddy found this cave back in the

1920s. Actually, it was his daughter, Fern, who was six at the time. I'm named after her."

She parked at the edge of the treed area and led them through the woods on a narrow path tracking the edge of a gully, Cam using a hiking stick to steady himself. Walking behind, he noticed that the soles of Fern's work boots appeared new and unsoiled. Odd, like her hands. He shrugged. Perhaps she just happened to be a neat farmer.

"When we get a lot of rain," she said, "this gully fills." A twelve-foot wall of stone ran along the opposite side of the gully. A few hundred yards in, she stopped and pointed. "See that shelf protruding from the wall of stone? About four feet up, there's a hole in the wall. See it?"

Cam snapped a picture and nodded. "Looks like it's about two feet in diameter."

Lowery Farm Cave Hole, Illinois

"A little less, actually. It's tight. But my great-granddaddy crawled in. It opens up into a cave system that goes on for hundreds of yards. But the artifacts were all near the entrance, stacked on stone ledges."

"Can we go in?" Astarte asked.

Fern nodded. "A little further up, there's a place to cross the gully and climb up to the ledge. That's how my grandmother found it. She was playing around the gully, looking for arrowheads. There was another rock in the hole, almost like a plug. They noticed it didn't really belong there."

Cam's phone dinged, signifying a text. Normally he would have ignored it, but something told him to take a second to read it. Rivka, the Mossad agent. Odd. He glanced down. *You are in danger.*

Swallowing, he touched Astarte on the arm. "Honey, can you go back to the pickup truck for me? I think my insulin pump fell off. It must be on the front seat." He shrugged at Fern. "I have diabetes."

Astarte looked at him funny, probably because she could see the bulge of the pump beneath his shirt.

He tugged at his earlobe. In softball, that was the sign the coach gave when he wanted the girls to pay close attention, as if saying, *Listen carefully to me.* "Thanks," Cam said. "We'll wait here for you."

"Sure, Dad." She gave him a long look, turned and began to jog back along the path.

He turned to Fern. What had Rivka meant by her warning? Did she mean they were in danger now, specifically? Or, rather, just in general? He had to assume the former. He should have listened to his gut when he noticed her hands and boots.

Fern allowed a tight smile to form slowly. "That was wise."

"What?"

Two men stepped from behind trees twenty yards away, each carrying a hunting rifle. "Sending your daughter away. Nice try."

A third man, not much older than Astarte, appeared on the path, pushing Astarte ahead of him.

*Damn.* "What exactly is it you want?" Cam asked.

"First, your phones. Hand them over. And your walking stick."

Cam stalled. "Where's the real Fern?"

"She and her husband had a conveniently-arranged minor car accident. Nothing serious, but they'll be occupied for a couple of hours." Her eyes narrowed. "Your phones. *Now,* Mr. Thorne."

One of the men lifted his rifle. Sighing, Cam complied, motioning for Astarte to do the same. There was a time in his life, before his injury, where he might have played it differently. But he couldn't now, especially with Astarte in danger.

The fake Fern motioned toward the cave, the men with the rifles following. "So here's the deal. I'm Fern's hairdresser. You'd be surprised what people confide while in the chair. These three boys are my brothers. Not rocket scientists, but they can keep their mouths shut and they sure as shit can handle a rifle. We grew up here. Heard the stories. We know there's a treasure in these parts. Fern told me what she knows about the cave." She turned. "But it's not enough. Nobody can figure out the writings and symbols."

"What makes you think I can?"

"Desperation, I suppose. There aren't many experts in pre-Columbus history running around out there. You're one of them." She set her jaw and took a rifle from one of her brothers. "And lost treasure makes people do, well, desperate things."

She led Cam and Astarte to the cave shelf and gestured toward the hole with her weapon. "I hope you don't mind snakes and bats." She shrugged. "Actually, it doesn't matter. In you go."

The hole was chest high. Cam didn't see that they had much choice. "I'll go first," he said to Astarte. Crawling, at least, was something he didn't really need his legs for. He hoisted himself up and wriggled forward at a slight downhill angle, his body blocking most of the outside light. He was glad they weren't wearing shorts. After about ten feet, he felt a cooling temperature change. Rolling out of the tube, he stood, the air thick, his eyes trying to adjust.

Astarte popped through a few seconds later. "We can't see anything," she yelled through the opening.

In response, Cam's phone slid toward him, clattering through the stone passageway.

"There's no cell coverage in there," Fern called, "so don't waste your time trying. The carvings are next to the entrance." She paused. "And don't bother to come out without answers."

Cam reached for his phone. As Fern said, no coverage. He flicked on the flashlight mode.

The carvings could wait. First, he needed to figure out what their options were. He had no delusions about what was likely to happen. If he couldn't help Fern and her brothers decipher the cave writings, he'd be of no use to them, and they'd likely at least consider blocking the entrance and leaving him and Astarte in the cave to die. And if he *could* decipher the carvings, well, they might meet the same fate, no longer being of any use to treasure hunters hoping to keep their find a secret. The key would be to split the difference, to give them just enough that they saw value in keeping him around. Or, alternatively, to find an escape route.

The cave was narrow, head-high, angling away from the opening toward their right, generally following the direction of the gulley. The sound of water dripping echoed around them, and the stone floor was wet and slick. "Watch your step," he warned. Stalactites hung from above like melted candles. He shined his flashlight up to the ceiling; a thick brown blanket of sleeping bats—thousands, from what Cam knew about bat colonies—pulsated. Cam swallowed.

"Gosh," Astarte said, "Look at all of them."

"I'd rather not. Hopefully, we'll be long gone before they wake for their evening meal."

"Good thing you have your fanny pack. We can squirt hand sanitizer at them."

Cam was glad Astarte was putting on a brave face. Fear, which they were both actuley feeling, could be paralyzing. The fact that she had made a witty comment meant that, well, she was keeping her wits about her.

He moved forward. His light danced on the walls. The underground waters had carved a passageway about two feet wide; on either side of the passageway, a half-wall rose like a line of hedges bordering a garden path.

"It looks like someone plowed a path after a big snowstorm," Astarte said.

About thirty feet in, Cam turned and snapped a picture, the circular cave opening shining back at him like a floodlight. The proverbial light at the end of the tunnel. But he knew it offered them no safe harbor.

Illinois Cave

"These must be the ledges where the artifacts were," she said, standing on her tip-toes to peer over them. "But there's nothing there now."

"These guys wouldn't have bothered to capture us without searching the cave themselves first. I'm sure it's been cleaned out."

"So what's the plan?" Astarte asked.

The air was thicker here, and Cam guessed it would get only worse the further in they ventured. On the other hand, if water was dripping in, it had to come from somewhere and also had to drain away somehow. This cave network probably had another exit point. He exhaled. Given the right equipment and training, they might even have had a chance at finding it. But it would be foolhardy to wander deeper.

"Let's take a look at the carvings," he said. "If we can figure them out, maybe they'll let us go."

He led her back toward the entrance and shined his phone flashlight on the wall. At eye level, a box of symbols or letters had been etched into the cave face.

Burrows Cave Script

Cam exhaled. He recognized the script immediately. "It's the same writing that's on a bunch of the Burrows Cave artifacts," he explained. "Nobody's been able to figure it out."

"It looks sort of Phoenician."

"Yes. Sort of. But not exactly. Some people say it's a combination of Latin and Etruscan, a language spoken in ancient Italy before the Roman Empire. Some say its Iberian. But nobody's really been able to offer a good translation for any of it."

"Which is why we're stuck in this cave."

"Right." Turning, Cam's fanny pack slapped against the cave wall, jingling faintly. He froze. "That's it."

"What?"

"I have an idea."

Astarte put her head into the cave opening. "Hey, we found something," she shouted, her words echoing.

"What?" the fake Fern replied.

"You're probably not going to believe it." She paused. "Treasure chests, filled with coins."

A few seconds passed. "The girl comes out first. No tricks."

Astarte wriggled through, blinking as the sunlight assaulted her eyes. A pair of strong hands grabbed her arms.

Fern called in. "Now you, Thorne. Slowly."

Cam crawled out, also blinking.

"Show me," the woman demanded.

"I need to reach into my pocket, okay?" Cam asked, pointing to his blue jeans.

One of the brothers trained his rifle on him. "Okay," Fern said. "Slowly."

Cam pulled out a half dozen coins and dropped them into Fern's outreached hand. "They're Roman," he said. "I think second and third century. There are, like, four or five big chests filled with them."

Fern angled her head. "We searched that cave. Where?"

"I decoded the writings. It was an old Phoenician box cipher," he explained. "The reason nobody could translate it is that more than half of the symbols are gobbledygook. What you need to do is start in the center, and then move outward like a Fibonacci spiral, only using the symbols that are actually touched by the spiral—"

Fern cut him off. "Get to the point."

"Sorry." He took a deep breath. "The writing is a set of instructions. It says to go 8 paces in. Now, a pace in Roman times was actually two steps, not one—"

"The point, Mr. Thorne."

Astarte held her breath. *Careful, Dad.*

"Right," Cam replied. "Sixteen paces in, there's a fake wall that pivots, like those bookshelves in old mansions leading to secret passageways. Behind the wall is another room." He paused. "With the treasure chests."

Fern examined the coins. "They don't look gold."

She handed them to Darrell, the brother who had escorted Astarte back to the cave. "These ain't gold."

Astarte almost made a snarky retort. What, a cache of ancient coins wasn't enough? If a genuine find, these coins would be worth a fortune just based on their historical value. But she bit her tongue.

Cam replied. "Most Roman coins were bronze and silver, though some were gold." He shrugged. "We didn't go through the chests. Just grabbed a handful to show you what we found." He lifted his chin. "Can we go now? You have your treasure."

Fern ignored him. "Darrell, guard the entrance. Buck and Billy, come with me." She turned to Cam. "You're not going anywhere until you show us exactly where this treasure is." She gestured. "Lead the way."

Astarte marched forward and tucked her head into the opening. So far, so good.

Using a flashlight Fern had given him, Cam led her and her two brothers away from the cave entrance, down the narrow path carved by water flowing through the limestone. Thirty feet in, standing just behind a cluster of stalactites which they had to duck under, he pointed to a cave wall.

"That's it. That wall pivots and swings open." He stepped back, allowing the group to come closer to examine the wall. Out of the corner of his eye, he saw Astarte edge back a few steps. She stood next to a ledge, on top of which she had earlier stacked a handful of rocks she collected from the floor of the cave.

"Show us," Fern ordered.

"Okay." Cam took a step toward the wall and coughed, signaling

Astarte. She didn't hesitate, heaving the handful of stones upward at the cave ceiling. As she did so, Cam flicked off his light and dove for the floor. Next to him, Astarte did the same.

The bats reacted instantly, screeching in panic and taking flight in response to the rocks. In the near-black, the entire cave erupted with the flap of wings as thousands of bats swarmed before regathering as a group to fly toward the cave entrance.

Fern screamed and her two brothers cursed; in the faint light Cam could see them huddling against a wall, arms covering their heads. "Now," he whispered to Astarte. The cave seemed almost alive, convulsing, as if the cavern itself might take flight.

As Astarte began to crawl toward the opening, the bats still swarming above them, Cam quickly removed the hand sanitizer and sunscreen from his fanny pack and squirted, emptying both containers on the wet cave floor. He then followed Astarte, ignoring the pain in his elbows and knees as they banged against the stone floor. Before leaving the cave, they had practiced crawling through the passageway in the dark. Which meant he only hit his head a couple of times.

Five or six seconds after Astarte had unleashed the bats, Fern reacted. "Get them! They're escaping."

They were, in fact, halfway down the passageway.

"Darrell's out there," came the reply. One of the brothers flicked on his flashlight, which only served further to distress the bats.

"I said, get them!" she shrieked.

A couple of heavy footsteps, then a curse and the sound of a body thumping to the ground as one of the brothers lost his footing on the slickened cave floor. Cam didn't dare look back, but he trusted his ears. Another tumble, the second man presumably stumbling over the first.

"Almost there," Cam said to Astarte. "You go through first." The bats still swarmed, though most of them seemed already to have poured out the entrance. Cam and Astarte had prepared beforehand, tucking their pant legs into their socks and psychologically readying themselves for nature's onslaught. But they both knew the crawl through the opening would make for a nightmarish few seconds.

Astarte stood, ran the final few steps, and dove for the tunnel. A gunshot rang out, the bullet ricocheting off the cave walls. Cam didn't wait for a second shot, following Astarte into the opening. Bats were repulsive. But not as repulsive as bullets.

He wriggled, head down and eyes closed, the bats slithering by him in the few inches of space between his body and the tunnel's walls. He fought back a wave of panic. Amanda's voice: *They're just scared animals, trying to get out, just like you.* He breathed. The plan had worked so far. But here was the crucial part. Had Darrell been neutralized?

Cam propelled himself halfway out—head and chest—and shaded his eyes. To his right, on the edge of the ledge, he was barely able to make out the figure of a bloody-faced man gyrating and slapping at his body as if on fire. Cam blinked. One bat had lodged in Darrell's hair, and, apparently, a few others had flown down his shirt. Cam guessed that, having heard Fern scream, the sentry had stuck his head into the cave hole to investigate, only to have been battered by an avalanche of panicked, sharp-toothed projectiles.

Astarte, who had popped through a few seconds before Cam, handed Cam Darrell's hunting rifle as Cam dropped from the hole. "That was fun," she said, smiling.

He shuddered. "I need a shower." *And a cocktail.*

Glancing at Darrell to make sure he was not a threat, Cam yelled into the cave. "Stand back!"

He waited a couple of seconds, stepped away from the opening, and, reaching in, fired a single shot into the cave. He didn't want to hit anyone, but he wouldn't have felt guilty if he had.

He turned to Darrell, who was now whimpering on the ground, his eyes wide in terror. "Give me your car keys," Cam ordered. "And those coins. And don't even think about following us."

Cam eyed the man. He took a deep breath, fighting against his rage, against the monster. Following them was the last thing on Darrell's mind. "If I were you, I'd go straight for a rabies shot." Cam lowered the rifle. "Then get some therapy."

Astarte sat in Darrell's pickup truck with the engine running, peering down the path, waiting for her dad. Cam had insisted she run ahead with the keys. He shuffled along with the rifle, moving as fast as he could. "If I'm not there in five minutes," he said, "go for help."

They both figured there was no way Darrell would rally. But Fern and her two brothers from the cave might still have some fight in them.

She had backed the vehicle as far down the path as she could, not caring that the overhanging branches were scratching its paint. As soon as her dad hopped in, she was ready to gun it.

She checked her watch. "Come on, Dad," she whispered. Almost five minutes. She'd give him an extra minute or two. They had both exerted a lot of energy in the cave, not to mention their earlier three-mile walk and his weightlifting in Clarksville.

There. A movement. Her dad trudging along, the rifle dragging behind. She exhaled.

With a loud sigh, he pulled himself into the truck. "Off we go," he said.

She hit the gas. "Where to?"

He slumped. "Anywhere but here."

"Back to our SUV?"

"That's the first place they'll come looking for us."

"If they come, it'll be on foot. I punctured Fern's tires."

He smiled. "Good job. Then, yes, back to the SUV. Then we get out of here." He sighed again. "Sorry about that. Burrows Cave is always a wildcard."

"So do you think that's the actual cave?"

He nodded, still panting. "That writing on the wall matches the artifacts I've seen. Hard to see how else it would have gotten there."

"Maybe someone is trying to put people off the scent?"

"That would make sense, except nobody really knows about this site except Fern. And, apparently, the fake Fern and her brothers. So nobody is on the scent. Everyone else thinks Burrows Cave is fifty miles east of here, in Olney."

They bounced along through the cornfields, Astarte frequently checking the rearview mirror. Ahead, Cam's SUV sat undisturbed in the driveway of Fern's ranch. "Your chariot, sir," she said with a smile.

"Well done, honey. I'm proud of you. You were not only resourceful back there, but very brave."

"Thanks. It was worth it. We learned the true location of Burrows Cave. And, more to the point, that the cave is real, not a hoax."

"And we learned something else very important also."

She turned, a quizzical look on her face. "What's that?"

He held her eyes and spoke slowly, somberly. "Never, ever underestimate a man with a fanny pack."

Caryn Collin sat at the kitchen table in the apartment above her hair salon and fingered the handful of Roman coins Cameron Thorne had used to fool her. She shook her head and fought back tears of frustration. This cave, this treasure, had tormented her family for forty years, for three generations. Was it time finally to let go?

She swigged her Coors Light. This time, she had thought, they were finally going to hit paydirt. She had cultivated her relationship with Fern, luring her into the salon (by telling her she had won a random drawing for a free cut and color), befriending her, encouraging her to confide. And Thorne was the expert who could decode the cave drawing. It all seemed so perfect. Until the bats erupted.

Opening another beer, she moved to the living room and flopped into the old recliner. Grandpa Jack's. He had been the first of the family to fall into Burrows Cave. Burrows had hired him to help haul artifacts from the cave. They had done so under the cover of darkness, until one night in 1989 Jack never came home. Burrows had knocked on the door at dawn, hat in hand, teary-eyed, claiming a booby trap in the cave had sent a cascade of rocks down on Jack like something out of an Indiana Jones movie. Jack's daughter, Caryn's mother, had accepted $20,000 in cash from Burrows in exchange for not contacting the authorities. It, plus the six Roman coins found today, constituted the entirety of wealth accumulated by the family over the past four decades from the cave.

Yet Grandpa Jack's stories haunted Caryn and her brothers. All except Darrell—he had been too young to hear them. Now Darrell had bats to haunt him instead.

She picked up a magazine, but Grandpa Jack's stories chirped at her like an earworm, his voice gravelly from the Winstons he chain-smoked. "I've seen it. Candelabras and goblets and trumpets all made of solid gold. Treasure chests. Burrows won't let us take anything out yet. But soon. Soon we'll be rich."

"Soon we'll all be dead," Caryn mouthed in reply, tossing the magazine aside.

Burrows had been too savvy to allow Jack to learn the location of the cave, insisting on a blindfold every time they got within ten miles. And Jack had been too trusting.

But Fern's property seemed to check all the boxes. Right location, right topography, a history of artifacts found on the farm. Not to mention ancient script on the walls. There were, really, only two possibilities: The treasure was in the cave and had been removed by Burrows. Or the treasure was in the cave still. And Burrows was currently living in a modest ranch on a quarter-acre lot outside of Denver which he paid $130,000 for. Hardly what Caryn imagined for herself if she found a treasure.

"Which means that fucking treasure is probably still in the cave," she said, before guzzling her beer and crushing the can.

"Did I mention I hate bats?" Cam said as Astarte drove west on the interstate in the late-afternoon sun. He jerked back from a plastic bag that brushed against his leg, then slapped at a burst of air from the vent. He might never sleep again.

"Dad, you're the one who said you had your heart set on seeing bats today. Now you're complaining?"

"Very funny." He shuddered.

"We should get one as a pet."

"Please stop. I'm begging you."

He closed the vent, ran his hand over the back of his neck and both arms and legs, and took a deep breath. "Okay." They needed to make a plan. He had already texted the real Fern, warning her about the fake Fern. He thought about calling the police, but didn't want to kill the rest of the day answering questions. "We're behind schedule. And we need to get rabies shots. If we do that and also check into a hotel for a shower, we're going to be a day late to Montana. It's your call, honey."

"If I show up smelling like a pair of old hockey gloves and drooling from rabies, Matthias isn't going to want to see me, anyway."

Cam chuckled. They had stopped at a rest area to wash the grime and bat guano from their hands and elbows. "All right. It's been a long day already. We're close to St. Louis. Let's find a hotel, grab a quick shower, head over to the emergency room, and then go to Cahokia Mounds. Then we can have a nice dinner, go to bed early, and get on the road by dawn."

"Are you sure we need shots?" she asked. "I don't think I got bit."

"Sorry, but yes. Bats have really small teeth so you might not even notice a bite. And even a scratch can transmit it."

She shuddered. "I feel bad for that Darrell guy. He was pretty freaked out."

"I'm guessing the people in the cave were also. We knew what was coming, and we were able to stay low. They had no idea."

"And no treasure, either," she said, smiling.

"Oh, I need to do something." Cam wasn't sure what the protocol was for thanking a Mossad agent for potentially saving his life. Especially since the agency had made it known it might later decide to take it. He figured simple was best. He texted Rivka. *Thanks for warning. We are safe and back on the road.*

When Cam looked up from checking his phone, he sensed a change in Astarte's mood. "You seem a little, I don't know, down," he said.

She bit her lip. "It's just that I've always thought of my ancestors as heroic. *Admirable.* They crossed the Atlantic, made their way inland, built forts, eventually befriended the natives."

"So what's changed?"

"Well, now I picture a bunch of them traipsing across the frontier wearing fanny packs." She shook her head and grinned. "It's just not working for me."

He laughed. "Good one. You got me."

"Hey," she said. "You never told me what gave the fake Fern away. You knew something was up; that's why you tried to send me back to the truck."

"Her hands and boots were too clean. Didn't look like a real farmer to me."

"You're right. She was a hairdresser. Wow, Dad, that's impressive."

"Don't be too impressed." He smiled. "I also got a text from the Mossad warning me we were in danger."

She rolled her eyes. "Jerk."

"What I can't figure out is how they knew. The Mossad."

"Are they tracking us?"

He shook his head. "I don't think so. I had the SUV checked before we left. And, even so, tracking us would just tell them where we were, not that we were in danger."

"So they must be somehow tracking the fake Fern. Or listening to her communications."

"That's the same conclusion I reached. But why? Why would the Mossad care about some treasure-hunting hairdresser looking for Burrows Cave?"

She chewed her lip. "If we play connect-the-dots, we can go from Burrows Cave to the Ninth Legion to the Bar Kokhba uprising to the Temple treasure. It would make sense that Israeli intelligence would be interested in ancient Jewish artifacts and treasures."

Cam nodded. "I like it. It holds together, at least."

"And if they are bothering to track Fern, they must feel she is on the right track. That it's possible the treasure is here someplace in America."

Cam nodded again. "Agreed." He thought about it. "If they were tracking her, maybe she's more than just a hairdresser."

"Aha. Good point."

His phone dinged, interrupting their musings. "It's an email from the woman with the coin collection we met at the hotel this morning." He read through it and sighed. "Maybe not so fast on the Bar Kokhba connections. She doesn't know about the coin we saw, but she says someone else from Louisville has a Bar Kokhba coin. Some Israeli coin expert looked at it and said it's a replica from the early 1900s. Not authentic."

"Does that mean the coin we saw last night at the hotel was a replica also?"

"Hold on. She sent a link to the article the Israeli coin expert wrote in some coin collecting magazine. It has a picture of the coin." Cam studied it. "Damn. It looks the same as the coin we saw. Temple on the front, lulav branch on the back." He shook his head. "I'm guessing the one we saw is a replica also. The expert says it was common for churches at the turn of the century to make commemorative religious coins and hand them out to parishioners. He thinks that's what this is."

"Like you said, that weakens our connection to the Temple treasure. Maybe it wasn't the Ninth Legion that was here."

"Maybe." Cam weighed the evidence in his mind. The Bar Kokhba coin had been, in legal parlance, 'highly probative.' Now it was 'highly rebutted.' But they had other pieces of evidence which were fairly compelling. "I think we might still be on the right track, even without that coin. We still have the other Roman coins and the forts and the skeletons with armor and the anchor and the Brandenberg Stone."

"And the Burrows Cave pieces." Astarte glanced sideways at him. "You might remember them. The ones we almost just died for."

"I'm trying not to think about it. Did I mention I hate bats?"

"A few times, yes."

He pointed. "Take this exit. And I call first shower."

Rivka picked at a Cobb salad at a half-empty Uno Pizzeria in a shopping mall parking lot north of Boston. She. Was. So. Damn. Bored. She had expected life as a Mossad agent to be thrilling, hectic, maybe dangerous. Car chases and hidden cameras and men in tuxedos drinking martinis. Obviously, she had seen too many movies. She sipped at her Diet Coke. Hell, she wasn't even allowed to have a glass of wine while on duty. Which was, basically, all the time.

Her phone dinged. Cameron Thorne, texting her that he was safe. That was something, at least. But even the act of texting him a warning had been unfulfilling. She had been ordered to send the message, but given only barebones context and background. There was a group searching for the Bar Kokhba treasure in a cave in southern Illinois. Was that where the treasure was secreted? Rivka didn't know. She wasn't even sure if the Mossad itself knew. Best she could discern, her superiors had a vague suspicion the treasure was hidden somewhere in America, but had no idea where. And it was not the type of thing—being some of the most holy artifacts in Jewish history—which could be ignored. So they had assigned the new girl to the case: Keep an eye on Thorne. Find out what he knows. Determine if this Roman shipwreck might be related.

What they hadn't told her was what to do in all the downtime. Other than not drink wine, of course. Next debriefing, she would ask for more information. Now that things had heated up, she had a legitimate need to know.

Tired of watching the painfully dull baseball game on the television above the bar, she pulled Thorne's file from the leather satchel at her feet. He, at least, was not dull.

In fact, he was full of contradictions.

As a young lawyer representing the Catholic Church in priest sex abuse cases, he became so disgusted with his client that he leaked incriminating information to the press. For that, his law license was suspended. So, Rivka had concluded, he was an idealist, a moralist, perhaps even a crusader.

Yet that was not how he lived his life. His law cases were mostly mundane real estate transactions. He didn't lead marches through the streets, hadn't run for office. Sure, he and his wife conducted research which dismantled the Columbus-first myth, but they had done so methodically, dispassionately. The research was not a crusade for him, merely a search for the truth, a curious, analytical mind following the bread crumbs through the woods. It was refreshing, in a way. The Middle East was full of zealots and impassioned causes and petty squabbles flaming into full-scale war.

In the end, tragically, the research cost Thorne his wife and left him, temporarily, a paraplegic. Apparently, America, too, had its zealots.

She put down the file. What the dossier didn't convey was his easy smile and soulful, penetrating brown eyes and toned physique. She realized, with a pang of sadness, that it had been years since she had developed a crush on anyone. Her last crush had led to a three-year relationship, at the end of which she had been, appropriately, crushed. Sari was her name. A lot like Thorne, in fact—soulful, with an easy smile and brown eyes and toned physique. Other than the vagina thing, of course.

She sat back, pushing the sadness away. It was a good thing that she found Thorne attractive. It meant she had healed, moved past Sari.

Not that it mattered. She could only imagine how the agency would react to her having an affair with an asset. That would never fly.

She allowed herself a small smile. *But what if she did it as a way to gain intelligence?*

It was just before five when, her dad driving, they pulled off the highway into the parking lot for the Cahokia Mounds site.

Astarte rotated her arm. "That was a freaking big needle."

"You're the one who wanted a bat as a pet." He shuddered. "And we're going to need another shot in three days." At least the emergency room got them in and out in less than an hour, giving them time to get to Cahokia.

He parked. "Hurry," he said. "The grounds are open until dusk, but the interpretive center closes in a few minutes. I want to show you the birdman carving."

Astarte had read about the site on her dad's phone while he drove from the hospital. Located on the flood plains on the eastern shore of the Mississippi River opposite St. Louis, the settlement was at the center of a trade network ranging from the Gulf Coast to the Great Lakes. At its peak, during the 13th century, Cahokia boasted a population of 20,000 people, making it more populated at the time than London. The city's most enduring legacy was a series of ceremonial earthen mounds, the largest being over ten stories in height with a base covering fourteen acres, about the same coverage as the Great Pyramid of Giza in Egypt. Unlike the Egyptian pyramids, however, the Cahokia mounds were constructed with earth, not stone.

Then, suddenly, in the late 14th century, the city basically disappeared.

Astarte pulled up a drawing of the settlement on her dad's phone, wondering what could have caused its demise.

Cahokia

As if anticipating her inquiry, Cam replied. "One possibility is that the Europeans brought the plague," he said. "Remember, the Kensington Rune Stone party was on the upper Mississippi, up in Minnesota, in the year 1362. If they came downriver, they could have wiped out the entire city." He shrugged. "The dates work."

They walked quickly across the parking lot toward the low-slung, sand-colored interpretive center, Astarte favoring her left knee which she had banged in the cave. Cam continued. "And don't forget the Kensington Rune Stone inscription itself. It talks about a fishing party coming back to camp and finding 'ten men red with blood and death.' That sounds a lot like people dying of the plague, which in Europe was called the 'red death.'"

A wave of bitter sadness washed over Astarte. Her people, the Mandan, had been essentially wiped out by a smallpox outbreak in the 1830s which killed more than ninety percent of the tribe; the few dozen survivors, including Astarte's ancestors, were absorbed by neighboring tribes. Many Indians, and a growing number of historians, believed that smallpox had been used as a weapon to clear Native Americans off their lands. What was not open to debate was that the U.S. government refused to send a smallpox vaccine to the Mandan, believing them to be unworthy of protection.

She refocused. "How do we think this fits in with the Romans?""It doesn't, directly," Cam replied. "It's more about the Templars. They're the ones who carved the Kensington Rune Stone and then would have brought the plague. I think what happened was that the Templars found their way here in the first place by following the Romans. What's interesting is that, in the early 1800s, the first white people to reoccupy Cahokia were Cistercian monks. That's why the largest mound is called 'Monks Mound.'"

She knew that the Cistercians were the sister order to the Templars.

He continued. "It's weird—or maybe not—that the Cistercians would have come back here, to the same spot, four hundred years later."

"Not if they left something here the first time," Astarte replied.

"Exactly. Oh, and one more thing. After the Lewis and Clark expedition, Sacagawea brought her baby all the way back here, to Cahokia, to be baptized by the Cistercians."

It was no small thing, Astarte knew, to travel a thousand miles from North Dakota to St. Louis in the early 1800s. Just to have her baby baptized? Astarte shook her head. Her dad was right—there had to be more to the story.

Cam pushed through the door and paid their admission a few minutes before closing time.

"Just enough time to see one thing," he said, leading her across the exhibition hall and stopping in front of a simple sandstone carving about the size of a cell phone. "They call it the Birdman."

Cahokia Birdman Carving

Astarte snapped a picture. "It reminds me of the Burrows Cave carvings."

"Thank you," he said. "That's exactly what I was hoping you'd say. One of the things skeptics always say about the Burrows Cave artifacts is that they must be fake because some of them are simple and rudimentary." He gestured toward the carving. "Well, so is this. And nobody is calling it a fake."

They spent the next hour walking the grounds in the fading daylight. "I don't think this was a Mandan settlement," Cam said. "But they definitely would have come here to trade."

She nodded. "From what I know, around the 13th century is when we started moving north, up the Missouri River."

"Makes sense. As the Cahokia settlement grew and became more powerful, other tribes got pushed out of the area." He looked at his watch. "Let's get some dinner. Then find you a new phone. The Missouri River can wait. That'll be tomorrow's adventure."

Shrugging, she smiled. "Does it have to be an adventure? Can't it just be a leisurely drive?"

## Chapter 5

Cam woke at the first glow of Monday's dawn. The day before, he had caught a flight back to Boston from Montana after helping Astarte set up her dorm room. Their two-day drive from St. Louis to Montana—basically following the Missouri River, as the Mandan tribe had done centuries earlier—had been long but uneventful. No Mossad, no bats, no gunshots.

Just a sad goodbye and a lonely flight home.

He had set his alarm for five because he knew himself. If he didn't keep busy, he'd risk spiraling into a funk of despair and misery. Already last night he had almost lost himself in half a bottle of spiced rum, the one benefit of which was that he knew he'd feel better in a few hours than he felt right now. Sometimes an upward trajectory, a little momentum, was all it took to kick off the day.

But first he had to actually get out of bed.

After putting Venus outside on her leash, he shuffled back down the hall to use the toilet, one hand on the wall to steady himself. He chose not to look at himself in the mirror, knowing the red-eyed face glaring back at him would be a disapproving one.

At least Amanda had not popped into his head to scold him. "Probably still asleep," he muttered to himself. "Like I should be."

Ten minutes later he was on the elliptical machine. An hour after that he stepped out of the shower. Still not yet seven o'clock. He felt almost human.

His phone rang. Marconi.

"I am in need of your services today."

Cam was planning to meet with a coin expert to examine Denise's Plum Island coins. "I have plans."

"You will need to change them. This cannot wait."

He sighed, swallowing his irritation. He wanted to keep busy, but that didn't mean serving as an on-call lackey for a tyrannical old car dealer. "I might be able to clear my schedule. Why?"

"Meet me at Hanscom Airport in two hours. We will be flying to Mexico City for the day on my jet. I realize this is short notice, but this just came together and I don't want to risk our window of opportunity closing. You have a passport, I assume?"

He resisted the urge to lie just to spite the old man. "I do."

"I will text you the details."

He hung up before Cam could ask any questions. *Mexico?* He stepped into a pair of cargo shorts, then reconsidered. Where were they going in Mexico? Marconi, in his usual reticent manner, hadn't said. Cam switched to khakis and a blue blazer, hoping that wherever they ended up had air-conditioning. Mexico in August would be brutal.

He wolfed down some breakfast, Venus looking up at him with sad eyes. She was smart enough to recognize his travel bag and understand its ramifications. He checked his watch. "Come on, girl, let's go for a quick walk." If he was a few minutes late, so be it.

The wind had shifted, causing the lake currents to flow east to west. Cam had been on the lake long enough to know that the shift portended inclement weather. Removing his blazer, he put on a baseball hat and windbreaker and grabbed Venus' leash.

The neighborhood around the lake was densely packed, the small summer cottages which once sat comfortably on the narrow lots having been replaced by taller, wider structures. A light mist began to fall as Venus pulled Cam along. She missed their morning runs, as did Cam; his therapist—the real one, that is—guessed he'd be able to begin light jogging again in a few weeks.

As if on cue, a dark sedan pulled up. Rivka—the fake therapist—stepped out. Cam was not surprised. His ribcage throbbed, as if reliving the trauma.

"Mind if I join you?" She wore a beige blazer over a pair of jeans, both of which were cut in a way to show off her toned figure.

"Do I have a choice?"

"Not really." She fell in by his side. "Would you like to hold hands?"

He stopped. That was not what he expected to hear. "No. Why?"

She bent to rub Venus's neck. The dog, normally a good judge of character, nuzzled against her thigh. "To make it look more natural," she said, standing. "These are your neighbors. They are bound to ask who you were walking with. It's been, what, four months? It would be understandable if you began dating again."

He shook his head. Again with the dating. He resumed walking. "That's okay. I'll think of something if they ask."

She turned to face him. "Perhaps you don't think I'm pretty enough?"

The rain began. "What? Why would you say that?"

"I think my eyes are too close together. And my nose is too long. I didn't use to think that, but here in America all the models and actresses have smaller noses."

"There are plenty who don't."

She smiled. "So you do think I'm pretty enough. Good." She did a little skip as they walked. "Since you are here, and seemingly in good health, I assume you received my text in time?"

"Actually, no." He explained the cave and their narrow escape.

Her eyes widened. "Impressive. Perhaps I should be recruiting you rather than merely turning you into an asset." She leaned in as she said it, almost flirtatiously. Probably just her training.

"Is that what you're doing, turning me into an asset?"

"Yes. You have information that we need."

"I thought an asset was someone who supplied information voluntarily."

She exhaled. "Yes, I'm sorry about that. I should have asked rather than taken." She shrugged, as if explaining away using the wrong fork for her salad. "I am still rather new at this. I was only recently recruited myself. I was in the army and then, for the past six years, I was a professional beach volleyball player." She angled her head. "But at some point I knew I needed to grow up and get a real job. Something where I wasn't always digging sand out of my ears." She shrugged. "Then I went through a breakup, which seemed like a good time to make a change."

Rivka was either more forthcoming than spies in the movies or she was just playing him. "So how did you know we were in danger?"

She leaned in again. "We know *everything*."

"Clearly not, or you wouldn't be here trying to get info from me." He checked his watch. "Look, I don't have much time. So what is it you want?"

They rounded a corner, Venus pulling harder as she spotted the beach ahead. "As I told you, we are interested in Marconi's Roman shipwreck. And we know you are going to Mexico with him today. I would like a full report when you return."

"You could have waited for me to return if that's all you wanted."

"Yes." She exhaled. "Like I said, I'm new at this. The truth is, it's not just the shipwreck we are interested in."

"I figured." He held her eyes. "The Bar Kokhba treasure."

"Yes. Very good. We believe it may be hidden here in America. Or lost. It disappeared from history almost two thousand years ago, as you probably know."

He scooped up Venus' mess with a plastic bag and turned to walk home. The rain was falling harder now. He thought about offering her his hat but decided against it. "Why me? I'm not an expert on Israeli artifacts."

"For the same reason Marconi hired you. You *are* an expert on pre-Columbus exploration of America. If anyone can put the jigsaw pieces together, it is you. Which is why I came to see you this morning. I need to know what you learned in the Ohio River Valley."

He knew better than to try to lie to her. Somehow the Mossad had tracked him to Illinois and ascertained he was in danger from the fake Fern. They probably knew other details of the trip as well. This was likely a test, to see how forthcoming he'd be.

Exhaling, he gave a ten-minute recount of the trip, showing Rivka pictures of the coins and artifacts and sites on his phone. "Everything fits together," he said as they stopped in front of his driveway. "Except, that is, for the Bar Kokhba coin in Louisville. We thought it was a key piece to all this. But it turned out to be a modern replica." He shrugged. "Even so, I think we're on the right track."

"Okay, thanks," she said, rainwater dripping down her face. "Thanks for being truthful with me."

"Did I really have a choice?"

"We always have choices, Mr. Thorne."

He turned. "Well, whatever."

"One more thing." He turned back; her eyes danced. She didn't seem in any kind of rush to get out of the rain. "Who was the expert who decided the Bar Kokhba coin was not authentic?"

"An Israeli coin collector. I forget his name."

"Interesting," she said, arching an eyebrow. "I suppose we have to take him at his word."

Cam froze. "Wait. You guys did that." *Of course.* "That expert was working for you. The coin really is authentic."

She offered an exaggerated shrug and smiled. "I can neither confirm nor deny. But I will say that it most decidedly would not be in our best interest to have a bunch of treasure hunters out there looking for *our* treasure." She waved. "Good day, Mr. Thorne. Safe travels."

Running behind schedule due to his encounter with the female Mossad agent, Cam quickly changed out of his wet clothes before jumping into his SUV. His mind raced as he drove in the light rain: It now appeared that the Bar Kokhba coin was authentic after all, further buttressing their Ninth Legion theory. At a stoplight, he texted Astarte with the news. The coin had been the weakest link in their argument. Now, it turned out to be one of the strongest. The Mossad wouldn't have bothered to go to the trouble of faking a numismatic report without good reason.

He merged onto the highway. Half of Boston was on vacation, so traffic was light as he cruised east on Route 2. Most commercial flights flew out of Logan Airport, but sports teams and business executives tended to frequent the smaller suburban airport in Bedford, northwest of the city.

Cam passed through security, entered a private lounge per his host's instructions, and was escorted across the tarmac to a ten-seat jet, its engines already running. Marconi, dressed in a gray, Italian-cut suit with yellow tie, stood to greet him. "Mr. Thorne," he said formally, offering another of his half-bows, "thank you for joining us. Allow me to introduce Robinson Roberts. He's a professor of archeology at Boston University."

Roberts turned to eye Cam but did not rise from his leather seat. He was a small, unsmiling man with tinted eyeglasses and a bushy brown mustache who greeted Cam's nod with a grudging lift of his chin.

Marconi reached into his jacket pocket and withdrew two plain white envelopes. "Before I forget." He handed each man an envelope filled with cash. Cam and Roberts both noticed that Cam's was the thicker of the two.

As Marconi turned to consult with the flight crew, Roberts said in a low voice, "I'll say the same thing to you that I said to Marconi. I'm only doing this because I've been ordered to."

Cam found himself instantly disliking the man. "By who?"

"The head of my department. Apparently, Marconi has funded some of our university digs." He rolled his eyes. "But this idea of a Roman shipwreck in New England? Come on."

"You have me at a bit of a disadvantage," Cam said, taking a seat in the opposite row. He hoped he didn't regret it and get caught listening to the archeologist complain for the entire five-hour flight. "I don't even know why we're going to Mexico."

Roberts held a blink for a few seconds, as if by closing his eyes this whole nightmare might disappear. "There's a Roman bust. Terracotta. Found during a pyramid dig in the 1930s at a layer that dates back to the eleventh century." He shook his head. "So of course people like you jump to the conclusion that the Romans must have sailed to Mexico."

Cam clenched his jaw. "Please don't presume to know what conclusions I might reach."

"Come on. I know about your research on the Templars. Why else would Marconi bring you along?"

"I could ask the same thing about you."

"Because he knows he needs an archeologist to support his claims. And he's hoping that he's given enough money to BU that I'll go along with it."

"Will you?"

"Not a fucking chance."

"Even if you conclude the bust really is evidence of Roman travel to America?"

Roberts sniffed. "There's not a fucking chance of that happening either."

Astarte awoke in her dorm room to see Matthias' dark eyes staring into hers in the purple light of dawn.

She smiled. "Hi there."

"Good morning." He smelled minty and fresh.

"No fair. You brushed your teeth."

He kissed her lightly. "I had to use the bathroom, anyway."

Sighing, she relaxed her body into his. It had been a couple of months since she had last seen him, and when they first arrived, she felt shy. She had never let anyone completely into her personal space before, and the time away had made him almost a stranger. But a night of holding hands and laughing lightly and watching the stars twinkle over the Rockies as Matthias strummed his guitar had washed away her bashfulness.

"You passed the test," she said.

"What test?"

"When you sleep, you breathe through your nose."

He raised his eyebrows. "Doesn't everyone?"

"I did a study for a science project. Sixty-one percent of people sleep with their mouths open. It's not healthy. It makes you dehydrated and can lead to dental problems." She smiled. "When I do sleepover parties with my friends, I always try to count. Humans are the only animal that breathes through its mouth when sleeping."

"Well, it's not sixty-one percent on an Indian reservation. Indian babies are taught not to breathe through their mouths."

"I've never heard of that." If her birth mother had taught her that before dying, Astarte had no memory of it.

"You have that book by Catlin, the guy who lived with the Mandan?"

"I'm reading it now."

"Well, he wrote another one. It's called *Shut Your Mouth and Save Your Life.*"

She pulled her head back to look at him. "No, he didn't."

"I'm serious. He was convinced that the Indians were healthier than the white man because we're taught to breathe through our nose. I think he lost a kid to pneumonia or something, so he was obsessed with breathing."

"That's crazy. But it shows how observant he was about Indian life."

"He also said that's why Indians have such good teeth. Like you said."

She touched his mouth, running her hand along his lips. Matthias did, indeed, have straight, white teeth. Not to mention a cute chin dimple and a chiseled jaw. The first time she met him, at freshmen orientation a few months ago, she thought he looked like a young Antonio Banderas, complete with ponytail.

He continued. "In the Blackfoot tribe, the elders talk say the white man has bad teeth because of all the lies that pass over them on the way out of his mouth."

She laughed. "I like that." In fact, she realized she would have been entertained by pretty much anything he said. "That breathing through the nose thing," she said, leaning in. "I bet it helps when kissing."

An hour later, they disentangled themselves from the bed sheets and threw on some clothes. As a student in the honors college, Astarte had been given a single room, which was a nice luxury on a morning like this. Matthias, an upperclassman, lived off campus with some friends.

"Breakfast?" she asked.

"Great," he replied. "I was worried you were going to have your way with me and then just kick me out."

She slipped her arm into his. "First, I have to teach some other boy how to breathe through his nose."

She had told him about their adventures in the Ohio River Valley. "You never told me about the second half of your drive," he said.

"Not much to tell. It took, like, forever. Did you know that the Missouri River is longer than the Mississippi?"

"Really?"

"Trust me. We drove every mile of it." They pushed through the dormitory exit and strolled slowly across the quad in the brisk mountain air.

"Did it help you understand your people?"

"It did, actually. From what I've read, the Mandan were always traders. The other tribes were larger and more powerful, so to protect ourselves we stayed on the river and built fortifications on the high ground. Seeing the rivers—both the Ohio and the Missouri—gave me a good feel for where, and even how, we lived."

"How does all this Roman stuff dovetail with the Templars?"

She had explained to him the Mandan legend about the Templars coming to America in the twelfth century and marrying into the Mandan tribe. "It may be that the Templars were not the first Europeans in the Mandan line. Based on what my dad and I saw on our trip, it looks like the Romans were here before them—maybe a thousand years earlier."

"Which explains the Burrows Cave artifacts," he said.

"Right. The Templars somehow must have known about the Romans coming here. Maybe the Church told them—I mean, the Romans came from Rome, where the Vatican is. Or maybe the

Templars learned about it while in Israel. Either way, the Templars probably came over looking for the Roman settlement."

Matthias nodded. "Didn't I read something about the Templars wanting to form a New Jerusalem in America?"

"That's right. They were butting heads with the Church on a lot of the dogma, especially about the Church being so patriarchal. They expected that someday the Church would turn on them. Which it did. So they were looking for a safe haven."

"Well, to make a New Jerusalem, it would help to have the artifacts and decorations from the original Temple in the old Jerusalem, right?"

"It would. The question then is, are the artifacts still here?"

He opened the dining hall door for her. It was still early, so most of the tables were empty. They grabbed trays.

She smiled. "Our friends in Illinois think they're in some cave being guarded by bats. It's also possible they're in a shipwreck off the coast. That's what my dad is working on now."

"Shipwrecks make sense. I mean, the Romans didn't swim to America."

She smiled, then sighed. "I'm getting to the point where I understand that I might never know the whole story. I mean, it all happened a thousand or even two thousand years ago."

"And now you're like the last one. The last Mandan."

"Right. And I don't know if I'm Native American with European blood mixed in, or European with Native American blood mixed in." She turned her palms up and lowered her voice. "And I don't know if I really do descend from Jesus and Mary Magdalene and Cleopatra." She sighed again. "Basically, I don't know anything."

Matthias took her hand. "I get that you want to know about your past. I do. But, for me, seeing what kind of person you are, I'm more curious about your *future*." He smiled. "That's where this whole fortieth princess prophecy is going to *really* get interesting."

Cam allowed his eyes to close in the dim light of the jet, pleased to have a chance both to nurse his hangover and avoid conversing with the surly archeologist, Robinson Roberts. For some reason, his mind turned to the Mossad agent. She was an interesting character study, whipsawing between solemnity and whimsy. Part of her cover, no doubt. A way to keep assets like himself off balance. And he liked that she hadn't been bothered by the rain. Again, probably part of her training—

Roberts' voice jarred him back to the present.

"Excuse me," he said to the flight attendant, "but I specifically asked for Diet Pepsi. This is Diet Coke."

"I'm sorry," she said politely, "that's all we have on board. Can I get you something else?"

"No," he replied, pushing the can toward her. "Take it away."

Cam exhaled. Just as Marconi had hired Cam to focus on the history, apparently he had retained Roberts to opine and advise on archeological matters. Which meant Cam would need to work with the man going forward. Amanda, who believed that how someone treated service people revealed their true character, would have probably dumped the Diet Coke onto his lap.

Cam took a deep breath and turned to the archeologist. "I read recently about that find in a Mexican cave showing that humans were in America 33,000 years ago." The previous dating had placed the earliest humans in America at around 15,000 years ago. Cam was curious to hear if Roberts would try to explain away this discrepancy.

Roberts glared at him, combing his mustache with his fingers. "The jury is still out on the Chiquihuite Cave dating." He sniffed. "Not everyone agrees."

"How so?"

"Well, did you notice that there were no American or European archeologists involved with the dig?" He sniffed. "Only Mexican."

Cam's eyes widened. It was a racist comment, and he couldn't resist a jab. "I thought you, as an archeologist, would know that Mexico *was* part of America."

Roberts' face turned pink. "You know what I mean."

"That's it? You don't have anything substantive?"

"The burden is on them to prove their case. Not on me to rebut it."

"But they did. What was it, over two hundred stone tools, all buried at the same level dating back more than 30,000 years?"

"The tools could have shifted or been pushed down by burrowing animals."

"Two hundred of them? All to the same level?" Cam chuckled sardonically. "Look, I know how much archeologists hate to be wrong. But to be wrong by so much, and for so long, and with such stubbornness and pomposity." And, apparently, racism. "You would think, at some point, you guys would stop being so damn smug."

Roberts' voice rose. "Okay, smart guy. Explain to me how it is possible that humans would have been archeologically invisible for more than 15,000 years? Shouldn't there be more evidence than this single cave?"

Cam pushed his advantage. "The reason they were 'archeologically invisible' is because you guys dig down to a certain level and then you stop. So of course you never find anything deeper down. It's called *confirmation bias*."

Roberts leaned forward. "At least we use some kind of scientific method. You and your ilk see plow marks in the shape of a cross on a boulder and suddenly the Templars were here in America with the Holy Grail."

"For the record, the Templars probably were here. There's plenty of evidence to prove it, if you ever took the time to actually go look at it. But it's easier to sit in faculty meetings and blow smoke up each other's ass."

Roberts smiled smugly. "In the end, you'll see. We'll be right."

"That's my point. That's all you care about. You'd rather *be* right than *get it* right."

That seemed to end the conversation; Roberts turned to stare out his window. But Amanda felt otherwise. Cam had noticed that she came to him more often when Astarte was not around, perhaps sensing he was lonelier.

*That was a good line about being right versus getting it right.*

"But?"

*You won the argument. But you might have lost the war.*

"How so?"

*Instead of turning Roberts into an ally, you made an enemy.*

"He was never going to be an ally."

*You don't know that. You might have dazzled him with your research findings. Now, he'll oppose you at every turn.*

"I see your point. In some weird way, I wonder if that's what Marconi wants. He made a point of letting Roberts see that he was paying me more."

*Perhaps he's playing you off of one another. Be careful.*

"Okay."

*And one more thing, Cameron. You seem angry, quick-tempered.*

"I am. Someone killed my wife, and then Marconi threatened me and Astarte. Not to mention chucklehead over there with his smug, racist attitude."

*I get it. And sometimes a little anger can go a long way. But don't be reckless. Astarte needs you.*

Marconi wandered back from his seat near the cockpit, ending Cam's conversation with Amanda. Still standing, he addressed Cam. "How is your research coming along?" He was cordial, affable. Almost as if he had flicked a switch. The death threat at the castle needed to be made, it had been made, and now it was behind them—so long as Cam performed his job. That Marconi could turn his dark side on and off so casually made him impossible to predict. And dangerous.

Cam took a deep breath, pushing aside his disdain for both of his travel companions. "I've found a number of Roman artifacts in and around Massachusetts. I've been on the road a lot, interviewing the discoverers and getting pictures." Now that Astarte was gone, he could devote even more time to the project. "And we found a number of artifacts along the Ohio River which I think are relevant." Marconi had been supportive of Cam's five-day trip, having himself been intrigued by the coins along the Ohio. "I should have a full report for you in the next couple of days."

"Are your finds limited to New England and the Ohio River?"

"No. There are actually coins all over the country. There's one in Heavener, Oklahoma, that I'm particularly intrigued by because there's also a rune stone nearby. Heavener's a tiny town, less than five square miles." Cam smiled. In his younger days, he could have jogged around its perimeter. "A medieval Scandinavian carving and a Roman coin both found in the middle of nowhere?" He shook his head. "I don't believe in those kinds of coincidences."

"Will you be able to investigate it?"

"Not unless you want me to delay my report and fly out there."

Marconi pursed his lips. "Our flight path takes us not far from Oklahoma. Perhaps we could make a stop on the way back." He shrugged. "We have the plane for the day, and I'm intrigued."

Cam nodded. "I'll try to track down the family that found the coins and see if they'll agree to meet with us."

Cam glanced over to see Roberts' face flushed and fists clenched, apparently unhappy about being dragged to see more 'fake' Roman artifacts.

Marconi followed Cam's eyes. He leaned toward Cam and whispered, "If you do arrange things with the family, we'll leave Mr. Roberts on the jet, I think."

Apparently, in Marconi's mind, it was perfectly okay to threaten to kill someone one day and then to conspire playfully with them the next. More to the point, Cam wondered why he had been threatened with his head being put into a box while Roberts' punishment was limited to being left on the plane in what amounted to a kindergarten-like timeout. Cam tried not to think about the obvious answer—that he was more expendable.

They landed early afternoon at the Mexico City airport and stepped from the plane onto the tarmac, the air thick with smog and stifling hot. Marconi handed out N95 masks.

"What," Roberts asked, "is COVID really bad here?"

"No. But pollution is. The combination of high altitude and smog means there is 25% less oxygen here than in other cities. These will help with the pollution, at least."

A minivan transported them to the terminal where they quickly cleared customs. A Mercedes limo waited for them at the curb; within a half hour, they had entered a massive forested area on a hill in the middle of the city. "This is Chapultepec Park," Marconi explained. "The Aztec rulers lived here. I mentioned the air quality. Were it not for this park, the city would be uninhabitable. It is said that the park serves as the lungs of the city."

The limo stopped in front of a sprawling, white-stoned, windowless block of a building. Marconi whisked them through security, where an attractive woman in her twenties who spoke impeccable English greeted them with a smile. "Follow me, Mr. Marconi. We have a private meeting room waiting for you."

She led them into an interior courtyard—featuring a pond with a concrete umbrella overhanging it—before pushing through a door into a white-walled meeting room. On a red cloth in the center of a table sat a terracotta head about the size of a pear.

"Gentlemen," she said, "may I present the Tecaxic-Calixtlahuaca Head."

Tecaxic-Calixtlahuaca Head, Mexico City

Cam's first reaction was that the scruffy little face was not all that impressive. But he knew better than to rush to judgment. And he did notice the full beard, which meant the man depicted was not Native American.

"What can you tell us about it?" Marconi asked.

She repeated what Roberts had said on the plane, about the artifact being found during a pyramid dig in the 1930s beneath a cement floor in a layer of soil which dated to the eleventh century, long before European contact. The piece was largely ignored until a researcher stumbled upon it in the 1990s. "The prevailing theory is that a Roman ship, either on a trade mission or blown off course, arrived in Mexico in ancient times and brought this piece, and then it was placed in the pyramid as a treasured keepsake." She added, "Professor Bernard

Andreae, director of the German Archaeological Institute in Rome, gave his opinion of the head in the year 2000." She read aloud from a sheet of paper:

> *It is Roman, without any doubt. The stylistic examination tells us, more precisely, that it is a Roman work of the second century after Christ. It presents, in the cut of the hair and the shape of the beard, traits typical of the Severian emperors, exactly the fashion of the period. On this there is no doubt.*

She continued. "Thermoluminescence was conducted on the piece by the Max Planck Institute for Nuclear Physics in Heidelberg, Germany. The tests revealed a date of approximately 1,800 years before present."

With that, she stepped aside. "Feel free to examine the artifact."

Cam's ears had perked up when he heard the second century date agreed upon by two different experts. He knew the artifact was pre-Columbus, but this date, obviously, synced up perfectly with his Ninth Legion theory.

Roberts spoke. "How do we know the piece wasn't planted? Or even that the artifact didn't fall out of someone's pocket?"

"We don't," the woman said cheerfully. She was more patient with Roberts than Cam, who had rolled his eyes at the fell-out-of-pocket suggestion. She continued. "But there is no credible evidence indicating that this is in any way an illegitimate find."

Roberts stepped forward and removed a jeweler's loupe from his pocket to examine the artifact. Scowling, he turned the piece over, scratched at it with a fingernail, even sniffed it. He then splashed some water onto the head, dabbed it with a handkerchief, and examined the carved areas with a flashlight held at low angle. Finally, he pulled a couple of reference books from his satchel and compared images in the books to the head. After about twenty minutes, he stepped back.

"I have no reason to doubt the conclusion reached by the German professor. It does, indeed, appear to be Roman and date to around the second century. But I still question whether the piece was planted."

Marconi nodded. "Thank you, Mr. Roberts. But please remember that you have been retained to analyze the piece, not solve a mystery."

Cam weighed in. "I had a law professor who used to say that the most important tool in our tool bag was our common sense. In this case, why would someone plant a piece at an archeological dig in the 1930s and then wait around for it to be rediscovered more than sixty years later? It makes no sense. If they had planted the piece to, say, embarrass someone, they would have brought attention to the piece soon after the dig."

Roberts lifted his chin. "You can't be sure of that."

"I don't have to be sure. I have the artifact. It speaks for itself." Cam turned to walk away, then stopped. "If you want to discredit it, you have to come up with a scenario that makes sense. Who planted it? Why? Otherwise you're just throwing shit against a wall."

An hour later, they were back on the plane at the Mexico City airport. Robinson Roberts had pouted during the limo ride back to the airport, answering Cam's inquiries with one-word, toneless responses. Cam had acted as if he didn't notice, tormenting the archeologist with a staccato fire of inane questions and commentary about the terracotta head.

"As I told Mr. Thorne," Marconi announced, his suit somehow unwrinkled, "we will be making an additional stop in Oklahoma to see a Roman coin." He fixed his eyes on Roberts. "I will, of course, compensate you for your time."

They ate sandwiches on the plane, landed in Oklahoma City, quickly cleared customs, and touched down again in eastern Oklahoma at a regional airport in the late afternoon. Marconi had a car waiting. Roberts, scowling, opted to remain on the plane.

It occurred to Cam that Marconi may have chosen the surly Roberts as a traveling companion as a way for Marconi to seem more likeable by comparison. "What's that expression?" Cam asked as they slid into the back seat of a minivan. "*It is impossible for a man to learn what he thinks he already knows.* Roberts thinks he knows the Romans weren't here. So no amount of evidence will change his mind."

"That is the problem with people in academia," Marconi said. "They are very rigid in their thinking. I have always preferred people who are street smart." He arched an eyebrow. "Or, better yet, who are both."

Twenty minutes after landing, they walked into the low-slung, stone-fronted Heavener Public Library. A white-bearded man in a wheelchair greeted them with a wave next to the circulation desk. "I'm your man," he grinned, his shaking hand holding up a coin about the size of a quarter.

The elderly gentleman explained how he had found the coin while cleaning out a ditch in a residential neighborhood in 1976. About 18 inches down, he pulled out a soda bottle. The coin was stuck to the bottle with some gummy mud. He handed it to Cam, who snapped a picture with his phone.

Roman Coin, Heavener, Oklahoma

"The front is a profile of Emperor Nero. The back is an eagle holding a thunderbolt and olive branch." He paused to catch his breath. "It's from the late first century, probably the year 63 AD."

Cam handed the coin to Marconi. Unlike Cam, who had examined it dispassionately, Marconi held it reverentially by the edges, as if he might soil it with his touch. "Emperor Nero," he whispered, holding the coin to the light. He looked down and smiled. "I don't suppose you'd be willing to sell this? I can make you a more-than-generous offer."

The man shook his head. "Thanks, but no. I'm by no means wealthy, but I've got all the money I need, and finding this coin is probably the one thing in my life I've done that anyone will remember."

"I understand," Marconi said, reluctantly handing the coin back. "We thank you for your time, sir."

They walked back to the waiting minivan. "We should head over to see the rune stone soon, before the park closes," Cam said.

As they drove, Marconi made a phone call. From what Cam could hear, he had phoned a medical supply company in Tulsa, fifty miles away. Hanging up, he smiled. "I've just arranged to have a new motorized wheelchair delivered to our elderly friend. That one he was using was barely functional."

Cam nodded. Marconi, despite the death threat, was beginning to grow on him. "That's very generous of you."

"Not generous, selfish. Had the man accepted my offer, I would have suspected his story was a fake. Now I believe it was an authentic find. Believe me, he has brought me far more joy than the price of a wheelchair."

Marconi cleared his throat. "Speaking of generosity, I may be in a position to offer you a bonus."

"You're paying me enough. More than enough, in fact." He had counted the cash in the envelope Marconi handed him on the plane—$30,000, with a note saying it was payment for his first week of work. Cam did not want to feel like he had been purchased.

As if Cam had not spoken, Marconi continued. "I told you that my son and wife recently died. I have a brother, also. He is a priest. He works at the Vatican. He is in a position of considerable authority, overseeing both the Vatican archives and its museums. I am familiar with your Templar research, as I told you. I would imagine that, for a researcher like yourself, having access to the Vatican's secret archives would be of some use."

Cam swallowed. Perhaps being purchased wasn't such a bad thing after all. "Honestly, that would be amazing." So many documents had been lost—or believed to be lost—to history; he could happily spend a month there.

Marconi nodded. "When we are done with our work on the Roman artifacts, I will arrange it. Have you ever been to Rome?"

"Only once, years ago. And only for a couple of days."

"A couple of days? You need at least a couple of weeks." He shook his head, scowling. "Rome is the very cradle of Western civilization. Who goes to Rome for a couple of days?"

The minivan ascended to a wooded area atop a rocky hillside and stopped, saving Cam from what surely would have been a lecture on Roman cultural superiority. They got out and, in the fading light, followed a dirt path to a sandstone cliff. From there, a series of stone stairs led down through a canyon to a rustic wooden visitor center. Behind a panel of glass stood a massive sand-colored stone slab about the size of a garage door. Eight symbols—called runes—were carved into the quartzite, each about a foot in height. Cam moved closer and took a picture, zooming in on the runes.

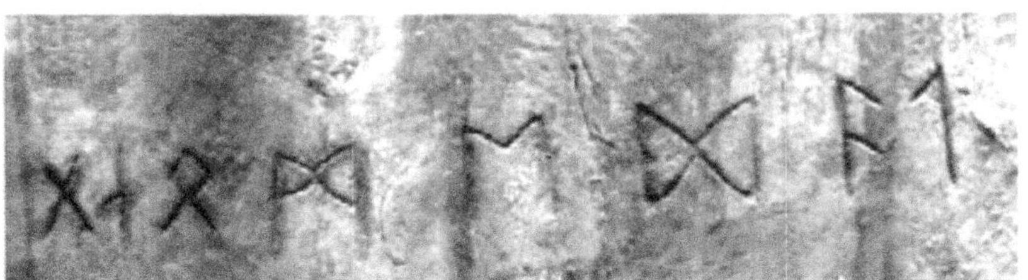

Heavener Rune Stone, Oklahoma

Cam shared what he knew. "The most likely translation is, 'Sundial.' This may have been part of some kind of astronomical site, like Stonehenge. The script is Scandinavian and probably dates to the medieval period."

"Is it related to the Kensington Rune Stone?" Marconi asked.

Cam much preferred Astarte as a travel companion, but at least the well-dressed car dealer shared his passion for history. "That would make the most sense." Cam had told Marconi about the possibility of the Kensington party traveling downriver and spreading the 'red with blood and death' plague to Cahokia. "Assuming they continued exploring, they would have made it to the Arkansas River and followed it west. The river is only about ten miles from here, accessible by a tributary. I'm guessing they knew where they were going. Probably looking for a Mandan trading outpost."

"Which explains the Roman coin."

"Right. Even though the Mandan moved out of the Ohio River Valley, they kept their European identity. Part of that identity would have been their artifacts, including the old Roman coins. This coin was probably brought over by one of the Ninth Legion soldiers and then kept as an heirloom."

"So, to be clear, it is your professional opinion that the coin we just viewed is authentic."

Cam turned to walk back to their vehicle. "It is. I know you hired me as a historian. But I'm a lawyer by training. I go where the evidence takes me."

## Chapter 6

Cam awoke in the middle of the night, his brain firing. Somehow, while he slept, his mind had been sorting, focusing, analyzing. And concluding. *Could it be?*

The second century date—and the volume of artifacts and events clustered during that time period—had been gnawing at him. While sleeping, his subconscious had proposed a shocking possibility. Rolling out of bed, he turned on his computer and pecked at the keys, a full moon over the lake keeping watch. Twenty minutes later, he sat back.

"Holy shit, girl," he said to Venus. "I might be on to something." She whined at him, wondering why they were out of bed at three in the morning. He laughed. "I know what you're thinking. Maybe I'm not on to something; maybe I'm just *on* something."

He and Astarte had assumed that the Roman Ninth Legion—consisting of Roman soldiers and camp followers from Hispania and England—had gone to Israel, helped put down the uprising, found the Bar Kokhba treasure, and fled across the Atlantic with it. But what if instead of *finding* the treasure, the legion had been offered the treasure as a reward?

He sent a quick text to Astarte. *What if the rebels in Israel made the Ninth Legion a deal? We'll give you the Temple treasure if you let us keep the Temple artifacts and ceremonial items and also take us with you to America. That would explain why some Burrows Cave artifacts are Jewish. There is more. Call me when you wake up.*

On his screen, he stared at one of the Burrows Cave artifacts, a menorah carved onto a black stone with the Phoenician-like script beneath it.

Burrows Cave Menorah Stone

The menorah, Cam knew, was an ancient Jewish symbol. And the seven-branched version (as opposed to the nine-branched candelabra used in modern times during the Hanukah celebration) was consistent with the Golden Menorah featured in the Temple in Jerusalem—the depiction of a seven-branched candelabra spoke to the piece's antiquity. What he was not sure about was the triangular base. Scrolling through the internet, he found that most ancient menorahs featured a round, square or hexagonal base. Only menorahs of the first and second century employed a triangular base. *Bingo.* There was no way Russell Burrows, he of no more than a high school education, could have faked a piece like this—how could he have ferreted out such an obscure piece of historical minutia in the days before the internet?

There was that date again. *Second century.*

Searching the internet, he quickly found another ancient seven-branched menorah with a triangular base, this one carved into a cave on the land of the Potawatomi tribe of Michigan. The tribe claimed it was the work of their ancient ancestors. Would skeptics argue that Burrows somehow carved this menorah as well?

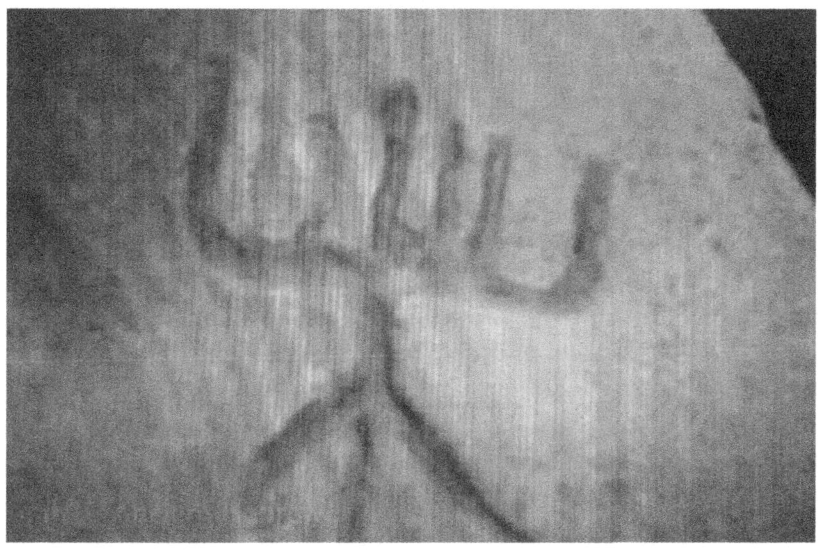

Potawatomi Menorah Carving

His mind racing now despite the hour, Cam turned to yet another artifact. He and Amanda had viewed the Bat Creek Stone a few years earlier while driving through Tennessee. The brown stone—about the size of a television remote control—featured an ancient script carved horizontally across its face.

Bat Creek Stone, Tennessee

The authenticity of the stone was beyond question—it had been unearthed by a Smithsonian archeologist excavating a Cherokee burial mound in the 1880s. For many decades it was displayed at the Smithsonian upside-down. Only in the 1960s did the chair of Mediterranean Studies at Brandeis University invert the stone and identify the script as Paleo-Hebrew, used in Israel only during the first and second centuries AD. Was the date a coincidence? Or was this artifact another piece in the Ninth Legion puzzle? Cam sat back. He didn't believe in coincidences. And his gut told him he was on the right track.

His gut proved to be right. Without much digging, Cam found a book written in the 1820s by the Chief Justice of the Tennessee Supreme Court, entitled *Natural and Aboriginal History of Tennessee.* In it, the judge described four different Roman coins found in Tennessee, all dating to the first and second centuries, brought to this continent, he believed, by some ancient mariners. Cam's research quickly found two more such coins. It was apparent that whoever had carved the Bat Creek Stone had been traveling with Roman coins.

Of course, there was no reason for the Roman soldiers of the Ninth Legion to carve a stone using the Hebrew language. The carving spoke to a Jewish presence. Digging further, Cam's eyes widened as he stared at a translation of the carving which tied everything together: The Bat Creek Stone inscription translated to, 'A Comet for the Jews.'

Cam had seen that before. 'A Comet for the Jews' was the Jewish battle cry of the Bar Kokhba revolt, a nod to its leader, Simon Bar Kokhba, whose name translated to, 'Son of the Star,' an ancient way to describe a comet.

It was times like these when Cam really missed Amanda. She would have shared his excitement, enthusiastically joining him in his deep dive down the rabbit hole. He looked at the moon and sighed. Maybe she was out there somewhere, serving as his muse. Maybe he would never have had his flash of inspiration were it not for her.

*There's another artifact, Cameron. Keep looking.*

"I don't know of any others."

*Yes, you do. The clues are right in front of you. You want Hebrew, you want second century, and you want Ohio River Valley.*

"Nothing rings a bell."

*Well, then, do a bloody Google search.*

Laughing to himself, Cam did just that. "Of course," he said aloud. "The Newark Decalogue Stone. I had forgotten about that." He had never seen the artifact in person, and it had been a decade since he had read about it. At the time, it was just another of those out-of-place artifacts, one of a hundred mysterious historical curiosities which seemed to bubble out of the American soil. He studied the image on his monitor.

Decalogue Stone, Newark, Ohio

The stone, about the size of a checkbook, was found in a Native American burial mound in Ohio in 1860. Inscribed in Hebrew along its perimeter was an abbreviated version of the Ten Commandments. In the center of the stone, a bearded man, captioned as Moses, stood holding a tablet. Based on the wear marks, one theory was that the piece was a talisman to be held during prayer. The stone had been found with a wooden burial platform resting beneath it—the platform wood was carbon-dated to 85-135 AD. And the "square" form of

Hebrew used on that tablet was consistent with that same time period.

Excitedly, he dug deeper and learned that the Decalogue Stone wasn't buried in just any burial mound. It was buried inside one of the Roman-style forts documented by the Smithsonian in the 1840s, similar to the fort schematic he had shown Astarte during their drive. He found the actual Smithsonian drawing of the elaborate Newark fortification in an online book.

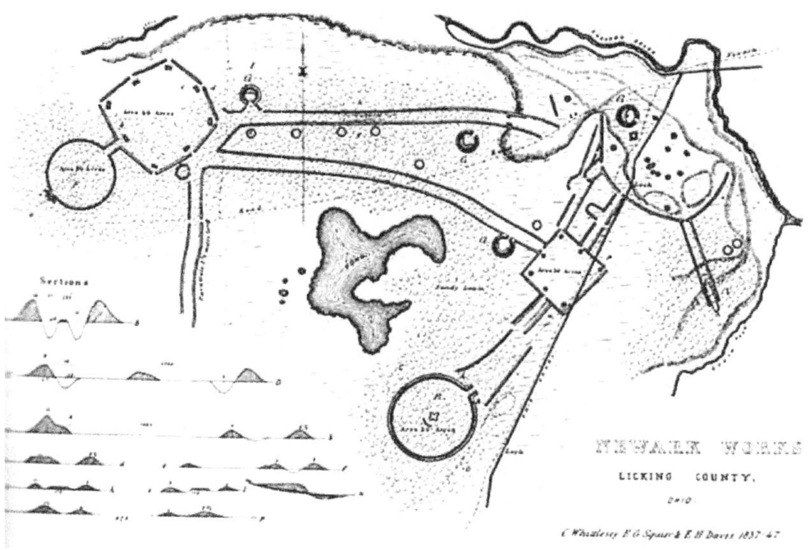


Ancient Fortification, Newark, Ohio

Cam sat back, thinking about the person holding the prayer talisman while inside the fort. Was the person who held it a refugee from the Bar Kokhba uprising? It added up. Here was another Jewish artifact, again dating to around the second century, again in the Ohio River Valley, again tied to the Romans.

He wasn't an expert on fortifications, much less Roman ones, but there was something about these Smithsonian drawings which intrigued him. As far as he knew, nobody else had tried to tie them to ancient Jews. Was it possible he might have noticed something others had missed?

He spent an hour scrolling through the scores of drawings laid out in the online Smithsonian book and was about ready to head back to bed when an extraordinary image jumped out at him—a fortification on the Little Miami River in southwestern Ohio, called the East Fork Works, from a map first drawn in 1823.

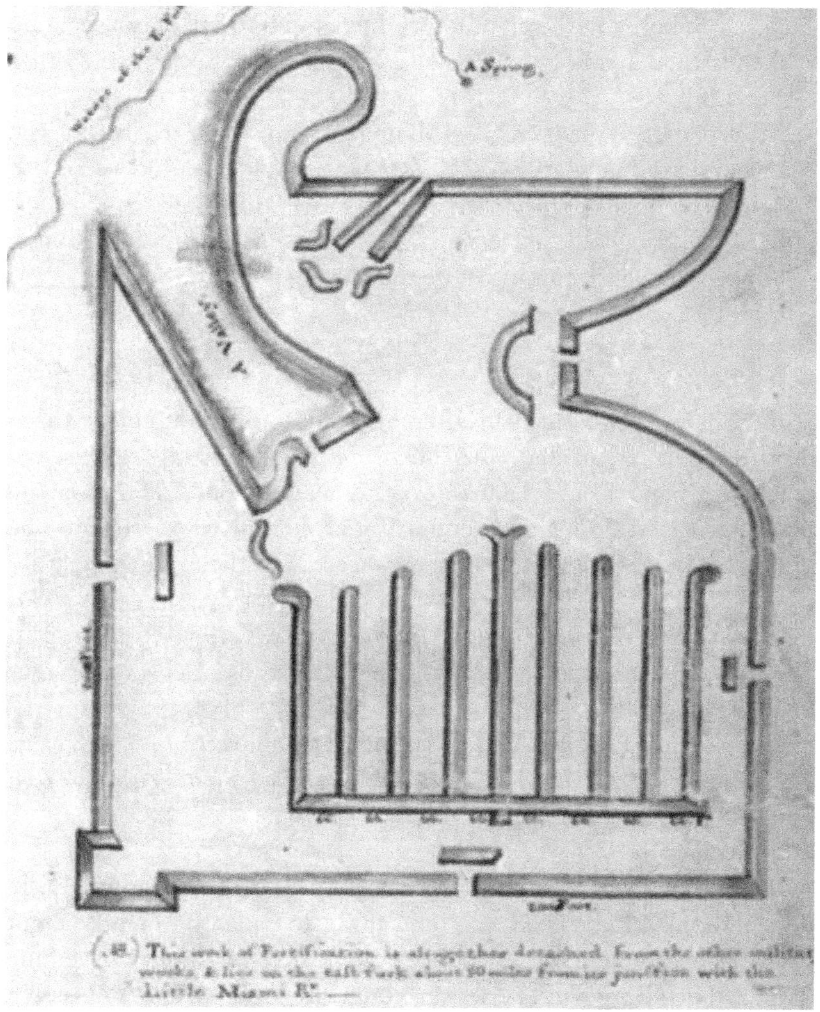


'Hanukah Fort,' Little Miami River, Southwestern Ohio

Cam blinked once, twice. He couldn't stop staring at the image. There was no doubt: The top portion of the fort mirrored the design of an oil lamp and the bottom portion was in the shape of a nine-branched menorah with the center arm standing tallest. The fortification design was a clear nod to the Hanukah story: There was only enough oil in the lamp to burn the holy Temple Menorah for one night, yet, by a miracle of God, the oil lasted for eight nights. The nine-armed menorah used during Hanukah (as opposed to the seven-armed menorah used at other times) featured nine candles—eight candles symbolizing the eight nights the lamp burned, plus a separate 'helper' candle symbolizing the oil lamp and used to light the other eight.

He typed up a quick email, with images, and sent it to Astarte. The conclusion was inescapable. The Romans would have no reason to design a 'Hanukah Fort,' nor would the Native Americans.

His theory about ancient Israelites accompanying the Roman Ninth Legion was becoming more than just a theory.

Cam had hoped to sleep in after his middle-of-the-night research marathon, but Venus had other ideas. He threw on some clothes and grabbed a banana and Venus' leash. A warm front had moved in, replacing yesterday's rain. Venus tugged at him to go toward the park, but he resisted, choosing the beach for their morning walk instead.

*Hoping to see that Mossad agent again? It's okay. I'm not jealous.*

"She might be able to shed more light on those Hebrew carvings and the Hanukah fort."

*And she might bat her eyelashes at you again also. Like I said, it's okay. There's something ... alluring about her. Dark and mysterious and a bit peculiar.*

"I like peculiar."

*I know.*

He shook his head. It was one thing to talk to Amanda about research or about Astarte. But he wasn't sure he should be taking dating advice from her. She was, of course (being a product of his own subconscious), correct—he was hoping to see Rivka. It made no sense, really. Just a few days ago he had told Astarte he was not ready to date. What had changed? Was it that, after being on the road and diving into a new research project, he felt more alive, more like his old self?

He'd have to figure it out later because, as he turned the corner, there she was, sitting at a picnic table with her bare feet kneading the sand. He wondered if she was thinking about her past as a beach volleyball player.

"Have you ever swum in the Dead Sea?" she asked abruptly.

"No."

"It's a surreal experience. You're in water, but because of all the minerals, your entire body is buoyant, like a beach ball. You can, literally, sit on the water as if it were a lounge chair. They think that may have been how Jesus did his walking on the water trick."

"That, or, you know, the whole son of God thing." Cam didn't believe it himself, but belief in Jesus' resurrection was probably the single most powerful force in the modern world.

She rolled her eyes. "Please."

"Why do you bring it up?"

She bent and rubbed Venus' neck, her blouse bowing off her chest. Cam did not look away, catching a glimpse of her olive-colored breast. He wondered if she had given him a peek on purpose.

"Because, so often, things are not as they seem. I'm sure you've seen that."

He nodded. "Sure. Sometimes a physical therapist is really a spy."

She angled her head. "Is that what you think I am?" She didn't wait for a reply. "A spy stays in the shadows and tries to get information by nefarious means. I think of myself as more of your ally. A partner, even."

"A partner who drops a barbell on my chest."

She smiled, her dark eyes playful. "That was *before* we were partners. Once you agreed, I've been on my best behavior. Well, maybe not my *best*," she teased.

He tried to keep his focus. The Mossad, like all intelligence operations, was not the least bit shy about using attractive female agents to promote its agenda; the tactic went back to Biblical times, with Delilah seducing Samson—and probably long before that. Cam would need to keep her fingers out of his hair. He sat, keeping a respectful distance from her on the picnic bench. "You were talking about things not being what they seemed."

"Yes. We wonder about Mr. Marconi. Has he really located a Roman shipwreck?"

"I don't know. I believe that he thinks he has."

"Is the ship important? I mean, haven't you found a bunch of other Roman artifacts already?"

"I have. But none of them are as impactful as the shipwreck. In law school, they taught us that our opening statement to the jury should summarize the case in about fifteen seconds—"

She interjected. "The elevator pitch. You have to make your case before the doors open."

"Exactly. So, if the shipwreck is legit, it's an easy opening statement, easy elevator pitch. A Roman shipwreck, 1800 years old, off the coast of Massachusetts." He shrugged. "Case is pretty much over, assuming you can prove what you say."

"It's not like that with the other artifacts."

"Right. You saw that with the coins—there is always a rebuttal. Get some expert to say they were replicas. Or claim a collector lost them. Or that they were ship's ballast. Or that a bird flew over with them in its beak." He thought about Robinson Roberts. "With the Mexican head, claim someone planted it during the archeological dig. With Burrows Cave, claim the whole thing is a fake. The problem is, especially with archeology, everyone can always make an excuse. That's why the shipwreck is so important. I mean, how can you fake it? It is what it is. And that's why Marconi is being very careful, very methodical."

"You say methodical. Isn't he dying?"

"Maybe methodical is the wrong word. 'Systematic' is probably better. He's pushing ahead quickly. In fact, he has a hearing later this week with the state commission—it's called the Board of Underwater Archeological Resources—to try to get a permit to bring up the shipwreck. But, in the meantime, he wants me to build a case for a Roman presence in America through the other artifacts. Sort of like paving the way for him. He thinks it will be easier for him to get a top dive team, and also for the experts and the press to believe in the find, if there is more evidence than just the wreck." Cam paused. "And he's right. If they were really here, there should be other stuff."

"Which you're finding."

He had told her about the Roman coins, the forts, the armor, the Brandenburg Stone, the Roman anchor, the Burrows Cave artifacts. For a second, he hesitated, not sure if he should share his work on the Jewish-related artifacts he had discovered in the middle of the night. But why not? He could see no downside, and, on the upside, he had no interest in making an enemy of the world's most efficient intelligence agency.

Rivka listened intently as he described the Bat Creek Stone, the Decalogue Stone and the Hanukah Fort. "I think they all tie in to the Bar Kokhba coins." He paused, searching her face for a reaction. "And the Temple treasure described in the Copper Scroll of Qumran. The scroll says it is one of two copies. I think the Romans, probably the Ninth Legion, found the other copy which led them to the treasure. They brought it here, maybe with the help of some of the rebelling Jews."

She merely nodded, her features revealing nothing. "This is good work. I can see why my bosses assigned me to recruit you. We knew about the coins, and we suspected the treasure might be here. But the Jewish artifacts are new to us."

"Be honest. Do you really think the Temple treasure might be here?"

She smiled and touched his arm as she stood. "Personally, I have no idea. But I think it's safe to say that the Mossad generally wouldn't waste its resources on a couple of old coins."

He watched the operative stroll away, her movements graceful and athletic. It struck him that she hadn't asked the obvious question, hadn't asked if he had any idea where the treasure might be. He knew from years of courtroom work that sometimes the questions not asked revealed the most about an opponent's thinking.

He tossed a tennis ball to Venus and mulled the issue over. The dog skidded to a stop in the sand and loped back to him. Cam threw again, then a third time. Finally, he gave up and put Venus back on her leash, having gained nothing other than a saliva-filled hand. At least for now, Rivka not asking about the treasure location didn't really help him better understand the Mossad. Or its mysterious agent.

Astarte jolted awake, the sun bright on her face. She couldn't remember the last time the sun woke her. She checked her phone. Nine-thirty. *Ugh.* She was supposed to be at her Psych class at ten. And it was the first day. No way could she skip.

She jostled Matthias. "Wake up, it's late."

He made a humming noise and tried to pull her to him.

Tempting. So very tempting. "Sorry, no." She rolled off the bed, threw on some sweats, and pattered down the hall to the bathroom.

She needed to get a handle on her schedule. In high school, she was in bed by eleven and out the door for the school bus by seven. Here, parties didn't even get started until eleven; some were probably still going at seven.

Ten minutes later, a cup of yogurt in one hand and her phone in the other, she half-walked, half-jogged across campus. Just her luck that her class was at the far edge. She stopped midstride when she scrolled down and read the text from her dad.

Was it possible the Jews had come with the ancient Romans? If so, did that mean that the Mandan descended from Jewish refugees rather than Roman ones?

She phoned him. "Sorry, just saw your text. It's earlier here."

"It's okay, I remember college, honey. Did you see my email?"

"No, just your text."

"Read the email, then call me."

What she really wanted to do was stop, sit on a bench, and read his message. But she had figured out that college cost $90 for each hour of class time, so it seemed irresponsible not to show up.

Even if it promised to be not nearly as interesting as what she might learn from her dad.

Cam downshifted Amanda's Subaru as he exited the interstate, relieved that the gears didn't grind. His legs, finally, were beginning to listen to his brain. Which meant Amanda, finally, might stop teasing him about not knowing how to drive a stick.

As he had told Rivka, the hearing in front of the Underwater Archeology Board was later this week, Thursday. Marconi wanted Robinson Roberts to present the case for the shipwreck itself, while Cam would present background information on other Roman artifacts found in the Plum Island area. Cam didn't like not being point man on this and he was far from convinced that Roberts' heart was into the project. But Cam understood that an archeology board would consist mostly of archeologists who would want to hear from one of their own. Most archeologists, like Roberts, didn't hold Cam in particularly high regard.

In any event, Cam had a few more artifacts he wanted to examine before completing his report. The first of them was a group of Roman coins found together on a beach in Beverly, Massachusetts by a metal detector in 1978, about ten miles southwest of Marconi's Plum Island shipwreck site. Cam parked in front of Beverly Historical Society, a grand, brick, Federalist-style mansion in downtown Beverly.

He had called ahead, and an intern showed him into a corner office decorated to match the building's 1781 construction date. Cam loved history and he appreciated the Colonial-era furnishings. But the building was an infant compared to the Roman coins which had been left on a mahogany table for him to examine. He snapped some pictures of the obverse sides, which, he had read, depicted four different emperors who reigned consecutively during the fourth century over a span of about fifty years.

Roman Coins, Beverly, MA

Cam sat back. On the one hand, the fourth-century date of these coins was inconsistent with his cluster of second-century finds. But he had always assumed that, had one ship come, others would have returned to trade. Is that what this collection of coins represented? Though it was possible a collector might have focused only on coins from a specific half-century, Cam doubted it. This particular period in time was not marked by many notable events or historical figures. And the odds of the four coins being clustered in date within the reign of four consecutive rulers (of 72 Roman emperors in total) were less than 1 in 5,000. A more likely and reasonable explanation was that the four coins came from a chest of recently-minted coins being carried on a fourth-century Roman merchant vessel.

Cam knew the odds were long on a Roman merchant ship safely reaching America. But they weren't 5,000 to 1 long.

Rivka peddled up the incline, pumping hard, relishing the sound of her heart in her ears and the feel of the bike surging to her will. As she rounded a corner, two more targets appeared ahead, perhaps a hundred yards. Two guys, both in racing jerseys, both riding at a good pace. She smiled and shifted gears. Time to reel them in.

She had found the Lexington Loop—a thirty-mile bike trail northwest of Boston—her first week living in Boston. The route, centered around where the American Revolution began, passed through back roads, meadows, farms, woodlands and marshes. Not a lot of car traffic, but enough other serious bikers for her to satisfy her competitive juices by engaging in impromptu races.

As her legs pumped and the sweat poured from her body, her mind raced. She had sat, thinking, at the picnic table for a full hour this morning after Cameron strolled away with his dog. And not just about him, though it was getting more and more difficult to purge him from her mind. Until now, she had never really understood her mission—or at least the reason *for* her mission. Why would the Mossad care so much about the Temple treasure? It was hardly a matter of national security. There had to be more to it, another layer.

That layer, she had concluded, dovetailed with research she had been assigned to do while in Israel, before being flown back to the U.S. on this assignment. She had not before now linked the research to her current mission, but of course she should have realized that with the Mossad nothing was random. She had been asked to analyze the possibility of certain groups in Israel attempting to build a Third Temple. The original, the Temple of Solomon, had been destroyed by the Babylonians; its replacement, King Herod's Temple, had been sacked by the Romans in the first century. The Jewish people had long yearned to rebuild atop the Temple Mount—in fact, that had been one of the primary goals of the Bar Kokhba revolt. But efforts to rebuild in the modern world were constrained by geopolitical realities: The Muslims had built two of their most holy sites—the Dome of the Rock and the Al-Aqsa Mosque—on the Temple Mount. There was simply no practical way to build over or around the sacred Islamic shrines.

But it wasn't just practicalities which kept most Jews, even religious ones, from pushing to rebuild the Temple. It was also that most of the Temple treasures—the holy items needed to furnish and decorate and sanctify the Temple—had been lost. Without these treasures, the Temple would never be more than walls and ceiling and floor. To many religious Jews, the Third Temple could be rebuilt only if and when God allowed for the Temple treasures to be recovered.

What, then, if the Temple treasures were, indeed, found?

With a surge, she flew past the two riders. She softened the blow by offering a smile and a friendly wave, which they returned. Most riders, especially men, hated it when she overtook them. Though not as much here as in Israel. Here, at least, men appreciated an athletic, fit woman. The men in Israel were more old-fashioned. They allowed women to serve in the military but, paradoxically, otherwise expected them to be subservient to men. Not as bad as in most other Middle-Easter countries, sure. But, as an example, in many areas of Israel, women were still expected to move to the back of the bus to allow men to sit in the front. Had she grown up in America, her athleticism would have been appreciated, even glorified. When she had first come to America, she had been amazed at the popularity of girls' sports in high school and college. In Israel, she was thought of as a bit of a freak. Girls called her an Amazon. Here, she would have been a team captain, probably one of the popular kids. Would it have made a difference in her life? She had to think so. What 13-year-old ever truly recovered from eating lunch alone every day in the school cafeteria?

Shaking the thought away, her mind turned back to the Temple treasures. Her analysis had concluded that, with the treasures, public sentiment might turn in favor of rebuilding. Orthodox theology called for rebuilding when the time was right. Militant groups would go along, as would nationalists. And there was another variable as well: Fundamentalist Christian groups, most of them based in the United States, believed that the Second Coming of Jesus could not occur until the Jerusalem Temple had been rebuilt. They, too, would therefore lend their support—and their significant political influence—to rebuilding efforts.

Would this support be enough to carry the day? It was unclear. But what was clear was that many groups in Israel would see the recovery of the Temple treasure as some kind of sign from God. A sign to rebuild.

Which explained, finally, why Rivka was here. What she was supposed to do, exactly, remained a mystery.

Ten minutes after leaving Beverly, Cam sat in a diner in Salem, only a few miles south. Phil, a burly man in work pants and a yellow t-shirt, greeted him with a smile. "I found this in 2006. You're only the second person to ask about it."

"Who was the first?"

"The local paper did a story. But, otherwise, nothing. I tried to get some of the universities to take a look. But, like I said, nothing."

After they ordered burgers, he handed Cam a small manila envelope. "I was rebuilding a wharf in Manchester-by-the-Sea," he began. Like Beverly, the town was less than ten miles from Plum Island. "I saw this coin in the sand. It looked irregular, you know. Not perfectly round. So I stuffed it in my pocket. When I got home, I cleaned it off. Then I brought it to a coin shop. The guy says it's from Tyre, which is part of modern-day Lebanon."

"The Phoenicians," Cam said, thinking aloud. The coin easily could have found its way to a soldier in the Ninth Legion.

"Yeah. The coin guy said it was probably from the first century." He chuckled. "I'll be damned how it got here."

Cam laid the coin down and snapped some pictures. "The back is pretty cool," he said. "Is that an eagle?"

Roman-Era Coin from Tyre, Manchester-by-the-Sea, MA

"Yeah," Phil replied. "The eagle's actually holding a rudder, like he's sailing a ship. They were big sailors, the Phoenicians. The front is pretty much worn away, but the guy said it was Baal, the sun god. He said the coin would have had to have been in the water for a long time to wear the front away."

Cam bent closer and nodded. *Probably almost two thousand years.*

The coin, like others he had seen, left no doubt as to its Roman-era origin. The only question was, how had it arrived at a beach along the Atlantic coast? A seagull? A clumsy collector? As ballast? Cam shook his head. At some point, the sheer number of these finds spoke of something more systemic. The question was, when would people start listening?

Back in his car, Cam continued his Roman coin tour of the North Shore, this time heading north toward the town of Georgetown. The town lay only five miles inland from Plum Island. Denise and her ex had found her coins near the northern end of the island; Cam was hoping to examine coins found on the southern tip, only yards from Marconi's shipwreck site at Emerson Rocks.

He found the hobby shop in the town's main square. Its proprietor, an elderly man with a kind face and twinkle in his eye, was happy to tell his story. "It was 1974. I had heard about a couple of guys who found Roman coins on Sandy Point Beach at the southern tip of the island back in 1960. So I went back to the same area after a storm and found one of my own. It's called a sestertius, from the third century. It's pretty worn away, but you can see the emperor profile on the front. I think that's Pax, the goddess of peace, on the back." He laid the coin on the countertop for Cam to examine and photograph.

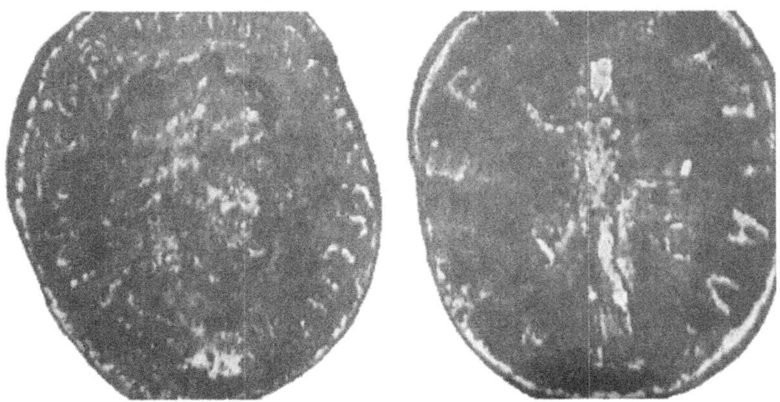

Roman Coin, Plum Island (Newburyport), MA

The man continued. "The other two that were found in 1960 were pretty much identical. Both third century. But those two coins were imbedded in a chunk of wood, like a ship's timber, that was encrusted with barnacles. The guys had to chip the wood away to find the metal. Wherever those coins came from, they'd been in the water a long, long time." He leaned forward. "In addition to the coins, they found two ship's spikes about six inches long."

Cam's eyes shot up. *Timber and ship's spikes.* "Any idea if the coins or those spikes are still around?"

"Sorry, no. That was sixty years ago."

He recalled the map he had seen showing the scores of shipwrecks along Plum Island. "You think that timber was from a wreck?"

"What else could it be? That area is notorious for wrecking ships."

Astarte lingered after class, chatting with a few other freshmen in the hallway outside the lecture hall. She knew she couldn't fall into the trap of limiting her social life to Matthias and the crowd of Native American students he hung out with.

She suggested lunch. She had read through her dad's email and wanted to call him, but it could wait an hour. In sweatshirts and jeans, they ambled across the campus toward the dining hall, exchanging names and hometowns and possible majors. After grabbing food, they sat at an outdoor table under a large maple tree, its leaves just beginning to turn.

Fifteen minutes into her meal, a gust of wind blew Astarte's napkin. As she turned to reach for it, her eyes settled on a boy in a cowboy hat and denim jacket sitting alone a few tables away. He tucked his chin when she looked up, but he looked familiar to her. And he definitely had been watching her. Was he just lonely? Maybe checking her out? Her arms tingled, her body sensing danger. She turned away but angled herself so she could study him. Where had she seen him before?

Her lunch group began to disperse—all going the opposite direction from her dorm, unfortunately. And Matthias was in a class. Okay. She could take care of herself. Assuming she wasn't being paranoid.

Sticking to the open areas of campus, she zigzagged her way toward her dorm. The clouds, which had been darkening and fattening during lunch, suddenly burst. She pulled her hood up. Holding her phone in front of her face as if reading a message, she reversed the camera and snapped a couple of pictures over her shoulder. Zooming in, she tried to make out the face. But his hat was pulled too low and he was too far back to get a good shot through the rain.

With a jolt of fear, she realized she had chosen a path which dead-ended at a duck pond near the center of campus. Normally, the pond area was crowded, but people had fled from the rain. Glancing back at a bend in the path, she saw he was still following, perhaps a hundred feet away. Enough of this heroine stuff. She dialed 911, quickly explaining to the campus police where she was. Just a couple of minutes, they promised.

She made a decision. Ducking behind a tree, she grabbed a couple of hockey puck-sized rocks. Years of softball pitching left little doubt that she could easily take him down with a throw to the head. She hefted a stone. But was she even certain he meant her harm?

Glancing back, she spotted him, now fifty feet away, trudging along, his eyes sweeping, searching. She made a split second decision. Winding up, she heaved the stone into the branches of a tree above his head. A flock of startled blackbirds erupted and took flight. She had intended to startle him and see how he reacted. But his reaction went way beyond alarm. Instantly, he dropped to the ground, covering his head with his hands. *That's it.* Darrell, from the cave, still on edge from the bats. Her chest tightened. Fern and her gang must have followed her to Montana, somehow. Perhaps a tracking device on the SUV.

She stayed hidden, watching. Slowly he rose, taking deep breaths, and dusted himself off. His eyes again searched, now angry. He had lost her.

But was he alone? Staying low, she peered out from behind her tree. In the distance, she saw a police cruiser speeding her way. She hefted a second rock. Darrell and crew likely would have left her and her dad in that cave to die. Stepping out, she whipped it, catching him square in the chest. For the second time, he fell. She rushed over and dropped her knee onto his chest just as a police officer, a woman not much older than Astarte, arrived.

"I'm the one who called you," she blurted. "This guy was following me."

"What are you talking about?" Darrell whined. "Get off of me."

The officer lifted Astarte from him.

"I know who you are, Darrell," Astarte spat.

"You're crazy," he protested. "I've never seen you before in my life. My name's Fred Hunter. I'm just here for the weekend visiting friends."

"Do you have ID?" the officer asked.

"Sure. Just let me up." On his feet, he dug out his wallet. "I got lost, trying to find my buddy's dorm."

Astarte edged closer. Could she have been mistaken? She studied his face. She had only seen him the one time. And she had been focused on other things, like surviving. Not to mention, sometimes people just looked alike. Maybe she was just being paranoid.

The officer handed his ID back to him and turned to Astarte. "His ID checks out."

She lifted her jaw. "Maybe it's a fake."

"You say he was following you? That's it?"

She was beginning to feel stupid. "From the dining hall. Yes."

"How far back?"

Her face burned. "I don't know, maybe a hundred feet."

Darrell, or whatever his name was, glared at her and rubbed his chest where the rock hit. "Don't flatter yourself. Why would I want to follow you?"

She clenched her teeth. Could she have been wrong?

"Can I press charges or something?" he said. "I mean, she attacked me."

Astarte listened to her gut. Pivoting, she swung her arm and cuffed him on the left deltoid muscle. Firmly, but not hard enough to do damage. Except to someone who just received a rabies shot.

"Ow!" he yelled, grimacing and bending at the waist in pain.

The officer stepped between them. Then she eyed at Astarte with a quizzical look. "Why's he reacting like that?"

"Because if it's the guy I think he is, he just had a rabies shot in that shoulder. If you lift his sleeve, you'll see the mark. Like I said, his name is Darrell. And he's been following me since Illinois."

Cam filled up the Subaru with gas on the North Shore and wove his way back to the highway. He had another appointment to keep. More coins—in Vermont, of all places. But if the Romans had come ashore in New England and eventually found their way to the Ohio River Valley, they would not have passed through Vermont. Cam had a theory, one he hoped to test when he arrived.

A call from Astarte interrupted his musings. "Did you read my email" he asked.

"Yes, but we have bigger issues. Fern, or whatever her name is, and one of her brothers tracked me to campus." She described the encounter. "He had his rifle in his pickup truck. Montana has loose gun laws, but you can't bring a gun onto campus. So they arrested him and confiscated the rifle."

Cam squeezed the steering wheel. He had assumed the Fern threat was behind them. They must still believe the treasure was in the cave and that Astarte and he could lead them to it. "I'm sorry, honey. Nobody should have to go through that on their first day of school."

"I think it'll be okay. Matthias heard the fake Fern on the phone at the police station, telling someone that they'd been watching me for three days and I hadn't left campus and that they were going back to Illinois. Maybe they thought I'd go looking for the treasure here in Montana."

He kept it light. "You mean you haven't yet?"

"You got me, Dad. I found it and it's under my bed. I just didn't want to share it with you."

He chuckled. "You sure you're okay?"

"Yeah. Like I said, they're leaving. In fact, they already left; the police followed them out of town for the first fifty miles. And they're assigning an officer to watch me." She paused. "Plus, Matthias is with me."

Cam didn't make the obvious retort, that they could just make a U-turn on the highway. Astarte was probably frightened enough as it was. "The police officer is staying all night in your dorm?"

"Yup. In the common area right outside my door. And following me to class and meals and whatever." She sighed. "It's worse than living with you, Dad."

He laughed again. "Okay." He paused. "You know, the fact that Fern hasn't given up tells me she's convinced the treasure is real. And that we are on its trail."

"I had the same thought. I wish we could have questioned her."

"All she had said was that the locals all believed the treasure was real."

"Don't forget the part about treasure making people do desperate things."

Cam exhaled and loosened his grip on the steering wheel. Astarte seemed fine. "You want to talk about my email?"

"It'll have to be later. I'm with some people."

"Okay. Love you. Be safe."

"Love you, too, Dad."

For the next half hour, Cam's stomach churned as he pictured

Astarte in all sorts of perilous situations. Finally, he opened the window and let the warm summer air wash his fears away. Forcing himself to focus, he tried to make good use of the second half of his two-hour drive. He began to organize the Roman artifacts report in his head, periodically dictating notes into his phone. For the purposes of Marconi's permit to salvage the Plum Island wreck, Cam would leave out his theory about the Ninth Legion and the Bar Kokhba treasure. He would keep it basic, limiting the report to the coins, the Mexican head and the Roman forts, along with evidence of earlier Phoenician exploration. He would leave out the Burrows Cave artifacts, knowing that many archeologists believed them to be a hoax. He would also omit the Hebrew artifacts and Hanukah Fort since they unnecessarily muddied the waters. His experience in the courtroom had taught him that, often, less was more. Keep it simple and don't overstate your case. All he needed to do was convince the board that the possibility existed that Roman explorers had crossed the Atlantic. For now, that was enough. Even if the story was so much richer than that.

Amanda's voice.

*'Rich.' I like that. You really have uncovered a treasure trove of artifacts and evidence.*

"Imagine what I would find if you were here helping."

*Astarte has done a nice job.*

"True. But I'm pretty sure she has other things on her mind. And I'm not just talking about Fern and her gang. I'm talking about Matthias."

*He seems like a nice boy. And he adores her. Not to mention, it's good to have him around if Fern and her gang come back.*

"Thanks for not being mad at me about that. I promised not to put her in danger."

*You weren't being reckless. Marconi really gave you no choice. And we can't lock her away in a tower.*

"As if she'd let us. Speaking of Matthias, did you, by the way, ever have the birth control talk with her?"

*Yes. Do you want details?*

"No. Definitely not."

*I thought not.*

What, Cam wondered, if he had answered yes? Could Amanda have supplied information to him that he otherwise had no way of knowing? Or would his subconscious just make things up, fabricate the conversation between Astarte and Amanda as Cam believed it would have taken place? He decided to ask.

How does it work? Are you, like, a ghost?

*No. I don't think so. I exist only in your head. I'm not floating around or anything like that. I see what you see, hear what you hear, know what you know.*

But sometimes you know things I don't.

*Those are things in your subconscious. Things you forgot. Or things you haven't quite put together yet.*

If I haven't put them together, and you're in *my* head, how could you know them?

*Simple, Cameron. I've always been smarter than you.*

Smiling, he drove northwest. He had crossed New Hampshire and half of Vermont before exiting Route 89 in Bethel, in the very center of the state. More importantly, the location was less than a day's walk from Vermont's largest copper mine, the Elizabeth Mine. If Cam was correct in his theory that ancient Phoenicians had come to America to mine for copper around three thousand years ago, it would make sense that Romans coming a thousand years later might revisit those mines to determine if they remained economically viable.

He met a husky, middle-aged man at a pizza place he owned downtown, along the White River. Wiping his hands, the man came out from behind the counter and greeted Cam. "This is a good time. In about an hour, the place gets hopping for dinner."

Cam asked about the coins.

"My buddy and I go out when we can with our detectors. There's a farm along the river where the owner lets us search. One year, this would be back in the early nineties, they plowed but for some reason didn't plant. We didn't find much, but did find two Roman coins. One was first century BC, the other first century AD." He shook his head and repeated almost the same thing Cam heard earlier from Phil in Salem. "Beats me how they got there." He stood the coins up in a little stand he had built for Cam to photograph.

Roman Coins, Bethel, VT

"Can I ask," Cam said, "which direction from here?"

"East, maybe ten miles."

Cam nodded. That brought the coins even closer to the Elizabeth Mine. "And you said, along the river?"

"Yup. We were only about fifty feet from the bank when we found them." The collector continued. "The first one is Emperor Titus with Jupiter on the back. The second one, the older one, is Marcus Aurelius with Victory on the back."

"And you said you didn't find anything else?" If the coins had been part of a lost collection, it stood to reason that they would have found other, more modern coins with them.

"No. And we spent a couple of days there, thinking it might be a rich spot."

Cam took a final look and shook his head. "Did you ever hear of other Roman coins around here?"

"In fact, there's been a couple. Not too far from here."

Cam didn't have time to track them down today, but it might be worth a return trip. He stood. "You know, I'm not surprised."

Munching on a turkey club from the Bethel pizza shop, Cam drove southeast down Route 89, the late afternoon sun at his back. His head was beginning to spin from all the Roman coins he had seen today. This next stop, at least, would not be coin-related. But it definitely was Roman.

He had arranged to meet with a professor of electrical engineering at Dartmouth. The professor was a student at MIT in the 1980s, where she served as a teaching assistant for Professor Harold Edgerton. Now deceased, Edgerton was a forerunner in the development of sonar and deep-sea photography, his equipment used by underwater explorers such as Jacques Cousteau. In the early 1980s, Edgerton traveled to Brazil to assist maritime archeologist Robert Marx in the analysis and exploration of a shipwreck near Rio de Janeiro.

Cam parked in front of the sprawling brick complex with a sign identifying it as the Thayer School of Engineering. Surprisingly, it was bereft of ivy. Perhaps, being engineers, they understood the damage the roots could do.

He wandered down a mostly-empty hallway, turned a corner, and knocked lightly on an office door. A smiling, middle-aged woman wearing a floral sundress greeted him in a German accent from behind a cluttered desk. "Come in, Mr. Thorne." She stood. "I am Hildegard Gurk."

"Your parents knew you were going to become a scientist when they named you," he replied with a smile. Hildegard of Bingen, later Saint Hildegard, overcame the patriarchy of the medieval time period to become one of Europe's leading scientific minds. Cam hoped the comment was not too forward, but something about the professor's face invited familiarity.

"Bravo to you for knowing who she is." She gestured for Cam to sit. "Of course, you are a historian."

"I actually learned of her through my research on the Knights Templar. When they found devices and tools and instruments in the

Middle East that they couldn't understand, they brought them to Hildegard."

"And your work on the Templars has, in turn, brought you to me. You are wondering if the Romans were in America before the Templars."

He nodded. "There's a lot of evidence that indicates they were."

"I know Professor Edgerton believed it. And he was as disciplined a thinker as I have ever known. He was quite a man. Not many male professors in those days were willing to take a chance on a female teaching assistant." She smiled. "Especially one with less-than-perfect English." When Cam had first reached out to her, she told him she had accompanied the professor on his trip to Brazil. "The professor was eighty-six when we flew to Brazil. It was an ordeal for him. But he insisted on going. You spoke of evidence. He, and the other members of their research team, believed the evidence was ... what is the word ... *ironclad*."

Cam was aware of the amphoras—tall ceramic jars used to transport olive oil and wine—found in the harbor. Almost two hundred jars were found by Marx, the archeologist, at a depth of about ninety feet. According to a pair of articles in the *New York Times*, the amphoras were identified by a UMass professor specializing in ancient pottery as being Roman and dating to the second or third century.

He pulled out his phone, where he had saved an image he found online of the amphoras. "Are these the amphoras?"

Roman Amphoras, Rio de Janeiro, Brazil

She leaned closer. "Yes. They were long and thin like that so they could nestle together, one facing one way and the other the opposite. Amphoras were called the shipping containers of the ancient world." Hildegard continued. "The locals called this the Bay of Jars—they have been pulling amphoras out for over a hundred years. Professor Edgerton was brought on to do a sonar scan of the ocean floor, beneath where the amphoras were found. He was convinced there was a ship buried there."

"So what happened?"

"Politics. Marx, the maritime archeologist, was … I think I am saying this correctly … a bull in the china shop. And some in the Brazilian government did not want to challenge the traditional narrative that the Portuguese explorer, Pedro Alvares Cabral, discovered Brazil. Portugal, in fact, issued a formal complaint that Marx was defaming Cabral." She smiled and shook her head. "As if that were not bad enough, the Italian ambassador to Brazil notified the government that, since the Romans were the first to 'discover' Brazil, all Italian immigrants should be granted immediate citizenship, just like Portuguese immigrants. It got pretty heated. In the end, the Brazilians kicked Marx out of the country and the navy dumped tons of silt over the find to cover it up."

"Wow. What a story." Cam focused on the amphoras, anticipating what skeptics might argue to refute the find. "Could the amphoras have been dumped into the harbor in modern times?" He couldn't see why, but anything was possible.

"No. The jars were encrusted with barnacles which had stopped growing in the harbor decades earlier because of pollution. You can see the growth on that picture you showed me. Then, later, the University of London performed thermoluminescence testing, dating the amphora to the Roman era." She sighed. "It was a legitimate find, probably lost to history forever. As I said, Professor Edgerton was a scientist. He just couldn't understand how politics and personalities could win out over the science." She lowered her head. "He died a few years later. And I read that Marx recently died as well. I fear that any chance of unearthing this ship died with them."

Cam nodded. He thought about Marconi, himself at death's door. Would the Plum Island wreck suffer a similar fate? "You'd be surprised how many stories I hear just like this one."

He had requested the meeting because he wanted to get a broader sense of the find, beyond what the newspaper articles could provide. Professor Edgerton clearly believed in its authenticity. As, apparently, did Hildegard.

Cam stood and thanked the professor. She held his eyes. "You seem like a good man. Don't let your story die, Mr. Thorne."

## Chapter 7

Two days after his trip to Vermont, Cam drove into Boston just before noon and pulled into a parking garage not far from the TD Garden, still known by most Bostonians as Boston Garden. He hated to pay for parking, but the hearing at the Board of Underwater Archeological Resources might go longer than the two-hour street meters. And it was Marconi's dime.

Carrying his briefcase and his suit coat, he walked half a block in the midday August humidity and entered a brick warehouse-style building. He pulled at his dress shirt, allowing the cool air in the lobby to dry his sweat, before slipping on his jacket and stepping into the elevator.

The rectangular meeting room—essentially an oversized conference room—featured a wall of windows which faced east, offering views of the Charles River as it dumped into the harbor. As Cam often did when he viewed the coastline, he tried to imagine what it might have looked like in ancient times. Would Romans have been attracted to Boston Harbor as the Colonists were? Or would they have preferred the North Shore, where the mighty Merrimack River met the Atlantic? Based on the number of artifacts found around the mouth of the Merrimack, Cam thought he knew the answer.

Cam hesitated in the doorway, scanning the room. The nine members of the board milled around tables arranged in a U at one end of the room, where they would sit. A smaller table sat in the opening of the U for petitioners and their spokespeople, the table equipped with a laptop and projector to allow for PowerPoint presentations. Eight or ten rows of audience chairs filled the other two-thirds of the room; two-thirds of those were empty. In the back corner, Marconi—dapper as always in a charcoal gray, double-breasted suit with powder blue tie and matching handkerchief—spoke into his phone while Robinson Roberts thumbed through a manila folder. As Cam strolled over, Roberts spotted him and snapped the folder closed.

Recovering, the archeologist, wearing an oversized blue blazer which smelled of pipe smoke, smirked at Cam, his eyes narrowing behind his tinted eyeglass lenses. He combed his mustache with the fingers on one hand. "You ready for your big day?"

"I'm ready with my presentation, if that's what you mean. What's so secret in your folder?"

Roberts flushed, his face matching his pink dress shirt. "You'll see."

Shrugging, Cam took a seat. Whatever Roberts was up to would be Marconi's headache, not his. Cam would speak first, his job to go through the laundry list of artifacts evidencing the possibility of a Roman ship crossing the Atlantic in ancient times. He had finished the report yesterday afternoon and sent it to Marconi for comments. Marconi had agreed that the better strategy would be to leave out the Hebrew artifacts, that sometimes less was more. Marconi also had been clear with his instructions. "We need to convince the board, and the local dive teams that will be listening, that it is possible that a Roman ship made it to the North Shore. That is all. Roberts will do the rest."

The board spent twenty minutes going through preliminary matters before calling Marconi's name. Cam, Roberts and the car dealer took seats at the table in front of the board; Cam quickly inserted his thumb drive and booted up his PowerPoint presentation. He stood, smiled and introduced himself, preparing to set forth his case as he had done hundreds of times in his professional life. "Mark Twain famously said, 'The very ink with which history is written is merely fluid prejudice.' What he meant was, when it comes to history, we are really just feeling our way along in the dark." Cam smiled again. "In just the past decade, in fact, we've seen this. Civilization began six thousand years ago in Mesopotamia; oops, make that twelve thousand years ago in Turkey, at Gobekli Tepe. The earliest humans arrived in America fifteen thousand years ago; oops, make that thirty-five thousand years ago, based on the recent find in Chiquihuite Cave in Mexico. The Neanderthal line of humanoids died out; oops, it now turns out that most of our genomes contain three or four percent Neanderthal DNA." He shrugged. "The point is, we need to keep an open mind." He knew he ran the risk of sounding patronizing. But boards like this often were composed of people from mainstream academia who rarely questioned established beliefs. As Cam had said to Marconi, it was impossible to teach someone something they already knew.

He continued. "When Mr. Marconi first asked me to conduct

research on Roman artifacts in America, I was, honestly, skeptical. Probably much as you are. But I was stunned at the sheer volume of artifacts I found." Beginning with the numerous coin finds, he next showed the terracotta head from Mexico, the amphoras from Brazil, and the ancient forts along the Ohio River. Images, he knew, were key, and he made sure his presentation was heavy on imagery and light on prose. Fifteen minutes later, to polite nods, he sat. Marconi surprised him by patting him on the shoulder.

Roberts inserted his thumb drive and stood. He cleared his throat, shifting back and forth on the balls of his feet.

"Mr. Thorne focused on the various Roman artifacts. I will be focusing on the shipwreck itself. As you know from our filing, Mr. Marconi has located a wreck off of the southern tip of Plum Island, beyond a reef known as Emerson Rocks." He clicked to his first image. "This is a mosaic from Tunisia of a Roman trireme ship. It is this type of ship that Mr. Marconi believes he has located off the reef."

Roman Trireme Ship Mosaic

"As you can see, a trireme was both sail- and oar-powered." He went into the history of the ship, how the Romans learned to build warships by copying the Phoenician design after capturing a Phoenician quinquereme, a larger sibling of the trireme, in battle during the Punic wars around 200 BC. "Triremes were about 120 feet in length. Compare this to Columbus' ships, the largest of which was 70 feet. Though triremes were designed for coastal use, rather than ocean voyage, they were known to sail from the Mediterranean to the

British Isles. Normally a trireme had a crew of around 200 men, with 170 of those being rowers. Without the rowers, the ship could hold enough provisions to last a couple of months at sea. In fact, the *Phoenicia,* a replica of a Phoenician trireme-style ship, recently completed an Atlantic crossing from Tunisia to the Dominican Republic. So it is not inconceivable that a trireme could have pulled in its oars and made the crossing with a skeleton crew." He smiled and shrugged. "But, of course I recognize that *could* have made the crossing is a far cry from *did* make the crossing."

He continued, his voice rising as his nerves calmed and he settled into his presentation. "We have heard from Mr. Thorne about the various Roman artifacts found in and around New England. Based on these, he argues, we should not be surprised to find a Roman ship in our waters. It is a compelling argument, I must admit." He paused for effect, again smoothing his mustache. "But I am here to tell you that it is, at least today, a losing one. I no longer believe that the shipwreck in question is of Roman origin."

*What?* Cam's stomach clenched. He had been concerned about Roberts. Was the archeologist more interested in his reputation in the archeological community than his obligation to his client? Leaning back, he studied Marconi. The car dealer remained impassive, chin up, attentive, as if his spokesman had not just sabotaged his efforts. Cam marveled at the man's self-control—*never let them see you sweat.* Then he thought about the severed skull of Columbus' crewman. Amanda's voice popped into his head. *Robinson Roberts bloody well better have a good exit strategy.*

Roberts switched to his next image, this one a grainy black-and-white photo of a dozen shirtless men posing on a pier, open water behind them. "This photo was taken in the summer of 1914, in Salem, Massachusetts." He held up what Cam guessed was the original photo, sheathed in plastic wrap—the object he had stuffed into the folder before the meeting so Cam couldn't see it. "I scanned it from this original, which I found in the archives of the Salem Historical Society. These men are all of Lebanese origin. In fact, most of them are sons or nephews of a wealthy Lebanese merchant by the name of Sameed 'Sammy' Haddad. Haddad emigrated from Lebanon as a youth. According to my research, he took a lot of pride in his Lebanese origin and was a generous supporter of the Lebanese community in Boston and on the North Shore."

Cam had no idea where this presentation was going. And from the looks on the faces of the board members, they didn't either. Robertson plowed ahead, now showing an image of Columbus' three ships. "Approximately twenty years before this photograph was taken, the nation celebrated the 400th anniversary of the Columbus crossing. As part of that celebration, replicas of Columbus' three ships—the *Nina, Pinta* and *Santa Maria*—were built and displayed at the World's Fair in Chicago. Eventually, the *Santa Maria* founds its way to Boston, in 1914. It was used as a tourist attraction, its promotors charging admission and sailing the vessel up and down the coast north of Boston. I even found an old picture of it in the harbor."

*Santa Maria* Replica at Sail

Roberts took a deep breath. "Enter Sammy Haddad. I was fortunate enough to find the journals of one of his sons, who put down in writing what I am about to tell you."

Roberts explained that Haddad believed that Italians were mediocre seafarers, especially when compared to the ancient Phoenicians. "And regarding the *Santa Maria,* Haddad often said that life was too short to sail an ugly boat. To prove his point, in the summer of 1914, he commissioned a Phoenician sailing ship to be built, which he named the *King Hiram*. It was an exact replica of a trireme, though built on a smaller scale. By the summer of 1915, the *King Hiram* was complete. He and his sons and nephews and other Lebanese immigrants—descendants of the ancient seafaring Phoenicians—quickly mastered the art of sailing the trireme. Often, when the *Santa Maria* sailed north of Boston toward Salem, Haddad would intercept it with the *King Hiram* and sail circles around it, mocking it and taunting its crew." He paused. "Its Italian crew."

Roberts now had everyone's full attention. "By the fall of 1915, the Italian crew had had enough. A few days before Columbus Day, on a moonlit night with a wind from the south, they commandeered the *King Hiram*. They sailed it north to Plum Island, where, at low tide, they ran the vessel aground on Emerson Rocks." He flicked to a new image, a faded copy of a 1915 newspaper article describing a ship being wrecked off the southern tip of Plum Island.

Roberts spread his arms. "It is that ship, the *King Hiram,* which Mr. Marconi has located."

All eyes turned to Marconi. The man let out a long breath and, with what Cam could see required an extreme effort, pulled himself to his feet. He nodded to the board, rubbed his face, and lifted his chin. "Ladies and gentleman, thank you for your time. I am sorry to have, as it turns out, wasted it. I, of course, accept the findings of the expert, Professor Roberts."

"Thank you, sir," the board chairwoman said, her tone somber. "I think it is safe to say that we were all skeptical about there being a Roman shipwreck in Massachusetts waters. Even more so now." She cleared her throat. "Based on the evidence presented, it is clear to me that this find is of no historical significance to the Commonwealth of Massachusetts." She looked at the other board members to see if anyone objected. None did. "Can I have a motion, then, waiving jurisdiction and relinquishing all rights to this find?"

A motion was made and seconded, the vote unanimous. That was it, then. Cam was no fan of Marconi, but he felt a pang of sympathy for the dying man. This had been his dream, his swan song. And now it was gone.

Roberts smirked at Cam as he gathered his papers. But at least he had the decency to linger in the conference room as Cam and Marconi made their way to the elevator in silence. Or perhaps, knowing Marconi's temper, self-preservation was his motivation. Cam began to speak, but Marconi touched him on the arm and shook his head. "Nothing need be said, Mr. Thorne. I thank you for your good work."

The elevator arrived at the ground floor and dinged. Marconi stepped aside, gesturing for Cam to go ahead. Cam nodded, his lips pursed. There was, truly, nothing to say. He held the man's gaze. "I had a few more sites with Roman artifacts to visit. I assume there's no reason to do so now."

Marconi angled his head. "Why would you assume that?"

The response confused Cam. "Well, aren't we done?"

The enigmatic millionaire straightened himself and adjusted his tie. "On the contrary, Mr. Thorne. We have just gotten started."

A warm wind buffeted Astarte as she strolled across campus, hand-in-hand with Matthias after a Thursday morning class. A plainclothes campus policewoman followed thirty feet behind, doing her best to stay unobtrusive. In the distance, over the mountains, a dry thunderstorm flashed and danced across the darkened sky.

Matthias stopped to watch the display. "It's beautiful, but also destructive. Lightning without rain causes wildfires."

"What is the Blackfoot legend about dry lightning?" she asked. There were many things she adored about Matthias, one of which was his wealth of knowledge about Indian culture.

His eyes focused on a spot high in the Rockies, still white with snow. "In our mythology, the thunderbird is a supernatural being of strength and power. It lives in the mountains and protects humankind from our enemy, the great horned serpent, by throwing lightning bolts at it. But the serpent is smart, and knows that when the thunderstorms come, it should take shelter underground. So sometimes the thunderbird tricks the serpent and throws lightning even without the rains."

"Neat. And interesting how the Native American representation of evil is a serpent, just like in Christianity."

"I had never thought of that."

"It's not a coincidence," she replied. "When cultures interact, they share their legends and beliefs. From what I've read, most Native American cultures historically worshiped the snake as a sign of fertility. It was only later that our beliefs changed. Think of the Serpent Mound in Ohio."

"Wait, what is that?"

"A giant earthen mound in the shape of a snake. It's on a tentative list to be approved as a UNESCO World Heritage Site, but most Americans have never even heard of it." Astarte pulled an image up on her phone. "It's over two thousand years old. Not far from the Roman forts. But it would have been built before the Romans arrived."

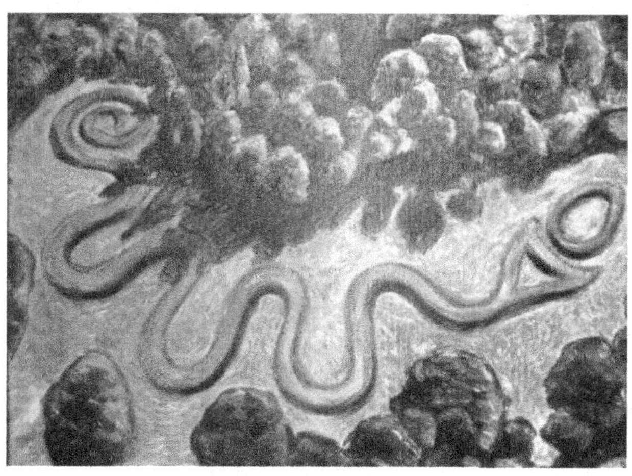

Serpent Mound, Ohio

"That's amazing. How long is it?"

"Over a thousand feet. And fifteen feet wide. See, at the end, it's about ready to eat an egg?" She continued. "Anyway, like I said, it's only after contact with Christian explorers that we start to see the serpent as a manifestation of evil in Native American culture."

He grinned. "I always learn something when I'm with you."

She lifted her chin and kissed him. "And I've learned that I can't be late to my physics lab. Last time I got stuck with a lab partner who spent the whole time on his phone. I had to do all the work."

"I can't believe you're taking that. You're a history major."

She shrugged. "I like physics." Smiling, she added, "And how else am I supposed to figure out the *real* story behind dry lightning?"

Two hours later, her stomach rumbling for food, she pushed through the doors of the lab building back into the midday sunlight. The lab had gone well—she had partnered with a new student, a tall woman with a foreign accent who seemed to know a lot about physics. The policewoman, who had waited in the hallway outside the lab, fell in beside her. Astarte sighed. At least she didn't follow her into the classroom. But having an escort only served to remind Astarte that she was in danger. It was like driving with someone in the back seat constantly saying, "Watch out!"

A Frisbee sailed her way, caught by the breeze. Astarte reacted, lunging to her side to snatch it inches from the paved path. She flung it back, welcoming the feeling of unleashing her body after days of inactivity. The past week, she suddenly realized, was the longest she had gone without participating in a sporting event since, well, since she could remember. It saddened her, as if college marked the end of her youth, the end of playing games for fun. It didn't have to, she knew.

She turned to her escort. "I feel like going for a run."

"Okay." The officer was wearing sneakers. "I can keep up if you don't go more than a couple of miles."

They headed back toward Astarte's dorm. Fifty yards away, Astarte froze. Two guys in cowboy hats leaned against trees in a wooded area to the side of the building. Could one be Darrell?

"I see them," the policewoman said.

And they saw Astarte. One of them moved toward her.

"Go!" the policewoman yelled, lifting her phone to call for back-up.

Astarte sprinted toward the front door, her key card ready to swipe. The man, running now, angled to intercept her, his buddy close behind. She doubted she could fight them off, but she might outsmart them. Recalling a trick her dad had taught her on the soccer pitch, she pumped her arms, appearing to be at full speed. Her pursuer, intuitively calculating their intersection point, raced toward her. As he closed to within five yards, Astarte shifted to another gear, surging past him as he lunged for her, barely swiping her hip with an outstretched arm. By the time he had righted himself, she was at the door. Sliding through, she shouldered it closed. For good measure, she grabbed a couple of coins from her pocket and jammed them between the door and the frame, wedging the door shut.

"What's going on?"

Astarte turned, gasping. The tall woman from physics, her lab partner. "Um, there are some guys out there who might be after me. Long story."

The woman, Becky was her name, stepped closer. "You mean the two guys in the cowboy hats?"

"Yeah."

Her eyes widened. "Two of their friends are in the stairwell. I saw them when I came in a few minutes ago."

Astarte's stomached clenched. That had been their plan, to chase her into the dorm and grab her on the way to her room, with the policewoman outside.

Becky turned. "Come on. There's a back staircase. My room's on the top floor. You can hide there."

Silently they raced down the hall, then up the rear stairs. On the fourth floor, Becky took Astarte by the arm. Before Astarte had a chance to react, Becky had spun her around and locked her in a chokehold. She spoke calmly into Astarte's ear. "Do as I say, and you won't be hurt. We're not going to my room. We're going to the roof."

"Wait, what?" Astarte's heart pounded. She began to writhe, but Becky tightened her hold.

Becky's arm was like a vice. Fighting her would not work. It occurred to Astarte that the man chasing her did not look familiar—not Darrell or either of his two brothers. Which meant the men in the cowboy hats could have been a diversion, a ruse to propel her into Becky's waiting clutches. "Becky, what are you doing? What do you want?"

"I want you on the roof. I can drag you up by your neck, or you can walk. Your choice. But we *are* going."

"I'll walk," Astarte sputtered. In the distance, she heard what sounded like the whop-whop-whop of a helicopter.

Becky loosened her hold a bit. "Good choice. Up we go. And you can call me by my Hebrew name. Rivka."

Robinson Roberts rarely drank in the afternoon, but today a warm glow washed over him as he lifted his mug at an outdoor table in a sports pub near the Boston Garden. "To history," he said. "The *real* history."

Three colleagues had joined him at the square table, two of them members of the Underwater Archeology Board. Technically, it was a conflict of interest for them to socialize with him. But the hearing was over, the vote taken, the ruling final. So the conflict was in the rear-view mirror. As was, thankfully, Mario Marconi.

The third colleague was Esmerelda Aparicio, an associate professor of archeology at B.U. Roberts had been trying to get into her Puerto Rican pants for months. Now, today, after his alpha dog performance, she seemed to be looking at him differently. In fact, she had slid into the chair next to his when they sat and, on more than one occasion, had allowed her leg to brush against his. He ordered another round, along with some nachos. "Did you see Marconi's face when I said his trireme wreck was a replica? He tried to hold it together, but I was sitting next to him. I swear, I could *smell* the desperation wafting off of him." Roberts chuckled. "But what was he going to say?"

One of the colleagues, a man in his fifties, laughed. "I half-expected him to pull you off stage with an umbrella, like in those old Vaudeville acts."

Esmerelda leaned her shoulder into Roberts. "I don't think even that would have worked. Robinson was on a *roll*." Roberts loved the way she rolled her 'r' when she spoke. God, what else could that tongue do?

An hour later, his two colleagues said their goodbyes. Roberts turned to Esmerelda and held her eyes. "Could I interest you in a shot of tequila?"

"Yes." She rested her hand on his. "But only one. Then we should go."

Arm in arm, giggling, they left the pub. Roberts checked his watch. Just past four. Esmerelda was smart to limit them to one tequila. He waived down a taxi and, giving her a knowing look, provided the driver with his home address. Esmerelda reacted by squeezing his thigh. Taking a deep breath, he turned and kissed her in the back seat, her taste a tantalizing mix of tequila and nachos and Latina spice. He kissed her again, sliding his tongue deep into her mouth. She hummed with pleasure.

The cab stopped. Even the traffic had been on his side today, allowing them to make it across town in less than fifteen minutes. He handed the driver a twenty, closed the door behind Esmerelda, and led her to his street level apartment. Not much space, but he kept it clean and the location in the Back Bay was ideal.

Inside, he flicked on a light. "Would you like another drink?"

"No." She looked at him knowingly. "But I would like to use your bathroom."

As she closed the door, a masked man stepped from the foyer closet. Roberts froze. The intruder lifted a pistol, his hand steady. "I have a message from Mr. Marconi."

A swirling torrent of wind and a deafening cacophony of noise met Astarte as she pushed open the roof door. Wide-eyed, she watched a helicopter land on her dormitory roof.

Rivka shoved her forward. "Stay low," she yelled.

Astarte knew that the best time to thwart an abduction was early on, at the site. She looked around, searching for a weapon or some way to impede the helicopter. But these were pros. By all appearances, the Mossad. With a sinking feeling in her chest, she trudged toward the open door.

Ten seconds later, they were airborne, she and Rivka in the back seat behind the pilot, who sat on the right. A scowling man with a pink and purple scar running from jawline to temple sat next to him. Rivka buckled Astarte's belt; as she did so, she snatched Astarte's phone from her pocket. She leaned closer, her clean, floral scent noticeable in the cramped cabin. "The man with the scar is Menachem Dodi," she yelled. It was like trying to be heard over a vacuum cleaner. "People think he's going to be mean because of the scar. They're right."

Astarte looked at her. What was she supposed to say to that? Was this some kind of good cop, bad cop thing?

Rivka continued. "Do what he says. I'll try to protect you as much as I can." She pulled away; her dark eyes, almost black, held Astarte's before leaning back in. "But there's not much I can do."

Again, good cop, bad cop? The copter banked, descending toward the Bozeman airport. Astarte swallowed. Apparently the copter was just the first leg of their journey. "Where are we going?" she shouted.

"Honestly, I don't know."

The rain shower had passed, so Cam took the opportunity to put Venus in the canoe and paddle around again before the midday heat arrived. Canoeing was good exercise. Plus, it also gave him a chance to swing by the beach to see if Rivka might have made her way there, bare feet kneading the sand.

The beach was full of toddlers and tweeners and a few elderly folks, but no volleyball players turned Mossad agents. Cam paddled along the shoreline, allowing the canoe to drift, deep in thought. What had Marconi meant when he said that they weren't done, that they had just gotten started? Was he just being brazen? Or did he have a backup plan?

One way to find out. Cam took out his phone.

"I don't understand how we move forward," Cam said.

"With all due respect, Mr. Thorne, you are merely a foot soldier in this. A valuable foot soldier, and a well-paid one. But merely a foot soldier, nonetheless. You will leave the strategizing to me."

Cam bit back a retort. No doubt Marconi had something unsavory planned, something it would probably be best if Cam knew nothing about. Perhaps he was planning to salvage the wreck furtively, though how that could be done near the busy Plum Island Sound waterway was a mystery to Cam. Or perhaps it was something as simple as a legal appeal of the Board's decision. Whatever.

"To be clear, you want me to keep documenting Roman artifacts? I've found a couple more that aren't in my report."

"Yes. With the Board ruling against us, your research takes on an even more important role. I will, of course, continue to pay you for your time."

The line went dead. Apparently, Marconi didn't feel very talkative. Not surprising, given the defeat he had just suffered.

Cam wasn't feeling particularly upbeat either. It was bad enough to be bested by Robinson Roberts. But, worse than that, despite having been forced into it initially, he had begun to believe in this project. Now it felt like it was on life support. He paddled home.

Twenty minutes later, now seated on his deck, Cam opened his laptop. He'd order a pizza in an hour, one of many meals he would likely be eating alone over the next many months. He was glad, at least, to have his research.

An email pinged. *Bingo.* A reply to a query he had made to a historical society in Maine, sparked by a call he had received from Professor Hildegard Gurk at Dartmouth. She had gone through some old files after his visit and found a reference to amphora jugs found in Maine in the early 1970s. Cam tracked down a 1971 newspaper article recounting how a diver found the two Roman-era amphoras in forty feet of water in Castine Bay. An expert opined that the clay paste of the jars matched amphoras produced on the Iberian Peninsula during the Roman era. Cam studied an image of one of the jars—about the size of a jug of wine—that the historical society sent.

Amphora, Castine Bay, Maine

*The Roman era again.* For the umpteenth time, Cam wondered if there was some kind of alternative explanation. The newspaper article suggested that perhaps the amphoras had been tossed overboard by a sailor from a nearby Revolutionary War shipwreck. But why would a sailor in the 1770s be in possession of Roman-era storage jars? And, even if so, why would he toss them overboard? Cam had a law professor who used to bellow, "Ladies and gentlemen, that is simply not how the world works!"

Cam had learned a lot about the world since then, had seen some crazy, unexplainable things. But, as the problem-solving principle known as Occam's razor stated, usually the simplest explanation was the correct one. Which meant that if there were Roman amphoras and Roman coins and Roman artifacts scattered around New England, it probably meant that *Romans* had brought them here.

Despite what the Underwater Archeology Board might believe.

The jet accelerated down the runway only minutes after Rivka had hustled Astarte aboard. As it rose, Astarte's stomach heaved. She fought to swallow back her digestive juices. A rollercoaster junky, she knew the sour taste in her throat had nothing to do with the motion of the plane.

She closed her eyes, her heart racing, uncomfortable in the plush, cream-colored leather seat. Rivka sat across a wide aisle, working her phone. The operative with the scar, Menachem, was in the cockpit. He had completely ignored her. Not even a glance her way. She hoped it would stay that way.

It didn't.

He appeared next to her like an apparition. One second she had been staring out the window, watching the mountains fade in the distance, and the next moment he was standing above her. She couldn't help but focus on the raised purple welt bisecting his cheek. "I was sorry to hear about your mother," he said somberly.

It was the last thing she expected to hear. "You knew her?"

"I did. We ... worked together in Belgium a couple of years ago."

"Wait, she worked for the Mossad?"

"No. She worked *with* the Mossad. There is a big difference. Those who work *for* us do it for the love of their country. Those who work *with* us do it for self-interest." He shrugged. "Or, more often, because they have no choice."

"Like me."

"Yes. Like you. We need your assistance. We will have it. The only thing yet to be determined is what happens between now and then."

She swallowed. She was brave, but she wasn't stupid. "What do you want?"

His expression softened. "You know, I have a granddaughter about your age." His accent sounded Russian, and she noticed a slight scent of salami on his breath. "I am sorry to frighten you. Truly. It is an ugly, dangerous world we live in." Perhaps subconsciously, he turned, hiding his scar from her. It looked fresh. She did not want to know the story behind it. "The reason I am here, now, rather than sitting in a café with my wife doing a crossword puzzle, is that I want to try to make things right, make things better for your generation." He smiled sadly. "But I am an old man. I am running out of time." He sighed. "And it is a big job, this fixing of the world."

She realized he had not answered her question. "Like I said, what do you want from me?"

"We are going to Illinois. You will show us the cave."

She relaxed a bit. It was not too onerous a request. Unless there was more to it than he was letting on. "Why?" she probed.

His features hardened. "Because I need to go there." With that, he spun and returned to the cockpit.

"Oh my God," Rivka said when he was out of earshot. "That was, like, the friendliest I've ever seen him."

"That was friendly?"

"Sort of, yes. He said he was sorry about your mother. He mentioned his granddaughter. I've known him for three months and he's never said anything to me other than give me an order."

Was it because he really did know her mother? And, if so, likely her father as well? Is that why Rivka had reached out to Cam, because the Mossad already had a level of comfort and trust with him? She tried to recall if they had said anything about a Mossad agent when they were in Belgium. Not that her parents would necessarily have shared those details with a fifteen-year-old. Now, of course, at the ripe-old age of seventeen, she was a full-grown adult, ready to be used as a pawn by one of the world's most ruthless spy agencies. She sighed. Life sure had been easier in high school.

Cam's eyes widened as he watched the evening news. He had never liked Roberts. But that did not mean he wanted to see the man dead. An intruder, the police were saying. A robbery interrupted.

Cam knew better. He phoned Marconi.

"I was expecting your call, Mr. Thorne."

"You did it."

"If you mean, do I have Professor Roberts' head in a box, the answer is no. But it is not a bad thing that people equate his death with his betrayal. It will prevent others from also betraying me."

"That is hardly a denial."

"As I told you when we first met, I am too close to death to follow the rules. And also too old for denials. But, I assure you, were I to have been responsible for Professor Roberts' death, I would also have been careful to cover my tracks. Nothing can be tied back to me. Our project will continue unabated."

Again, not a denial. But not quite an admission. "I don't care about the project. I care that Roberts is dead."

"Don't you see, Mr. Thorne, that the two are inextricably linked? Careful you don't make the same mistake Professor Roberts made."

Cam ended the call. He didn't appreciate being threatened. On the other hand, he—unlike Roberts—had not been disloyal to the dying sociopath. Hopefully that would keep him safe. The key, he knew, would be to continue to make himself valuable. And that meant finding more Roman artifacts. With a long sigh, he flipped open his laptop. There was nothing he could do about Roberts other than to try not to meet the same fate.

The coins he had first shown Astarte—and then later used to lure the fake Fern into the Illinois cave—had come from Marshfield, south of Boston. The guy who gave them to Cam said there was a shield found with them, but that it had ended up in a private collection and disappeared. Cam logged on to the New England Antiquities Research Association database, figuring if anyone had a record of the shield, it would be the folks at NEARA, who had been researching historical anomalies around New England for more than fifty years. Sure enough, within twenty minutes he hit pay dirt, albeit with a photo that left a lot to be desired.

Roman Shield, Marshfield, MA

Cam read the information card accompanying the image: "A bronze shield thickly cemented with sea growth is brought up from the shallows off Marshfield, Massachusetts by a fisherman in 1954."

While he was on the NEARA site, he searched for other Roman-era artifacts. He found a Roman-era oil lamp from Clinton, CT in the 1960s:

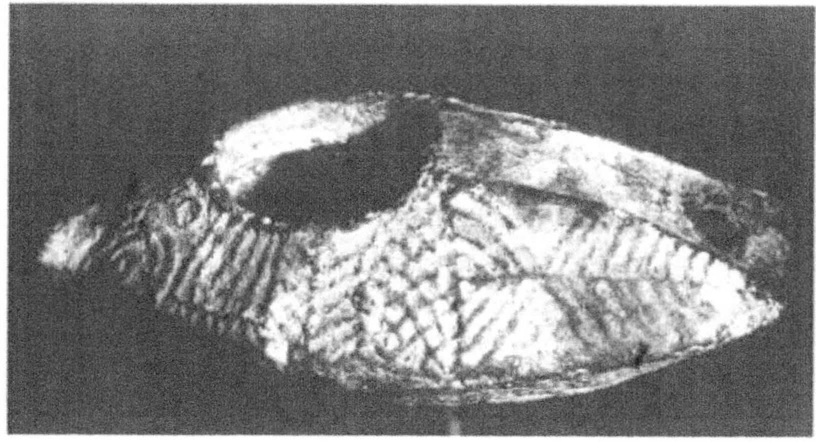

Roman Oil Lamp, Clinton, CT

He also found another Roman-era coin, this one recovered off the coast of Cumberland, Maine:

Roman-Era Coin, Cumberland, ME

Venus whined, needing to go out. Cam would look for more artifacts later; for now, this would suffice. He wanted to have a reservoir of artifacts to feed Marconi. Again, to keep himself valuable. Within months, the millionaire would be dead. Cam just needed enough artifacts to outlast him.

The jet landed at a small airport surrounded by miles of cornfields in what Astarte assumed was southern Illinois. A black SUV raced across the tarmac to them. Rivka escorted her down the plane's stairs in the late afternoon sun, Menachem close behind. Two men, both somber, sat in the front, nodding as Menachem gave instructions from the rear. A second SUV followed.

It didn't take a rocket scientist to figure out what they wanted. Her dad must have been correct: The Bar Kokhba treasures—including the Temple's holy vessels and implements—had somehow made their way here. And the Mossad, understandably, wanted to recover the priceless artifacts.

Twenty minutes later, they cut through the cornfields on a rutted path and parked in the same spot the fake Fern had left her pickup. The two men from the front seat exited and began to gather equipment from the cargo area. The second SUV, also containing two men, idled nearby.

"We tracked you and your father this far," Menachem said. "Now I need you to bring me to the cave."

Astarte swallowed. "I'd like to call my dad."

"Why?" Menachem replied.

"Because I'm scared. I want to ask him what to do." She swallowed. "Think how your granddaughter would feel right now."

Pursing his lips, Menachem nodded. "I tell you what, I will call him." He turned to Rivka. "Give me her phone."

On speaker, her dad answered. "Mr. Thorne, this is Menachem Dodi. You may recall we met in Belgium, in Ghent, a couple of years ago."

His voice was hard. "Why have you abducted my daughter?"

Astarte realized the campus police would have alerted him.

"Relax, my friend, she is safe."

"You are not my friend."

Menachem's eyes danced. "Then you are my enemy, perhaps?"

"No. I'm not you're enemy."

"In *my* world, not being an enemy is the very definition of friend. I am glad we have that settled." He handed the phone to Astarte, his hand over the speaker. "Speak. But be quick. And do *not* tell him where you are."

She nodded. "Dad, I'm okay." She fought to steady her voice. "But I'm scared."

He didn't hesitate. "Whatever they want, do it."

"Okay. That's what I thought."

"Just don't give that guy Menachem any reason to get mad."

Rivka motioned for her to end the call. "Got it. I have to go." She tried to keep her voice from cracking. "Love you."

"Lead the way," Menachem said. The two men had hoisted full packs onto their backs. She had no doubt they were armed.

Astarte turned to follow the path. Hard to believe it was only a week ago when she and her dad had innocently strolled this way into a trap. There was no innocence this time. Rivka fell in next to her and tapped her on the shoulder. "I listened to your call. Thanks for not telling your dad it was me that abducted you."

"What?"

"Just now. On the phone. You kept me out of it."

Astarte blinked. "Whatever." Was it possible the agent had a thing for her dad? Was that why she was being helpful? If so, was now really the time to be thinking about it? Apparently, abducting a college student from her dorm by helicopter was just part of a normal day for these people.

Astarte had no trouble finding the cave and the shelf extending out from the cliff face. "See that hole? You crawl in there, about ten feet. Then the cave opens up inside."

Menachem turned to one of the men carrying a pack and nodded. "So the Collins woman was telling the truth. This is the spot."

They must be talking about the fake Fern, Astarte realized.

His henchman replied, "The Sodium Pentothal told us that."

"Truth serum results are only about ninety percent reliable. We need one hundred. There are dozens of caves out in these woods. And she has plenty of incentive to lie. Unlike the girl."

The man leered. "If you wanted a hundred percent, you should have let me put the jumper cables on her nipples."

Menachem's eyes narrowed. "Under torture, people will tell you what they think you want to hear to make the torture stop. That is often not the same as the truth. You would do well to remember that."

He turned back to Astarte. "Is that hole the only way in?"

She shrugged. "I don't know. But we assumed it was, because they let us go in by ourselves. If there was another way out, they probably would have kept more of an eye on us."

He nodded, apparently satisfied by her logic.

She decided to be as forthcoming as possible. "There were some strange carvings on the wall near the entrance. My dad thought they might be an ancient script."

Menachem shrugged. "It is of no concern."

That seemed odd. She assumed they were here to recover—or at least search for—the treasure. Maybe they somehow knew exactly where it was and didn't need the carving to piece it together. But that didn't make sense. How would they know where in the cave the treasure was located, but not know the location of the cave itself?

The men with the packs entered. After about thirty minutes, during which Astarte sat against a tree under Rivka's watchful eye, one of them emerged from the cave hole and gave a thumbs-up sign. Did that mean they had found the treasure? Had she and her dad somehow missed it? Thinking back, they hadn't really searched for it; they were more concerned about escaping. But had the fake Fern also missed it? Perhaps the Mossad had some kind of map of the cave interior. It was the only thing that made sense given Menachem's disinterest in the script carved near the entrance.

Menachem turned to Rivka. "Take her away. Back to the vehicle. As we discussed."

Rivka nodded. "Come on."

Astarte was okay with that. She had no desire to go back into the cave. In fact, she had half-feared they might lock her in and leave her there. With the bats.

"What are they going to do?" she asked Rivka as the agent loped along.

She shrugged. "They don't tell me much."

They made the quarter-mile trek in less than five minutes, rushing as the bugs began to swarm in the fading light. They climbed into the idling SUV. Rivka nodded to the driver. "Go."

About ten minutes later, just as they had left the cornfield and turned onto a county highway, Astarte heard a deep rumble and felt the vehicle shake. "What was that?"

Rivka shrugged. "Sounded like an explosion of some kind."

Another followed in its wake, then a third.

Astarte tried to get a sense of its direction. "Did they come from the direction of the cave?"

Rivka shrugged again. "Hard to tell. The sound echoes. When I was in the army, you could go crazy trying to figure out where the shells were landing. Especially in the mountains."

"Yeah, but we're not in the mountains," Astarte replied. Rivka remained silent. "Seriously, do you think they blew up the cave?"

"I don't know. But I don't know why they would. You said there's treasure in there. Maybe they blew a hole in a wall to get to it."

Astarte nodded. That, at least, made sense. For some reason, she thought of the bats, thousands of them nestled together on the cave ceiling. "I hope they didn't kill the bats."

"Not a chance. One thing everyone knows about Menachem is that he loves animals. Even bats."

"Wait, what?"

"Seriously. He's killed plenty of people, I'm sure. But not animals. He says they are God's creatures."

"Aren't people God's creatures also?"

Rivka shook her head. "Not according to Menachem. I heard him say once, 'People do all the work, and Satan takes all the credit.' He thinks most people are evil."

A cold realization swept over Astarte—she herself was people.

Cam paced the living room, alternately staring at his phone and cursing his fate. "Call back, dammit."

After receiving Menachem's call on Astarte's phone, he had tried to phone Rivka. No answer, probably because she was ducking him. So he had reached out to the one person who might be able to help. Georgia Johnston, a retired CIA operative who was like an aunt to Astarte. In fact, Astarte had spent a long weekend visiting her in Washington, DC earlier in the summer.

After what seemed like a couple of hours, but was really only twenty minutes, his phone rang. "Just so you know, Cameron, I'm halfway through my second cocktail."

"This will sober you up. The Mossad kidnapped Astarte."

Her voice took on a steely edge. "Tell me what you know."

Five minutes later, they hung up. Cam exhaled. At least someone was doing *something*. Georgia would make some calls, twist some arms. She had been retired now for a couple of years, but she still had plenty of connections. A country girl from rural Texas, she had combined a folksy friendliness and a keen intellect to forge her way in what had been, for most of her career, a male-dominated profession. She had once laughingly said to Cam and Amanda over dinner, "With my pear-shaped body and foul mouth and taste for whiskey, the good old boys thought I was one of them. I fit right in."

Hopefully, some of those good old boys could help.

In the meantime, maybe Cam could figure out how to give the Mossad what they wanted so he could trade it for Astarte's safety. The most obvious conclusion to draw was that the Mossad was interested in the Temple treasure. But what was that treasure, exactly? Answering that question may provide insights into the Mossad's thinking. Cam opened his laptop and dove in, researching the history of the Jewish Temple in Jerusalem.

The First Temple, built by King Solomon, was destroyed by the Babylonians in 586 BC. It was rebuilt by King Herod around 20 BC. This Second Temple, in turn, was sacked twice by the Romans. The first and most famous sacking occurred when Rome put down the Jewish uprising around 70 AD; this was the revolt which included the famous stand—and mass suicide—made by the Jews at the Masada fortress. The Romans looted the Temple and paraded through the streets of Rome with Temple treasures including the Golden Menorah, golden trumpets, and the golden and bejeweled Table of Shewbread (which held loaves of bread always present in the Temple as an offering to God). The items were then deposited in a Roman shrine called the Temple of Peace. The procession of these treasures was memorialized by a carving on the Arch of Titus in Rome, built to commemorate Titus' putdown of the rebellion. Cam found a photograph of the arch, which still stood today in Rome.

Arch of Titus, South Inner Panel, Rome

Of these looted Temple treasures, the Golden Menorah—the candelabra used by Moses in the wilderness and later brought to Jerusalem—would have been the prize. There is a record of the Menorah being seen in the second century in the Temple of Peace but, after that, it seems to have disappeared from history. One rumor claimed that it and the other treasures were melted down; another that the holy treasures were taken by the Vandals when Rome fell; still another that they were being kept hidden by the Vatican. Cam made a note to himself: Perhaps Marconi's brother, in charge of the Vatican Archive, would be able to shed light on the Vatican possibility. One final rumor, which Cam found the most intriguing, was that the Golden Menorah and other Temple treasures had been mysteriously loaded onto a ship, never to be seen again.

Cam now turned to the second looting of the Temple by the Romans, this when the Bar Kokhba uprising was put down in 135 AD. Many historians believed that, before the revolt was quashed, the Jews were able partially to rebuild the Temple and resume worship. Though lacking the Golden Menorah and other holy items such as the Ark of the Covenant, worshippers were able to fill the Temple with valuable gold accoutrements such as vestments, platters, goblets, candlesticks, and musical instruments, many of which were also encrusted with precious stones. Many of these items were itemized in the Copper Scroll of Qumran. These treasures—like the Golden Menorah, Temple of Shewbread and golden trumpets—then mysteriously disappeared.

Cam sat back. The Ark of the Covenant, he knew, had been hidden from the Romans. But an argument could be made that pretty much all the other Temple treasures had been taken by the Romans and then, shortly thereafter, lost to history. He and Astarte had already postulated that the Ninth Legion—perhaps with the assistance of Jewish rebels—had sailed with many of the Temple treasures to America. Was it possible they had made a stop in Rome on their way west through the Mediterranean and grabbed the rest of the treasures, including the Golden Menorah, before searching for a safe haven? There was no evidence directly supporting the possibility, but the dates worked and it would explain the disappearance from Rome of the holy treasures. And, of course, it would explain why the Mossad was so interested.

But it did nothing to help him find Astarte.

They cruised at seventy down the county highway as night began to fall, Astarte in the back with Rivka.

"Are we heading back to the airport?" Astarte asked innocently. She studied the driver's eyes in the rearview mirror. They shifted nervously.

Rivka replied, perhaps a beat late. "Yes. To the airport."

It was a lie. They were driving toward the setting sun, just as they had been when they left the airport a couple of hours ago.

Rivka's words, about Menachem's willingness to kill, echoed in Astarte's head. And here she was, in the middle of nowhere, with three Mossad agents who seemed to have no further use for her. She had to do something.

A lifetime of road trips provided the obvious option. "Um," she said sweetly, "I really have to go to the bathroom."

The driver glanced into the rearview mirror, waiting for direction from Rivka, who sat behind him. Rivka exhaled. "Can you use the woods?"

"Fine with me, as long as you have some paper."

The agent in front open the glove box and passed back a wad of napkins. "Pull over up here," Rivka said. "I'll go with her."

Astarte knew she couldn't outmuscle the agent. And, though a fast runner, she probably couldn't outrun her, either. But, in the thick woods, sometimes the smaller rabbit had the advantage over the faster hound.

While the SUV idled on the shoulder, Astarte led Rivka into the woods. "That's far enough."

Astarte stopped and looked at her sheepishly. "Can we go a little further? I don't want the men watching."

"Whatever."

Fifty feet in, Astarte circled around behind a tree, pulled down her jeans, and squatted. With one hand, she searched the ground for a rock. "Sorry," she said. "Now it won't come. I'm nervous."

Rivka exhaled. "Close your eyes. Think of a waterfall."

There. A pineapple-sized stone. "Okay. Thanks." She peed, wiped herself, and pulled up her pants. Suddenly she let out a short shriek—not loud enough to alert the agents in the car, but enough to alarm Rivka.

"What is it?"

"A snake! It bit me on the ankle!" She pointed toward the tree. "There he is!"

As Rivka bent to peer in the dim light, Astarte rotated her body and swung the stone, catching Rivka on the side of her temple. The agent staggered and moaned before dropping to one knee.

Astarte reacted instantly. Racing away, she angled deeper into the woods, ducking under branches and dodging trees and shrubs.

"Astarte, come back!" The sound of branches breaking told Astarte the agent was in pursuit. But, dazed and a head taller than Astarte, she would struggle to fight through the undergrowth. And Astarte had a decent head start.

Cam answered the phone a microsecond after it began to ring. He had stopped pacing the living room and moved instead to the outdoor deck, as if being under the same stars as Astarte somehow brought him closer to her. "Georgia. Talk to me."

"You're right. It's the Mossad. My sources say one of their jets left Montana and landed in southern Illinois a couple hours ago."

Cam clenched his jaw. They wanted her to bring them to the cave. "The question is, why do they care about that damn cave so much?" And, though he dared not voice the words, did they care so much that they would eliminate any possibility of others finding it?

"I think it's what you told me. The Temple treasures."

It didn't add up. "I get it. Old and gold. So really valuable. But enough to kidnap a girl on American soil?" *Or worse.*

"You're right, it doesn't add up. From what I'm hearing, it's more than that. There are groups in Israel who want to rebuild the Temple. In simple terms, before you can rebuild, you need to find the Temple treasures."

Cam had read about this when researching the Bar Kokhba uprising. This desire to build the Third Temple went back almost two thousand years. In fact, the Bar Kokhba coins they had seen featured the Temple of Solomon—the reason for the uprising—on the front. So it wasn't about gold. It was about God. Cam's chest tightened. When religion got involved, reason often left the room.

"Can you do anything?"

"A call has been made. From the White House to Tel Aviv. Telling them to stand down." She lowered her voice. "But it has to go through channels. And agents in the field don't exactly check their phones like teenagers at the mall. It's going to take a while, at least an hour." She paused. "Honestly, Cam, I don't know if it's too late or not."

Astarte had been lumbering through the woods for about five minutes. At her pace, not even half a mile. Not nearly far enough. No doubt Rivka had gone back—or phoned back—to the SUV and the three agents were now in pursuit.

The forest filtered out most of what little daylight remained, but Astarte could make out shapes and outlines even in the dim light. Counterintuitively, she ran toward the thickest growth, searching for the path of greatest resistance—whatever obstructed her would doubly obstruct the larger Mossad agents. Branches slapped at her face and arms, scratching and slicing. But she forged on.

Down a gully, then back up the other side, pulling herself along by grabbing at underbrush. Hands bleeding, she reached the ridge. She dared a glance back, panting in the thick air. Nothing. Holding her breath, she listened in the darkness. Again, nothing. Had they stopped pursuing her? She pictured Menachem's reaction to them reporting Astarte had escaped. *No way would they give up their pursuit.*

In the distance, between the trees, a speck of light. She squinted. Perhaps a farmhouse on the far side of this copse? Back on level ground, she angled toward the light in a slow jog, head down, arms up to protect her face, trading stealth now for speed. Stumbling, she bashed her knee. Blood trickled down her cheek and from her hands. *Keep going.* A low-lying branch smacked her on the forehead, dazing her. She fought back tears. *Don't cry. It's hard enough to see as it is.*

The woods began to thin. She increased her pace, ignoring the throbbing in her knee as she ran. The light intensified, the outline of a structure forming in the distance. Or perhaps it was just her imagination. She pushed on, panting now, every step bringing her closer to—

"Astarte, stop!" Rivka stepped from the shadows, barely visible. She hissed rather than spoke. "Listen to me."

*No.* Astarte felt her entire body sag. It was all for nothing. The agent must have circled around, probably after looking at satellite imagery on her phone and deducing that Astarte would angle toward the light. But why was she keeping her voice down? And why was she crouching? Something didn't add up. Astarte resisted the urge to flee. "What?"

Rivka reached out, put a hard object into her hand.

*My phone.*

The agent stepped closer, Astarte now able to see the nasty gash on her temple where Astarte had smacked her. "Keep going, toward that light. There's a house there. I'll keep the guys away. When you get there, call 911."

"Wait, why are you helping me?"

"I had no choice but to help abduct you so you could show us the cave. But I had no idea they were going to kill you afterward. I draw the line at killing innocent girls." Rivka smiled, her teeth shining in the night. "Besides, you have a good soul."

"A good soul? How do you know that?"

"The bats. Most people wouldn't have cared about them. But you did." She looked around. "Now, go!"

Cam collapsed into a deck chair when he heard Astarte's voice. "Are you okay? You want me to fly out there?"

"No, I'm fine. And by the time you get here, I'll hopefully be gone. I'm at the police station. I have some cuts and bruises. But nothing compared to the gash on Rivka's head."

"Wait, she was involved?"

"Yup."

Damn. So much for his ability to read people. "The gash on her head—is that how you escaped?" No way could the stand-down orders from Tel Aviv have reached Rivka that quickly.

"Actually, no. She let me go. I mean, she did it without anyone knowing. But, still."

"Seriously?" Maybe he wasn't such a bad judge of character after all. "Why would she let you go?"

"She says it's because I have a good soul. I wanted to save the bats in the cave."

"You know, I really do love those bats."

She managed a chuckle. "Yeah, right."

Hearing her laugh made him want to cry; he dabbed at his eyes with his sleeve and took a deep breath. "Save the bats from what, honey?"

"I think there were explosions at the cave. It was after I left with Rivka. Rivka thought maybe they were blowing a hole in the wall or something."

"I suppose it's possible there really was a treasure in there. Maybe they were able to translate the script. Or maybe they had a map or something." He explained the desire among some Jews to rebuild the Third Temple.

"Wow, so the Mossad must really believe the treasure is here."

"Which means the Romans were here, and probably some Jewish rebels also."

She finished his thought. "Which explains the origin of the Mandan tribe. Just like we thought."

None of that really mattered at the moment. He took a deep breath. "Do you really think they were going to kill you?"

"I think Rivka thought that. Otherwise, she wouldn't have risked her job to help me escape."

"Good point." Even if it felt like a kick to the gut.

"I actually thought of you in the woods, when I was running away. That stupid *Meatballs* movie you made Mum and me watch with you. Rudy Rabbit. That was me. Darting through the woods."

He laughed. "Like I tried to tell you guys, the movie's a classic. Full of life lessons." He really did want to get on a plane. "Where are you staying tonight?"

"One of the female deputies is letting me stay at her place. Then I catch a flight out of St. Louis tomorrow morning."

"I could meet you there, and we could drive to Montana again together."

"Like I said, hopefully I'll be long gone. Besides, love your company, Dad, but not a chance I'm doing that drive again."

## Chapter 8

Cam rolled out of bed early Friday morning, waking Venus from a sound sleep. "Come on, lazybones. Let's go for a walk." Humming, his entire mood buoyed by Astarte being safe, he led the dog outside. "Beach or park? I know, park. Last time I dragged you to the beach." Plus, he had no interest in seeing Rivka, even in the unlikely event she had made it back from Illinois. Yes, she had saved Astarte in the end. But, still.

As he and Venus walked, Cam turned his attention back to his work with Marconi. Specifically, he needed to riddle out an inconsistency in the pile of evidence he had gathered. He had learned in law school that all evidence should point to the same conclusion. If it did not, then either the conclusion was wrong or some of the evidence was faulty. Given that, by all appearances, the Temple treasure had indeed been hidden in or around southern Illinois, it was likely that the shipwreck off of Plum Island really was a Roman trireme. But that flew in the face of Roberts' research showing the trireme belonged to the Lebanese businessman, Sammy Haddad. Again, either the conclusion was wrong—which meant the Mossad and Marconi, as well as he and Astarte, were mistaken—or Roberts had somehow bungled his research.

Cam replayed the details of the Underwater Archeology Board hearing—and the past few weeks—in his mind. It was Marconi's final words to him which resonated. Cam had asked if the Board's decision meant the project was over, done. Marconi's response had surprised him. "On the contrary, Mr. Thorne. We have just gotten started."

Why the term, *on the contrary*? A normal response would have been that the Board's decision was a hurdle to be overcome. Instead, Marconi seemed to imply that the ruling had not been a setback at all but rather some kind of step *forward*.

By the time Cam had reached the park and let Venus loose off her leash to chase a squirrel up a tree, he had some clarity. "I got played," he said, rubbing the dog's neck as she trotted back to him. "Played like a carnival accordion."

Though the sun had barely risen, he phoned Marconi.

"You assumed I'd be awake because I don't have much longer to live." He chuckled. "You assumed correctly. I almost never sleep anymore."

Cam was in no mood for small talk. "I think I know what you did, but I want the details."

"I was wondering how long it would take you to tease it out."

"That whole story about Sammy Haddad and his boat was a fake, right? There never was a boat like that in Salem."

"Correct."

"Explain. I'm listening."

"I learned early in life that the key to being a good salesman was to give people what they wanted. The difficulty, of course, is determining just what that is." Marconi cleared his throat, apparently warming to the task. "For selling cars, it is relatively simple. Some people come in and just want to believe they are getting the best deal. Others are there to show off their negotiation skills in front of, say, their daughter. Still others want to be treated like a big shot. A few are nervous or scared and simply want to believe they are being treated fairly. Some even just want to bully the salesman. Like I said, the key is to figure out which button to push with which customer."

"Okay."

"So, what does the Underwater Archeology Board want? Most of all, they don't want their worldview challenged. The members, being part of the archeological community, part of mainstream academia, firmly believe Columbus was the first European to cross the Atlantic. They are happy, comfortable, in this belief. All this about Roman exploration? It is ... what is the word ... *vexatious*, to them. So they are more than willing to believe the ludicrous story of a wealthy Lebanese man building a trireme and having it scuttled on the rocks off of Plum Island." Cam knew that what Marconi was describing was something called *confirmation bias*—the human tendency to seek out information which confirms rather than refutes current beliefs.

Marconi continued. "What is their alternative? Taking a vote that recognizes the possibility of the wreck actually being Roman?" He chuckled. "Unthinkable. They would then have to defend their action to colleagues and peers at cocktail parties and conferences and faculty meetings. Can't you hear it now? *Did you really think it was possible a Roman trireme crossed the Atlantic 1800 years ago?* Not to mention questions from the press." He offered another short laugh. "No, they slept well last night, having put this behind them."

"But the story's not true. What if they had dug deeper?"

"Part of it is true. The *Santa Maria* replica really was brought to Boston in 1914 as a tourist attraction. And there really is a newspaper article about a ship sinking off of Plum Island in October of 1915."

"But not the rest of it."

"No. But, again, why would anyone dig deeper? They have the result they wanted. And who would suspect a petitioner of purposefully sabotaging his own project?"

Marconi made a good point. Skeptics would climb all over themselves to debunk a claim of pre-Columbus exploration. But nobody would bother debunking evidence claiming that the ancient Romans did *not* sail to America—it was what everyone believed, anyway. It would be like scientists conducting a study to prove that the Tooth Fairy wasn't real.

"What about Roberts? How did you fool him?" Cam reconsidered the question. "You did fool him, right? He wasn't in on this?"

"You're first assumption is correct. Again, the question is, what does Professor Roberts want? Or, I should say, what *did* he want?" He paused. "To be honest, Mr. Thorne, more than anything else, he wanted to best you. To put you in your place. To humiliate you. In that sense, he probably died a happy man."

Cam nodded. Of course. Marconi had intentionally faced the two men off against each other. Beginning with insulting the professor by paying Cam more than him. And then continuing by forcing the professor to concede to the possible validity of the Mexican terracotta head. Of course, once Roberts was of no further use to Marconi, he was disposed of. The irony was that Roberts had been disloyal in exactly the way Marconi wanted him to be. And it still cost him his life. Cam would need to be careful not to meet a similar fate.

Marconi continued. "I planted the photo of Haddad's family in the archives of the Salem Historical Society. And paid to have the journal of Haddad's son forged and placed where Professor Roberts would find it. But I needed to make sure he had the incentive to dig down, to follow the bread crumbs deep into the woods. You, Mr. Thorne, were that incentive."

"So Roberts, too, got what he wanted. Public vindication. He was right, I was wrong."

"Not only that, he saved face with his colleagues. He, like them, was never comfortable with the idea of a Roman wreck."

"Which is what made him a perfect hire for you."

"Precisely."

"I haven't quite figured it out, but you wouldn't have done all this if *you* hadn't also gotten what you wanted. After all, a good businessman always looks out for himself most of all."

Marconi chuckled. "Touché. And you are correct. Let's walk through it. What would have happened if I had played it straight, if we had convinced the Board that the find was legitimate? First, under Massachusetts law, the state would be entitled to twenty-five percent of whatever I salvaged. That is twenty-five percent off the top, without having to pay a penny of the costs or take an ounce of risk." He snorted. "Second, even worse, I would have had a bunch of bureaucrats breathing down my neck, micromanaging the project, delaying me. Third, can you imagine the publicity if they had acknowledged that the wreck might indeed be an ancient Roman ship? Every treasure hunter on the East Coast would have tried to sneak in and vulture my find."

Cam recalled the end of the hearing, the motion made by the Board chairwoman. The Board voted to *waive jurisdiction and relinquish all rights to the wreck.* He nodded. Essentially, the Board, believing the wreck to be a modern one of no historical significance, handed the wreck over to Marconi and gave him *carte blanche* to do what he wanted.

"I get it," Cam said. "The way it stands now, you have full rights to the site and nobody will bother you. Not the state and not the other treasure hunters."

"As you said, Mr. Thorne, a good businessman always looks out for himself most of all."

Rivka jolted awake as the jet's wheels touched down. Her first thought was that her head hurt. Her second thought was that she was lucky it was still attached to her body.

Menachem had been livid the night before when he learned she had let Astarte escape. "She's just a little girl. How could you possibly have lost her?"

"She surprised me. I'm sorry. She got me good with a rock. By the time I cleared my head and called the other agents, she was gone."

But the question held an unspoken accusation. He sensed she was not being truthful. She would need to be careful. Betraying the Mossad was not something many people lived to brag about.

As if on cue, her phone rang. Menachem. "Yes?"

"The girl didn't escape. You let her go. Why?"

She should have known she couldn't fool Menachem. "You were going to kill her. I couldn't allow that."

"You couldn't *allow* it?" he bellowed. "First of all, I don't recall you being promoted over me. Do I now take orders from you, a silly girl?"

"No, sir."

"Secondly, we were not going to kill her. We were taking her to a facility to have her memory erased. That's why we needed her, not Thorne, to bring us to the cave. We still need his help; we can't risk him being foggy-brained. But it was important to the operation that nobody know we were at the cave, much less set off those explosions."

"Why does it matter?"

"Because I say it does. In case you haven't figured it out, that's what we do. We keep secrets."

"So that was it. You were just going to erase her memory?"

"An unpleasant experience, I concede. And not without some risks. But a long way from death."

Rivka knew the Mossad had been developing treatments to suppress memory, especially short-term memory. Apparently, short-term memory was stored in a different part of the brain, which is why people who suffered a concussion often couldn't remember what they had for breakfast that day but otherwise had no memory loss.

"Well, why didn't you tell me the plan? Why do you always keep me in the dark?"

"The answer, I would think, is obvious: Because you can't be trusted." He hung up.

Well, she had sure messed up. Blinking back tears, she rubbed her face and peered out the airplane window in the morning light. Boston. Last night, nobody had told her where the plane was going, the other agents avoiding her for fear of being guilty by association. She hoped she had, at least, won their gratitude for taking all the blame for Astarte's escape.

Reversing the camera on her phone, she studied her wound. She was lucky not to have a concussion and short-term memory loss herself. She had cleaned the gash and used a butterfly bandage to stop the bleeding, but she would need stitches to close it properly. And she'd likely have a scar. Whatever.

"Anyone who would reject me because of a stupid scar is not worthy of me in the first place." She voiced the sentiment aloud, as if it would have more meaning that way. "And I'm not just a silly girl."

But with her head throbbing and her career falling apart and her love life a complete nothing, she didn't feel nearly as brave as her words.

After breakfast and a shower, Cam did a couple of hours of law work before peering out at the lake. The surface was calm, so Cam took the opportunity to put Venus in the canoe and paddle around more before the midday heat arrived. He phoned Marconi again.

"One thing I still don't get. Why hire me at all? Why have me put on that dog and pony show with the Roman artifacts if you didn't want the Board to buy it?"

Marconi offered another of his short laughs. "I was wondering when you'd get to this. The answer is, because there were a couple of divemasters and marine archeologists in the audience, attending at my request. I wanted them to hear your presentation. Not read it. Not have me describe it to them. I wanted them to hear you and witness for themselves the mountain of evidence you have collected. I am a salesman. I know that nothing compares to a face-to-face presentation. As I said to you on the first day we met, I need to convince one of these top dive teams to join me on this project. I can offer them money. But that's not what motivates them. They are treasure hunters. They like the treasure, but, more than that, they are hunters. They like the thrill of the chase."

It made sense. Marconi would need to surround himself with respected professionals and document every step in the process. This operation would be subject to the highest level of scrutiny, especially once it was established that the shipwreck dated back to the Roman era.

"So have any dive teams agreed?"

"Not quite. But I have a meeting this afternoon. They will. I will tell them what I told you, that the Sammy Haddad story was made up. But I don't think that will be necessary. I watched them as you spoke. What is that expression? They drank your Kool-Aid."

"What about the dive team from Italy, the one you used when you went down and verified the ship was a trireme?"

Marconi exhaled. "That was last summer. I would love to use the Italian team again—they were good men, handpicked by my brother. But I am aware of the political realities. I need to use an American team, someone respected by the authorities in this country."

Cam understood. "So you want to dive, what, in a few weeks?"

"I don't have the luxury of a few weeks, Mr. Thorne. What is that expression? As between fast, good and cheap, you can only have two of the three. I don't care a whit about cheap. That leaves me with both good and fast." He paused. "If I have my way, we start tomorrow."

Caryn Collins made the fifteen-minute drive from her salon to Fern's farm in ten minutes, her mouth dry and her armpits dripping. Billy had called. A farmhand he knew reported hearing explosions near the cave yesterday afternoon. *Please don't let it be the cave.*

She raced through the cornfields, her pickup bouncing and jerking like a bad skier fighting the moguls. She didn't care. And didn't care if Fern saw her. She could buy a new truck, find new friends. Her family only had one cave, one shot at a treasure.

At the edge of the woods, she jumped from the truck and ran the quarter of a mile to the cave. Even from a distance, she sensed something amiss. The forest was quiet, and a gritty haze hung in the air. She pushed on, then froze. The limestone shelf outside the cave entrance was gone. As was the cave opening. In their place, a pile of gray stone rubble stood, dust swirling around it in the breeze. Dropping to a knee, she vomited, her eyes never leaving the pile of debris.

Someone had dynamited the entrance to the cave. The only way in.

Had they—whoever it was—found the treasure and removed it? It didn't matter. Either it was gone, or it was destroyed by the blast. Just like her dreams.

Astarte stepped out of the cab in front of her dorm carrying a small plastic bag with her dirty clothes and a toothbrush the deputy had given her.

Her face looked like one of those old hockey goalie masks with the stitches painted on, the kind from the horror movies. The cuts weren't deep, but the branches and underbrush had done a job on her. Not just on her face, but her arms as well. Even the security guys at the airport commented. "You one of those MMA fighters?"

"You should see the other girl," Astarte had replied.

The truth was, the other girl—Rivka—had probably saved her life. Of course, that was after kidnapping her and putting it in jeopardy in the first place. But something didn't add up. Why the need to kill her? She got it—that's what the Mossad did. But even they had to have a good reason to kill an American citizen on American soil. Was finding the Temple treasure that reason? It couldn't be—she had brought them to the cave, as they asked. So it must be because they wanted to keep the treasure secret and didn't trust her to keep her mouth shut. But why the need for secrecy? She pushed through the dorm's front door in the lobby, the same lobby Rivka had abducted her from.

She let out a long breath. The mystery would have to wait. Dad had assured her that Georgia had gotten the Mossad to stand down, and Georgia was not the type to make assurances that would not stand. Even so, she felt on edge, skittish. Who knew when another helicopter might land on her dormitory roof?

In the meantime, she was hoping she could just go back to being a normal college freshman for a little while.

## Chapter 9

As the sun rose over the Atlantic, Cam drove through the back roads of Ipswich, mirroring the route he had taken two weeks earlier. Hard to believe it had only been fifteen days since he first met with Marconi and dove down the Roman artifact rabbit hole. A lot had changed. But not the amazing views from the castle's hilltop.

This time, however, Cam did not park in front of the castle. Instead, he veered down a service road angling away from the main structure. As he approached a beach area along Plum Island Sound, he stopped and pulled out a pair of binoculars. The tip of Plum Island teemed with activity. At least a dozen SUVs and pickup trucks filled the small parking lot next to the beach at Sandy Point. A score of men carried supplies to the shoreline where a couple of small motorboats ferried equipment and workers out to a motorized barge anchored a few hundred yards offshore.

Yesterday, Marconi had said he planned to start the dive operation today. From the looks of things, he was right on schedule. Cam checked his watch. 7:30. Money had a way of getting people out of bed.

He drove back to the castle. "Mr. Thorne," Marconi sang as Cam parked and stepped from his vehicle. Dapper in a blue blazer and pressed khakis, he actually sounded glad to see Cam. "Join me. I am about to head out to the barge."

He took Cam by the elbow. "We have spent the past twelve hours preparing. I learned long ago, it is always better to begin projects on Friday night. If there is a problem—say, for example, one of the neighbors complains or there is a question about permits—nothing can be done until Monday at the earliest because city hall is closed. By then, it is often too late."

"Like with your barge?"

He led Cam around the castle, the rising sun in their eyes. "Exactly. Technically, I probably need a permit. But you know what they say about forgiveness being easier to get than permission."

Better yet, this was Labor Day weekend, meaning city hall

wouldn't open until Tuesday. "And you have the one permit you really need. From the Underwater Archeology Board."

"Correct. Releasing the wreck to me."

They climbed into the golf cart and drove down the Grand Allée toward the shore. Cam was glad he had grabbed a windbreaker; it was ten degrees cooler here along the coast, with a brisk, briny breeze. Before they reached the bluff overlooking the water, they veered left along a dirt path through a forested area. They broke through not far from the beach Cam had just visited. Marconi stopped in front of a long aluminum gangway connected to a floating wooden pier. "This dock was installed overnight, brought here on the barge. It is probably illegal." He shrugged. "But it will be gone in a few days."

Cam nodded. Again, the weekend.

A cabin cruiser bobbed alongside the dock, straining at its lines. A portly man with a bald head and a wide smile put down the pastry he was eating and stood as they approached from the gangway. "Mr. Thorne," Mario said, "may I introduce you to my brother, Cardinal Palo Marconi."

The cardinal's smile widened further as he offered a half bow. He wore a black cardigan over a gray dress shirt with a white priest's collar at the neck. "Here, I am just Palo. It is a pleasure to meet you."

"You came all the way from Italy?"

"How could I miss such a big day?" he said, his arm sweeping toward the ocean. Unlike the self-possessed Marconi, Palo seemed demonstrative and unrestrained. Odd that each had chosen a profession more suited to the other's personality. "The Vatican Archive contains many secrets. But none as exciting as this promises to be."

A captain dressed in white stood ready to ferry them out to the barge. Palo leaned in. "Perhaps we should pray?"

Shaking his head, Mario took his brother's hand. "Please excuse Palo," he said to Cam. "Personally, I don't trust people who say they speak to God. Except my brother, of course."

Palo feigned a hurt expression. "I said nothing about speaking to God. I only want to beseech His blessing over this project."

"Well, I suppose that cannot hurt." Marconi bowed his head. They stood silently in the stern of the boat while Palo offered a short prayer.

Marconi chuckled as the boat lurched into reverse. "You see what is happening, Mr. Thorne? If the project is a success, Palo will say it was because of his prayers. If it fails, Palo will say it was because my prayers were not earnest and heartfelt enough. I cannot win."

The barge loomed a quarter of a mile away, anchored off of Emerson Rocks. Marconi must have arranged the logistics weeks ago, on the assumption he would both succeed at the Board hearing and secure a dive team. Again, it was just a question of foresight and money, especially the latter.

Cam half-listened as the brothers bantered. Their family, Cam had learned, had moved to Gloucester from Italy when the brothers were boys. But Palo had returned to spend his entire adult life in Italy.

"If Catholicism is the one true religion," Marconi said to his brother, "then explain to me why the letters of the word 'Presbyterian,' when rearranged, spell out 'best in prayer.'"

Palo tilted his head back and laughed heartily. Marconi, Cam had noticed, often chuckled. But he never laughed from the belly as his brother did. Palo retorted, "Just for that, you must listen to one of my jokes." He took a deep breath. "A priest and a rabbi are friends. Together, they buy a car, from Marconi Motors, of course. The rabbi walks out and sees the priest sprinkling water over the hood. He asks, 'What are you doing?' 'I'm blessing the car,' the priest replies. 'Oh, as long as we're doing *that,*' the rabbi says. He walks into the garage and comes back out with a hacksaw. Dropping to one knee, he says a quick prayer and cuts two inches off the tailpipe."

Cam laughed politely, saved from more banter by the boat pulling up to the seaward side of the barge. The barge, clean and modern, was the size of a fenced-in tennis court. One end featured a bridge area with a rooftop viewing platform. A massive crane arm extended from the center of the barge. The remaining areas of the vessel were littered with divers and their gear and supplies. Four anchor lines, one at each corner, held the barge in place about fifty feet from the tip of the comma-shaped reef known as Emerson Rocks. "You can see the reef now because it is low tide," Marconi said. "During high tide, it is hidden. Which is what makes it so deadly." Making it a metaphor for many things in life, Cam mused.

Marconi led Cam into the bridge of the vessel while Palo circulated, greeting the divers, offering short prayers for those who desired them and a pat on the back for those who didn't. Marconi had laminated copies of the Underwater Archeology Board decision and hung them prominently on both the interior and exterior walls of the bridge. Marconi was probably correct in his assumption that the official-looking document would suffice for the weekend if someone happened to investigate.

Laid out on folding tables inside the bridge were poster-sized images of the ocean floor, clearly showing the outline of a ship. These images were overlaid with colorful, crosshatched schematics. Marconi explained, "These are the results of sonar testing, both side-scan sonar and sub-bottom profiling." He smiled. "This is something my family knows a bit about—the best sonar systems are manufactured by Marconi Underwater Systems, founded by my grandfather. Professor Edgerton, from MIT, who did the sonar work in Brazil with the amphoras, was a more recent leader in the field."

Cam nodded. It was hard not to be impressed with the science. Or with Marconi—despite his age, he was adept at using the most modern technology. Perhaps not surprising given who his grandfather was. "You've been busy," Cam offered.

"This work was done earlier in the summer. Discretely, of course. Fortunately, the water is not deep—less than fifty feet—and we know the exact location of the wreck. It was a simple matter to tow the sonar scanning device beneath our boat."

"I assume the results confirm your assumptions."

"We wouldn't be here otherwise, Mr. Thorne."

"And I also assume you chose not to show these images to the Underwater Archeology Board because they reveal too much."

Marconi put a finger to his lips and ushered Cam to a corner of the room. "That thin man there, in the ponytail, he is the lead archeologist for this operation. We should be careful about what we say around him."

Cam noticed Marconi had not yet introduced him to the archeologist. Probably smart—no reason to antagonize the man. And also smart to hire a mainstream maritime archeologist and put him in charge today. As Cam had noted, the project needed to be professional and beyond reproach.

Marconi responded to Cam's comment. "You are correct about not showing the images to the Board. They had, in their minds, a quaint picture of Sammy Haddad's trireme and its sad ending. No reason to show them the real thing and invite more investigation."

They left the bridge and climbed a set of outside metal steps to the observation platform, Palo huffing in the rear. From here, peering north, Cam could see the beach where Denise and her husband had found the Roman coins in 2016 after a storm came up from the south. Had they washed ashore from this very wreck? Or was it possible there was another Roman wreck buried nearby? Cam shook his head —one wreck at a time. And, more to the point, it didn't really matter. He was standing above a Roman-era wreck and, nearby, a cache of Roman coins had washed ashore after a storm. It strained credulity to imagine the two were not somehow related.

He refocused on the activity at the barge. The divers had been divided into four teams of two divers each. "The teams will alternate," Marconi explained. "Two teams of divers will be in the water at all times, one working the front of the wreck and the other in the rear. Each will wear a camera mounted on his or her mask, recording and documenting every second of their dive. The camera feed will be displayed on monitors here on the barge. Each diver will be using a state-of-the-art underwater metal detector."

Cam nodded. He had seen the detectors—which looked like space guns—when he boarded.

Marconi continued. "First, we will set the detectors to search for non-ferrous metals."

"Gold, you mean."

"Correct. Later, we will focus on other historical items which are iron-based, ferrous."

Cam remembered from chemistry class that the symbol for iron was Fe, Latin for ferrum. "What makes you think there is gold on the ship?"

"We believe there is cargo in the rear of the ship—the boat sank rear-end first, we think because of the weight of the cargo. In addition to sonar scanning, we used an underwater magnetometer to measure magnetic field strength. The cargo, whatever it is, is non-ferrous."

Gold in this wreck? For the first time, it occurred to Cam that perhaps the Bar Kokhba treasure never made it inland. Which begged the question: Did Marconi have a hidden agenda here, beyond his avowed Italian nationalism?

Marconi continued. "See, next to the crane, there is a hatch in the center of the barge? That is so we can pull things up from the bottom without having to swing them out over the side."

Cam understood: By coming up this way, nobody from the shore could see what things were being hoisted. Shiny things, perhaps.

A splash announced that the first dive team had entered the water. Marconi let out a long breath. "Finally, the day has come."

"Hallelujah," Palo replied.

Rivka stood in a forested area along the Plum Island shore, only a stone toss from where the Atlantic lapped gently against the sandy coastline. Unlike some areas of the North Shore where the ocean unleashed a violent, full-fledged assault on the unyielding bedrock, the sand here seemed to soften and cushion the encounter. Here, today at least, land and sea were at peace. Even the dreaded greenhead flies, normally anxious to take chunks of flesh from Plum Island visitors like a swarm of flying piranhas, were dormant today. Rivka lifted her binoculars and peered out at the barge. Hopefully, the peace would hold.

Something rustled in the woods behind her. She dropped to a knee and peered through the brush. She had followed a short trail through the forest after parking at a lot along the main island road. This stretch of the island preserve was closed, except to hikers and birdwatchers. Had she been followed? A second rustle, this time closer. She grabbed a rock, wishing she had thought to bring a weapon. Moving slowly and keeping low, she inched forward. A third rustle, closer still. Holding her breath, she peered around a tree and gasped. From less than ten feet away, a pair of dark eyes stared at her. A doe. Behind her stood a pair of white-speckled fawns.

"Well, hello," Rivka said, staying motionless. She had read a lot about symbolism and knew that a deer sighting was nature's way of reminding you to listen to your intuition. "Okay," she whispered. "Message received."

Message delivered, the doe and her fawns pranced away. Rivka watched them, hand on her heart, until they had disappeared into the woods.

Exhaling, but more at peace than she had been in days, she returned to her task. From her perch she could see both the barge off of Emerson Rocks and, across the bay, the beaches and wooded areas surrounding Crane Castle. She adjusted the field glasses, the morning sun rising over the Atlantic warming her face. She didn't like lying to herself. So she admitted that the first thing she would be looking for on the barge was Cameron Thorne.

There. On the observation platform with Marconi, his hair blowing in the wind, his still-recovering legs plenty muscular enough to anchor him to the bobbing deck. She liked that he was fit and active. Just as she liked that he was smart and witty and kind. In fact, she had found nothing she didn't like about him—other than the inconvenient fact that he might refuse to have anything further to do with her, of course. Rivka had abducted his daughter and then helped her escape. Which would he be more influenced by? She supposed the two actions offset each other, resulting in some kind of moral ambiguity. She also supposed moral ambiguity would not be high on the list of qualities Thorne desired in a woman. Still, her intuition told her that he was attracted to her. And the deer told her to listen to her intuition.

So what was the next step?

Technically, she wasn't even supposed to be here. Menachem had reassigned her, punishment for what he viewed as negligence in allowing Astarte's escape. She assumed from his action that the mission involving the Bar Kokhba treasure was largely complete—otherwise he would have waited a few days to reassign her. They had found the cave in Illinois and, she assumed, dynamited it shut. Presumably after removing the treasure. Assumptions and presumptions. Nobody had told her anything for certain. Other than she had been taken off the case, of course.

Menachem really had no right to be peeved at her. She had been assigned to Thorne, and it was Thorne who led them to the Ohio River artifacts and the Illinois cave. Menachem had been focused on Marconi, thinking he was the key to finding the treasure. Were it not for Rivka's work co-opting Thorne, the mission could not have succeeded. Instead of suspending her, they should have given her a commendation.

The worse part was being kept in the dark. That's what had caused all the *mishegas*, the craziness, with Astarte.

Other than Astarte's memory not being erased, Rivka assumed the mission had succeeded. But what did that mean? She pictured a strutting Menachem getting off the plane in Tel Aviv, being met by dignitaries and VIPs, escorting them into the cargo hold to view the treasure, accepting pats on the back and salutations. But perhaps she had it wrong. Had the mission succeeded? And, again, what exactly did that mean?

On a hunch, she called Menachem's cell. He answered on the first ring. "Yes?"

"*Erev tov,* good evening." It was seven hours later in Israel.

"What do you want? And why say *erev tov*? It is morning. Where are you?"

Wide eyed, she looked at the phone. So Menachem was not in Israel. She stammered, "Um, I was hoping you would reconsider and keep me on the case."

"Rivka, this is not a volleyball game, where it is okay to lose a point. A lost point for us could mean lost lives. Or worse. You screwed up. Accept your punishment, learn from it, and move on. You will receive a new assignment shortly. Use it to prove you can be a good agent, not just a silly girl. Goodbye."

*A good agent.* In her mind, she was. And again with the *silly girl* insult. Her jaw clenched. She had a keen mind, read people well, paid attention to detail. And her gut told her something was amiss. Why was Menachem not back in Israel? Assuming he had recovered the treasure, there was no way he would have allowed underlings to escort it home. He would have insisted on guarding it himself. No. If Menachem had not flown back to Israel, neither had the Temple treasure.

So where was it?

Cam kept out of the way, sticking to a shady area underneath where the observation deck overhung the bridge. He took the time to observe and to think. A lot had happened over the past two weeks. It might be good to allow his subconscious a couple of hours on a cool morning to try to arrange and make sense of things.

Late morning, a text arrived as he drank from a carton of orange juice. From Fern, the real one. He read through it quickly, then reread it more slowly. Apparently, last night a truck had sped through the cornfields by Fern's farm, from the direction of the cave. At first light, Fern had investigated. The cave had been dynamited shut. Just as Astarte suspected.

Cam cursed. It was unfortunate for a number of reasons. Most basically, it meant that whatever story the cave could tell would now go untold. The history—whatever it was—would be lost. As, of course, would any treasure left inside. And he felt bad for Fern. She had invited him onto her family's property, and her kind hospitality had been repaid with dynamite. He texted Astarte to share the news.

An hour later, close to noon, a fresh team of divers arrived at the barge. The current divers, numbering eight, stood in line to board the motorboats for the return trip to Sandy Point beach.

"Wait," Marconi called from the observation deck. He ambled down the steps and reached for a hand-held metal detector, about the size of a flashlight. Walking among the divers, he swept the detector over them, up one side of their body and down the other. At the fifth diver in line, a red-haired man with a large Adam's apple, the device rang out as it passed over a pocket in his cargo shorts. The man's Adam's apple bobbed.

Marconi stepped back and motioned for one of his staff—in fact, the same henchman who had held the knife to Cam's neck—to approach. With a practiced movement, the henchman removed a gold coin from the diver's pocket and handed it to Marconi. Marconi held it to the light, making a show of things, all eyes on him. "The emperor, Augustus. It is Roman era," he announced." Marconi beamed with joy. Not that it would help the diver.

With a sigh, Marconi approached the man. "What is your name?"

"Micah. Micah Horvat."

"I had offered a reward for the first Roman-era artifact. Micah here has found it." From his pocket, Marconi counted out ten one-hundred-dollar bills and stuffed them into the pocket which had concealed the gold coin.

Marconi continued. "If I recall, Micah was the name of a thief in the Bible." Marconi turned to his brother. "Palo, do I have this correct?" Cam noticed that one of Marconi's assistants had escorted the ponytailed archeologist out of the bridge, apparently so he could witness this theater.

"Yes. He stole eleven hundred shekels from his own mother."

"I see." The car dealer made a subtle gesture with his hand.

With cat-like quickness, Marconi's henchman kicked out Micah's feet, sending him sprawling to the barge's deck. Moving like a blur, the henchman snatched his wrist, spread his fingers, and sliced off his pinky finger with a diving knife, like a sous chef chopping carrots.

Screaming in pain, Micah grabbed at his hand, writhing. Before Cam could turn away, the henchman tossed the bleeding chunk of finger into the Atlantic.

"Let that be a lesson to all of you," Marconi said, his low, hard voice slicing through the sound of Micah's whimpering. "I pay you well. But what we find here belongs to *me*. The next time I catch a thief, it will not just be his finger we cut off."

Cam sat alone in a folding chair at the rear of the barge, staring out at the ocean, half a turkey sandwich in his lap. A few seagulls circled, hoping for remains from the crew's lunch. He shook his head. Why hadn't he left after Marconi cut off the diver's finger? The truth, he knew, was that the monster within had hardened him to violence, made him almost immune to its effects. What was a finger compared to losing his wife, having his daughter kidnapped, being paralyzed himself? Still, he didn't like who he had become. He tossed the sandwich overboard. Another snack, along with the finger, for the creatures of the ocean.

He hadn't left, of course, because he was intrigued, excited. They had found a gold coin of the Roman era. Amazing. How could he leave now, when they were about to rewrite history?

A text pinged his phone, interrupting his musings. *Rivka*. He took a deep breath. Did he even want to communicate with her? He knew he at least had to read the message.

*You Americans waste too much food. Why did you make such a large sandwich if you weren't going to finish it?*

Wait, what? He scanned the shoreline. Was she out there, watching? Obviously, she was. He offered a half-wave, feeling a lot like a fish in a fishbowl. Good thing he hadn't been picking his nose.

His text pinged again. *Best I can tell, Temple treasure is still in America. At least, it's not back in Israel. Possible they didn't find it?*

Odd. For the second time today, he wondered if the treasure could be here, on the coast, less than fifty feet beneath where he sat. If so, what had Menachem blown up at the Illinois cave? Astarte had said they were only at the cave site for about forty-five minutes before the explosions. Enough time to find the treasure, remove it, and then blow up the cave. But not enough time to do a thorough search and satisfy yourself it was not there. But if they did find it, where was it? Could Menachem have kept it for himself? Cam replayed the Micah incident in his mind. It was stupid to try to cheat Marconi. It would be downright ludicrous to try to cheat the Mossad. No way could Menachem hope to get away with it. Like Rivka suggested, something didn't add up.

He texted back. *Is it possible Menachem hid it someplace here?*

The return came right away. *Doubtful. Standard operating procedure is to repatriate ASAP. Too much risk in foreign land.*

Cam nodded. Her message made sense. Which meant that Menachem's behavior did not.

A shout from Palo interrupted him. "Mr. Thorne, come quickly. You will want to see this."

Cam strode across the barge and into the bridge. Laid out atop a black mesh diving bag, its surface still wet with seawater, sat an ornate gold goblet.

Cam swallowed, his eyes wide. "That just came up?"

Marconi, beaming, nodded. "The style dates back to the Roman era."

Moving closer, Cam stared at the object, almost afraid to touch it. And not because of what happened to Micah. "Is it fragile?"

Marconi chuckled. "No, not at all. Salt water has no effect on gold. Wood, copper, iron—everything else decays or rusts. Not gold."

Which explained why it was still so shiny.

Cam couldn't take his eyes off the goblet. Was it really almost two thousand years old, a part of the ancient Jewish Temple?

"Is there more?" he asked. For the first time, he noticed that four of Marconi's henchmen were now carrying side arms.

Marconi shrugged. "Only Poseidon knows." He smiled. "But I don't think he will be able to keep his secrets from us for long."

Astarte played with her hair in front of the mirror in her dorm room, trying to decide how to wear it. Matthias liked it down. But she thought it looked messy and wild that way. And neither messy nor wild was the impression she wanted to make on his parents.

He had invited her to an afternoon powwow at a campground outside Helena. His parents were driving down from the Blackfoot

Reservation near the Canadian border. "There's someone I want you to meet," he had said.

"You mean other than your parents?"

He had blushed. "Well, them too. But this is one of our tribal elders. When I mentioned Burrows Cave to her, she got this faraway look in her eyes and just nodded. Then she asked if she could meet you. She's driving down with my mom and dad."

"Just to meet me?"

Matthias had smiled. "Well, she's also my great aunt. I think she's curious, like my parents."

"Okay, no pressure."

She had chosen an Indian-style brown suede vest inlaid with cobalt-colored beads which Amanda had given her for her birthday last year. "I want you to be with me, Mum," she whispered. The beads brought the blue out in her eyes. Tassels of the vest hung over her hips down to her knees, giving the look a stylish flair. Her favorite pair of jeans made her feel comfortable, as did twisting her hair into two braids. Stylish and comfortable. Definitely better than messy and wild. Unfortunately, there was nothing she could do about the cuts on her face. She shrugged. Indians wore their battle scars with pride. She'd do the same.

Rain was forecast, so Matthias had borrowed a car rather than taking his bike. They made the trip in an hour and a half—the blink of an eye compared to the marathon journey with her dad.

Tents and campers and RVs ringed a central park area at the campground. She had been to powwows before, but never anything like this—the music was louder, the costumes more feathered and elaborate, the dancers more fervent, the laughter more joyous. Even the smoke from the cooking fires smelled more succulent. Not to mention that the crowd was three or four times what she had ever seen at a powwow. The difference, she guessed, was that the Indians in New England lived in towns and cities among other Americans. Here in Montana, most lived on the reservations, where their culture was celebrated and nurtured every day, not just once a month. She took Matthias' hand. "Thanks for bringing me. *This* is why I came to college here."

He smiled. "I know."

They wandered around, content not to find his family right away. When they did, the family greeted Astarte with warmth and more than a bit of curiosity—apparently Matthias had never brought a girl home before. Not to mention the whole fortieth princess thing, details of which had begun to spread through the Native American community.

It didn't take long for his great aunt, Flowing River, to take her by the arm and escort her away from the tumult. Tall and handsome and serene, she reminded Astarte a bit of Matthias. She wore her dark, gray-streaked hair like Astarte, braided on both sides. Matthias had told Astarte she was part of the Blackfoot ruling council. "Will you walk with me?" she asked. Thick clouds hovered overhead, but the rain held off, as if in deference to the tribal elder.

"Of course."

She led Astarte down a path toward a small lake. "I sense a kindness in you."

"My mother used to always say to me that kindness was the new cool." Astarte felt a pang of melancholy. "She would have been happy to hear you say that."

"Your adopted mother, you mean. Amanda."

"She's the only mother I remember."

"There were many of us who did not want you placed with a white family. We believed you belonged with your own kind. But they have raised you well. And now you have come back to us. I know you have come for answers."

The comment did not call for a response. And Astarte knew she would learn far more by listening than by speaking. They walked in silence for a few seconds, content in each other's company.

"Have you heard of the Yuchi tribe?' Flowing River asked.

"Just the name. Weren't they from the Ohio River Valley?"

"In fact, they have a history remarkably similar to the Mandan. Many Indian historians believe they were related. The Yuchi lived in trading villages scattered along riverways, just like the Mandan. And the tribe name they called themselves was 'Children of the Sun,' because they came from a land far to the east. Their shamans supervised the Great Medicine Society—what we call the Midewin—that spiritually bound most of the tribes of North America."

Astarte recalled something her father had said. "Aren't the Midewin ceremonies similar to Freemasonry?"

Flowing River nodded. "Very. Some believe the Yuchi shamans were taught the Midewin rituals by traveling Europeans. Personally, I believe those Europeans either were the Mandan themselves or Europeans who came to trade with the Mandan."

Her father had said something similar, that waves of Europeans would have come back and forth over the centuries to trade.

Flowing River turned to face Astarte. "Here, finally, is my point. I know you have been investigating Burrows Cave. I also know many people doubt its authenticity. But you should know this: In the 1950s, a quarter-century before Burrows stumbled into his cave, the Yuchi chief recorded the Yuchi history for posterity. He described how foreigners from across the sea arrived in what is now southern Illinois." She paused for effect. "There, they built a large underground mausoleum. Into it they placed ancient treasures and an archive of ancient knowledge.

"Wow," Astarte replied, realizing her response did not do justice to the revelation.

"Matthias said you and your father were not certain if the Burrows Cave legends were real. I think you now have your answer."

Rivka picked a leaf from a tree and tossed it skyward, watching the wind lift and buffet it before it began to flutter downward. What path would it take, what random forces would act on it and change its fate? She often lately felt like that leaf, allowing forces beyond her control to influence her life's path.

Enough of that. It was time to drive. No more sitting in the passenger seat. No more silly girl.

She texted Cameron. *Meet me at Michael's Harborside in Newburyport. We need to talk.*

A minute passed, then his response. *When?*

*When you're done at the dive site.*

*That might be a few hours.*

*Okay. I'll be at the bar. Maybe under it, if you're late.*

*Ha. I'll be there by four.*

She checked her watch. Just after two. And it had been months since she'd had a drink. She'd need to be careful. Or maybe not.

Cam stood under the overhanging deck on the barge, listening as the ponytailed maritime archeologist explained to Marconi the need to slow things down. Though his real name was Jack, everyone called him Jacques, apparently a nod to the famous French diver, Jacques Cousteau. From what Cam knew, Jacques was well-regarded, with affiliations at both Harvard and Oxford. Marconi had chosen wisely—it would be hard to discredit his discoveries. Cam hoped, for Jacques' sake, that he did not meet the same fate as Marconi's last archeologist.

"We have found what appears to be an ancient artifact. Now is the time to be very methodical." Jacques pushed a pair of John Lennon glasses up his nose as he chewed on a beef jerky. "If there is one object, there are probably more. But this is our only chance to study them *in situ*, as they were when the ship sank. We need to stop the salvage operation. To rush now would be reckless, almost criminal." He took a deep breath. "And we should call the authorities."

Marconi's dark eyes narrowed; he took a step closer. "We will *not* be calling the authorities. Do I make myself clear?"

The memory of Micah's finger probably fresh in his mind, Jacques lowered his head. "I understand."

Marconi stepped back. "As for stopping the salvage operation, how long a delay are you suggesting?"

"Perhaps three or four days."

"You can have the rest of the afternoon. Tomorrow morning, we continue our work." He turned to Cam. "You told me once that you dive?"

Cam nodded. "I'm certified."

"Good. Tomorrow, you go down with the archeologist."

Jacques worked the jerky around in his mouth. "I already have an assistant. A *trained* one."

Marconi turned to walk away. "Well, now you have a new one. One I know I can trust."

Cam thought about objecting. He was certified; that did not mean he was qualified. But this was a shallow dive, nothing particularly difficult about it. The truth was, he was excited about the possibility. How often did one get to be part of making history?

Cam decided there was no reason to stick around. The archeologist and his assistant—his real one—would spend the rest of the day documenting and photographing the find. Cam surreptitiously took a picture of the goblet with his phone, then stepped out onto the bridge to wait for the cabin cruiser to ferry him back to the castle. Twenty minutes later, he was at his car. He checked his watch. Still time to meet Rivka at the bar.

But did he want to? He avoided answering that question by telling himself he had no choice. On the one hand, she had helped kidnap Astarte. On the other hand—

*No*. There was no other hand. No amount of attraction he may have felt for her could overcome such an odious act.

She said she needed to talk to him, presumably about the treasure. He couldn't not go—too much was at stake. But it would be a business meeting, nothing more.

A half-hour drive brought him to Newburyport's downtown area along the Merrimack River. He spotted Rivka at a corner table on the upper deck of Michael's, a sprawling seafood restaurant with upper and lower decks hanging over the river. She seemed lost in thought, staring out at the mix of sailboats and yachts crammed into marinas on both sides of the waterway. An empty beer bottle stood next to a full one on the table in front of her, along with a plate of half-eaten fried calamari.

She offered a tentative smile as he approached. "I wasn't sure you would come." The late afternoon sun lit her face, angling beneath the table umbrella.

"I wasn't sure I wanted to."

"Fair enough. But now that you are here, you might as well sit."

Rivka pushed out the chair catty corner to her, but he sat across from her instead. The waitress appeared, and Cam ordered a beer of his own.

"Is Astarte okay?" she asked tentatively.

"Yes." This was not the conversation he wanted to have. It was a personal question; this was business.

"I want you to know that it turns out her life was not in danger. I was wrong. I can't tell you more than that. But I swear it is the truth."

He exhaled. "Okay." Hopefully she was right.

"I wanted to talk to you about the Temple treasure," she said. "I think it's still in America." She explained her reasoning. "No way would Menachem send it back without guarding it himself."

"So where is it?"

"I don't know."

"Could it be still in the cave?" he asked.

"I suppose so. But then what were the explosions for?"

She was right, Menachem's actions didn't make sense. "There must be something we are missing."

His beer arrived.

"Do you want some calamari?" She pushed the plate toward him.

"No."

"Do you think I poisoned it?" She reached across, snared a piece, and popped it into her mouth. Holding each other's eyes, neither spoke. After a few seconds, Cam turned away and sipped his beer.

She broke the silence. "You were just looking at me for a long time. I asked you a couple of weeks ago if you thought I was pretty, but you didn't really answer."

He blinked. "I think you're direct."

"I grew up on a kibbutz. Everyone there was direct. In the real world, you might not tell a coworker her breath was bad. But you would tell your sister—you know, because you were family." She exhaled. "A kibbutz was like that. Always truth. Sometimes brutally so."

"Okay. Here's a brutal truth." He leaned forward. "You go near Astarte again, and I'll hunt you down. I promise."

She held up her beer and smiled sadly. "Fair enough" Eyeing him, she took a couple of long swigs. "How about this: I'll stop asking if you think I'm pretty if you agree to tell me when you start thinking I am."

"Whatever."

"You may have noticed, I'm not very good at people. I'm good at things—I can play sports, I can fix things, I did well in school, I'm artistic. But people and relationships confuse me." She shrugged, her eyes beginning to get misty. "So, sorry if I say inappropriate things."

He wondered how many beers came before this one. And whether, now that they had discussed the treasure, he should make an excuse to leave. Instead, he told her about the gold goblet and coin—he had, after all, promised to keep the Mossad informed of Marconi's actions.

She blinked her tears away. "Really? So is part of the treasure here and part in Illinois?"

"I don't know. It's possible the goblet is just some Colonial-era artifact and the ship is also Colonial."

"What about the gold coin?"

"Playing devil's advocate, part of me wonders if Marconi and the diver arranged that beforehand, as a way to intimidate the other divers. Nobody actually saw him with a missing finger. It could have been staged." Cam took another sip and thought about the misdirection play with the Sammy Haddad trireme. "In fact, it's exactly the kind of thing Marconi would do."

"So we're just guessing here."

"Right."

"Well, how about doing a shot of tequila then?" She leaned forward. "I mean, if we're just making it up as we go along, anyway."

Frowning, Cam shook his head. "I'll pass, thanks. Tequila and I don't get along. And I should call it a day."

She let out a long sigh and stared out at the river. "Okay, I get it. But, tell me the truth: Is it the tequila, or is it me? Like I said, I'm not any good at this stuff."

He set his beer down. "Honestly, Rivka, it's a ridiculous question. You almost killed me with a barbell, then you kidnapped my daughter. It hasn't exactly been a harmless flirtation."

"Well," she replied with another sad smile. "At least I'm not boring."

On his drive back to Westford from his beer with Rivka, Cam phoned Georgia. He held off on telling her what they had pulled up from the wreck today. She was a dear friend, and normally he would have been candid with her. But, though technically retired, she was an agent for the CIA. He didn't want to have to ask her to lie for him.

"I'm thinking of flying out to Montana to keep an eye on Astarte," she said by way of greeting.

Cam chuckled. "I think she's fine. Turns out the Mossad wasn't going to kill her. At least I think that's the case. And she's got a boyfriend who's very devoted, so she won't be alone."

"Any chance he has a friend for me?"

"I don't think the college kids can keep up with you, Georgia."

"Speaking of which, it's cocktail hour. I'm going to fix myself a drink while you tell me what you want."

Cam explained why he thought the Temple treasure might still be in America. "Have you heard anything?"

"That's interesting. And it sort of dovetails with something I did hear."

"And that is?"

"That Menachem may have gone rogue. Apparently, he suffered an ugly knife wound last year. Not only did it carve up his face, but the wound was deep enough to cause some brain damage. People say his personality has changed."

"Do you think he's trying to keep the treasure for himself?"

"I don't know. I'll keep digging."

"Thanks. Any luck on Palo Marconi?" Cam had asked her to look into him, just in case.

"Not much. Like you said, he's head of the Vatican Archive. That's pretty high up. Well-liked, well-respected. A bit of a glutton, but doesn't drink and doesn't whore around." She sniffed. "What a waste. No scandals or anything like that. Grew up here in the states. Comes back every summer to visit. You know about his family. The only controversial thing I heard was that he espouses a few religious views which are out of the mainstream."

"Such as?"

"As one example, he gives more weight to the writings of Paul than do most other Church authorities. Apparently, sometimes Paul's teachings differ from those of Jesus."

"Whatever. Maybe it's because Paul is his namesake."

"To me, it's all arguing over how many angels can dance on the head of a pin. Love thy neighbor. The rest of the Bible is all just commentary."

Cam had never thought of it that way. Leave it to Georgia to distill eight hundred thousand words down to three.

"All right," he said. "I'll let you go. Thanks."

"Rugby player," she said.

"I'm sorry, what?"

"The college guy you're going to fix me up with. I like rugby players. Always have."

"That's because they go to the pub after their matches."

"Right. In short shorts."

He grinned. "Goodnight, Georgia."

"Goodnight, Massachusetts."

## Chapter 10

Cam made a point of getting up before five on Sunday, not wanting to be late to the dive site. Amanda joined him as he walked Venus in the purple light of dawn.

"You're up early," he said to her.

*Different time zone.*

He smiled and unzipped his sweatshirt, the day already warming. "Of course."

*And I know you're excited about diving.*

"Can you believe it? What if there really are Temple treasures down there? Short of the Holy Grail or the Ark of the Covenant, they would probably be the most amazing things anyone could find." He turned down the road toward the beach.

*I can leave if you want. I know you like to meet Rivka there.*

"That's okay. I think, after yesterday, she'll keep her distance a bit. Which is fine with me."

*That's your head talking. And your anger. But a part of you is still attracted to her. I can tell.*

It doesn't really matter if I am or not. I could never forgive her for putting Astarte in danger.

*Careful, never is a long time. And she did risk her job to save Astarte. In the end, she did the right thing. And don't forget, even if she had refused to help abduct Astarte, some other agent would have stepped in to do it. At least this way, she was around to help.*

I suppose.

*But you're right. Now's not the time. You're not ready, and she's not necessarily a good choice, given that her job is to spy on you. By the way, you never answered her question.*

"Which one?"

*When she asked if you thought she was pretty.*

"Not pretty in the conventional sense. But attractive in her own way. What do you think?"

*I agree. Her features are anything but classical, but the overall gestalt is pleasing. But you can't trust my taste. Look who I ended up marrying.*

Skipping his regular morning workout, Cam ate a quick breakfast and repeated yesterday's drive east. He parked at the castle and walked the few hundred yards to the pier, glad for the exercise. He peered across the sound: Even at just after six o'clock, the barge was a beehive of activity.

Marconi greeted Cam with a tired smile as Cam stepped off the cabin cruiser and onto the barge. "Cameron, come aboard. We have a big day in front of us."

Marconi had never used Cam's first name. Cam ambled over. As always, Marconi wore a blazer, today with a gold tie. But the clothes could not hide his pallor and the yellow tinge to his eyes. Somehow he was keeping up a frenetic pace, even as the cancer ate at him from within. He fingered the tie. "I chose this color on purpose for today."

Cam knew it was not because it matched his eyes. "Did Jacques find more stuff?" The archeologist, another beef jerky in his mouth, had nodded gruffly at Cam when he saw him.

"It is as we hoped," Marconi replied. "The goblet appears to have fallen out of a wooden chest or crate in the cargo hold area. Much of the wood has, in fact, decayed. He has dug the sand away by hand. The chest is full of artifacts." He paused for effect. "Including what looks to be a seven-branched candelabra."

Cam was almost afraid to ask. "Gold?"

"It appears to be. In fact, it matches this almost perfectly." Marconi held up a laminated image. "This is a replica of the Temple Menorah, built to the specifications laid out in the Book of Exodus." He handed the illustration to Cam.

Temple Menorah Replica

Cam swallowed. "So what's in the chest down there is not just any candelabra. It's the Temple Menorah."

"So it appears." Marconi let out a long sigh. He, like Cam, was trying to keep control of his emotions. "Whatever it is, it will, obviously, be our priority for this morning's dive. *Your* priority. Don't let him talk you out of it."

Cam found the divemaster and collected his gear. A charged sense of anticipation rippled through the barge, the divers and crew sensing the potential magnitude of their find.

Palo walked over and, with a loud sigh, dropped into a folding chair next to where Cam was pulling on his suit. "*Buongiorno,* Mr. Thorne. May I join you?" he asked, offering a box of pastries.

"Of course. But I ate already."

Palo wiped some crumbs from his mouth. "I know my brother can be a bit … harsh in his ways. But he values your contributions to this project."

"Honestly, he's paying me more than what is fair."

Palo waved the comment away, as if money were a nuisance which had no place in the life of a spiritual man like himself. "When I say value, I don't mean money." He touched his chest. "I mean appreciation. Besides, money means nothing to Mario. At least not anymore." He lowered his eyes. "Now, he just wants to complete his life's work."

Cam nodded. "I get that. Truly. But he needs to stop cutting off people's fingers. He told me he didn't like it when people think of Italian-Americans as mobsters. But he behaves like one."

"Not always. Only since the death of his son and wife." He crossed himself. "May they rest in peace. Since then, he seems to have lost his moral compass. That is one of the reasons I came home. I try to temper him." He grinned, the curve of his mouth accentuating the roundness of his face. "Though sometimes I fear that my bad jokes only serve to irritate him."

"For what it's worth, he seems to be more upbeat since you've arrived."

Another grin. "That has nothing to do with me. He is upbeat because of this shipwreck. Which brings us back to the beginning of our conversation." Palo filled his lungs and lowered his voice. "The doctors say Mario does not have much time. And I cannot stay away from Rome indefinitely. When he is gone, someone will need to continue this work. Recover the artifacts, get everything tested and dated. And then, hopefully, put all this history on display. Mario envisions a small museum, perhaps here at the castle. And he and I think you would be the perfect person to carry things forward."

Cam blinked. It would have been an ideal job for Amanda, who had been trained as a museum curator. But it was not what he did. "I'll help finish the recovery efforts." With Marconi gone, it would actually be an appealing project. "But I'm not really the right person for the museum stuff."

Palo patted Cam's knee. "I understand. I'm glad at least you will see this project through. I fear that, no matter how careful we are, and no matter how many top professionals we employ, there will be those who question our results."

Cam thought of Robinson Roberts, and his comment to the effect that no amount of evidence would change his mind about explorers coming to America before Columbus. "Well," he replied with a sigh, "I'm used to that."

Marconi strolled over and joined them. He had just cleared the barge, leaving only a skeleton crew along with his armed henchmen. He was taking no chances.

"Have you thought about what I said?" Palo asked his brother.

Marconi shook his head. "I am sorry, Palo. But there is no time."

"No time to recover the dead? No time for a proper burial?"

Marconi turned to Cam. "Palo is concerned that we might find human remains in the wreckage. And, if so, what we should do with them."

Cam put up a hand. "I can end this debate now. There's no way that bones can survive that long in the ocean. When we find really old bones, it's because they were sealed in a dry environment where no bacteria or organisms could get to them. Like a mummy in a sarcophagus."

His words seemed to comfort Palo. Cam wondered if he knew about the skull his brother kept in a copper box. From what he could discern, Palo was as spiritual as Marconi was ruthless. In some ways, that might make the cardinal the more dangerous of the two. At least Marconi could be counted on to do what was best for Marconi. With Palo, who knew what he might do because he believed it was God's will?

Just as the sun crested over the Atlantic, Cam flopped backward off the edge of the barge. Even after a long, hot summer, the waters remained cold, fed from the Arctic. Not, however, as cold as they used to be—great white sharks, which in the past rarely ventured north of Cape Cod, had recently been spotted along the North Shore. If a great white appeared today, Cam hoped he preferred the smell of beef jerky.

He and Jacques descended slowly, each wearing a camera on his mask. Using hand signals, the archeologist led Cam toward the stern of the wreck. They ducked through a jagged, refrigerator-size hole torn from the hull and into the cargo hold. Jacques came at the wooden chest from one side, Cam from the other. The chest, like the ship, was damaged. The lid, especially, had rotted—probably because it, not needing to support the weight of the chest's contents, had been constructed with thinner planks of wood than the other five sides.

While on the barge, Cam had listened to Jacques and Marconi decide on a plan. Though the opening at the top of the chest was wide enough to retrieve whatever might be within, they decided that the wiser course would be to break the remaining pieces of the lid away and bring them up for testing. That would allow easier access to the artifacts and also minimize the chance of a diver getting hung up on a sharp edge. And, of course, testing the chest's wood would go a long way to dating the artifacts within—the science of dendrochronology allowed wood to be dated and its place of origin determined.

The two divers again exchanged hand gestures and began breaking the lid pieces away. Cam was surprised at how easy it was, like snapping twigs from a tree branch. After tucking the wood pieces into their dive bags, they turned to the contents of the chest.

*This is it.*

Jacques had acceded to Marconi's demand that Cam dive with him, but there was no way he was going to allow Cam to be the one to retrieve the candelabra. Which was fine with Cam. When it came time to establish the chain of custody for the artifact, it would be best if the respected professional archeologist—not the controversial revisionist historian—had been the one to lift the object from its resting place.

Using two hands, Jacques gently worked the candelabra side to side. Then he tried to hoist it. He was able to get one side up, but the weight was too much for him, even underwater. Grudgingly, he motioned for Cam to help.

Peering into the chest, Cam was struck first by the size of the menorah—perhaps four feet tall, including its hexagonal base, with a candelabra section three feet in width. He slid his hands under the base, while Jacques grabbed the middle stem of the candelabra. Bracing their legs against the inside of the hull, they pulled the object free and set it down next to the crate. Cam knew that rocks lost about a third of their weight underwater; assuming a similar ratio for gold, and guessing they had together just lifted two hundred pounds, he was looking at about three hundred pounds of solid gold. He did the arithmetic in his head—about eight million dollars at today's gold prices. Which, of course, paled in comparison to the actual Golden

Menorah's historical and religious worth. Marconi had been smart to clear the barge.

After a few seconds to catch their breath, they hoisted it again, this time sliding it through the opening in the hull. They placed it base-down on the ocean floor, where it settled into the sand.

Cam moved closer. Even in the dim light, the artifact gleamed. He held his head still, allowing his camera to document the find. Jacques did the same from the other side. They traded places, each happy for the excuse to stare for a few seconds at the priceless treasure.

Above them, a large metal basket broke the surface and descended toward them, suspended from the crane arm by a thick chain. Cam guided the basket toward the menorah. He and Jacques lifted the candelabra into the basket.

Cam pointed toward the surface, but Jacques shook his head and instead climbed into the basket next to the menorah. Using his dive slate, he wrote, 'chain of custody.' Cam nodded. At some point, Jacques might need to testify that the menorah never left his sight.

Cam began to ascend, but Jacques stopped him with a gesture and gave him a thumbs-up sign. Then he reached out to shake Cam's hand. They had little in common and didn't particularly care for each other. But only two people on the planet had ever seen the golden Temple Menorah, and, at least for that moment, their bond was as strong as the thick chain hoisting the menorah from its watery grave.

As Cam broke the surface of the water, he immediately noticed the sound of a helicopter overhead. He watched as it descended, disappearing behind the trees behind Crane Castle. Marconi didn't waste any time.

Cam clambered aboard and quickly stripped off his gear. Marconi and Palo stood on either side of the basket, which had been freed from the crane. Jacques remained in the basket with the menorah, still in his wetsuit. Someone had thrown a tarp over the menorah. The men were arguing.

"No," Jacques said. "I will not let you damage a priceless artifact."

"I do not want to *damage* it," Marconi replied. "I merely want to scrape half a milligram of gold from the bottom of the base. We need this for testing."

Jacques shook his head. "To do so is *desecration*. The proper procedure is to first notify the authorities. Then bring experts in to determine the least intrusive way to test it. Not to mention, since it is a sacred artifact, we should bring in religious leaders as well." He folded his arms across his chest. "There is a process that must be followed. I cannot be a part of this ... recklessness."

"Then move aside," Marconi hissed. He motioned toward one of his henchmen. "I will not ask twice."

Jacques turned to Palo. "You're okay with this? You are a man of God. And this object is a religious treasure. Not to mention sacred."

Palo swallowed. "I am. It is necessary. The Golden Menorah, if this is truly what it is, was forged by the hand of man; so, too, may it be sullied."

The archeologist turned to Cam. Cam met his look with a shrug. "The only way people are going to believe this is if we prove it scientifically. And I don't trust the authorities. Once they get their hands on it, we may never see it again."

Cursing and red-faced with anger, Jacques stepped out of the basket. The issue, Cam knew, was that Jacques—as lead archeologist—would be blamed for the failure to follow protocol. So be it. He was, no doubt, being paid well to be the scapegoat. "I wish to object in the strongest possible terms," Jacques sputtered.

"Duly noted," Marconi said dryly. But he had already dropped to a knee and begun to use a metal tool to scrape at the underside of the candelabra's base as Palo titled the candelabra back. Using a Ziploc bag, he caught a few shavings of gold and held them up to the sun. "That should do the trick."

Marconi held the bag out to the archeologist. "What do you expect me to do with this?" Jacques said, leaning away.

"This needs to be brought to a laboratory at MIT. The helicopter is waiting. As is the scientist. He already has a sample I took from the goblet."

Marconi shook his head. "I'm not letting the candelabra out of my sight."

Cam stepped forward. "He's right. He should stay with the menorah and finish studying and documenting it." Cam addressed Jacques. "Can your assistant bring the sample to MIT? It needs to be someone beyond reproach."

Jacques let out a long breath. He was still angry, but he also didn't want to do anything to delegitimize this find. "You're right. It should be my assistant."

He called her over and explained the situation. Marconi handed her the bag and gave her instructions on where to go at MIT. She boarded the cabin cruiser, which would take her to the helicopter.

Jacques, still in his wetsuit, turned back to Marconi. "What is this testing? And why wasn't I told about it?"

Marconi's tone turned hard. "You weren't told because your job is to be the archeologist, not the metallurgy expert."

Palo interjected, "As for the testing, it is called uranium thorium–helium dating. It is new, developed by a Swiss scientist. Just over the border from Italy, in fact. I have used it to test artifacts in the Vatican collection. Until recently, there was no way to date gold artifacts. This methodology changes that. You see, all gold contains traces of uranium and thorium which, when they decay, produce helium. When gold is put into a molten form to manufacture an art object, the helium is lost. But once the gold cools again, the helium is locked in anew. By taking a sample of the object and melting it down, the age of the helium—that is, how long it has been locked in the gold—can be ascertained by measuring its rate of decay in a laboratory, giving us the manufacture date. It is not exact, but it can get us within a few hundred years."

"So, if this is authentic," Cam said, "we'd expect a date of around 3,300 years before present. That's when Moses was wandering in the desert. And that's when the Golden Menorah was made."

"Yes," Palo replied. "Anything close to that date would convince me that this menorah is authentic. Again, there is a margin of error of a few hundred years." He shrugged. "But how many four-foot-tall ancient golden menorahs could there be?"

Cam nibbled on a corn muffin on the observation deck of the barge in the mid-morning sun. Things had settled down a bit. Jacques' assistant had delivered the gold shavings to the MIT lab. The helicopter was a bit much, Cam thought—what did it save, maybe an hour? But when you only have weeks to live, an hour here or there took on added importance.

The dive teams had been called back to the barge and were

collecting more artifacts from the cargo hold area. Marconi's men had wrapped the menorah in the tarp and muscled it onto the cabin cruiser; Marconi and Palo, with Jacques, had escorted it back to the castle. Presumably they had some kind of secure lab set up in which to study it.

Cam had stuck around at the dive site because he wanted to see what else might be found. The gold goblet had been an amazing find. It, in turn, had been dwarfed by the menorah. Both of these items were among the Temple objects supposedly lost. If the chest was, indeed, the repository for the lost Temple treasures, there should be more objects. Trumpets. The Table of Shewbread. Incense holders. Candlesticks. Priestly breastplates. Other goblets. Platters. But Cam had seen nothing else in the chest. And nothing shiny had come to the surface in the past couple of hours.

There could be a second chest, obviously. And it could have fallen from the ship during the wreck and be buried under 1,800 years' worth of sand. But it made no sense for there to be some of the Temple treasures and not the rest. He shrugged. Maybe they just hadn't found the second chest yet.

He yawned. Not surprising, given his short night's sleep and the warm sun and an inevitable post-adrenaline crash following his morning discovery. He ambled over to the cabin cruiser for a ride to shore. He had parked at the castle rather than at Plum Island with the other divers because he knew whatever valuables they found would end up on the Ipswich side of the harbor.

Back at the castle, he found Jacques in a windowless basement room that smelled like an old oil furnace. An armed guard sat behind a desk in the hallway outside the door. The menorah stood upright on the cement floor beneath a row of fluorescent lights, between a floor drain and a shelf stacked with cans of paint. An extension cord hung from the ceiling. Cam decided to take a light tone and try to build on their comradery. "A state-of-the-art lab, I see."

The archeologist replied with a wry smile. "Sort of like a dungeon. Which is what I deserve. I should never have let him take those gold shavings."

"Let's be honest. You didn't have a choice."

He turned and looked at Cam over his John Lennon glasses. "You referring to the diver with the finger?" He paused. "Or to Robinson Roberts?"

"Both." As Cam had hoped, they were finding common ground over their disdain for—and fear of—Marconi. "So are you going to sleep down here? Maybe get a cot?"

"Don't laugh. I might. This is the find of a lifetime."

Cam stepped closer and studied the menorah. "It's redder than I thought it would be. Or is that the light?"

"Most gold you see in jewelry is mixed with copper and silver and zinc, which makes it more yellow. This is pure." He pointed to one of the arms, bent slightly askew. "But pure gold is not very strong. And it scratches easily."

"Did you learn anything from studying it yesterday *in situ*?"

"A little. It was covered by sand and silt. I found all sorts of marine life in the sand—worms, amphipods, mussels, even a sand dollar."

"A sand dollar?" Cam smiled. "So it was a worthwhile dive after all."

"Right. If it turns out this menorah is just some theater prop, we at least have that."

"Getting back to the marine life. What does that tell you?"

"Not much, actually. It does mean that the artifact wasn't planted there recently. It takes time for the little critters to move in. Same thing with the seabed. The soils in the chest were mixed together, like after a number of storms."

"So the artifact's been down there awhile?"

"At least a year." He shrugged. "Beyond that, it's impossible to tell. Could be two years, could be two thousand."

Rivka had thought ahead and brought a lawn chair to her secluded Plum Island vantage point today. It was not that she didn't have the stamina to stand for hours on end. It was that last night's tequila—and the headache in its wake—had left her unwilling to attempt it.

She lifted the binoculars, focusing again on the barge. Shaking her head, she made a decision. She dialed Menachem's cell. After six rings, it went to voicemail. She hung up and tried again thirty seconds later. Same result. She tried a third time.

"For God's sake, Rivka, what do you want?"

"I'm on Plum Island. Something's up at the dive site."

"You're supposed to be off the case."

She plowed on. "This morning, they pulled up something large, about the size of a basketball backboard. I couldn't see what it was because they kept it under wrap. Then they brought it ashore."

"Maybe it was an anchor."

"That's what I thought when I first saw it. But then a helicopter landed at the castle and quickly took off again about fifteen minutes after the anchor thing made it to shore."

This seemed to get his attention. "Did they load the anchor thing on board?"

"I couldn't see from where I am. But the helicopter flew south, toward Boston."

"What else did you see?"

"It's what I *didn't* see. The lead archeologist went with it back to the castle. That was four hours ago. He hasn't come back to the barge yet."

"So?"

"He's supposed to be supervising at all times. It's standard procedure. And there are divers still down there. Yesterday, he was on the barge all day, didn't leave once. I'm thinking maybe they found something really valuable and he's studying it. That would explain why they wrapped it—they didn't want anyone to see what it was. And they sent part of it to some lab to be tested."

"And what do you think it might be, this mysterious valuable object?"

"You know exactly what I think it might be."

He let out a long breath. "I doubt very seriously that you are correct. But I do agree the archeologist's behavior is curious. Stay on it."

She allowed herself a small smile. At least he hadn't called her a silly girl.

Cam climbed a set of stairs, leaving Jacques in his dungeon lab, and found Marconi and Palo cutting into a hunk of cheese at a table on the outside terrace. The same table where Columbus' crewman's head once sat.

"May I join you?" Cam asked. A lot had happened in the past two weeks.

"Please," Marconi replied, gesturing toward a chair. "We were just discussing our next steps. The divers are almost done with artifact recovery. The next step is to try to raise the ship."

"Raise it? How? And why?" Cam assumed that the ship would be dated by taking wood samples and having them tested. But most shipwrecks were allowed to lie where they sank.

"The why is obvious: I want the ship to be the centerpiece for our museum."

"Are you even certain it's Roman era?"

Marconi's eyes narrowed. "Yes. Aren't you? What else could it be? What other ship would have the Temple Menorah?"

"Well, for one possibility, the Templars could have found the Temple treasure in Jerusalem in the twelfth century and decided to bring it to America. This could be a Templar ship."

"No. It could not. It is a trireme, not a medieval cog."

Cam had been doing some reading in the last day. "Actually, the medieval galley ships were very similar in design to the trireme."

"But galleys were not used for trans-Atlantic voyages."

"Neither were triremes, generally. You can't have it both ways. If a Roman trireme could make the crossing, so could a Templar galley."

Swallowing his cheese, Palo leaned forward. "He has you there, brother."

Marconi waved the disagreement away with his hand. "I am confident the testing will reveal this to be a Roman-era ship. As I said, it will be the centerpiece of our museum."

Cam, too, had no interest in continuing the debate. But part of him hoped the ship would end up being Templar. He was, after all, a Templar historian and aficionado. He also recognized it was entirely possible that the Templars could have found their way across using ancient Roman maps or travel logs in possession of the medieval Church. "How are you planning to raise it?" Cam asked.

"Using air bags, we will raise the hull just enough to slide slings beneath it. Front, back and middle. We will attach those slings to the crane. Then, again using air bags, we will float the ship toward the surface, using the crane to keep it stable." He shrugged. "It is a simple process, though the execution can be a bit challenging. The salvage team arrives tomorrow, Monday."

"That soon?"

"We have already received a visit from the Coast Guard inquiring about permits. I was able to put them off. But we don't have the luxury of time." He coughed into his handkerchief; Cam noticed flecks of blood on the white cloth. "And, more to the point, *I myself* don't have the luxury of time."

Seated in the front seat of her beaten-down Honda Civic in the fading daylight, Rivka slid out of her shorts and wriggled into an extra pair of jeans she kept in the car. A fresh shirt, a brush through her hair, some eyeshadow and lipstick, and a swig of mouthwash completed her makeover. She angled the visor mirror. Not bad. She undid the top button on her blouse. Men didn't tend to spend much time looking at her face, anyway. Especially in a bar.

She had followed a couple of the dive team members after they left Plum Island, figuring they might head to a local pub. The last thing she wanted was more tequila. But a glass of wine and some nachos would be nice. Not to mention some answers.

She pushed through the door of the Beachcoma pub. Not bad—she half-expected the divers to find a dive bar. But soft music played and the place seemed clean and well-kept. She wandered through and spotted a group of the divers at a table on an outdoor patio. She strolled over. "I'm looking for a guy named Raymond? He's a friend of Jenny's."

They looked back at her with blank faces. But one of them, presumably the sharpest of the group, quickly sized up the situation. "No Raymond here. But you're welcome to pull up a seat and wait."

She did so, but not next to the sharp guy. Tonight, she was looking for dumb.

An hour later, twilight having set in, Raymond was long-forgotten. Rivka was sharing potato skins with a preppy-looking guy with a sunburnt nose and light blue eyes named Thompson. Rivka wasn't sure if that was his first name or his last. She leaned in, her knee brushing against his thigh under the table. "So, Thompson, what were you guys diving for?"

"I can't really say. They made us sign a non-disclosure."

"Seems a little over the top. What could be that important at a dive site on Plum Island?" She dried her hands on a napkin and turned away, making a show of starting a conversation with the guy on her other side.

Thompson drew her back. "Actually, it turned out to be pretty amazing."

She glanced sideways at him. "Whatever. You just said you couldn't talk about it."

A few seconds passed. "No. Seriously. Amazing."

"A dead body?"

"No. Better."

"So tell me."

"I can't."

She let out a long, exasperated sigh. "You have too many lawyers in this country. Everyone acts like every little thing is this major secret."

"It's not a little thing."

"Look. You said you couldn't talk about it. But then you keep talking about it. Please make up your mind." She turned away again, this time angling her body so Thompson could peer down her shirt.

He edged closer and lowered his voice. "Okay, but you need to promise not to tell anyone."

Twenty minutes later, she excused herself to use the ladies' room and slipped out the front. She felt bad about it, actually. Not because of ditching Thompson. But because she should have left some cash for her share of the tab.

Cam left Crane Castle in the twilight, no longer needing his GPS to find the way back to Westford. He had stuck around until the last of the divers left the barge. But there had been no additional finds. Odd. Gold goblet. Then gold menorah. Then nothing.

Ten minutes into the drive, Astarte called. They made small talk for a few minutes. "I met Matthias' parents today. We were at a powwow."

"I'm sure they loved you."

"They didn't make me eat at the kids' table, so there's that." Amanda often told the story of being asked to supervise the children's table when visiting a boyfriend's family. "And, actually, his great aunt took me aside." She told Cam about the Yuchi legend. "It seems to confirm that Burrows Cave is real. And also that the Romans—or some other Europeans—were in the Ohio River Valley in ancient times."

"Interesting. And it's fascinating that the Midewin ritual matches Freemasonry." He chuckled. "The Freemasons are at the bottom of all these rabbit holes I go down."

"You never joined, right?"

"No. Maybe someday."

"Aren't they really secretive?"

"They are. But I don't think it's as dark and mysterious as everyone thinks it is. I spend a lot of time in lodges, and they pretty much are normal guys. I read something recently to the effect that their secrecy is like the water at the bottom of a well. The men who built the well know how deep it is. The rest of us can only peer down and wonder what might lurk below, while the dark surface mirrors back our fears."

"Somebody said something like that about our heroes and heroines. Their faces mirror back our hopes and dreams."

"Interesting insight." He took a deep breath. "So I have some news for you." He told her about the menorah salvage. "Pretty amazing to see it in person."

"Is it, you know, authentic?"

"It's at a lab right now." He explained the gold testing process. "We should have results in a day or two."

"That soon?"

"Honey, you'd be surprised how fast things can happen when you hand someone a blank check."

## Chapter 11

When Cam arrived at the castle early Monday morning, he went first to the basement rather than taking the ferry to the barge. He nodded a good morning to the two armed guards at the end of the hallway and found Jacques in the same clothes he had been wearing the night before, studying the sacred relic with a jeweler's loupe.

"Good morning," Cam called.

Jacques blinked twice. "Christ, is it morning already? There are no windows in here."

"Just past six. Cold morning, actually." His car thermometer had read 44 when he arrived. "So what's the verdict, doctor?"

"I can't find anything to make me think it's a fake." He gestured toward a piece of paper on a folding table. "That's a passage from the Book of Exodus, where it describes how to make the menorah." He reached over, lifted it, and read aloud.

> *Make a lampstand of pure gold. Hammer out its base and shaft, and make its flowerlike cups, buds and blossoms of one piece with them. Six branches are to extend from the sides of the lampstand—three on one side and three on the other. Three cups shaped like almond flowers with buds and blossoms are to be on one branch, three on the next branch, and the same for all six branches extending from the lampstand. And on the lampstand are to be four cups shaped like almond flowers with buds and blossoms. One bud shall be under the first pair of branches extending from the lampstand, a second bud under the second pair, and a third bud under the third pair—six branches in all.*

Jacques continued. "I had to find an image of an almond flower on the internet. As far as I can tell, this menorah matches the description in the Bible."

"Playing devil's advocate, that doesn't really prove anything. A modern replica could still match."

"Of course. But if it *didn't* match, that would tell us something."

"Fair point."

"What will really tell us something is that helium decay testing."

Cam didn't point out that Jacques had originally opposed taking a sample of the gold for testing. "When can we expect some results?"

"Marconi said preliminary results from the goblet should be back this morning. Then tonight for the menorah. Final results tomorrow."

"Wow." Cam let his mind wander. The world had no idea that history was about to be rewritten. Would Marconi allow the results to be released right away? He couldn't wait long, obviously. Not if he wanted to see his life's work completed. "I'm surprised Marconi's not in here with you."

Jacques sniffed. "Please, he's been looking over my shoulder all night."

"Maybe he finally went to get some sleep." Unlike the past couple of days, there were few people moving about at the castle. "I know the salvage team is supposed to arrive late morning to try to raise the wreck."

A gunshot shattered the morning tranquility.

"What the—?" Jacques sputtered.

A second shot, this one closer.

Cam moved toward the door. The guards had already mobilized, semiautomatic rifles drawn.

"Lock the deadbolt," one of them said, pushing the heavy door closed. "Don't come out until we tell you to."

Cam set the lock. But hiding in a locked room was hardly an inspired escape plan. Marconi had installed a monitor, connected to his security system, in the basement room. Cam strode across the room and studied it. Six camera angles, each covering a different pie wedge of the perimeter. *There*. Four men, paramilitary, on the rear stone terrace, assault weapons drawn. And four more closing on the front door. That must be where the gunshots came from. Cam guessed there were more than just these eight. One of the men turned to give an order. Cam peered at the monitor. An ugly scar. *Menachem*.

"Shit," he hissed.

"What?"

"It's the Mossad. Only one reason they would be here."

Cam was not a coward, but he had no interest in making some kind of heroic last stand to save an artifact. Even one as valuable and important as this one.

He went for the door. "I'm getting out of here. I suggest you do the same."

"Without the Menorah?"

"Yup. Unless you can hide it in your pocket."

Cam unbolted the door and pulled it toward him. Slowly, he leaned out. A series of gunshots erupted, bullets ricocheting down the hall. One thudded into the door inches from his ear. *Fuck.* He slammed the door. "That's not going to work." From what he had observed, Marconi had a security detail of eight men. The Mossad likely had twice that. And, well, this was the Mossad.

Cam played it out in his mind. All Menachem needed was one prisoner or informant to tell him where the Menorah was being kept. Then it would be full-scale assault time. Which meant he and Jacques were at ground zero. Marconi had been smart to put them in the basement—it offered privacy and security. But now it was like a jail cell in the middle of a shooting gallery. Even if they weren't being targeted, there were too many bullets flying around, ricocheting off of cement walls, to risk staying. "Like I said, we need to get out of here. Forget the Menorah," Cam said.

"How? There's only one door." Jacques cringed as another volley of shots rang out.

Cam studied the HVAC duct work running along the ceiling to the corner of the room, where it turned up and through to the next level. It might hold a grown man. But there was no way to get in without some kind of metal-cutting tool. The floor beneath them, along with two of the walls, was concrete. Cam ran his hand along the other two walls, which presumably were interior walls leading to other rooms in the basement. He stopped. One of the walls, near where it met an exterior cement wall, felt cold.

"Put your hand there," he told Jacques. "Does that feel cool to you? Like it's open to the outside?"

As if on cue, Cam heard movement on the other side of the wall. "Shh," he ordered. He stepped back and grabbed a metal pipe leaning in the corner, ready to use it if necessary. He put his ear to the wall. Definitely movement on the other side. Mossad? Staffers in hiding? Mice?

He grabbed the tarp which had been covering the Menorah, pulled Jacques to him, and retreated to the corner, dragging the tarp over them. Cam peered through an eyehole. A few seconds passed. Suddenly, a metal shelving unit against the wall seemed to creak. Cam lifted the pipe. With a groan, one side of the shelving swung away from the wall, as if on a hinge. *A secret door.* Cam and Jacques held their breaths.

Marconi's head appeared in the void behind the shelving unit. His eyes moved from the locked door to the tarp. Reaching over, he yanked the tarp away. "Hurry. Come with me." He maneuvered a flat, four-wheeled dolly through the opening. "And bring the Menorah."

*Of course.* As was the case in most castles, this one had been equipped with hidden doors and passageways to allow its owners to make a furtive escape if necessary.

Cam and Jacques muscled the Menorah onto the dolly and steered through the opening. A dank, musty smell greeted them. Marconi, carrying what looked to be a semiautomatic handgun, maneuvered the secret door back into place and gestured with his chin. "This way."

Cam had no delusions about Marconi's priority. He needed Cam and Jacques to help him rescue the Menorah. Beyond that, they'd have to find another way to be useful to him.

The concrete floor of the secret passageway sloped toward the ocean, Cam and Jacques fighting gravity's effect on the dolly. Cam guessed they were beneath the Grand Allée—it made sense to have an escape route to the sea. The gunshots were barely audible now, muffled by earth and stone.

Struggling against the weight of the Menorah against his still-recovering legs, Cam addressed Marconi. "Why not just let them have it? You have the ship. The carbon-dating will prove it's Roman."

Marconi scowled. "No. The carbon-dating will prove it's Roman *era*. It could be Phoenician, Greek, Persian—they all built triremes. But only the Romans had access to the Golden Menorah."

Cam nodded. The ship itself brought them close to the goal line. But the Menorah pushed them into the end zone. Unless it got them shot first.

They continued, loping along as gravity did the work of transporting the Menorah. The air was heavy here, and Marconi struggled to keep up. After a few minutes, the passageway leveled out and ended abruptly. A door set into a wooden wall rose in front of them. With a key, a wheezing Marconi opened it. The sound of ocean lapping against sand met them. Marconi pulled a flashlight from his pocket. They were in some kind of wooden boathouse built into the ridge along the shoreline. Cam blinked. He was staring at the back of a duck boat, the amphibious tour buses used to ferry tourists around Boston and other cities.

Palo emerged from the shadows. "Thank God you made it," he said, touching his brother's arm.

"God had nothing to do with it. If he did, he would have prevented the Mossad from attacking in the first place."

"How do you know it is the Mossad?" Palo replied.

Panting, Marconi replied. "Golden Menorah. Elite assault squad. You do the math." Marconi glanced at the duck boat. "Move that ramp closer," he said to his brother.

Cam and Jacques, with Palo's help, wrestled the Menorah up the ramp and onto the stern of the duck boat. Cam didn't wait to be asked to be useful. He knew how to drive both a car and a boat—how hard could it be? He jumped into the driver's seat and turned the key. The engine roared to life.

Cam powered the duck boat out of the boathouse.

"Thorne," Marconi instructed. "You need to drive across the beach out to that Boston Whaler moored offshore."

Cam glanced up, seeing the Whaler bobbing in the sound. "Why not just stay in this?" he asked as they bounced across the rocky shoreline.

"Maximum water speed is ten miles-per-hour," Marconi replied matter-of-factly.

"Oh."

Shots rang out even before they reached the surf. Cam ducked reflexively, then turned. Two operatives on the bluff. Marconi's secret passage had given them a head start, but of course the Mossad would be watching the shoreline.

Another shot sounded, pinging off the metal gunwale. Cam hunched in his seat. At least the boat was designed for combat. And the metal canopy overhead gave them some protection from the men shooting down on them.

The boat splashed into the water. Marconi reached over and hit a switch, apparently engaging the propeller. "Go!" he yelled.

Cam set a course. Ten mph was being generous—he could have swum to the Whaler faster. Another set of shots pierced the morning air, clanging off the canopy. Cam glanced over his shoulder again—more Mossad men, now gathering on the pier.

Marconi yelled over the engine. "We are fortunate they are using weapons designed for short-range combat, not sharpshooting." Another bullet pinged off the metal hull.

"Brother," Palo said, lying prone on the deck, "fortunate is not the word I would use to describe how I feel at the moment."

Spinning the wheel, Cam slammed the duck boat sideways up against the Whaler, using the amphibious vehicle as a shield while they worked to transfer the Menorah. While Marconi held the two boats together with a line, the other three men dragged the Menorah over the gunwale of the duck boat and into the Whaler. "Gentle, gentle," Marconi ordered.

Diving aboard, Cam turned the key—an outboard engine roared to life. "Where to?" he asked Marconi.

"Away," came the simple response.

Dropping to the deck, Cam wedged himself between the captain's seat and the steering column. Unlike the military boat, the Whaler offered no protection. Holding the bottom of the wheel, Cam pointed the bow toward what he hoped was open ocean and jerked the throttle forward. The boat surged ahead.

Crouched as he was, Cam couldn't see forward. But he had a good view of what was happening onshore. Four operatives had gathered at the cabin cruiser at the end of the pier. He caught Marconi's eye. The larger boat could easily overtake the Whaler. Marconi grinned. "I thought something like this might happen. Late last night, I pulled the battery from the cabin cruiser."

Cam nodded. Good move. But Menachem would not be so easily deterred. As if on cue, a bullet thudded against the captain's seat. Cam swerved, working the wheel erratically, hoping to keep the shooters from homing in.

Marconi crawled past Cam, onto the bow, staying low. "Head to starboard twenty degrees," Marconi yelled over the engine. "Stay on this course, and you'll hit Emerson Rocks." Cam did as told. He appreciated a good irony, but that would be taking things too far.

Twenty seconds later, now clear of Emerson Rocks, he angled back to port, now racing north along the coast at thirty mph. The buzzing of a distant helicopter—probably picking up Menachem's men at the castle—reminded Cam that this could only end one way.

No doubt the Mossad had a boat, or boats, ready to launch as well. He considered their odds. An elderly priest, a dying car dealer, an archeologist, and Cam. Versus the Mossad. What was he doing?

Cam caught Jacques' eye and motioned for him to crawl forward to grab the wheel. Jacques did so, his face pale, eyes wide. Spinning forward, Cam spotted Marconi kneeling in the bow, peering ahead, chin on the bow point like some kind of hood ornament. Cam reached out and snatched the handgun from Marconi's waistband.

"Thorne, what are you doing?"

Cam tossed the gun overboard. "Disarming you."

"Why in the world would you do that? We might need that gun."

"*You* might need that gun." Cam lifted one of the bow's cushioned seats and grabbed a pair of life jackets stored underneath. He slid one to Jacques. "But I'm not going to die for some artifact, no matter how valuable." He slipped the life jacket on, crawled back to the captain's seat, brought the Whaler to a stop, and, a half-mile off the coast of Plum Island, jumped overboard. Jacques followed.

Marconi leered down at them. "What's to stop me from cutting you to pieces with my propeller?"

"Provenance," Cam replied, bobbing in the salt water. "We're the only two people who can vouch for the validity of your find. You can kill us, but your dreams will die too." He locked eyes on Marconi. "Not to mention, that prop may kill us, but it will also become disabled. Bone is hard. You'd be a sitting duck for the Mossad."

Standing just off the secluded Plum Island shoreline in the morning light, Rivka adjusted her binoculars. One of the great things about working for the Mossad was the amazing technology. The Boston Whaler was no more than a blip on the horizon to her naked eye, over a mile away, but these field glasses magnified to 160x, allowing her to see that Cameron hadn't shaved this morning.

She almost dropped the binoculars when, a few seconds later, Cameron jumped overboard. What was he doing?

The obvious answer dawned on her. Saving himself, of course. Poor guy. He didn't deserve to be dragged into all this ugliness.

Figuring a passing boater would rescue Cameron and the archeologist, she shifted her gaze back to the racing Whaler. Marconi was now driving, still on a northerly course, apparently trying to stay out of sight of the Mossad stationed on the Crane Castle bluff by hugging the coastline. She shook her head. Nice try. But unless Marconi's boat had stealth technology, his time was limited.

Marconi made a slight course adjustment, angling away from the coast now. She tracked him for another half-minute. Suddenly, the boat came to another stop, well short of the mouth of Merrimack. What was he doing now? She blinked. Marconi and his brother were on their knees, side by side, heads bowed. Were they praying? Then his brother suddenly bashed Marconi over the head with what looked like a fire extinguisher. Marconi toppled, apparently unconscious.

*What the—?*

Palo stood over his fallen brother, tears in his eyes. He reached down, touched him tenderly on his cheek as blood pooled beneath him. "I am sorry, Mario. So very sorry. But it is God's will."

With a heavy heart, he tied a rope tightly around Mario's ankle, then secured the other side to the center stem of the Menorah. Safely out of sight of both the Mossad and any boat traffic near the mouth of the Merrimack, he hoisted his brother onto the boat's rear seat, surprised at how light he had gotten—once muscular, his brother had become emaciated and frail. But there was still enough body mass in him to do the trick. If Palo had the will.

Exhaling, Palo looked to the sky. "Must I do this?" he whispered.

God's voice spoke in his head, firm and unyielding. "Never did I proclaim your path would be an easy one. There is no other way."

"We could make a run for it."

"No! *They must not get the Menorah.*"

He bowed his head. "But, my Lord, you are all powerful. A miracle perhaps? Like with Moses and the Red Sea?"

God's voice rose. "Enough! Dare you question me? I have shown you your path. Now follow it."

Palo nodded. There really was no other way. At three hundred pounds, the Menorah weighed too much for Palo, alone, to hoist over the side. Even with Thorne's and the archeologist's help, they had struggled to wrestle it onto the boat. He had begged Mario to go along with his plan, to go along with *God's* plan. He had even convinced

Mario to pray with him, to allow God to guide him. But his brother had refused. "I am an old man. Why would I throw my life's work overboard when I only have days to live?" Without Mario's help—and, in fact, with his resistance—how could Palo possibly hoist the artifact out of the boat?

But God, in His infinite wisdom, had provided a solution. A painful one, yes. But God didn't ask for more than we could give. *If Jesus Christ died for me, then no sacrifice can be too great for me to make for Him.*

The solution, which God had shown him, was to employ a counterweight to offset the bulk of the Menorah. Tenderly, Palo lifted Mario's legs over the gunwale. Mario moaned, beginning to stir. *Not much time, better hurry.* Crossing himself, Palo kissed his brother on the forehead. "I love you, brother. Please forgive me." As gently as he could, Palo pushed more parts of Mario's body over the gunwale until, like a ragdoll, Mario flipped over the side, making a light splash. The four feet of slack in the rope snapped tight from the jerk of Mario's mass, jamming the Menorah against the gunwale. Palo prayed that the jolt did not wake his brother—drowning was a horrible way to die. Peering over the side, he saw Mario hanging upside down, his head and chest underwater, the rest of his body suspended just above the Atlantic.

Palo now turned to the Menorah. In some ways, casting it into the sea was as bad as what he had done to Mario. But God had lit Palo's path. With Mario's dangling mass serving as a counterweight, Palo grabbed the Menorah and, knees bent, used all his strength to lift. The Menorah rose a few inches, just enough for Palo to kick a life jacket under it. Resting, he repeated the process, grunting and grimacing, this time sliding the fire extinguisher under. Inch by inch the Menorah rose, becoming increasingly heavier as Mario's sinking body grew more buoyant. A wave hit them broadside, and the weight of both men and the Menorah together on one side caused the boat to teeter precariously. Reacting quickly, Palo dove for the high side, righting the vessel. He exhaled. Most boats would have flipped, but the Boston Whaler was nothing if not sturdy in the water.

Returning to his task, sweat running down his face, Palo muscled the Menorah upward. Finally, with a grunting burst of exertion, Palo was able to fulcrum the candelabra up and flip it over the side. The sacred artifact broke through the water's surface and plunged, toddling back and forth like a leaf in the wind.

Palo, panting, watched the Golden Menorah descend, Mario tethered to it, now head up, trailing. The bright yellow of the candelabra faded to gold, to brown, to black, to nothing.

Nothing except Mario, eyes wide, staring up at him.

The distant sound of a boat engine shook Palo from his stupor. Blinking, he took a deep breath and rushed to the captain's seat to restart the boat.

With his phone, he took a quick GPS reading. Closing his eyes, he forced himself to focus and memorize the coordinates. It was one thing to throw the sacred Golden Menorah overboard. It would be quite another to forget to mark its location.

He restarted the engine and changed his heading, now pointing straight at Plum Island. He removed a strap from a life jacket. Spotting a barren stretch of shoreline, he angled toward it. No other boat traffic in the area. Now was his chance. Holding the steering wheel with one hand, he looped the strap through the spokes of the wheel. He then tied off each end of the strap, essentially locking the steering wheel in place.

Throwing the life jacket over his shoulders, he let go of the wheel, confirmed the boat was on its desired course, took three strides toward the rear of the boat, and jumped.

He hit the water with a thump, churning and tumbling. Bobbing to the surface, he gasped and wiped the water from his face. He was sore, but all body parts seemed to be working. He wriggled out of the life jacket. He would hold on to it, but did not want to bob so high in the water that the Mossad—no doubt close on his heels—could spot him. A passing boater would surely pick him up once he waved and yelled, just as Thorne had figured. And, though still early morning, there should be plenty of boat traffic soon, brought on by the Boston Whaler crashing ashore in what he hoped would be a violent, fiery crash.

A crash that should attract the attention of the Mossad for enough time for Palo to get away. And if it did not, well, then God had other plans for him—and the Golden Menorah—today.

Still shaking her head over what she had witnessed with Marconi and his brother, Rivka bounced north along Plum Island's rutted main thoroughfare, one eye on the empty road and the other peering through the low brush to track the boat which had picked up Cameron and the archeologist. Some kind of crash echoed behind her. She chose to ignore it, instead focusing on Cameron. She lost sight of the rescue boat a few times, but when it circled around the northern tip of Plum Island—as she figured it would—and cruised in to dock near the Newburyport public beach, Rivka parked and jumped from her car to meet it. Not that she had any reason to believe Cameron would be happy to see her. But he would want to hear what she had seen.

Ten minutes later, Cameron—his lips still blue from the cold Atlantic—was in her car. Jacques had opted to wait for his wife. Rivka turned on the heat.

"Just so you know, I had no idea Menachem was going to attack. He's gone off the deep end. This was not what I signed up for."

Cameron studied her. If he was as good a judge of character as she thought he was, he would sense her sincerity.

"Okay," he said, finally. "I believe you."

She swallowed, surprised at how his words made her feel warm inside. "Thanks." But enough of that. She told him what she had witnessed with the Marconi brothers.

"Wait, Mario Marconi is dead?"

She nodded. "Either that, or it was a great show."

"But that makes no sense," Cameron said, rubbing his face. "I get why Palo would throw the Menorah overboard. That way the Mossad couldn't take it. And he can come back later with a dive team to retrieve it."

"I agree. And he was smart about it. He stayed close enough to the island so they were hidden from view from the Crane Castle grounds. No way could Menachem and his men see where they dumped it."

"But why kill his brother?"

Rivka knew Cameron didn't really care for Marconi. But he was clearly shaken by the man's death. "Maybe Marconi wouldn't go along with the plan. Maybe he thought they could elude Menachem's team."

"But why the need to kill him?"

She replayed the scene in her head. "I think that was the only way for him to lift the Menorah overboard. He needed Marconi as a counterweight."

Cameron shook his head in disgust. "He needed a counterweight, so he killed his own brother. Sick. But with Jacques and me gone, and Marconi not willing to help, the Menorah wasn't going anywhere." He turned to face her. "Could you find it?"

"I think so. With binoculars, if you know an object's height, you can calculate distance, which I did. And I drew a line in the sand to mark the angle, then put large stones on the line. So I can get close."

"Good. We can't leave the Menorah there—at some point, we need to go find it." He held her eyes. "And then you'll need to decide whether you're going to give it to Menachem."

She exhaled. "I know one thing. I'm not giving it to him until I understand what he's going to do with it."

Cameron lifted his chin. "I'm not sure why you told him about it in the first place."

"Cameron, I work for the Mossad, remember? And, like I said, I didn't know he was going to do the whole commando raid thing."

He let out a long breath. "Okay. I get it. Nobody can tell what that guy's going to do. But one thing is clear: Palo doesn't trust Menachem with the Menorah, either."

"I don't get that. It belongs to us, to Israel, after all. What does the Vatican care?"

Cameron shifted in his seat. "If we can get to Palo before Menachem does, we can ask him ourselves."

"I'm guessing Menachem is way ahead of us. But maybe not." Her phone rang. "Speak of the devil," she said to Cameron, smiling.

"Are you still at your observation spot on Plum Island?" Menachem asked tersely.

She bit back a retort. Menachem didn't trust her enough to be part of the assault team but still expected her to be blindly loyal to him. "No, sir. I left about fifteen minutes ago."

"Did you see anything before you left?"

She told him about Palo stopping the boat. "I'm not sure what they were doing," she lied. "It was hard to see." There was no way Menachem could know which binoculars she happened to be using. "After about ten minutes, they started up again, heading toward shore." That was when she had left; she truly didn't know what happened next.

Menachem filled her in. "There was a crash. The boat ran ashore. But nobody was in it. And no Menorah." He paused. "We *need* the Menorah."

"Yes, sir," she replied noncommittally before hanging up. She looked out over the ocean and spoke to herself. "But you need it for *what?*"

Cam sat in Rivka's old Honda behind a police barrier a few hundred yards from Crane Castle. His car was parked in the front lot, but there was no getting near the scene of so much carnage. Based on what he had seen and heard of the gunfight, Cam guessed there had been at least a few casualties. Most of them on the side of Marconi. And for what? Why had the Mossad felt the need to conduct a military-style assault on the castle? And why had Marconi not commanded his security forces to stand down in the face of such an onslaught?

The answer to both questions, of course, was the Golden Menorah. But it was like one of those high school test questions: Give your answer, and explain why. The Menorah was the answer. The 'why' eluded him.

"So, what's the plan?" Rivka asked.

Cam let out a long breath. "Honestly, I don't know." The original plan for today had been to try to raise the trireme. But with Marconi dead and the castle a crime scene, any hope for a salvage may have died as well. The salvage permit would, at a minimum, be suspended. Cam turned on the radio, hoping to get some news about the carnage at the castle.

"Should we try to find Palo?" he asked.

"He must have jumped off before the boat crashed. I doubt he wants to be found. Especially after murdering his brother."

"But nobody knows he did that. Except you. And, now, me."

"So we're a team."

Cam ignored the comment. "At some point, people will notice Mario Marconi is missing." He sighed. "Can you drive me to the police station? I better tell them what I know."

She put the car in reverse. "Sure."

The whole thing was a mess. It would take days for the police to unravel it…

A news update on the radio interrupted his thoughts. "An MIT professor was abducted overnight, and his lab ransacked, in what authorities are describing as a possible burglary gone bad."

"Holy shit," Cam said. "That's not a burglary." He turned to Rivka. "That was you guys, wasn't it? The guy doing the gold testing."

Her shoulders fell. "I don't know. Honestly. But it sounds like us. Are you sure it's the same professor?"

"No. But, yes. It has to be." He stared out the window. With the Menorah gone, and the lab ransacked, and the trireme still at the bottom of the ocean, and Marconi dead, it was becoming increasingly difficult to prove their case, as if someone was intent on suppressing this discovery. Presumably the 'someone' was the Mossad. But, again, why?

Cam walked out of the modest brick Ipswich police station into the bright, midday sun. Shielding his eyes, he saw Rivka climb from her Honda and wave to him from up the street. He stopped, unsure what to do.

She read his thoughts. "I have sandwiches." She held up a paper bag. "And I waited three hours. That must count for something."

He smiled. "What kind of sandwiches?"

"Turkey. One on wheat, one on rye. Your choice."

He jogged over. After a morning of interrogation, he was, in fact, famished. "I'll take the wheat if you don't mind."

They ate in silence for a few seconds.

"Remarkably, nobody got killed at the castle," he said. "Four guys in the hospital, one serious."

"Believe it or not, we're trained to shoot to disable, not kill. It doesn't always go down like that, but we try."

"How thoughtful of you."

"It's actually strategic. We're usually on foreign soil. Dead bodies tend to garner a lot of attention. We don't like attention, generally." She offered a coy smile. "At least not that kind."

He took another bite.

"So, what'd you tell the police?" she asked.

"Pretty much the truth. Not the stuff you told me, but everything I witnessed myself. We tried to escape in a boat, then Jacques and I jumped out when we had a chance."

"You told them about the Menorah?"

He nodded. "There's no way to keep something like that secret. But I didn't tell them where it was, obviously. I told them I thought it was the Mossad trying to steal it." He smiled. "At first they thought I was a kook. But that got their attention."

"I'm sure the FBI will be here soon, if they're not already." She took a bite. "You were right. It was the same MIT professor."

*Damn*. The professor would not be released until he was no longer a risk to the Mossad's mission. If ever. "So we'll never get the lab results on the gold."

"Not unless we can find the Menorah."

"I have to think Palo is hoping to beat us to it."

"Except for one thing," she replied. "He doesn't know about us. He thinks he's the only one who knows where it is. So he might take his time, lay low for a while." She paused. "You know, I dive. I'm certified."

He nodded. "How deep is the water there?"

"I pulled up a nautical chart on my phone. Between 90 and 120 feet."

"That's cutting it close." Recreational divers were not supposed to go below 40 meters, or 130 feet.

"It's worth it. I say we go for it."

Cam wasn't sure he wanted to trust her as his partner on a deep dive—figuratively or literally. "If we do, we're going to need some kind of cover story. Maybe find another wreck out there that we say we want to explore." He looked at her. "And also make sure Menachem doesn't find out." Could he trust her not to tell her boss? Probably. She had nothing to gain by double-crossing Cam—if she was planning to tell Menachem where the Menorah rested, she could have just left Cam out of it.

"Okay, it's a date," she said cheerfully. "So where to next?"

"I think we call it a day. Let the dust settle and then figure out what to do. My head's spinning right now."

"Okay. Want me to drive you back to Westford?"

"Will this old car make it that far?"

She gave him a dirty look. "You can insult me all you want, but leave my car out of it. She runs just fine, even if she does have a few dings and some rust. Besides, you Americans care too much about your cars."

"Fair enough. I'll direct all future insults at you."

Cam had showered, walked Venus, and phoned Astarte to update her on his adventures. Now he sat on the deck in a sweatshirt and jeans, enjoying the brisk, sunny day as the wind whipped across the lake. Venus whined, pointing her nose toward the water.

"No canoe ride today, sorry. I'm going to stay off the water for a while."

Suddenly she turned, barking at something in the house. Cam stood. "What do you hear, girl?"

He slid into the living room, holding Venus by the collar. A fireplace poker offered a welcome weapon. He stood next to the hearth, silent. He had rebuilt the house himself and knew its creaky boards, its smells, the way the sunlight played off its windows. Something was amiss. Venus barked again, in agreement.

Edging forward, Cam turned a corner into the kitchen area. Empty. And front door closed. But a baseball cap Cam had hung near the front door had fallen to the floor, as if someone had opened the front door and let in a breeze. Sniffing now, Venus pulled at him, toward the other side of the house. Cam traded the poker for a carving knife and allowed her to lead the way.

Down a hallway, past the bathroom and laundry area, toward what had been Amanda's office. The door was ajar. Had Cam left it that way? He rarely entered the room, not yet having the will to go through her things and dispose of them. With his foot, he pushed the door open. Empty. But the window was open. Someone had been here.

Retracing his steps, Cam led Venus up the stairs. They checked the bedrooms, then the bathrooms and closets. Nothing. Unlike her reaction downstairs, she didn't seem to be disturbed by strange smells or sounds up here. Cam returned to the main level.

Planning to check the basement, he instead allowed Venus to tug him back through the living room and onto the deck. He froze when he saw Menachem standing at the far end. Venus growled, her fur bristling. Cam, too, felt the hair on the back of his neck rise.

The operative waved his handgun. "Restrain your dog." His dark eyes surveilled his surroundings, analyzing and calculating. Were there weapons? Escape routes? Witnesses? Other risks? He had probably done this a thousand times.

Cam swallowed, fought to steady his voice. "Were you just in the house?"

"I was. I wanted you to see how easy it was for me to violate your space. But I thought it would be best to talk out here, out of respect for you."

"How very considerate."

Menachem nodded, either not noticing or choosing to ignore the sarcasm in Cam's voice.

"What do you want?" Cam asked.

Menachem stepped forward, cutting the distance between them from twenty to ten feet. "Answers. Something doesn't add up."

"What doesn't add up is all the bloodshed. I get that you want to recover the Menorah. But, come on."

Menachem scratched at his scar. "Actually, you don't *get it* at all, Thorne."

"So enlighten me."

"No." He waved his gun. "I am here for answers, not questions. Where is Marconi?"

"I don't know. I jumped from the boat, and he drove off."

"What about his brother?"

"His brother was in the boat with him."

"And they had the Menorah? You are certain?"

"I helped put it in the boat myself. When I jumped out, it was still there."

Menachem gazed at a distant spot above Cam's head. "No." He shook his head. "There is more to this story. Something you are not telling me."

Cam held his eyes. "Go talk to the archeologist, Jacques. He'll confirm everything I just told you."

"I did. And he did. But not lying is not the same as telling the truth."

"You want me to start making shit up?"

Menachem took another step forward. "Let's try it this way. If you had to bet, say, on the life of your daughter, where would you say the Menorah is right now?"

There it was again, Menachem's trump card. He seemed like just the type to ignore an order to stand down if he thought it essential to his mission. Cam lowered his chin. "I'd say they threw it overboard to keep you from getting it. And they plan to go back later to get it." He shrugged. "But I wasn't there when it happened, so this is just a guess, and I have no idea where exactly it might be."

A movement behind the Mossad agent caught Cam's eye. *Rivka*, peering over the edge of the deck. Cam kept his gaze fixed on Menachem and put a hand on Venus' head, quieting her.

Menachem replied. "That is our working theory as well. So we need to find the Marconi brothers. Where might they be?"

"I have no idea. Mario had the duck boat and Boston Whaler ready for a quick escape. I'm guessing he had other contingency plans in place—"

Silently, Rivka dashed across the deck, interrupting Cam's words. With a side kick, she knocked the gun from Menachem's hand. As he turned, she dropped to a knee and snapped a lightning-quick, open-palm jab into his solar plexus. Staggering, he doubled over, gasping. She followed up with a karate chop to the back of his neck, sending him to the ground, motionless.

Panting, she stood over him. "I ... am ... not ... a ... silly girl," she spat.

Cam pulled her away. "Thanks. But that's probably not going to get you a promotion."

"Fuck it. This life is not for me, anyway. These people are crazy."

"So, now what?"

She took a deep breath and smiled. "You invite me in for a drink?"

"Seriously, what are we going to do about Menachem? Either he's dead, or he's going to wake up. I'm not sure which is worse."

"He's not dead. It'll take more than that to kill that old bastard."

"So should we tie him up?"

"I suppose that's as good a plan as any."

"Wait, you don't have a plan?"

"My plan was to stop him from hurting you. He had a gun."

Fair enough. "You're right. Thanks." He took a deep breath. "I guess we tie him up."

Palo thanked the Good Samaritan who had rescued him from the Atlantic and given him a ride to the Gloucester harborfront, away from the crash and Plum Island and, hopefully, the Mossad. He purchased a sweatshirt, a baseball cap, and a pair of flip-flops in a convenience store, along with an egg and cheese sandwich. He then shuffled a few blocks inland to the hulking, gray-stoned Saint Ann's Church, where God had first spoken to him as a young boy. He pushed through the massive mahogany doors, breathed in the familiar incense-scented air, and, with a loud sigh, flopped onto a pew in the rear corner of the nave.

Lowering his head, he began to pray. The prayers quickly turned to tears. He let them flow, emptying himself. Of guilt, of remorse, of doubt, of pain. He had done God's will. There could be no higher calling. Hopefully, he would meet Mario again and his brother would forgive him. But, in the end, true forgiveness was not Mario's to give.

An hour later, at peace again, Palo stood. In order for his brother's death not to be in vain, Palo had to find the Menorah. The time for prayer had ended. He had work to do.

Bound in an Adirondack chair on Cam's deck, Menachem began to stir. Cam was tempted to hit him with a baseball bat. Instead, Rivka tossed a cup of cold water in his face.

Coughing, his eyes flew open. He swore in Hebrew. Rivka threw more water at him.

"I'm awake, goddammit," he growled.

"I know. The second cup was just for fun." She lowered her face to his. "I'm not sure you heard me the first time. I'm not a *silly girl*."

Nodding, he grimaced. "I see that now. You may have broken my ribs."

"If you start spitting up blood, we'll take you to a hospital," she replied. "After you answer our questions, that is."

"You know this is a mistake."

"One mistake was joining the Mossad. Another mistake, perhaps, was attacking you. This, now, questioning you, is no mistake at all. It is the obvious course of action."

"If I have learned anything over my forty years of service, it is that nothing is obvious."

She shrugged. "Whatever. We are still going to question you. And you are going to give us answers."

"How can you be so sure? Torture won't work. You know what kind of training we go through."

"Correct. I do. Which is why we're going to use honey rather than vinegar. Tell us what's going on. Everything. Convince us that your cause is just." She eyed him as Cam eyed her. This was a side of her Cam had never seen. Strong. Savvy. Confident. *Formidable* was probably the best word. "If you do," she continued, "we'll bring you to the Menorah."

Menachem's head jerked forward. "You know where it is?"

"*Convince us.*"

"How do I know you're not bluffing?"

"Because if we are, you'll hunt us down. Maybe not Cameron, but definitely me. I'm not an idiot. I may have been dumb enough to attack you. But I'm not dumb enough to think I can sabotage an entire mission and live to tell about it."

Menachem closed his eyes and leaned back, as if in meditation. After ten or fifteen seconds, he let out a long breath and lifted his chin. "Very well. We'll do it your way." He leaned forward. "Rivka, you're too young to really understand this. And Thorne, though I know you are half-Jewish, as an American the same goes for you." He lowered his voice. "For the Jewish people, the Golden Menorah is more than just a priceless holy object. It is everything to us. It is the symbol of our people. It is on our emblem, our coat of arms. It was used in ancient times, used in medieval times, and also now used in modern times—it has been a constant in our history. It embodies universal enlightenment, as it is written in the Book of Isaiah: 'Nations will come to your light, and kings to the brightness of your dawn.' And its seven candles symbolize the branches of human knowledge, represented by the six candles inclined inwards towards, and guided by, the light of God as represented by the central flame." Somehow his scar made his words more powerful, more potent. This was a man of action, who normally had no time or use for oratory. "It is the one object that is uniquely Jewish. Unlike so many of our sites and artifacts, the Christians make no claim to it, nor do the Muslims."

"Okay," Cam said. "I get that. Continue."

"So here we are, after two thousand years of it missing, the Golden

Menorah is at our fingertips. So close. How can we not grab for it, not scratch and claw and even kill for it?"

"Even kill?" Rivka asked.

"Yes, if necessary." His eyes shone, revealing the fire burning in his soul. "Think about what would happen if the Menorah fell into our enemies' hands." The words came out in a hiss. "They would parade it through the streets, desecrate it, defile it. Just as the Romans did two thousand years ago. It would symbolize how God has turned his back on us, abandoned us. And it would serve as a rallying cry for the Arab world, a symbol from Allah that the time had come to lay siege to the Jewish state." He fought to control his breathing. "I am not exaggerating when I say the very survival of Israel would be at stake."

Cam glanced at Rivka. She, like him, had clearly been moved by Menachem's words.

"I've never heard you speak like this, Menachem," she said. "Normally, you are more ... measured."

"Now is not the time to be dispassionate. Everything I have fought for, everything I live for, is in jeopardy." He set his jaw. "We *must* find the Menorah."

Moved as he was, Cam knew he needed to continue to think rationally, critically. There were some things that still didn't make sense. "Okay. Then why did you bomb the Illinois cave?"

"It had nothing to do with the Menorah. There were some artifacts in the cave, yes. And they were Jewish. But nothing particularly important. What was important was that there were bodies buried with them. Jewish bodies. Our ancestors. We could not have treasure hunters desecrating their burial place looking for trinkets. So we closed the cave forever."

Cam nodded. It made sense. He and Astarte had not ventured beyond the front of the cave, so would not have seen the bodies. And the bodies were consistent with what he and Astarte had theorized about refugees from the Bar Kokhba uprising having come over with the Roman Ninth Legion.

Menachem continued. "I'll be honest. Much of this is my fault. I never thought you'd actually find the Menorah. It all seemed so damned outlandish." He glanced at Rivka. "Nothing personal, but if I had taken this more seriously, I would have assigned a more senior operative to the case."

She sniffed. "Not some silly girl, you mean?"

"I stand corrected on that, obviously. Were it not for you, the Menorah would be lost. You have proven yourself worthy." He leaned forward against his restraints. "Now prove yourself heroic, Rivka. Help us recover our sacred treasure."

After leaving the church, Palo found a taxi. "North," he said, "to Newburyport." He needed to lay low, to avoid the Mossad. But he also needed to remain in the area, close to the Menorah.

Seated on a bench near the mouth of the Merrimack River, overlooking the clam beds at Joppa Park as he nibbled, appropriately, on fried clams, Palo made a call. "It is time," he said in Italian.

"Very well. We fly tomorrow. We will be ready to dive the next day. Same location as last year?"

"No. Close by, but deeper. Thirty to forty meters."

"And our fee?"

"I will triple your normal daily rate. And, of course, pay all expenses." In truth, he would have paid more than that to have a team he could trust, but it was always dangerous to put too much blood in the water when sharks were around. "We will use the same dive shop we used last year, near the airport. And their boat as well. I will text you the information."

It would be risky, out on the open water. The Mossad would be looking for him. For the Menorah. But what choice did he have? He would do what he could and leave the rest up to God.

Palo stood in Farley's men's shop on State Street in downtown Newburyport. Unlike his brother, he didn't spend much time worrying about his appearance. But he couldn't very well waltz into the local Catholic church as a Vatican emissary dressed in a sweatshirt and flip-flops.

Outfitted now in a dark blue suit and maroon tie with matching pocket square, and carrying another bag filled with a couple of sets of casual clothes, Palo strolled west a few blocks to the stately brick Immaculate Conception church. He had phoned ahead, the parish priest more than pleased to host a high-ranking Vatican official even on short notice.

After a quick tour, the balding, mustached priest smiled at Palo. "With due respect, Your Eminence, I have trouble believing God sent you all this way merely to visit our humble church."

Palo nodded, appreciative of the man's prescience. "You are correct. I have a favor to ask. A peculiar one, at that."

"Anything I can do. You need only speak it."

Palo led the priest back to the altar. He had been prepared to visit other churches tonight if necessary, but the Lord had seen fit to make simple his task. He smiled and bowed his head. "Actually, it is not for me." He pointed. "It is for the Almighty. A gift."

Cam grabbed a couple of beers from the fridge as Rivka sliced a cucumber and some tomatoes for a simple salad. A pizza was on its way. As, apparently, was a nasty thunderstorm. He had never actually invited her to stay. But he hadn't sent her home, either. She had, after all, rescued him from Menachem.

Menachem, on the other hand, had rushed off. Cam had half-expected him to exact some revenge for being bested, but he had bowed his head to them, winced, and shuffled back to his car. They had agreed to reconnoiter at dawn on Plum Island, where Menachem would have a boat and dive equipment ready. Hopefully, the storm would be over by then.

While Rivka went to use the bathroom, Cam checked email on his phone. In all the commotion of the day, he had not done so since late last night. He scrolled through. Mostly junk. But the word 'gold' in a subject line caught his eye. He peered closer. Arrival time of 3:22 AM. He opened it. Eyes wide, he dropped into a chair. Ten simple words. He reread them to make sure he got them right.

*Final results of helium testing reveal date of 3150 BP.*

The professor must have sent the email—including an attachment with the full lab report—before being abducted. Apparently, at Marconi's instruction, he had copied Cam on the message. Unbelievable. It was authentic. Cam had hoped, dreamed, fantasized. But now it was a reality. A scientific reality. The Romans were here, and they had brought the Golden Menorah with them.

Rivka stared at her reflection in Cam's bathroom mirror. "Okay, now what?"

She was here, in his home. They had bonded during the day, teaming up to face—and defeat—common enemies. Now they had settled into an easy, effortless coexistence. She saw the evening unfolding; one beer would lead to another, perhaps an after-dinner swim in the rain, maybe a movie and a bottle of wine and some thunder and lightning and eventually their knees brushing against each other on the couch. She wanted it. But did he? And if not, was she wise to let the alcohol and inertia do her work for her?

The old Rivka would have said yes. And the new Rivka wanted to. But the last thing she needed was for him to feel pressured or trapped or confused. He had—by both his words and actions—indicated he wasn't ready yet. She smiled at herself in the mirror. Actually, that was a bit of revisionist theory. He had indicated he wasn't ready for anything with *her*. She had decided to interpret that to mean he just wasn't ready in general, that it had nothing to do with her. Was she correct? She shrugged. It didn't matter. It was her interpretation, wishful or not, and she was going to run with it.

Tonight she would eat her pizza and drink her beer and then say goodnight. Today they had bested the Mossad. Tomorrow they would, together, make a discovery that would change history.

If that didn't spark a romance, nothing would.

## Chapter 12

Cam awoke from a dead sleep in the black of a stormy, moonless night. A noise, some kind of thump, echoed in his subconscious. He reached for Venus, who had slept next to him every night since Amanda's death. His hand found only sheets.

"Venus?" he whispered, sitting up. The sound, as best he could tell, had come from inside the house. Had Venus also heard the noise and gone to investigate? If so, why no barking? A pit formed in his stomach. His gut spoke to him. *Menachem.* Had the Mossad agent's speech been a ruse? Had he returned to silence Cam and make sure the Golden Menorah remained a secret? It was impossible to dismiss the possibility. A bolt of thunder clapped, as if confirming his fear. He heard the dim whir of his generator; power must be out.

Opening his side table drawer, Cam found a flashlight and his pistol safe, which he quickly opened using the fingerprint scan mode. He swung his feet out of bed and removed the Smith & Wesson Bodyguard .380 from the case. With his thumb, he slid the safety lock off. He took a deep breath. He had never fired the weapon, other than at the range. But he had purchased it for times just like this. Someone had invaded his home. He doubted they were here on a social visit. His trigger finger twitched.

Finding his phone, he called 911. "I think I have an intruder in my house," he whispered. He gave his address as he slid into a pair of sweatpants.

"Most of our officers are out on emergency calls," the woman said. "There's trees and power lines down, especially around the lake. It may be awhile before anyone can reach you. I suggest you flee the premises and seek shelter at a neighbor's house."

Great.

Moving slowly, keeping to the edge of the stairs to minimize squeaking, he tip-toed downward. A distant, soft glow—probably coming from the basement—served as a beacon. He considered slipping outside and trying to peer in through a window, but rejected the idea—Menachem would have brought backup to stand guard outside. Plus, if they had Venus, he would need to act quickly to rescue her.

His trigger finger twitched. Yes, she was just a dog. But, other than Astarte and his parents, he loved that dog as much as anything on earth. A random thought popped into his head, something Astarte had said about Menachem: He was an animal lover. It gave Cam hope. He took the last two steps to the first floor.

The light in the finished basement now glowed brighter. He also thought he heard a low murmur. Was someone with Menachem? If so, what were they doing? Perhaps they were searching the house for laptops and computers, wanting to make sure no evidence of the Menorah would be left behind. Evidence such as an email from MIT documenting the gold testing results.

Creeping forward, he stopped for a second to wipe the sweat from his hand. His mouth felt dry, and every step he took pounded in his ears like a drumbeat. But he knew the floor was thick and relatively soundproof. He arrived at the top of the basement stairs. He froze, paralyzed with indecision. Did he really want to confront a Mossad team and engage in a firefight? Could he really hope to survive such an encounter?

A thunderclap sounded again, once more providing an answer. He exhaled. He hadn't heard a single bark or whimper. The truth was, Venus was probably already dead. His best bet would be to take the 911 operator's advice and get the hell out of here. With a heavy heart, he turned and began to edge toward the front door.

The sound of someone bounding up the basement stairs froze him in his tracks. *They had heard him.* He ducked around a corner and turned off his flashlight, gun at the ready. Could he actually pull the trigger? He swallowed. They had probably killed Venus. And planned the same for him. He had no choice. And he'd better not miss.

But it was dark, and his hand was shaking. He had an inspiration. He pointed the flashlight at the stairs with his left hand, finger on the button. When it came time to fire, he'd shine the light at his target, giving him a split second to aim. The action might also blind the operative, giving Cam another advantage. He peered out. The top of a head appeared, ascending. Then an entire head. Cam leaned out, flicked on the light, aimed the gun—

"Dad! What are you doing?" Astarte stood in the stairwell, shielding her eyes. "I can't see. Turn that off."

Cam collapsed to one knee, quickly tucking the gun into a pocked of his sweatpants. *Holy shit, holy shit, holy shit.* He flicked the light off and turned away, vomiting, nauseated at what he had almost done.

"Dad, what's wrong? Are you sick?"

He coughed and sucked for air. "No. No. I was just afraid. I thought you were an intruder." Outside, a police light flashed. He would be happy to send them on their way.

"We came home to surprise you. Matthias and I. I was just making the bed up for him down in the basement."

"Oh." That explained why Venus hadn't barked.

"I let us in the back door so we wouldn't wake you."

"Oh," he repeated, forcing a smile.

She stepped forward, Venus at her heels. "I thought we could help find the Menorah. I mean, how often do you get to be part of history? And, before you say anything, I attended class today via Zoom."

He managed to pull himself to a standing position. "Great idea, honey." Holding the wall, he hugged her, keeping the pocket with his gun turned away. "Whew." He forced a smile. "You're right. I am surprised." The gun felt hot—almost scorching—in his hand.

"Sorry. Our flight was delayed because of the storm." He noticed her hair was wet. "It's nasty out there. We had to walk in from Route 40 because there are power lines down. I didn't want to wake you and give you a start."

"No. I mean, thanks." He rubbed his face, swallowing a mouthful of bile. "Good idea, not giving me a start."

Cam had been unable to fall back asleep, even after half a tumbler of Irish whiskey. He had been micro-seconds from pulling the trigger. The suffocating, crushing guilt he felt from almost murdering his daughter made the bench press weights Rivka had dropped on his chest feel like a silk robe in comparison. Who was he? What kind of trigger-happy, anger-fueled monster had he become?

Amanda's reply came to him in the purple light of pre-dawn, the storm having moved on as quickly as it had arrived.

*A monster trying to protect his family. A monster not perfect. A monster put into an impossible situation. In other words, a human monster.*

"Humans don't kill their young."

*Neither did you. You stopped, of course, when you saw who it was. What more could you do?*

"I could be more careful."

*No, Cameron. You were careful. That's why she's alive. It was a crazy, daft set of circumstances, that's all.*

"Maybe I just need to find a different line of work."

*Right. Because being a historian is generally a very high-risk profession. Maybe you should become a test pilot or one of those steel workers on skyscrapers instead.*

"Well, it's been high risk for us."

*Yes. But it's also been high reward. You love what you do. And Astarte loves it also. How many college kids fly home just to spend extra time with their dad?*

"More to the point, how many of them almost don't live to tell about it."

*Enough, Cameron. She's fine. And she's here to share an adventure with you. Take advantage of it. Heaven knows, I wish I could.*

With a long sigh, he rolled out of bed. Amanda, of course, was right. A near miss was still a miss.

With the storm over, they'd be able to get started early at Plum Island, as planned. It was 4:30 now. The sun rose at around six. Which meant it was time to send Venus down the hall. "Go wake Astarte, girl!"

Twenty minutes later, after walking Venus, Cam joined Astarte at the kitchen table for a quick breakfast.

"Matthias will be right up," Astarte said. "So, what's the plan?"

Cam outlined things, including the part about Menachem breaking in yesterday and Rivka turning the tables on him.

"Yes!" Astarte exclaimed. "Way to go, Rivka. We owed him one. She's starting to grow on me, Dad."

"Yeah, well, it could just be a rash," he said, chuckling. "Anyway, we've agreed to help Menachem find the Menorah. It does, after all, belong in Israel. Rivka marked the location. She can get us close. Hopefully, last night's storm didn't stir things up so much that it's completely buried."

Seated in an armchair of his room at the Essex Street Inn in downtown Newburyport, Palo prayed all night for the storm to pass. At around four, his prayers were answered. And he was ready.

The night before, after leaving the Immaculate Conception church, he had walked down to the waterfront and rented a sixteen-foot aluminum fishing boat with a small outboard motor at a local marina. Explaining that he was a fisherman wanting to get an early start, Palo had paid for the boat up front and also rented fishing gear and supplies. The fish, of course, was a symbol of Jesus—Palo took it as a sign that he remained on the righteous, holy path.

Now, in the purple light of dawn, dressed in blue jeans and a windbreaker he had purchased yesterday and toting a breakfast the innkeeper had prepared for him, he returned to the marina with a duffel bag over one shoulder. Yanking the starter rope, Palo coaxed the engine to life. He headed west toward the mouth of the river and then swung south, hugging the Plum Island coast. He cruised at about fifteen mph, the ocean calm, passing the site where the Whaler had crashed harmlessly ashore. Twenty minutes after leaving the river, he reached his destination two-thirds of the way down the island's length. He then veered due east, toward the open ocean.

Using the GPS app on his phone, he cut the engine two hundred yards short of where he had deposited the Menorah. For the same reason he had chosen not to sleep last night, he refused to allow his eyes to settle on the actual spot where Mario and the Menorah rested. He would, eventually, need to face up to—and pay for—the crime he had committed against his brother. But, for now, denial was best. For now, he would focus on doing what the Good Lord commanded.

He removed from the duffel bag the object he had taken from the church, the so-called gift to God—a large brass altar candelabra. He tied a 200-foot line of nylon rope to it and tossed the candelabra overboard. It weighed probably only a quarter of the 300-pound real Menorah, but it was a dense artifact and made a loud splash before it began its plummet toward the ocean floor. Fifteen seconds later, the line slackened. He nodded. About 90 feet, just as he estimated. In the orange glow of pre-dawn, he cut the line, tied the free end to a white vinyl buoy he had purchased from the marina, and flipped the buoy overboard.

Again being careful not to look toward Mario's burial location, Palo restarted the boat. Heart heavy, but still resolute, he motored back toward shore. There, tucked alongside a sandbar, he threw an anchor over the side, took out his binoculars, and watched to see if the Jewish fish would take his Catholic bait.

Cam, Astarte and Matthias took an Uber to Ipswich to pick up Cam's car before driving up the coast, arriving at the Sandy Point beach just after six. The barge remained anchored offshore, empty. Cam spotted Menachem on the beach, backlit by the eastern glow, wearing fatigue pants and a black pullover, staring out toward where the Golden Menorah was buried. "I'll be right back," Cam said, jogging toward the shore. He guessed Astarte would want to keep her distance from Menachem. Which was fine with Cam.

"You know," he said by way of greeting, "nobody is using the barge. We could commandeer it."

Menachem's mouth slowly formed itself into a smile, his scar purple in the morning light. He had a cup of coffee in one hand and a cigarette in the other. "I like the way you think. But I don't want to draw any unnecessary attention to ourselves."

"So what's the plan? Where are your men?"

He took a puff. Cam imagined that nicotine was not the only drug coursing through his veins. He knew how painful cracked ribs could be. "There are no men, other than the boat captain. Just you and Rivka and me. We are all certified. Two of us will dive while the other stays in the boat."

"I have Astarte and her boyfriend to help as well." Menachem began to object. Cam held up his hand. "Not negotiable. I want a couple extra sets of eyes, especially if I'm going to be underwater."

"Are you saying you don't trust me, Thorne?"

"Yes."

"I suppose that is understandable. But there is no room for them on the boat. They can stay on shore, keep an eye on things with binoculars."

"No room?"

"Lots of gear." He smiled. "And I had a large breakfast."

Cam didn't push it. Truthfully, he was happy for the excuse to keep Astarte out of harm's way. She would not be happy, but so be it.

"Why the skeleton crew?" Cam asked.

"This is a very delicate operation. Sometimes less is more."

Rivka had texted, telling Cam she was in place. Cam led Menachem north along the shore a couple of hundred yards. Rivka, on her hands and knees in the sand, was peering northeast, out to sea, using the stones she had placed yesterday as a sight line. She hopped to her feet and brushed the sand from her jeans. "Good morning," she said brightly, smiling at Cam.

Menachem merely grunted. Cam replied, "You're in a good mood."

"Why wouldn't I be? It's a beautiful morning." The day had dawned bright and dry, with a light breeze. "And this promises to be an exciting adventure."

"Talk to me," Menachem said, flicking his cigarette into the sand, even that simple gesture causing him to wince in pain.

"This line should be pretty accurate," she said. "I suggest you bring the boat here and get on this bearing. Once you're on it, the captain should be able to hold it."

"Astarte and Matthias can direct us from shore," Cam offered.

"How far out?" Menachem asked.

"About two miles."

"You're going to need to do better than that."

She shook her head. "If I give you an exact distance," she replied, "you won't need us."

"Don't forget who you work for, Rivka."

"That reminds me." She reached into the back pocket of her jeans and pulled out a folded envelope. "My resignation letter."

His brow furrowed. "You can't resign from the Mossad."

"I just did."

Shaking his head, Menachem walked away, the envelope still in Rivka's hand.

Cam leaned in. "That's ballsy. How do you know he won't kill you?"

"He might. But not until after we find the Menorah." She shrugged and smiled. "Hopefully, by then, he'll be in such a good mood that he lets it go."

"That's cavalier."

She smiled. "I'm guessing God doesn't want me. And the devil isn't finished with me yet."

Chuckling, Cam walked off to find Astarte and Matthias. Rivka wasn't lacking in brashness, that was for sure.

Ten minutes later, the dive boat—featuring a large open area in the stern and a raised, enclosed cockpit toward the bow—arrived. The captain beached the boat and they climbed aboard, absent Astarte and Matthias. Cam swallowed. Menachem and the burly captain on the one hand, he and Rivka on the other. And he still wasn't certain he could trust her. Not great odds if things went sideways.

Communicating with Astarte via cell phone, Cam directed the captain as he angled away from shore. Fortunately, the waters were calm, making it fairly easy to keep their bearing.

"We've gone almost two miles," Menachem announced, turning to Rivka. "Time for a more precise measurement."

She nodded. "Keep going."

Menachem began to push for more, but Cam interrupted. "What's that? Floating off the port bow, maybe fifty yards out?"

The captain changed course.

Menachem shielded his eyes with a hand. "Rivka, did Palo Marconi drop a buoy after throwing the Menorah overboard?"

"Not that I saw. But he was working on the seaward side of the boat. And once he threw the Menorah over, I focused on getting a bearing and distance. He easily could have done so without me noticing."

"Are we near the correct location?" Menachem asked.

She frowned. "Sort of. But not exactly. It should be further out."

"Well, maybe your readings were off." The thought seemed to please the Mossad leader, as if validating his opinion of her.

The captain pulled alongside the buoy. Menachem leaned over the gunwale and, wincing, grabbed it. "It's clean. Hasn't been in the water for long." He lifted it into the boat and examined the rope tied to it. "Rope is also clean. I think this might be it." He tugged on the line. "There's something on the other end."

"Want me to get it?" Cam asked.

Menachem ignored the question. Working alone, hand over hand, the Mossad agent stubbornly hoisted the line, haphazardly tossing rope into the boat. Cam and Rivka leaned over the side, peering into the depths. The shadow of something appeared, rising.

"It looks yellow-ish," Rivka said.

Seconds later, Menachem gave a final heave and a brass-colored candelabra broke through the surface. "Ha!" he exclaimed with a rare show of emotion, grabbing it with two arms and setting it gently on the rear seat. "We found it."

Cam recoiled in surprise. Before Rivka could say anything, Cam touched her arm, shaking his head.

Silently, they all stared at the ornate object—measuring about two feet tall and three feet wide—for a few seconds.

"I thought it would be bigger," Menachem said, finally. "There is a replica in Jerusalem. It is nearly twice the size of this."

Cam swallowed. "I had the same reaction when I first saw it at the wreck site," he lied. "But you know how things get exaggerated in the Biblical era. Goliath standing almost ten feet tall, Abraham living to 175."

Menachem studied Cam. "This is the menorah you recovered?"

"Of course." He angled his head. "Do you think there are two of them floating around out here?" It was a good thing Rivka hadn't told Menachem there was supposed to be a dead body tied to the Menorah.

The Mossad leader turned back to the candelabra. "I believe you received preliminary results from MIT? Before the lab was destroyed." He said it matter-of-factly, as if he had played no part in the destruction.

Cam nodded. "Yes. Approximately 3,000 years before present."

Rivka weighed in. "Look at how the gold has faded over the centuries. It needs a good polishing."

Menachem straightened himself. "Like you said, there cannot be two menorahs buried out here. So it is what it is, undersized or not." He nodded his head and lifted his eyes to the heavens. "We have done it, accomplished the impossible. We have found the Golden Menorah."

While Menachem conferred with the captain in the cockpit, Cam huddled with Rivka in the stern, making a show of examining the menorah.

"This is not the candelabra I saw Palo throw overboard yesterday," she whispered.

"And it's not the one I recovered at the dive site," he replied.

She bit her lip. "Palo must have planted this for us to find."

"Agreed. So, now what?"

She shook her head. "I don't know. But I still don't completely trust Menachem. Let's let him make the next move."

Cam's phone rang. Astarte. "Did you find it?" she asked excitedly.

"As Mum would have said, things are a bit dodgy."

"Really? You can't talk, right?"

"Correct."

"Okay. Then just listen. I just spoke to Georgia. She spoke to one of their analysts. She thinks Israel may not want to recover the Menorah after all."

That made no sense. It would be like the Catholic Church not wanting to find the Holy Grail. "Why would that be?"

"Because it would be destabilizing."

"How so?"

"Because finding the Golden Menorah would renew calls to build the Third Temple. Most Jewish scholars agree you can't build a new Temple without all the holy objects. God's commandment to build the Temple included filling it with the Menorah and other sacred furnishings and fixtures—you can't have one without the others. But if you had the Menorah, the most sacred of all the objects, things would change. People, especially Orthodox Jews, would take that as a sign from God that it was time to rebuild. In fact, rebuilding is one of the sacred tenets of Judaism—Georgia said that praying for the reconstruction of a Third Temple is a required part of the daily Jewish prayer."

Cam nodded. "And, like you said, rebuilding would be incredibly destabilizing." Both the Al Aqsa Mosque and the Dome of the Rock, two of the most holy sites in Islam, sat atop the Temple Mount. Any attempt to build a Third Temple in their place would inevitably lead to a holy war.

It occurred to Cam that there was a symmetry, a cosmic balance, in the fact that his research journey both began and ended with efforts to rebuild the Temple. The Bar Kokhba uprising, which had triggered the Ninth Legion trip to America, was itself sparked by Jewish rebels' desire to rebuild the Temple, as evidenced by the Temple image featured on the Bar Kokhba coins found along the Ohio River. And now here they were again, with the Menorah potentially triggering another attempt to rebuild.

Cam hung up and recounted the conversation to Rivka. "Astarte's right," Rivka replied. "And it's not just Orthodox Jews who would push for the Third Temple. Many fundamentalist Christians would as well. Even some Catholic groups. They all see the Third Temple as a necessary step leading up to the Messianic age. Some of them have been calling for rebuilding even without the Golden Menorah."

Cam stared out over the Atlantic. Was that what was going on here? Was the Mossad trying to *prevent* the Menorah from being found as a way to prevent a holy war? Is that why Menachem had destroyed the caves in Illinois, as a way to erase any history of ancient Jews being in America, a history which in turn was an important clue leading to the Menorah?

As if in response to his questions, the dive boat roared to life, turned, and began racing straight out to sea.

"This is not good," Cam said under his breath to Rivka.

Menachem bounced down the cockpit stairs and pulled a gun from his pants, confirming Cam's fears. He shouted over the engine. "I need your cell phones." He tossed a couple of canvas bags at them. "And I need you to put these over your heads."

"Let me guess," Cam replied. "You're going to dump the Menorah again."

The Mossad agent nodded, chin up but eyes sad. "Yes. For the last time."

Seated in the rented fishing boat along the coast of Plum Island, Palo raised his field glasses and watched as the dive boat raced away. He smiled. They had found the candelabra, obviously. Palo would need to make it up somehow to the kind priest at the Immaculate Conception Church. There was no way that candelabra would be escaping a watery grave.

He yanked the engine alive. It had been a pleasant morning here along the shore. And a successful one. But God's work was not done. There was a Third Temple that needed rebuilding.

Unable to see, Cam did his best to estimate time and distance as the boat roared out to sea. He had counted out forty minutes and guessed they were traveling at about thirty mph. So twenty miles. And from the angle of the sun sifting through the bag covering his face, it seemed like they were headed just north of due east. None of which was worth a damn. If that menorah went overboard, they'd never find it again.

Which, of course, was fine.

But they still had to sell the ruse to Menachem.

The captain cut the engine, and the boat coasted to a stop. "You may remove your hoods," Menachem said.

Blinking, Cam glared at him. Rivka, catching on quickly, did the same.

"You can't do it, Menachem," Cam pleaded. "Last night, you told us how important the Menorah is to the Jewish people. And you were right. There must be another way."

"Nothing is more important than peace," he replied simply. "And you are wrong. There is no other way. I wish there were."

With a sad shrug, he lifted the candelabra over his head with both hands and, reciting a short prayer in Hebrew, tossed it off the back of the boat.

Rivka, who had already kicked off her shoes, reacted instantly. She dove after it, slicing into the water and resurfacing ten seconds later twenty yards from the stern of the boat. "I have it," she sputtered, one hand working furiously to tread water while the other clutched the candelabra.

Cam moved to the gunwale, ready to jump in to help.

"Don't move, Thorne. Not if you love your daughter."

Cam froze. "But she'll drown. No way can she tread water with that thing weighing her down."

"I know."

Cam reached for a seat cushion.

"I said, don't move." Menachem lifted the gun. "Again, remember your daughter."

"It's okay," Rivka called. "I can do it."

Cam leaned toward her. "But for how long?" He looked around. "There are no other boats out here."

Menachem ordered the captain to start the boat. "Last chance, Rivka. We are leaving. I suggest you come with us."

"We can't just leave it." Her voice cracked in frustration. "It's *sacred*. It's the *Golden Menorah*."

"And it's going to kill you if you don't let it go," Menachem replied icily.

"He's right," Cam called to her. "You'll never last out here. You have to let it go."

"No." She shook her head. But she was already beginning to flail.

"Rivka, listen to me. It's over. He's won. Now, please, come back to the boat."

Rivka swore and let out a scream of frustration that would have made even the banshees proud. "God himself will punish you for this, Menachem," she said. "You and your line will be cursed forever."

"You may very well be right," he replied. "Now get in the boat."

Cam waved at Astarte, barely visible a couple of hundred yards down the barren Plum Island beach. Menachem hadn't even bothered to beach the dive boat, instead warning Cam and Rivka to keep their mouths shut and then forcing them to jump over the side and swim ashore. But Cam didn't mind. He had half-expected Menachem to put a bullet in their heads and dump them twenty miles offshore.

Astarte and Matthias jogged to them. "How did it go?" she asked.

Cam smiled at Rivka. "Academy Award performance." Cam quickly explained how they had found the replica menorah left by Palo and convinced Menachem it was the real thing. "I thought Rivka really was going to go down with that candelabra."

"Well, I had to sell it. Menachem is no idiot. He knew I had seen the Menorah when it was in the boat with the Marconi brothers. He was suspicious that the candelabra was so small. But my willingness to drown to save it convinced him it was the real thing."

"Like I said, Academy Award. You should have heard her curse Menachem." Cam turned to Astarte. "And you were right. The Mossad doesn't want the Menorah to be found. Just like Georgia said. Too destabilizing."

"He didn't suspect anything?" Astarte asked.

Rivka replied, "He *always* suspects *something*. But no more than usual, I think."

"I, for one, will be happy if I've seen the last of Menachem," Cam said. They had played tug-of-war with the Temple treasures for the last time, hopefully.

"So where's the real Menorah?" Matthias asked.

"Must still be out there," Rivka answered. "Based on my calculations, a couple hundred yards from where Palo dumped the replica."

"So how do we get it?" Astarte asked. "Our dive boat just drove away."

Cam gestured with his chin toward the barge, still anchored offshore near the southern tip of the island. "There's equipment for eight divers still on that barge. All we have to do is drive it out to the dive site."

"Anyone have the key?" Astarte asked.

Rivka smiled. "Who needs a stinking key?"

Hesitantly, Matthias spoke. "Um, do we really want to recover it? Maybe the Mossad is right. Maybe it is too destabilizing."

"What do you mean?" Astarte asked.

"I know my perspective is unique. Being Indian, I really have no connection to Israel and its history. But I look at what's happening in the Middle East and I want to pull my hair out. Not just in Jerusalem, but the fights between the Sunni and Shiite also. So many people killed, over nothing." He shrugged. "I'm not sure what to do. But we should at least think about it before rushing back out there."

Cam weighed his words and nodded. "You make a good point. But the reality is, if we don't get the Menorah, Palo will. I don't know what his agenda is, but he's a senior Vatican official. It's safe to say he probably has one. An agenda so powerful he killed his own brother for it." He held Matthias' eyes. "Let's do this. Let's recover the Menorah first, then have the discussion about what to do with it. Fair?"

Matthias nodded. "Yes. Fair."

Two hours later, they had successfully commandeered the barge and were motoring back toward the white buoy location. Not being totally comfortable with a deep dive, Cam had phoned Jacques and convinced him to join them. Jacques, in turn, brought his assistant, who remained onshore at Rivka's rocks to direct them on the proper bearing. More importantly, Jacques had also recruited a divemaster he often worked with, giving them all an extra level of comfort before they dove. By lunchtime, with Jacques skippering the motorized barge, they were in position over what Rivka had calculated was the Golden Menorah dump location.

Cam turned to Jacques. "I wasn't sure you'd come."

"Why? I like being shot at and then almost drowned."

"I know. Fun day."

"Besides, find of a lifetime." He smiled. "Where's Marconi?"

Cam kept it vague. "I think he's dead."

Jacques nodded respectfully. "What makes you so sure the Mossad won't come for us?"

"They found another candelabra. They think that's the Menorah." Again, vague. Cam glanced around them. "But you're right. They could come back. If they do, we'll give them what they want."

"Agreed."

"You know, this is a bit of a needle in the haystack. Rivka is only estimating at the location. She was watching from shore and saw them dump the Menorah overboard after we jumped."

"Hopefully it'll be clear down there."

"You want first dive?" Cam asked.

"You with me?" Jacques replied. "We found it together the first time."

Rivka interrupted. "Um, Cam, aren't you forgetting something?"

"What?"

She pulled him aside. "Marconi is still tied to the Menorah. How are you going to explain that to Jacques?"

"Good point."

"The good news is that his body will actually make it easier to find the Menorah—two needles to look for rather than just one." She paused. "The bad news is, we're going to need to figure out what to do with the body once we find it."

Palo motored north along the secluded Plum Island coast, one eye on the barge and the other on the woman standing on the shore who seemed to have been directing it. He fought to slow his breathing, angry at himself for not renting a boat with a bigger engine. What had promised to be a sublime day had suddenly turned cataclysmic.

He made a quick phone call, shouting over the engine. "This is Palo. I have orders from Mario. We have another situation. Gather the team and stand by." Mario was dead, but his operatives didn't know that.

How had the barge known exactly where to go? And who, exactly, was on it? Palo had watched the Mossad agent, Menachem, race away in his dive boat, blissfully unaware that he had been duped. Now, apparently, it was Palo who was being played. But, again, by whom?

Palo offered a friendly wave to the bookish woman on the shore. He hoped her intelligence didn't extend to street smarts.

"Pardon me," he called. "Did you by chance find a wallet in the sand? I was fishing there earlier this morning and seem to have lost it."

She glanced around her. "No, sorry."

"Would it bother you if I came ashore to look for it myself?"

Ten minutes later, he had her tied up in the woods, cowering, her back against a tree. He leaned closer, speaking in a soothing voice. "As God is my witness, I'm not going to hurt you." His tone changed. "Unless, of course, you refuse to tell me what you know about the people on that barge."

Cam stood by a video monitor in the cabin of the barge. He had come up with a new plan, one that hopefully would make it easier to find the Golden Menorah. And also to deal with the issue of Marconi's body.

One of the tools Marconi had equipped the barge with was an underwater camera. Two of them, actually. The technology was simple, often used by fishermen—drag a camera on a power cord beneath the boat so you can see what's down there. Jacques, Rivka, the divemaster and Matthias had donned snorkeling equipment and were swimming in a grid pattern, cameras dangling, switching off in pairs to stay fresh. Cam and Astarte manned the monitors, the benefit being that neither Jacques nor the divemaster would be able to see Marconi's body on the video feed.

After about fifteen minutes, Astarte called out. "I think I see something." She stuck her head out the door and yelled to Rivka. "Tell Matthias to go to his right about ten feet."

Cam switched to her monitor. "There," she said, smiling. "That's it."

Cam nodded. "And I see the body also. Turn off the monitor."

He strode out to the railing and tossed Rivka a yellow buoy similar to the one they had found tied to the candelabra this morning. "Tell Matthias to let his camera drop to the ocean floor and tie this buoy to the line. Don't say anything to Jacques and the divemaster quite yet. And come aboard right away."

Quickly, Cam began to put on his dive suit. No reason to open things up for debate. Rivka did the same. By the time the snorkelers came aboard, Cam and Rivka were ready to dive.

Jacques eyed them. "I guess the decision has been made who's going down."

Cam squeezed his shoulder. "We're already geared up. No reason to be out here even one minute longer than necessary. Who knows when the Mossad might come back."

The divemaster gave thumbs up, and Cam and Rivka splashed over the side. The plan was simple: Follow Matthias' camera cord to the bottom, tie a rope to the Menorah, and winch it aboard. It would have been easier to use the barge's crane and metal basket to hoist the Menorah, as they had done on Sunday, but Cam didn't want to take the extra time.

Before any salvage could take place, of course, they would have to deal with Marconi.

They descended methodically, following the cord, Rivka leading. Sensing his anxiety, Rivka turned and gave him a thumbs up. Cam had never gone this deep, and he concentrated on slowing his breathing. They would need to move quickly. They had enough oxygen for a twenty-minute dive. Of that, they would need to set aside eight minutes for their ascent—rising from the 90-foot depth at no faster than thirty feet per minute, then taking an additional five-minute safety stop twenty feet from the surface. Assuming three minutes on the descent, that left them nine minutes at the bottom. It sounded like plenty of time. But there was something disquieting about knowing that death loomed only minutes away.

Flashlights on, they approached the ocean floor. The Menorah, resting on its side, glowed eerily in the diffused light of their beams. But, as agreed, Rivka ignored it, instead going for Marconi's splayed body. Cam glanced over, thankful he had landed face down. Cam had descended with one end of a thick marine rope, the other secured to a winch on the barge, and he began to tie it around the Menorah. He felt sluggish at this depth, almost as if the water were thicker here. And his gloved hands struggled with the knot. But, eventually, he forged a crude but secure knot.

Rivka, meanwhile, worked to untie the line wrapped around

Marconi's ankle. They had talked about just cutting it, but a cut rope tied to a dead body might, eventually, cause the authorities to look harder at Marconi's death. As it was, in a few days the body would float to the surface and likely wash ashore. The medical examiner would see the wound on his head and also determine that death had been from drowning. Attention would naturally focus on Palo, who had been alone in the Boston Whaler with him just before his death. That was enough. There was no need for the authorities to find another clue, one which might lead them to the Menorah.

Cam watched her for a few seconds, working proficiently, the wetsuit accentuating her curves. Oddly, he trusted her, which was quite a thing to say about someone who had kidnapped your daughter only a few days earlier. As she turned and gave him another thumbs up, he wondered if they had any kind of future together. Shaking the thought away, he gave three quick tugs to the rope. Almost instantly, the Golden Menorah began to rise.

In sync, Cam and Rivka followed.

Cam broke the surface, pulled off his mask, and opened his eyes to see a semiautomatic rifle pointed at his head from the deck of the barge. He spat out brackish sea water. *Palo*. Their ascent had been a leisurely one. But it must have been quite an eleven minutes on the surface.

"Thank you, Mr. Thorne, for retrieving the Menorah for me," Palo called. "Please, now, come aboard. I have a few questions for you, then I will be on my way." He held up his hand. "And, yes, your daughter is safe. I am not a monster." He gestured toward the bow, where Astarte and Matthias sat, watched by a guard.

Rivka surfaced next to him. He touched her shoulder. "We need to do what he says."

They climbed aboard. Armed men—members of Mario's team—stood over them as they sat on the deck of the barge not far from the dripping Golden Menorah. A couple of life jackets had been buckled to the Menorah, apparently in case someone tried to throw it overboard. The sight of the sacred Menorah adorned with orange flotation devices would have been farcical were the situation not so grave.

Still in their wetsuits, they answered Palo's questions. "As far as I know, the Mossad doesn't suspect anything," Cam said. "They fell for your ruse."

The cleric glanced at Rivka. "Then why is she here?"

"I used to work for the Mossad." Rivka lifted her chin. "But I do no longer."

Palo turned to the guards. "Give us space." He lowered his voice. "Where is my brother's body?"

"Still down there," Cam answered. The guards were not so far away for Cam to risk trying something rash.

"At that depth, in the cold water, it will take at least a few days to surface, if it surfaces at all," Rivka added.

Palo nodded, probably thinking that, in a few days, he hoped to be safely back in Rome. Staring out at the horizon, he weighed his options. With a long sigh, he turned back to them.

"This may come as a shock to you, but I do not want to keep the Menorah."

Cam blinked. He had assumed Palo wanted the sacred object as a prize to bring back to the Vatican. "Why not?"

"It belongs in Jerusalem. Not the Vatican, not America, definitely not at the bottom of the Atlantic. Jerusalem." He paused. "The problem is, how to get it there? The Mossad has made it clear that they, presumably acting on orders from the Israeli government, don't want it. But the Golden Menorah belongs to the Jewish people. The Bible makes that clear. We, mere mortals, cannot presume to defy God's will."

Cam's mind raced. Things certainly had turned on their heads. The Vatican was trying to give a sacred Jewish treasure back to the Israelis, who were refusing the offer. Bizarro world. Not that Cam trusted Palo. After all, he had murdered his own brother. There was more at play here than simply the desire to do right by the Jewish people. What that was, Cam had no idea. He needed to buy some time, then get Georgia on the phone.

"You say no man can presume to defy God's will," Cam replied. "I say, no man can presume to know it."

"You are correct, with one exception. God has expressed his will in the Bible. There is no need to interpret or construe. His words are clear. All we must do is read and obey."

"Not always. The words of the Bible are sometimes anything but clear."

Palo straightened himself. "That may be. But not in this case. The commandments laid out in the Book of Exodus, Chapter 25, leave no doubt. The Lord said, 'Let them make Me a sanctuary, that I may dwell among them.' And in that sanctuary, he commanded: 'And thou shalt make a candlestick of pure gold... And there shall be six branches going out of the sides thereof: three branches of the candlestick out of the one side thereof, and three branches of the candlestick out of the other side thereof.'" Palo paused for effect. "The Lord commanded that the Israelites build a sanctuary, a temple. And in that temple, place a golden menorah. The words cannot be more clear."

"So," Cam said, "you support rebuilding the Temple. Even if doing so brings war."

Palo's dark eyes held Cam's. "Yes. If that is God's will, so be it. He has told us, His children, that we must build Him a temple and put a golden menorah in it. So we must. The Lord works in mysterious ways, Mr. Thorne. We would be fools to attempt to divine His ultimate plan."

Rivka, Cam knew, had studied and researched the question of a Third Temple. "But I thought Catholics don't support rebuilding the Temple," she said. "I thought you believed that Jesus himself was the new Temple."

Palo shook his head. "Yes, that is, indeed, the official Vatican belief. But it is ... unconvincing. Jesus is many things." Palo counted them off on his fingers. "The Son of God. Our Lord and Savior. The Christ. The Master. The Logos. Our guiding light. The Lamb of God. Our King." Palo shook his head. "But Jesus is *not* something inanimate, made of wood and bricks and marble. How can a person, even the son of God, be a building? No. We pray *to* Jesus, not *within* him." He paused, waiting for Cam and Rivka to nod their approval. Cam did so, the point being a valid one.

Palo continued. "The writings of Paul, my namesake, confirm my interpretation. He states in 2 Thessalonians, chapter 2, verse 3, that Jesus will not return until the Antichrist—and I quote—'takes his seat in the temple of God.' Well, I ask, how can the Antichrist take a seat in the Temple if there is no Temple?"

Rivka glanced at the Menorah. "You are a senior Vatican official. Are there others who agree with this interpretation?"

Palo smiled. "Let's just say there are others who understand the clear meaning of words."

"So, what next?" Cam asked. "You have the Menorah. And you have the guns. That means you get to make the next move."

Palo smiled again. "A press conference. We will put our guns away, of course. But it is time to introduce—or reintroduce—the Golden Menorah to the world."

Astarte sat on the deck of the barge's bow, her back against the enclosed bridge, as Palo questioned her father and Rivka. She texted furiously while Matthias stood watch. Palo and his operatives, in their arrogance, didn't see the two teenagers as much of a threat.

Had he known she was texting with a CIA operative, he would have thought differently.

Georgia, not surprisingly, had put the puzzle pieces together. And the picture was not a pretty one.

The Mossad, it turned out, was right to be worried that the Golden Menorah might destabilize things in the Middle East. But that worry would have turned to panic had they known what Palo really had in mind.

The Vatican, Georgia explained, had long sought to control Jerusalem. For a thousand years, in fact. That was what the Crusades had been all about. But with the city occupied predominantly by Jews and Muslims, the Vatican played third fiddle, essentially exercising power by playing one side off the other and serving as a de facto tie-breaking vote.

"In fact," Georgia concluded, "even as far back as the formation of Israel after World War II, the Vatican was trying to keep control of the city, pushing for an international commission controlled by them to govern the city. Their statement read, 'Let Palestine be internationalized rather than someday be the servant of Zionism.'"

Astarte explained all this to Matthias. He was pre-law, majoring in history; his analytical mind had no trouble connecting the dots.

"So that's what's going on. The Vatican wants to give the Menorah to the Israelis because they know it will explode in their faces."

"Pretty much. Georgia thinks that's why other senior Vatican officials went along with this. I think Palo legitimately wants to rebuild the Third Temple. But the Vatican is looking at the bigger picture. The Menorah appears, the Orthodox Jews and Fundamentalist Christians push for rebuilding, the Muslims of course object, things get ugly—"

Matthias finished the thought. "And the Vatican steps in as peacemaker, convincing the United Nations that the only way to stop World War III is to appoint a neutral party as caretaker of the Temple Mount area. The Pope."

"Right. Neither the Jews nor the Muslims will support the choice. Which is what makes him the obvious selection. Neither side would ever agree to a caretaker it thought the other side approves of."

Matthias nodded. "Classic Middle East. The enemy of my enemy is my friend."

Cam stood on the back of the barge with Rivka, Astarte and Matthias as the vessel chugged around Plum Island and turned up the Merrimack River, the life-jacketed Menorah now covered with a blue tarp. The river was wide here at its mouth, the waters swirling as the waterway's outflow met the incoming tide. Jacques, unfamiliar with the currents, nearly ran the barge aground on a sandbar. Cam half-wished he had.

Astarte had explained Georgia's theory. Rivka concurred. "Not a day goes by when the Vatican doesn't angle for more power in Jerusalem. They have a lot of holy sites there. And they hate not being in control of them."

"Well, a more immediate concern is this press conference," Cam replied, looking at his watch. "It begins at three, less than ninety minutes. Apparently the Vatican public relations office sent out a press release promising major news. There's going to be a big turnout."

Astarte smiled. "What a tragedy, Dad. All those cameras and you forgot your fanny pack."

"Very funny."

Watching the gulls circling the barge, Cam tried to play things out in his mind. Palo would unveil the Golden Menorah, explain how it had been recovered from the Plum Island wreck site, show pictures of the Roman trireme wreck, reveal how preliminary testing showed the artifact dated back to Biblical times. He would probably go along with Mario's timeline and Cam's theory, suggesting that the Menorah had been brought over by the Roman Ninth Legion along with refugees of the Bar Kokhba uprising in the early second century. And Jacques, with his Harvard and Oxford affiliations, would be there to confirm the legitimacy of the find.

It would be quite a bombshell, both from a historical and a religious perspective. But its most immediate—and drastic—effect would be a political one, setting off a chain of events certain to destabilize the Middle East and perhaps the world.

The barge angled toward shore. Palo had apparently made arrangements to tie up along the public docks at Waterfront Park, in the heart of Newburyport's commercial district. The city's historical downtown and vibrant urban lifestyle made it a popular destination for both tourists and residents. Though Labor Day weekend had passed, the park was filled with boaters, dog-walkers, shoppers and picnickers, most of whom had at least one eye on the massive rectangular barge approaching the shoreline like some kind of alien capsule.

Rivka touched his arm. "We can't allow this press conference to happen."

"I know. But how do we stop it?"

She exhaled. "I only know one way. Menachem."

His chest tightened. "No."

"Listen. It turns out, he was right all along. Well, maybe not right. But at least he had good reasons for what he did."

"He shot up Crane Castle. Kidnapped Astarte. And he would have let you drown."

She smiled. "Only because he knew you would have saved me."

"Seriously, I want nothing more to do with that guy. Asking for his help would be like pouring gasoline on a fire." He took a deep breath, picturing Menachem and his goons shooting up the Newburyport waterfront area. "We have to come up with a different plan."

Astarte surprised Cam. "I don't know, Dad. Maybe Rivka's right."

Cam shook his head. "Look, if there's one thing that has become clear, it's that we can't trust that guy. There has to be another way."

As the barge settled against the stone pier, the portly Palo—still dressed in blue jeans and maroon windbreaker—ordered two of his henchman to rotate the Menorah so that it faced the shoreline. "But don't take the tarp off," he said. "I don't want to unveil it until the press are all here. Leave the life jackets on for now. And not too close to the railing. I want people to be able to be able to see it, not touch it." They did as instructed, wrestling it into place just in front of the barge's center hatch ten feet from the port railing.

Spotting Cam and his group, Palo ambled over. "Plotting against me, no doubt," he said with a smile.

They all merely stared back at him.

He continued. "But why? Thorne, this is the find of a lifetime. Jacques has resigned himself to making the best of it; he is, in fact, purchasing more appropriate clothes even as we speak. And Rivka, your country will soon see the return of a national treasure. You should be rejoicing."

Cam played what might end up being his last card. "We could tell the authorities what you did to your brother. Bring them to the body. Rivka could tell them what she saw."

"Yes, you could. They would question me, perhaps even arrest me. But that won't change anything." He gestured toward the blue tarp. "What happens to me won't change the fact that we found the Golden Menorah. God has made known his plan. We are helpless to fight it."

They hadn't eaten since breakfast, so Astarte and Matthias volunteered to grab sandwiches while Cam and Rivka stayed on the barge.

"One hour until the press conference," Matthias said as they exited the sandwich shop.

"I know." Astarte's phone dinged. "Hold on, a text from Georgia." She read it quickly and looked up. "Well, this is interesting. Georgia went back over security videos from Logan Airport. Palo came to Boston last summer. He flew with diplomatic privileges, so his bags weren't examined. But one of the things he checked through was a large wooden crate."

"Large enough for a giant menorah?"

"Yup. And my dad said the Marconi brothers did a dive last summer at the wreck site, with an Italian dive team."

"So what are you saying? He planted the Golden Menorah? Why? It makes no sense."

Walking faster, she replied. "Actually, it does. One of the possibilities has always been that the Vatican had the Menorah hidden away in its vaults. Israel has asked for it over the years, but the Vatican always denied they had it. So, if Palo wanted to put it in play, he'd need to be cute about it. They couldn't just suddenly find it and hand it over. What are they going to say—*sorry, it was hidden in a broom closet?* Everyone would know they had been lying for decades, probably longer."

"Okay. Keep going."

They were on the boardwalk now, perhaps a hundred yards from the hulking barge. "But if the Menorah is found in America, in a second-century Roman ship, well, that's a different story entirely. The Vatican is five thousand miles away. So they leave the Menorah there for a year, letting the underwater critters burrow into the sand all around it. Then they have my dad do all this research so the Romans-in-America story holds together."

"And then they get a top marine archeologist to go down and make the discovery. Pretty good plan." Matthias paused. "But why would Mario go along with it?"

"Because having the Golden Menorah in the wreck conclusively ties the trireme to the Romans. Otherwise, the ship could have been Phoenician or Greek or Persian. But only the Romans had access to the Temple treasures."

Matthias nodded. "It holds together. And it fits in with what we knew before, about Palo and the Vatican wanting Israel to rediscover the Menorah so they try to rebuild the Third Temple."

Astarte hopped aboard the barge. "Dad, we need to talk."

Cam and Rivka listened as Astarte summarized her theory about Palo planting the Menorah. Rivka had pulled out four folding chairs from the bridge and set them up at the far end of the barge. They ate as they conferred.

"I don't know all the details, Dad. But does this make sense based on what you know?"

Cam thought through the past few weeks. "It does. Perfectly, in fact. I think you nailed it, honey."

Rivka nodded. "I agree. But it still doesn't change anything. It's still the actual Menorah. And it's still incredibly destabilizing." She turned to Cam. "Cameron, can you try one more time to talk to Palo? Maybe he'll listen to reason. Try to convince him that his brother would not have wanted this. Maybe offer to share the gold test results with him if he at least delays a few days. Tell him you can convince me to keep quiet." Her shoulders dropped. "Anything to buy some time."

He took another bite and tossed the rest of his sandwich down. "Okay. I'll try." He checked his watch. Forty minutes. A few members of the press had already begun to gather along the park area lining the pier. "Astarte and Matthias, I want you guys off the barge."

"Why?" Astarte replied.

"Because there are men here with guns. And Palo is a whack job. And Menachem is still out there somewhere. You can watch from shore. We all can, in fact. I'll join you in a few minutes."

Cam found Palo seated on the bridge, feet up, eyes shifting back and forth between the tarp-covered Menorah and the boat traffic moving up and down the river. He was guarded by two henchmen with semiautomatic rifles. Two more stood on the pier in front of the barge, unarmed but with scowls sufficient to keep onlookers at a distance. Palo had changed out of his blue jeans and windbreaker into a beige suit. His round face was sunburned and his eyes bloodshot from apparent lack of sleep, but there was no mistaking the look of satisfaction on his face.

Cam made his case, Rivka by his side. "All we're asking for is a little time. It's in your best interests also. I know you want to pressure the Israelis into building a Third Temple. Give us a couple of days and we can help line up support behind it. That way you can hit the ground running."

"And why would I trust you to do that?"

"Because it's better than doing it all willy-nilly like this press conference. If your ultimate goal is to build a Third Temple, your best bet is to be more methodical."

Palo touched his ten fingers together in front of his chest, as if in prayer. He weighed Cam's words. "You are probably correct. But, still, the answer is no."

"That makes no sense."

"It makes perfect sense, Mr. Thorne."

"Why is that?"

"Because the game is over. I have won. Why do anything to prolong it, to open the door to unnecessary risks? I have worked too hard, waited too long. The future, alone, is my enemy."

The cleric turned to Rivka. "Would you be so kind as to remove the life jackets from the Menorah?" He smiled. "And tidy up the area. We want her looking her best for the photo op."

Rivka glared at him for a few seconds, offended by the sexist nature of the request, before marching away.

As she left, a tall, twenty-something man wearing work pants, a t-shirt, and hat with the word 'Yeat' on the brim approached the bow of the barge. The two henchmen stopped him. "What do you want?" one asked.

"Easy, dude. I work for the harbormaster. I just need to see your docking permit."

He tried to push past, which caused the other henchman to grab his arm. The man threw an elbow, which led to a punch, and soon all three men were rolling around on the ground, grunting and writhing.

"Enough," Palo yelled. "The last thing we need is for the police to come." He clicked at his phone and handed the device to one of the armed guards. "The permit is here, on my phone. Show it to him. And make sure those two knuckleheads stand down." The other guard, now alone, focused his full attention on Cam.

Palo, too, turned to Cam. "And that's another reason I must say no to you. There is a reason I live in Italy. I truly do despise most Americans. They are so churlish, so uncivilized. The sooner I can complete my mission here, the sooner I can return to Rome."

Rivka took advantage of the commotion caused by the altercation. She slipped under the tarp and, using the crane's pedestal to shield herself from Palo, dragged the four folding chairs under the tarp with her. As instructed, she removed the two life jackets wrapped around the arms of the Menorah. She began to remove the third flotation device, secured to its base, but reconsidered and left it. She then quickly opened the chairs, stacked them in pairs, separated them a bit, and slid them against the face of the Menorah, the back of each upper chair flush against the candelabra's arms. *Good.* As she had calculated, the arranged chairs approximated the height and width of the Menorah. Lifting the tarp slightly, she ran her fingers around the inside of the cup area of the center arm. A few seconds later, still on one knee, she pivoted and, reaching out from underneath the tarp, released the latches to the barge's center hatch.

Exhaling, she slipped from beneath the tarp, holding the life jackets, and studied the results. The tarp looked slightly fatter than it should because of the chairs, but it had already been bowed outward due to the life jackets. She doubted anyone would notice.

Smiling, she strolled away. She wasn't so bad at this tidying up thing after all.

Cam shuffled out of the enclosed bridge to find Rivka standing along the rail, peering out toward the mouth of the river.

"Hoping for the cavalry?" he said with a smile.

"Hoping we wouldn't need it, actually." She read his face. "No luck with Palo, huh?"

"Nope." He held up his watch. "Twenty minutes."

She smiled sadly and slipped her phone from her back pocket. "Just enough time for me to call my family in Israel and tell them to lock their doors. It's going to be ugly." She edged away and made a quick call.

When she finished, Cam took her gently by the elbow. He felt bad. This was personal to her. Her country, her family, her friends were being affected. "Come on. Let's get off this barge."

She leaned into him. "Is that a proposition?"

He smiled. "No. But I will buy you a beer once this stupid press conference is over."

Palo made no effort to stop them from leaving. They found Astarte and Matthias sitting on a stone bench on the boardwalk running along the waterfront, perhaps fifty feet from the stern of the barge. A dozen or so reporters had gathered, many with camera crews, along the boardwalk near the barge. Palo was tapping at a microphone, testing the sound system he had somehow acquired. Cam checked his watch. Ten minutes.

"We could call in a bomb threat," Astarte joked.

"What we need is a real bomb, not just a threat," Rivka replied. She was pacing, her eyes on the river, perhaps hoping for some kind of miracle. But the only boats on the waterway were a couple of sailboats, a group of kayakers, and a fishing trawler chugging toward the ocean. "It would be best if the Menorah disappeared from the face of the earth."

Cam thought about arguing the point. After all, history was neither good nor evil. It just was. It was people who chose to interpret it in ways that led to death and destruction and misery. But he let it go.

Palo tapped at the microphone again. He stood behind the barge railing and in front of the blue tarp, facing the boardwalk. "Thank you all for coming," he said with a smile. Cam now counted more than twenty reporters, including a crew from CNN. "We will begin a few minutes early, if that is okay."

"Why?" Astarte whispered.

"Because he's afraid," Rivka replied. "Afraid God will smote him down for the evil he is doing."

"Some of you may know the history of the Golden Menorah of the Bible, forged by Moses and then later placed in Solomon's Temple in Jerusalem." He went on to describe how the Menorah was later placed in the Second Temple and then taken by the Romans after the Jewish uprising in 70 AD. "Soon thereafter, the Menorah disappeared from history." He paused. "Until now."

Smiling, he waited for the murmuring to die down. His words had their desired effect, focusing all attention on the barge. "Over the past many days, an underwater archeology team has been removing artifacts from a wreck off the southern tip of Plum Island, perhaps ten miles from here. Leading this team is world-renowned marine archeologist, Jacques Burnett." He motioned to Jacques, who nodded to the crowd. "The ship is a Roman-era trireme, dating to the second century. That, in and of itself, is an extraordinary find. But it pales in comparison to one of the objects found on board." He paused as two of his men marched toward the tarp. He raised his voice. "Ladies and gentlemen, may I present to you the sacred Golden Menorah of Jerusalem!"

With a flourish, Palo's men ripped the tarp away. Four folding chairs stood, stacked in pairs, teetering. One of the chairs tumbled, thumping to the deck, coming to rest inches from the open hatch in the middle of the barge.

A stunned silence filled the park area. Rivka, grinning, filled it with a round of applause.

## Epilogue

***Two Weeks Later***

Cam sat at the outdoor heated patio behind the Sea Level restaurant, overlooking the Merrimack River only yards from where, two weeks earlier, Palo had docked the barge. He thought it was appropriate to meet Rivka here—at the scene of the crime, as it were. It was a cool fall evening, the leaves in Waterfront Park just beginning to change.

She strolled toward him along an outdoor path, stylish in a black blazer and linen slacks. The scar on her forehead had healed, and she seemed to have an air of self-assuredness about her that he hadn't noticed before. He stood to greet her, accepting a quick kiss on the cheek, noticing she had been careful to stay away from his lips. They hadn't spoken since what Cam and Astarte had come to refer to as Palo's Folly. Each of them probably had a lot to say. Some of it might even be the truth.

"Would you like a drink?" he asked.

She smiled "You promised me a beer once this was all over. I'll take it now, if that's okay."

"So is it? Over, I mean?"

"I guess it depends on how you define that."

He smiled. "I'm supposed to be the lawyer here." He ordered the beers nonetheless.

They made small talk until the beers arrived. They clinked. "To doing the right thing," Cam said.

She made a face. "Really? We can do better than that, can't we?"

"Okay, I'm listening."

She stared out over the river. "To history. As Maya Angelou said, 'History, despite its wrenching pain, cannot be unlived, but if faced with courage, need not be lived again.'"

Cam nodded. "Well said." It struck him suddenly that Amanda hadn't spoken to him in the past three days, since he had texted Rivka to set up this dinner. "Actually, now that I think about it, shouldn't the toast have been, *to courage*? So we don't repeat our painful history?"

"I was hoping you'd say that."

"Because what you did was courageous."

"I'd like to think so. I did something that was not in my self-interest, but that I knew needed to be done to prevent another Mid-East war. To prevent us from reliving our painful history."

"What do you mean by not in your self-interest?"

"I knew it would anger you. I betrayed you. Lied to you. That's the last thing I wanted to do." She held his eyes. "I think you know that."

"But you did it for your country." He was beginning to appreciate the strength of her character. Standing up to Menachem. Resigning. Even lying to Cam when she felt duty-bound.

"Yes. Above all us, we must prevent war. Menachem was correct."

He nodded. "I get that. And I'm not angry. Hurt, a little. Like you said, you lied to me. But I'm a big boy." He smiled. "Or I became one, after Astarte told me to stop acting like a three-year-old."

She laughed lightly. "Good for her, wise beyond her years."

"So, you want to tell me how you pulled it off?"

She leaned forward. "Do I ever! I've been holding it in for two weeks now. There's really nobody else I can tell."

"I assume you had Menachem's help?"

She nodded. "As soon as I knew what Palo intended, I called Menachem. Told him that the menorah he dumped was a replica and that the real one was on the barge in Newburyport. When he finished swearing at me, he gathered a team of divers across the river. While they swam across, I opened the hatch on the barge. It was during that fight with the harbormaster's assistant, which we staged to distract Palo and his men. It worked even better that Palo ordered me to remove the life jackets and tidy up. The divers came up from underneath and slipped the Menorah through—it helped that I left one of the life jackets attached, giving it some buoyancy in the water so they could swim it back across. As you saw, I piled the chairs under the tarp so that when they took the Menorah, the tarp didn't fall."

Cam smiled. "That was fun, seeing Palo's face as the cameras flashed. They got some great pictures of those folding chairs." He turned serious. "I assume Menachem dumped the Menorah someplace way out in the Atlantic?"

"Yes. As I understand it, he took only one of his men with him. And made him wear a hood, like he did to us."

"Well, I guess it's not a bad thing to be paranoid in that line of work."

She shifted in her chair. "I saw the story in the newspaper. At least nobody is questioning the trireme. I was worried that the stink from the Menorah fiasco would attach to the wreck, to your research."

"It did, a little. If you noticed, they didn't get any academic types to go on the record. It's weird—normally we have the artifacts but not the science to back them up. This time, we have the MIT lab report, but the Menorah is gone. Not having both makes it hard to prove the case."

"You have photographs of the Menorah, right?"

"People will argue they're fakes."

"What about the ship? That's an artifact."

"But it's going to be a least a year before we can raise it. Remember, the permit was in Marconi's name. And now that the Underwater Archeology Board knows they got duped by Marconi with the 1914 replica ship story, they're going to be extra careful and methodical. It's going to take a while. Jacques is still on board, so hopefully he can push it through. The danger is that everyone knows about the wreck now, and it's just sitting there, a few hundred yards offshore. The poachers and amateur divers are going to have a field day. It's exactly what Marconi was worried about." He sighed. "There might not be anything left of the ship by the time we raise it."

"But you have carbon-dating on the wood, right?"

"We do." He shook his head. "And I can hear the naysayers already, arguing that the ship might have been built with really old wood." He smiled. "Just like the coins were brought over by seagulls in their beaks."

"People can say what they want. That doesn't make them right."

"I know. And we still have the gold goblet we found next to the Menorah—the dates came back on that as ancient." He sat up. "Plus the coins and the amphora and terracotta head and all the stuff in the Ohio River Valley. So we can still make a strong case that the Romans were here. But it's not as ironclad as it could have been."

"Seems pretty ironclad to me."

Cam sipped his beer and smiled. "Well, you saw the actual Menorah. So you're a bit biased."

"Right. It did leave quite an impression."

"Not many of us can say they saw it. You and me. Astarte and Matthias. Jacques. Menachem. Palo. Maybe a couple of men working on the barge, assuming they even knew what they were looking at."

"Speaking of Palo, do you know what happened to him? The FBI questioned me, but then I didn't hear anything more."

"He tried to claim diplomatic immunity, but after the fiasco on the barge and murdering his brother, the Vatican wants nothing to do with him. Not to mention, he, you know, *lost the Golden Menorah.* They're saying he's unhinged, that the whole Menorah thing was a figment of his imagination."

"I suppose that works," Rivka replied.

"Well, the truth is, as far as any of us can prove, the Menorah really is just a figment of our imaginations. I mean, we saw it. But we can't prove it. Other than Menachem, of course."

She tilted her head. "And me."

"What do you mean?"

"Other than Menachem. And me."

"I don't understand."

With a smile, Rivka help up a black key fob-like device. "I glued a tracking device into one of the arms of the Menorah. I just couldn't see letting it be lost to history forever."

"No way." He slapped the table. "So you know where it is?"

"Right down to the square meter. This tracker is Mossad technology, guaranteed for life."

Jokingly, he started to push back his chair and stand. "So, what are we waiting for?"

She smiled sadly. "A new world, unfortunately."

"Right." He retook his seat. "Good point."

They sat in silence for a few seconds.

Cam broke it. "Seriously, what are you going to do? About the Menorah?"

"Well, my apartment is too small for it now, so nothing right away."

"I get it. Can't have a garish Menorah blocking the fireplace."

"Not to mention how hard it would be to find candles that fit."

"And people would expect some *really* big Hanukah gifts if you pulled that thing out."

Smiling, she squeezed his hand quickly before pulling back. "I like this."

"What?"

"Bantering with you. Being with you. Like I told you, I'm not good with people. But with you, I don't feel that way." She smiled. "Even though I did lie to you."

"It was for a good reason. Like I said, I get it."

"So, what next?" she asked.

"Well, I say we start with some dinner."

She leaned forward. "And then?"

"We'll work our way up to other things."

"Such as?"

"Well, down the road, if things go well, and we're still getting along, and we haven't gotten sick of each other…"

"Yes?"

"Maybe we could, I don't know, take that fob of yours and go on a dive?"

Laughing, she shook her head. "You can be such a jerk. How do you know I won't drown you out there?"

"I don't, actually," he said, smiling. Her question was tongue-in-cheek, of course, but the truth was that he didn't really know what she might do. Which, he realized, was one of the things he liked about her.

*Me, too,* Amanda chimed in. *She's got spunk. You need that. But don't worry, I'm not staying. I'll always love you, Cameron. You know that. But you're on your own for the rest of the night.*

Rivka eyed him. "And you're okay with that? With not knowing what I might do?"

He took a deep breath. "I am. Life is full of risks. And it hurts sometimes. But you can't hide in your room." He held her eyes. "Sometimes you just have to take the plunge and hope things work out."

***The End***

## Dear Reader

I love to get reader feedback, both to help me continue to write about things that you (hopefully) enjoy and also to improve on the things you don't. Please feel free to reach out to me at dsbrody@comcast.net, and/or also to leave a review at Amazon or Goodreads.

If you enjoyed *Romerica,* you may want to read the other books featuring Cameron and Astarte in my "Templars in America" series, all of which have been Kindle Top 10 Bestsellers in their categories (see below). And if you enjoy legal thrillers, please check out the three legal thrillers in my "Boston Law" series, *Unlawful Deeds, Blood of the Tribe,* and *The Wrong Abraham:*

https://www.amazon.com/gp/product/B0753CRT9D

### "Templars in America" Series

***Cabal of the Westford Knight***
***Templars at the Newport Tower*** (2009)
https://www.amazon.com/dp/B00GWTZYLS
Set in Boston and Newport, RI, inspired by artifacts evidencing that Scottish explorers and Templar Knights traveled to New England in 1398.

***Thief on the Cross***
***Templar Secrets in America*** (2011)
https://www.amazon.com/dp/B006OQIXCG
Set in the Catskill Mountains of New York, sparked by an ancient Templar codex calling into question fundamental teachings of the Catholic Church.

***Powdered Gold***
***Templars and the American Ark of the Covenant*** (2013)
https://www.amazon.com/dp/B00GWTYJ5K
Set in Arizona, exploring the secrets and mysteries of both the Ark of the Covenant and a manna-like powdered substance.

***The Oath of Nimrod***
***Giants, MK-Ultra and the Smithsonian Cover-up*** (2014)
https://www.amazon.com/dp/B00NW13QTG
Set in Massachusetts and Washington, DC, triggered by the mystery of hundreds of giant human skeletons found buried across North America.

***The Isaac Question***
***Templars and the Secret of the Old Testament*** (2015)
https://www.amazon.com/dp/B016E3X2QK
Set in Massachusetts and Scotland, focusing on ancient stone chambers, the mysterious Druids and a stunning reinterpretation of the Biblical Isaac story.

***Echoes of Atlantis***
***Crones, Templars and the Lost Continent*** (2016)
https://www.amazon.com/dp/B01MXJ0BNX
Set in New England, focusing on artifacts and other evidence indicating that the lost colony of Atlantis, featuring an advanced civilization, did exist 12,000 years ago.

***The Cult of Venus***
***Templars and the Ancient Goddess*** (2017)
https://www.amazon.com/dp/B0767Q4N1S
Set in New England, triggered by the discovery of a medieval journal revealing that the Knights Templar came to America before Columbus because they were secretly worshiping the ancient Goddess.

***The Swagger Sword***
***Templars, Columbus and the Vatican Cover-up*** (2018)
https://www.amazon.com/gp/product/B07HCRNYVN
Set in Rhode Island and Ireland, inspired by the 1980s Vatican Bank Scandal and featuring a treasure map, carved on a sword, indicating that Christopher Columbus may have aided the Templars in secreting a treasure in America.

***Treasure Templari***
***Templars, Nazis and the Holy Grail*** (2019)
https://www.amazon.com/gp/product/B07XV9QJNZ
Set in New England, New York and Belgium, triggered by a 15$^{th}$-century Dutch Masterpiece which Hitler believed was a secret map to the Templar treasure and the Holy Grail.

***Watchtower of Turtle Island***
***Templars and the Antichrist*** (2020)
https://www.amazon.com/gp/product/B089QWSGM1
Set in New England and Montana, sparked by occultists who believe that a stone tower in Newport, RI—built by the medieval Knights Templar—is a portal through which the Antichrist will appear.

***Available at Amazon as Paperbacks and as Kindle eBooks***

## Author's Note

For centuries, historians have tried to explain away the plethora of Roman-era coins and artifacts found on American shores. The coins were brought across the Atlantic in the beaks of seagulls (sneaky devils). Or they were used as ballast in Colonial ships (because, you know, there are no rocks in Europe). Or coin collectors brought their collections to the beach and lost them there (I always swing by the safe deposit box before a swim in the ocean). I had heard about some of these coins and artifacts and had always meant to look into the mystery surrounding them. But, boy, was I blown away by the sheer number of them. Up and down the East Coast, and all along the Ohio River Valley. Clearly, there was more at work here than sneaky seagulls.

Fellow researcher Rick Osmon suggested one possibility in his 2011 book, *The Graves of the Golden Bear* (Grave Distractions 2011). Offering forts and coins and artifacts in support of his theory, Rick speculated that the Roman Ninth Legion, which essentially disappeared from history in the second century, may have crossed the Atlantic and settled in the Ohio River Valley. The theory made a lot of sense, especially in light of the fact that so many of the coins and artifacts dated specifically to the second century.

Rick's theory also helped explain the Burrows Cave mystery. Most historians dismiss the Burrows Cave artifacts as a hoax, but the hoax story never added up to me. There are simply too many artifacts, many of them exhibiting an advanced knowledge of obscure and subtle points of history, to be the work of a hoaxster. Russell Burrows did indeed earn a few bucks from selling the artifacts, but not nearly enough to justify the time and effort needed to create the artifacts in the first place. Rick's suggestion that members of the Ninth Legion—consisting of soldiers from across the Mediterranean—may have carved the artifacts and secreted them in the Ohio River Valley is an explanation that makes sense to me.

When I did more research on the Ninth Legion and learned that it had been deployed in Jerusalem to help put down the Bar Kokhba rebellion in 130 AD, I sensed that the plot for this story was taking shape. The Romans, after putting down the rebellion, looted the city. According to the Copper Scroll of Qumran (one of the Dead Sea

Scrolls), the amount of treasure hidden during the rebellion was valued at $1.5 billion in today's dollars. Here, now, was a possible motive for the Ninth Legion fleeing Europe and heading to America.

The story really came together when I got a phone call from a longtime reader of my books. An amateur treasure hunter, he explained that he had discovered what he believed to be a Roman-era shipwreck off the coat of Cape Ann, north of Boston. He showed me ingots, tools and coins he had retrieved from the site. I asked the obvious question: Why haven't you sent an underwater archeological team down? He explained that the permitting process was so arduous and time-consuming (made more so by the state archeologist's hostility to any project involving possible pre-Columbus contact) that it would take years to get the permits needed. In the meantime, due to the public nature of the permitting process, the location of the wreck would be disclosed, allowing others to poach his find. In the end, it just wasn't worth it to him to move ahead. So there the wreck sits, undiscovered in the real world but the subject of Marconi's obsession in a fictional one.

In the end, this book came together very quickly. I was able to complete the first draft in 101 days, about half of what it usually takes me. Of course, writing during a pandemic, with so few distractions, didn't hurt.

As is the case with all the books in this series, if an artifact, site or object of art is pictured, it is real—except as specifically noted otherwise. (To state the obvious, the discovery of the Golden Menorah is purely fictional.) And if I claim it is of a certain age or of a certain provenance or features certain characteristics, that information is correct or believed to be correct. Likewise, the historical and literary references are accurate. How I use these objects and references to weave a story is, of course, where the fiction takes root.

For inquisitive readers, perhaps curious about some of the specific historical assertions made and evidence presented in this novel, more information is available here (in order of appearance in the story):

*For a good history of shipwrecks around Plum Island, see https://historicipswich.org/2016/08/29/the-shipwrecks-at-ipswich-bar/.

*Information in this book about the Crane Estate is true, other than that the castle has not been leased by a millionaire and is, as of this writing, still available for rental as a function venue. For a summary of the history of the property, see https://historicipswich.org/crane-estate-history/.

*Catlin's discussion of and observations concerning the Mandan tribe can be found in Volume 1, at pages 93-94, of his 2-volume set: *Letters and Notes on the Manners, Customs and Condition of the North American Indians, Vol. 1 and 2* (Dover Publications 1973), by George Catlin.

*For information on the September, 2016 Plum Island Roman coin find, see decision of Massachusetts Board of Underwater Archeological Resources: https://www.mass.gov/files/documents/2017/06/bac/uabmarch17.pdf, at pages 3-4. This decision is a good example of the unsupported assumptions and conclusions some governmental authorities will adopt in order to avoid giving credence to possible pre-Columbus artifacts. The Board's decision to cede jurisdiction of the find to the finder is what triggered the "Sammy Haddad" twist in my plot.

*For the Smithsonian's documentation of pre-Colonial forts in the Ohio River Valley, see *Ancient Monuments of the Mississippi Valley*, by E.G. Squire and E.H. Davis, which can be found here: https://www.gutenberg.org/files/49668/49668-h/49668-h.htm#chap11

*For a thorough discussion of the Copper Scroll of Qumran, see *The Mystery of the Copper Scroll of Qumran* (Bear & Company 1999), by Robert Feather. The $1.5 billion treasure valuation can be found at page 15.

*For a discussion of Great Lakes copper, including the Uluburun shipwreck off the coast of Turkey, see article by Jay Wakefield, here: https://www.migration-diffusion.info/article.php?id=174

*The 1989 newspaper article discussing the Devil's Backbone fort can be found here: https://www.latimes.com/archives/la-xpm-1989-09-03-mn-2117-story.html

*Information about the soldiers with breastplates dug up in 1799 and the armor and shield found in 1895 can be found here: *Footprints of the Welsh Indians* (Algora 2004), by William L. Traxel, at pages 93-94.

*For a thorough discussion of Burrows Cave, see *The Lost Treasure of King Juba* (Bear & Company 2003), by Frank Joseph. Also see *Atlantic Rising*, Issue 111 (May/June 2015), in particular for the point regarding the artisic ability evidenced by the Burrows Cave artists.

*For a discussion of the carvings at Cave-in-Rock in Illinois, see *American Antiquities and Discoveries in the West* (Hoffman and White 1835), by Josiah Priest, at page 148.

*Information on the Old Stone Fort in Makanda, Illinios can be found in *The Lost Treasure of King Juba* (Bear & Company 2003), by Frank Joseph, at pages 201-203.

*Source materail for the Lowery Farm in Illinois can be found in research posted by "Zelph," here: http://www.bplite.com/viewtopic.php?t=6058. See also *A Guide to Treasure in Illinois and Indiana* (Carter/Latham Pub. 1977), by Michael Paul Henson. See also *Atlantic Rising*, Issue 111 (May/June 2015). The interior of the cave pictured in the story is not the Lowery Farm cave. Likewise, the carved script pictured inside the cave in the story is not from the Lowery Farm cave; the carved script, however, does come from a Burrows Cave artifact.

*For information tying the Kensington Rune Stone party to a possible plague outbreak at Cahokia Mounds, see *The Kensington Rune Stone: Its Place in History* (Pogo Press 2001), by Thomas E. Reiersgord, at pages 71-80.

*For the assertion that Sacagawea brougth her baby to Cahokia to be baptized by Cistercian monks, see http://lewisandclarktrail.com/section1/illinoiscities/mounds.htm.

*For background information on the Tecaxix-Calixtlahuaca head in Mexico City, see *Templars in America: From the Crusades to the New World* (Weiser Books2004), by Tim Wallace-Murphy and Marilyn

Hopkins, at page 70. For the quote from Professor Andreae that the head is Roman, see https://www.asc.ohio-state.edu/mcculloch.2/arch/calix.htm.

Regarding the assertion that thermoluminescence testing showed a date of 1,800 years BP for the head, see http://www.andrewcollins.com/page/articles/romanbust.htm

*For the discovery of the Bat Creek Stone carving being Hebrew, see https://ensignmessage.com/articles/stone-inscription-found-in-tennessee-proves-that-america-was-discovered-1-500-years-before-columbus/

For the assertion that the carving translates to "A Comet for the Jews," see *Old World Roots of the Cherokee* (McFarland 2012), by Donald N. Yates, at page 121.

*For the book entitled, *Natural and Aboriginal History of Tennessee*, and the discussion of Roman coins therein, see page 183, here: https://archive.org/stream/naturalaborigina00hayw?ref=ol#page/n10/mode/2up/search/roman+coin

*For a good background discussion of the Hanukah Fort of Ohio, see http://bookofmormonresources.blogspot.com/2018/10/ohio-mound-found.html

*For the argument that it was unlikely to have four Roman coins found clustered in date within the reign of four consecutive rulers, and that a more reasonable explanation was that the four coins came from a chest of recently-minted coins being carried on a fourth-century Roman merchant vessel, see *Saga America* (Three Rivers Press 1983), by Barry Fell, at page 32.

*For information on the Manchester-by-the-Sea coin, see https://www.salemnews.com/news/local_news/salem-man-finds--year-old-shekel-on-the-shore/article_d1b1dc77-839a-5601-83dd-f71a06cb937a.html

*The *New York Times* article discussing the amphora found in Brazil can be seen here: https://www.nytimes.com/1985/06/25/science/underwater-exploring-is-banned-in-brazil.html.

For information dating these amphora to the Roman era, see http://pamle.blogspot.com/2008/06/romans-in-brazil-during-second-third.html

*For information on the replica Santa Maria's journey from Chicago to Boston, see https://magicmastsandsturdyships.weebly.com/does-columbus-sail-his-ships-in-jackson-park-lagoon.html

*For the assertion that the clay paste of the Castine Bay jars matched amphora produced on the Iberian Peninsula during the Roman era, see https://www.science-frontiers.com/sf001/sf001p02.htm

*For a discussion of the possible location of the Golden Menorah, see https://www.biblicalarchaeology.org/daily/biblical-sites-places/temple-at-jerusalem/where-did-the-temple-menorah-go/

*For assertion that Yuchi tribe have history similar to Mandan, see https://accessgenealogy.com/native/earth-lodges-of-the-mandan-arikara-and-hidatsa.htm

For Yuchi involvement with Midewin ceremony, contact the ZSR Library at Wake Forest University for a pdf file entitled "Alexander and Burrows Cave," by Cyclone Covey.

For the assertion that the Yuchi built an underground mausoleum in southern Illinois, see *The Lost Treasure of King Juba* (Bear & Company 2003), by Frank Joseph, at page 22.

*A good summary of uranium thorium–helium testing of gold objects can be found here: https://link.springer.com/article/10.1007/s13404-018-0238-z#:~:text=Geologic%20gold%20deposits%20can%20be,of%20the%20investigated%20gold%20occurrences

*For a discussion of the Vatican's historical stance regarding the statehood of Israel, see https://jcpa.org/the-vaticans-path-toward-official-recognition-of-israel/

So do I think ancient Roman visited our shores? As Cam often says, my training as a lawyer tells me to follow the evidence. At some point, it becomes impossible to otherwise explain all the coins and artifacts found along the Atlantic Coast and in the Ohio River Valley. And if they did come, it provides an explanation as to where the Templars may have obtained maps and logs allowing them to cross later. I know this for certain: I'm a lot more willing to believe that Roman-era ships crossed the Atlantic than that seagulls flew across with coins in their beaks.

As always, thanks for reading and coming on this journey with me.

David S. Brody, November, 2020
Newburyport, Massachusetts

## Acknowledgements

Readers may not realize that the finished version of a novel is often the fifth or sixth draft of the story, each draft becoming iteratively improved (hopefully) over the prior version. Those who volunteer to read these early versions, armed only with red pens and caffeine, perform an invaluable task. I offer my heartfelt thanks—for their astute insights, observations and comments—to the following individuals (in alphabetical order) for allowing me to rope them into being my beta readers:

Mary K. Baier
Jonathan Blasczak
Benjamin Brody
Jeffrey Brody
Carol A. Bye MacLeod
Robert Cronin
Randy Dickey
Derek Gunn
Michael Hauptly-Pierce
Mark Hickox
Bart Leavens
Richard Lynch
Matthew McMahon
Paul McNamee
Scott Eric Miller

In addition to these readers, a number of individuals provided information and guidance to me as I researched and wrote this book. In particular, I wish to thank (in alphabetical order) Jonathan Blasczak, Mark Eddy, Bruce Grimes, Derek Gunn, Daniel Irving, Rick Osmon, Lee Pennington, Brian St. Pierre and Eric Wysk for their contributions and assistance. Any mistakes in the story are mine, not theirs. And the fact that they may have assisted me does not mean they endorse or support any of the things written.

My research was greatly aided by the extensive files and archives maintained by the New England Antiquities Research Association (NEARA). I strongly encourage anyone who has an interest in ancient sites and artifacts in and around New England to join NEARA (visit www.NEARA.org).

I relied on the following books as resource material and encourage curious readers to dive deeper into these materials by consulting these sources (listed alphabetically):

**The Graves of the Golden Bear* (Grave Distractions 2011), by Rick Osmon.

**Letters and Notes on the Manners, Customs and Condition of the North American Indians, Vol. 1 and 2* (Dover Publications 1973), by George Catlin.

**New England's Ancient Mysteries* (Old Salt Box 1993), by Robert Ellis Cahill.

**Saga America* (Three Rivers Press 1983), by Barry Fell.

Finally, this is an old refrain, but I can't imagine writing these books without my wife Kim's help and advice. She brings just the right balance of helpful enthusiasm and a skeptical eye. In short, she is both inspirational muse and cold-blooded editor. Makes for some fun dinner table conversations, and I adore her for it.

## Photo Credits

Images used in this book are the property of the author, in the public domain, and/or are attributed as follows (images listed in order of appearance in the story):

*Crane Castle/Estate, Ipswich, MA credit Jay Burnham, Wikipedia
*Roman Coin, Marshfield, MA, credit Matt Adams
*Plum Island Coins, credit Eric Wysk
*Sacrificial Table, America's Stonehenge, credit Rick Lynch
*Phoenician-Style Ship Petroglyph, Lake Superior, credit Library of Congress
*Falls of the Ohio Roman Coins, credit https://www.asc.ohio-state.edu/mcculloch.2/arch/coins/fallsoh.htm
*Map of Roman Coins Found in U.S., credit Lee Pennington
*Roman Coin with Solar Crown, Indiana, credit Lee Pennington
*Roman Coin Collection, Indiana & Kentucky, credit Lee Pennington (part of David Wells collection)
*Brandenburg Stone, credit Lee Pennington
*Stone Anchor, Derby, Kentucky, credit Bruce Grimes
*Roman-Era Ship, Burrows Cave, credit https://faculty.ucr.edu/~legneref/archeol/htm/arc577.htm
*Cave-in-Rock, credit https://www.flickr.com/photos/davidwilson1949/6286936069
*Old Stone Fort, Giant City, Makanda, Illinois, credit https://www2.illinois.gov/dnr/NaturalResources/cultural/Documents/UnsolvedPrehistoryWallOfMystery.pdf
*Lowery Farm Cave Hole, credit Zelph, http://www.woodgaz-stove.com
*Illinois Cave, credit https://littleegyptgrotto.org/
*Cahokia Illustration, credit Cahokia Mounds State Historic Site
*Tecaxic-Calixtlahuaca Head, credit Romeo Hristov
*Roman Coin, Heavener, Oklahoma, credit http://www.gloriafarley.com/chap11.htm
*Heavener Rune Stone, credit Wikipedia
*Potawatomi Menorah Carving, credit https://www.youtube.com/watch?v=1vcem3miWvY (22 minute mark)

*Decalogue Stone, credit J. Huston McCulloch
*Roman Coins, Beverly, MA, credit New England Antiquities Research Association
*Roman-Era Coin, Manchester-by-the-Sea, MA, credit https://www.salemnews.com/news/local_news/salem-man-finds--year-old-shekel-on-the-shore/article_d1b1dc77-839a-5601-83dd-f71a06cb937a.html
*Roman Coin, Plum Island (Newburyport), MA, credit Malcolm Pearson (James Whittall papers)
* Roman Coins, Bethel, VT, credit *America's Ancient Stone Relics*, by Warren W. Dexter & Donna Martin
*Roman Amphoras, Rio de Janeiro, Brazil, credit David Pratt
*Roman Trireme Ship Mosaic, credit Matthias Stephanius, Wikipedia
**Santa Maria* Replica at Sail, credit https://magicmastsandsturdyships.weebly.com/does-columbus-sail-his-ships-in-jackson-park-lagoon.html
* Serpent Mound, Ohio, credit https://columbusfreepress.com/article/ohio-earthworks-verge-taking-world%E2%80%99s-stage
* Amphora, Castine Bay, Maine, credit Rick Lynhc
*Roman Shield, Marshfield, MA, credit New England Antiquities Research Association
*Roman Oil Lamp, Clinton, CT, credit New England Antiquities Research Association
*Roman-Era Coin, Cumberland, ME, credit New England Antiquities Research Association
*Arch of Titus, Rome, credit Dnalor 01, Wikipedia
*Temple Menorah Replica, credit the Temple Institute

Made in the USA
Monee, IL
22 February 2021

61126560R00164